With great concentration Lord Kilrood then took the loosened lock of her hair and tucked it beneath a braid that circled her crown.

"When you look up at me like that—especially when you are curious rather than angry—you are utterly alluring. Any man you were to look upon just so would be bound to feel a, well, a quickening."

When he dropped his hand Finch patted her hair and felt flustered. No man had ever spoken to her in such a manner. "I am a plain woman, and I know it. I should be grateful if you state your business plainly. Flattery has never been inspiring to me. If there is something you need, if I can help you in some manner, I will, simply because my brother thinks highly of you."

"Good," he said. "Very good." Kilrood bent closer until she could feel his breath on her mouth. "I have need of you, Finch."

"Lush and provocative . . . another fine, wickedly sexy tale from the talented Ms. Cameron."
—*Romantic Times* on *Beloved*

"Her plots and subplots are wonderfully dark and devious, with an atmosphere that heightens all tensions and dangers to the breaking point."
—*Affaire de Coeur* on *Bride*

"A suspenseful, tightly written historical romance. . . . This is a satisfying, highly sensual read with some unexpected twists."
—*Publishers Weekly* on *Beloved*

"Her narrative is rich, her style distinct, and her characters wonderfully wicked."
—*Publishers Weekly* on *Charmed*

"A sensual, rollicking love story about the mischievous, madcap side of love."
—*A Little Romance* on *Bride*

"A marvelously talented historical author."
—*Romantic Times*

"Stella Cameron works magic with our hearts and casts a seductive spell."
—Katherine Stone, bestselling author of *Thief of Hearts*

BOOKS BY STELLA CAMERON

STELLA CAMERON

MORE and MORE

WARNER BOOKS

A Time Warner Company

WARNER BOOKS EDITION

Copyright © 1998 by Stella Cameron
All rights reserved.

Cover design by Rachel McClain
Cover illustration by Franco Accornero
Hand lettering by David Gatti

Warner Books, Inc.
1271 Avenue of the Americas
New York, NY 10020

Visit our Web site at
www.warnerbooks.com

A Time Warner Company

Printed in the United States of America

First Warner printing: April 2000

10 9 8 7 6 5 4 3 2 1

WARNER BOOKS EDITION

Cover design by Rachel McClain
Cover illustration by Vince McIndoe
Hand lettering by David Gatti
Text illustrations by Laurie Standish Abel

Warner Books, Inc.
1271 Avenue of the Americas
New York, NY 10020

Visit our Web site at
www.warnerbooks.com

 A Time Warner Company

Printed in the United States of America

First Printing: April, 1999

10 9 8 7 6 5 4 3 2 1

For Maureen Walters, Maria Angelico, and the entire fabulous team at Curtis Brown, Ltd.
There are agents, and there are agents.
And then there are AGENTS . . .

...meet Lady Hester's blue eyes.

❧ Prologue ❧

7 Mayfair Square, London. 1820

"You cannot trust the young.

"I thought I had made myself very clear: I am too old and too busy and too important to waste time on tasks that should not require my superior talents. To this end I expected to be free of my more youthful relatives' muddles by now.

"They are impossible.

"They have squandered the opportunities I provided them.

"Ah, well. And so it goes. Once more I must be the one to step in and save the day. Without me foolish Hester and that boy Hunter will undoubtedly lose this beautiful house entirely. I must rescue the family—yet again—and do so without revealing my fine hand in the matter for even an instant.

*As I have today, I must find disgracefully devious, but nec-
essary ways to gain information on the lay of the land.*

*"When I left Mayfair Square—that was some years ago,
but considerably later than should have been necessary—
when I left I said I'd done everything I intended to do, that
they had benefited greatly from my endeavors and did not
deserve further assistance. I told them that in future they
must manage without me. To allow them to know I have
weakened would only make them more demanding, more de-
pendent.*

*"I will warn you at once that my patience and my re-
strained sensibilities will doubtless be tried almost beyond
endurance. There will be moments when I shall simply have
to absent myself from events that I cannot condone or control. Please understand that if I could, I would shield you
from the more flamboyant escapades I expect from those
who have not learned to suppress the impulses of the heart
(and body) and listen to intellect alone. Unfortunately I
know matters will get out of hand and there won't be a thing
I can do about this.*

"There are lodgers at 7 Mayfair Square. Lodgers!

*"In a house that was once a center of culture, of musi-
cales and soirees, to say nothing of intimate gatherings
where only the most elite could hope to share the delicious
honor of being invited—in this house there are, even as I
write to you, three floors occupied by paying strangers.*

*"The shame of it nearly overwhelms me, but I do not have
time for such self-indulgence. I must act, and act quickly.
And I ask you to forgive me if my methods become—from necessity—less than, shall we say, conventional?*

*"You will? Of course, you will, I knew you were too sen-
sible not to support me.*

*"So, it is time to begin. I am persuaded that my best
chance of speedy success lies in dealing with these interlop-
ers one by one, or should I say, floor by floor. First we will
convince the brother and sister on the ground floor (offspring of a Cornish merchant—I shudder at the thought—a*

merchant involved in China Clay) to leave. Latimer and Finch More. Common names, but what can one expect of a tradesman's family? Latimer has a small import business. Oddities and rarities, so I'm told. And Finch catalogs offerings and deals with clients. More & More they call themselves. No doubt they consider that quite clever, but I have little patience with these new and flippant ideas embraced by those with little understanding of the value of well-bred reserve.

"Fortnum and Mason, Limited. Of Piccadilly, of course. Now there's a solid, no-nonsense name for a company. The original Mason owned a small shop on his own at first. Then his friend Fortnum—that was William who was a footman in the royal household—Fortnum retired and they became partners. Traded through the East India Company. They imported really exotic stuff. Hartshorn, Gable Worm Seed, Dirty White Candy. Those are items you will remember because they are worth remembering. Fortnum and Mason's cocoa powder even went on the expedition to find the Northwest Passage last year.

"I only remind you of these things to make a point. Fortnum and Mason always knew their places. Straightforward tradesmen. You wouldn't find them getting above their station by insinuatin' themselves into the households of the ton.

"I must collect myself.

"The challenge will be to bring about events that will encourage the upstart Mores to move along. At present they are much too happy at Number 7, but I do have a plan.

"Young Ross, Viscount Kilrood, lives next door at 8 Mayfair Square. He's a Scotsman who bought the property from Lord and Lady St. Germaine, not that we are concerned with such details here. But Ross will definitely play a large part in what will happen during the weeks to come.

"He is a glowering fellow. Angry, I rather think. I have heard a rumor that he was engaged, but his intended married his brother instead, and Kilrood has never recovered, or some such poppycock. But he has visited with the Mores *on occasion. Something to do with a commission he has for them. Anyway, I am given to believe that he has looked a little longer than might be expected—at Miss More. Can't imagine why myself. Plain stick of a thing from my observance. But no matter. The man has obviously deprived himself of female company for too long and consequently is no longer a fair judge of feminine attributes. I shall take advantage of his growing need.*

"Ahem. Forgive me if I am less than subtle. However, as I've told you, these young blades will stoop to less-than-admirable behavior anyway. I am simply forced to take advantage of human nature—for a higher cause, of course. But I shall, you may rest assured, choose to avoid actually watching.

"I grow tired. As I have said, I am old and deserve to rest upon my laurels. I shall do so, at least for tonight.

"Tomorrow the work truly begins. And it may be a great deal of work to ensure that Viscount Kilrood is forced to take More & More into his home—and away from Number 7.

"Hah. It is time to embark on Kilrood's seduction of Miss Finch More."

❧ Chapter 1 ❧

If there was one thing Finch More couldn't abide, it was being wrong and having to admit as much.

She was wrong.

She should not have returned to Whitechapel alone, and on foot, and when it was growing dark, and colder.

She should not have placed herself in the way of being frightened out of her wits by her own imagination—which could be overactive. Why, a moment ago she'd even mistaken a slight sound for someone speaking her name.

"Finch."

There it was again. She looked in every direction. The streets were all but empty, and the few muffler-swathed people still abroad walked with the certainty of folk who knew where they were going and were in a hurry to get there. Not one of them spared her as much as a glance.

"Silly female," she said aloud, and glared at a grinning boy with a big, sticky bun in one hand, who poked out his crumb-covered tongue as he passed. What did she care if a mannerless boy thought she was light-brained for talking to herself?

"They puts people the likes of you in asylums, they does," the boy said. He held the bun in his teeth, crossed his eyes, and rushed away with his arms flailing.

Why did Latimer insist upon keeping the business down here in Whitechapel, where all manner of sordid events occurred? "Cheap," she said, and glanced furtively behind her to make sure the boy was well enough away not to hear. Latimer watched every penny and insisted she do likewise. That was why she'd decided to walk rather than get a cab after she'd made the delivery of a small package. She should have continued home as Latimer had expected, but he was likely to stay at the warehouse all night, very possibly without eating, if she left him alone there.

"Fi-inch."

A great bound of her heart made her feel quite odd. There, she thought, that *was* her name. Very softly spoken, to be sure, but definitely her name. Someone she couldn't see said, no, sang her name in a foolish manner to try to make her afraid. The back of her neck prickled.

Who? She didn't know anyone in London apart from the rest of the people who lived at Number 7. And the people Latimer did business with. Hardly likely candidates for playing tricks on her in the street.

Very soon she would be there, at the warehouse, and safe. Not that she wasn't safe now. After all, what could happen to her with buildings on either side of the street and people . . . There had been people only a moment ago, and there would be more any second. She pulled the looped ribbons of her reticule into the crook of an elbow. Only a country girl, a girl from a Cornish village or some such backward place, would start dreaming voices just because she was in London.

"Fi-inch."

She whirled about. This time it had sounded closer.

A hand, clamped over her mouth, caught her next breath

in her throat. Her bonnet tipped forward, and she couldn't see past the brim. She choked, and kicked at whoever stood behind her, but her slippered heels undoubtedly fared worse than what felt like a pair of solid boots.

The bonnet slipped sideways until it hung beneath her chin.

"This won't take no great time, miss," a voice said against her ear. Seams on his heavy glove bit into her face. "Better to keep your feet for walking, if you please." With that she was bundled through a gap in a high wooden fence and into a yard between two buildings. A squalid yard strewn with rubbish from what she could make out. And the buildings were of blackened brick with no windows and had roofs that blurred into a darkening sky where smoke scarred a faint purple haze.

Why would anyone bother to murder her? That's what he would do, wasn't it? This man was going to kill her.

Finch tried to scream.

"'Ere, 'ere," her captor said, and shook her. "You'd do well enough to 'eed my warnings and do what I tell you."

She had no opportunity to do otherwise before a shape materialized from the shadowed wall to her right, a tall figure with head bowed. His billowing cloak and top hat cast a fuzzy silhouette behind him.

Like a great bat.

Squeezing her eyes shut, Finch struggled, kicked, and squirmed, and bit hard at the gloved hand over her mouth. A muffled curse was her only reward. For the rest, she was lifted from the ground and flung down.

Flung down, but caught by the cloaked creature the moment before she would have hit muddy ground. When she tried to look at him, he spun her around, relieving her of her reticule as he did so, and finished what the other had started by depositing her facedown in a heap on the ground.

"Remain as you are if you please, and you will be unharmed," she was told in a voice so low of tone it echoed from its owner's depths. The man did not sound English, did he?

A shower of objects hit her back, and she cried out.

"Silence."

Shaking, placing her hands over her mouth, Finch did her best to do as she was told. She would die here in this filthy, smelly place with smoke burning her eyes and stinging her nose. Die in the chill of a young winter's night.

"Remember my words, Miss Finch More," said the voice from the earth. "The time is coming soon. The old tiger will give way to the new. Then the young tiger will eat its predecessor. So it reads. Each of us has a purpose whether it be great or small. Your small purpose will be served, and you will no longer be required—but you might be overlooked if you cause no irritation."

The speaker fell silent, but his speech echoed on. A meaningless dissertation. Part of their evil design to terrify their victims into complete submission.

Finch bowed even lower. What made them think she could do anything but be submissive?

Another hard article, and another, then several more bounced from her shoulders and neck to land among the stones and debris.

These creatures were tossing down the contents of her reticule. She opened her mouth to say she had nothing of value, but thought better of the notion. They would discover what a poor prize they had chosen soon enough, then there would be no need to wait longer to dispose of her.

"Keep your eyes closed, Miss Finch More. And you will put your hands on your ears. There will be loud noise. Like the roar of the tiger. It will be easier if you do not see or hear." She didn't know which of the men spoke, but she quickly clapped her hands over her ears. Her eyes were already tightly shut.

A loud noise? An explosion, perhaps? A pistol shot?

Finch moaned, and curled into as small a ball as she could make of herself.

Poor Latimer. He was so absentminded about anything but his treasures from the Indies and China—and the pieces he'd recently obtained from Egypt. What would he do without her? How would he remember to eat, or put on a neckcloth, or make sure the accounts for the business were kept in order, to say nothing of paying the rent to Lady Hester Bingham?

Latimer would never go to Papa for help because their father had disinherited his son when Latimer insisted on studying antiquities rather than going into Papa's business.

Poor Papa. He was a hard man but not without feelings, and he did love her. Finch just knew Papa loved her, and Latimer, of course. And since Papa was a widower of many years, he didn't have a wife to turn to in times of grief.

Finch's mind spun and spun—and spun. Everyone she loved would be distraught at her death. When her pale, lifeless body . . .

She held her breath and parted her hands from her ears a scant distance.

Not a sound.

No one spoke harshly to her, or tried to stop her from moving.

She opened her eyes, and when she could see a little made out a shiny coin nearby. When she dared to raise her head a fraction she saw several more coins, and the silver cross that had been her mother's and which Finch always kept with her. Also there were a number of large buttons she'd bought for her collection—and the *Hydrobia ulvae* she'd been fortunate to find for her shell collection.

Finch sniffed. Tears spattered the backs of her hands.

Crying, for goodness sake.

She knelt more upright and checked around. Her attackers had definitely left.

They had left.

She was still alive.

They had not shot her.

"Of course I'm crying. I am not made of stone. I almost

di-di-died here." She wiped her face with the back of a sleeve and kept on sobbing. Such a terrible shock was bound to make a woman cry and shake and feel unwell.

"I have been too strong for too long," she said into her sleeve. It was true. Always the strong one. Always the one to deal with the more unpleasant aspects of trying to make a life with only her own small allowance, Latimer's meager inheritance from their mother (portioned out in minuscule amounts), and what little profit could be squeezed from the fledgling business.

Still weeping, she clumsily retrieved her spilled treasures. Why hadn't those beasts taken her money? Little enough, it was true—just the coins she carried for emergencies—but thieves weren't supposed to leave money behind.

Her hands hurt, and her knees, and her face, and other parts of her.

Oh how horrified Latimer would be when he saw her, and how angry that she had returned to him rather than go home.

When she stood up every bit of her ached. Now she must collect herself as best she could and try to ensure Latimer had no idea of exactly what had occurred. She must devise a suitable story. True, she abhorred lies, but on this occasion she would invent a small untruth for the purpose of saving her dear brother's temper.

A *large* untruth.

She did what she could to pin up escaped locks of hair and replaced her bonnet. Fortunately her pelisse and gown were of sensible brown chintz. The darkness made it impossible to see well, but she thought mud might be scarcely noticeable.

At last she could do nothing more to improve her appearance, and she set off to go the short distance left to the warehouse. The building was in a mean alley and flanked by two similar hulks at present unoccupied. On the opposite side of the alley hovels slunk together in a dismal line. Those who lived there were seldom seen.

The night was all but black now. A sullen moon barely bothered to stroke the edges of a single cloud break. Finch's soft half boots scuffed the cobbles. Cold struck through the thin leather to her feet.

She reached the door where a small (Latimer called it "discreet") sign announced, More & More, Importers, in white letters on a piece of polished wood.

Pushing her way inside the echoing cavern, Finch finally decided what she would tell Latimer and felt hugely relieved.

"Latimer," she called, hurrying between crates containing items Latimer had obtained from abroad. The space reeked of dust and mildew. "Latimer, it's Finch." A light shone through the open door to the large office they called their showroom. In truth they could only show certain items in the office. Anything too big, or too heavy, required that a customer make the best of viewing it in the warehouse itself, not an ideal arrangement but the best that could be offered at present.

"My what a day," Finch said, affecting a cheerfully exasperated tone. She walked quickly into the office.

With his back to her, Latimer bent over an open crate.

Lord Kilrood faced her from behind the desk.

Drat, Finch thought, and felt her false cheer sink beneath gloom. Of all the rotten luck. How could she have the misfortune to find him here tonight of all nights?

A number of weeks earlier they had met Lord Kilrood through Hunter Lloyd, the nephew of Lady Hester Bingham who owned 7 Mayfair Square. Kilrood had started doing some business with them. He seemed a decent enough sort, despite the superior manner one could expect from someone of his station, but he had an uncanny way of staring at her as if he found her a puzzle. Or perhaps she shocked him . . . Perhaps he could not believe that in his privileged life where he could surround himself with nothing but pretty women, he occasionally found himself in the company of a plain one.

She bobbed an abbreviated curtsy, not that it was worth the effort since he showed no sign of noticing.

He *really* stared.

Finch attempted to stare back, but he had the kind of disquietingly brilliant blue eyes that didn't blink. In fact they didn't even flicker. His eyelashes were very black and cast a shadow in that blue stare.

How *rude*. He should have been taught from childhood that open curiosity was incredibly rude.

She cleared her throat and made a great deal of cinching the ribbons on her reticule. When she glanced downward she noted with disgust that there were jagged rips in her skirt. And mud did show when it began to dry—even on brown chintz.

"Latimer—"

He interrupted her, "A moment, Finch. I'm looking for something."

Just as well. She prayed her hastily fabricated tale would be convincing.

Lord Kilrood came from behind the desk. He lowered his head slightly and peered at her more closely.

Finch nodded politely—although restraint cost her considerably—and she even smiled a little. But then she felt what she had felt on more than one occasion when in the company of this imposing man: wobbly inside.

Oh fie, of all the treacherous tricks of silly female vulnerability to the male. The man appealed—well, he caused some strangely exciting sensations, and she actually felt drawn to him. It was as if she wished, no, she *did* wish she were other than plain. And she did wish that he might look at her as a man interested in a woman—as a woman—looked at that woman.

This was most muddling. After all, she was nine-and-twenty and had known love once. These feelings had not been associated with that pure and tragically lost love, not at all. Naturally there could be no question of loving a stranger anyway, but tonight's events, the manner in which she felt bemused in his company, suggested that her reaction to Lord Kilrood was motivated by something quite other than a pure spirit. Why it felt . . . *carnal*.

"Are you all right, Miss More?"

"Don't mind Finnie, Your Lordship," Latimer said from the depths of his crate. "You know how quiet she is. She has lived a very simple life in the country and is unaccustomed to making polite conversation."

Sometimes Latimer could be intensely irritating.

Lord Kilrood paid no attention to Latimer's comment. He did come a little closer to Finch.

She felt warm, which was ridiculous since she was obviously cold. Oh, her fearful experiences this night had been too much. They had made her—she hoped temporarily—feebleminded.

"Miss More," he said, very quietly, "what has happened to you?"

Finch looked to Latimer's back and was grateful to see that he hadn't heard. She placed a finger on her lips and shook her head.

Lord Kilrood narrowed his eyes.

The wobbly sensation returned. He was a well-made man. A very well made man. Taller than she had thought she cared for because she didn't like feeling overpowered by another's size, but she felt differently about this man's person. He was tall, and broad of shoulder, and he had a solid presence that suggested his fine figure would be just as fine without his well-cut clothes.

A wild heat overtook Finch, and she couldn't stop her mouth from falling open. What had come over her? She closed her eyes tightly, then opened them again. Had she hit her head when that creature threw her down? She didn't remember doing so, but then, perhaps she wouldn't if it were bad enough.

Amnesia.

A change of personality.

Without clothes? Of all the terrible, absolutely unsuitable, completely unforgivable thoughts.

"You should sit down," he said, blessedly keeping his voice low. "You do not look well."

She looked awful. Greville had liked the way she looked, God rest his soul, but that was because of their long familiarity. Everyone else said she was a fright.

"Miss More?"

Finch shook her head again, more violently this time. Lord Kilrood had a pleasing face. His cheekbones were high, his mouth . . . he had a most pleasing mouth. A finely cut face, that's how she would describe it. Finely cut but very much the face of a strong man. A strong, handsome man. Pleasing was a pathetic word that did little to convey a person's true feelings if those feelings were about something she thought marvelous.

He had a slow manner of speech, slow and considered, with the faintest hint of that most intriguing Scottish accent. There was a touch of red in his dark hair.

"Miss More," he said, sounding less concerned than determined this time, "I insist that you take a seat. You are not yourself."

Latimer stood up and turned around.

Finch braced herself. She must not cause him more worry. Providing for their livelihood was already enough strain on him. "Latimer, I don't want you to worry about me."

"Hm?" His thick, brown hair fell over his brow. He was examining a white figurine of a naked woman.

She would not allow him to blame himself for the outcome of her own careless actions. "I had a little accident. Nothing serious."

At that Latimer looked up sharply. "Did it break?"

"Break?"

"That perfect Grecian amulet. Not particularly old, but without a flaw. Did you break it, Finnie?"

"Er, no." She felt foolish. "I delivered it safely. Then I decided to come back here after all."

"Good, good," he said, smiling at her. "I say, Finnie, that dress is getting a bit tatty, isn't it? Even for you? Never mind. You wouldn't be good old Finnie if you gave a fig for such things. See if you can make some tea for His Lordship, would you?"

§ Chapter 2 §

Ross laced his hands together behind his back and studied Finch More. Continued to study her. He found Latimer More's careless attention to his sister's welfare deplorable. True the man was an academic and removed from most of the rest of the world, but that did not excuse callous neglect.

Latimer said, "I shall have to go out to the warehouse." He handed the figurine he held to Ross. "Very nice piece. Also Greek. I haven't dated it precisely yet. If you'll excuse me." He left the office and could be heard humming, or rather, "pom-pomming" to himself in the spaces beyond.

"They knew my name," Finch said. Her expression became stricken.

"I beg your pardon?" They had become acquainted, at least in a casual sense, some weeks prior, but the lady had remained respectfully withdrawn. "Who knew your name?"

With a flurry, she went about the business of untying her bonnet strings as if she were preparing to go to work. Then, with the bonnet in one hand, and her amazingly bright red hair rapidly sliding to fall in tangles at her shoulders, she paused. "Oh, dear," she said and proceeded to cram the headpiece back on hard enough to smash its crown. She said, "Oh, dear" again.

There were times when convention must be put aside. "I insist that you sit down, Miss More," he said, pulling forward an armchair covered in faded puce velvet. *"Down."*

She sat—or rather plopped—and put her hands together in her lap.

"I asked what has happened to you," he said. "And what did you mean when you said someone knew your name?"

"Nothing." Slim almost in the extreme, the lady had the pale skin of the red-haired and a considerable endowment of freckles over her pointed nose. Her eyelashes were also red. At the moment they were downcast.

He would not be so easily diverted. "Your hair is awry." Carefully, he removed her hat and was surprised when she made no attempt to stop him. "And your hat was askew, and is sadly damaged. You have torn your gown in numerous places, and there is mud in evidence."

"As I tried to tell my brother, I had an accident. It was nothing serious."

Ross was unsure why, but he found her an unexpectedly interesting creature. "What kind of accident?"

"I fell."

He wished she would look at him. He thought her light brown eyes . . . interesting. "How did you fall?"

"I fell," she said, her face snapping up. "How many ways are there to fall? I fell *down*."

He waited until she looked at him fully. "I don't think you misunderstood the question," he said. "You are upset. No—do not deny it. I have had the opportunity to observe you since I've known you and your brother, and by nature you are a calm woman, or at least you are a woman who does not display great emotion. You were upset when you arrived here, and are upset now. A fall, even though disconcerting, should not cause either so much damage to your *toilette,* or render you so disquieted. Neither should there be anything about the event to make you want to hide the details from your brother. And you did indicate a wish to do so."

After far too long a pause, she said, "It was a bad fall," but when she closed her mouth, her lips trembled. Ross had taken note of her lips before—not at all the lips of a woman intended for the spinsterhood her brother insisted she desired.

Now he noted what he hadn't noted before, several thin, red marks on her face. He put the bonnet on the desk and bent over to see more clearly.

Miss More shrank back in her chair.

"How was your face injured?" he asked, and touched one of the marks with a gentle forefinger.

She sat absolutely still while he touched her. "Does this hurt?" He looked into her eyes and stilled his fingers. Her intelligence was something he'd divined the first time they met. He'd also felt an unusual kinship with her, as if they shared some connection as yet to be revealed. Today he felt that connection again, and its nature became at least somewhat clearer. They could come to understand each other—a state he had never before attained with a lady. "I asked if this hurts," he said.

"No." She cleared her throat, and said more clearly. "No."

"I am no expert at such matters, but I wonder what manner of fall would produce such widely diverse injuries."

Finch More stared up into his face, and he experienced a catch in his breathing. A unique creature. True, all people were unique, but they almost always had similarities to others of their kind. Not so Finch More, as far as Ross could discern. And then he realized his fingers had come to rest on her cheek.

She remained quite still.

"These were not the result of a fall, were they?" he said. "Someone did this to you." He had an unpleasant conviction that he was correct. "Struck you, perhaps?"

"Please don't persist with this."

So, he had deduced accurately. "Since I see that you are determined to hide the truth from Latimer, I must insist that you reveal it to me. I would be remiss if I left you alone with what is obviously a matter of great trial to you."

"It is a matter of great puzzle and annoyance," she announced, so abruptly and with such force, that she flinched at her own vehemence. "Oh, please, leave the matter alone."

Ross wavered. After all, it was really none of his affair. Or was it? Surely what had happened to her wasn't connected with his own business, with the commission he had undertaken. He considered. Could this be the start of what he had hoped to avoid? If those with a reason to stop him from succeeding had discovered his dealings with the Mores . . . Dash it all, the last thing he'd considered possible was that he might lead them into danger, but he could not go back now. Too many lives depended upon what he intended to complete in London before the year was out.

"Shouldn't you like to set the figurine down?" she said, regarding his left hand.

Ross glanced, too, and was mildly amused to see that he gripped the well-endowed figurine by a very personal part of her anatomy. "I had forgotten her," he said, and stroked the small, perfect face, a shoulder, a breast. "Beautiful, don't you think?"

"Quite."

Unsure why he was resorting to subtly baiting her, he continued examining the piece. Each breast received his scrutiny, and his touch. He massaged the cool creature's body with a thumb while he returned his attention to Finch. "Men have always been enchanted with the female form. I wonder how many centuries have passed since the artist made this with such care. I'm sure he enjoyed his work."

"The artist could have been a woman," she pointed out.

"I think not." He turned the figure in his hand. "Only look at the angle of the head, the thrust . . . well, there is an eroticism in the artist's rendition. As if his subject aroused him. Ah, yes, I'm sure it was a man." There was no excuse for his making such an unsuitable comment to an unmarried lady. She would be correct in demanding an apology.

Miss More regarded him direct. "You may be right. Perhaps he was in love with his model." Brave words, but there were spots of color in the lady's cheeks and the slightest tremble in her voice. He did admire her, though. She was indomitable. Oddly, that indomitability had the effect—possibly an unforgivable effect—of making him want to shock her.

"You are a great help to your brother," he said. "He has told me so. You assist in cataloging acquisitions for him, which must mean you have a degree of knowledge yourself."

"Some," she said, "but my own area of interest is glass. A cold medium, but mysterious, subtle—and rarely as obvious as the piece that so intrigues you."

He put the figurine on the desk. "Very well, Miss More, we have feinted long enough. Who knew your name?"

Using the arms of the chair, Finch got up—and let out a sharp cry.

"What is it?" He caught her by the shoulders. "What have they done to you?"

She turned her face away, but a movement caused him to look to her hands. With the palms against her body and her wrists crossed, she nursed them awkwardly.

"Your hands," Ross said, and held each of her forearms carefully but firmly while he turned them over. "Your gloves are in ribbons. My dear woman, your *hands* are in ribbons."

"Yes," she told him quietly. "They hurt."

Horrified, Ross began to peel off a glove, but she drew breath so sharply he felt her pain himself and paused. "You were attacked? You attempted to fight back, perhaps. Tell me, please. I shall know the truth, miss. I shall not be diverted."

"I don't know who it was," she said finally. She helped him take off a glove with a ruined, blood-spattered palm.

"But I did not fight. Nothing nearly so romantic and heroic. These wounds were made by debris on the ground."

"Latimer must know about this at once."

"No!" She would have pulled away had he not restrained her. "No, I tell you. Latimer has more than enough to concern him. If he learns about this, he may try to make me remain in Mayfair Square when he needs me here."

"I should certainly agree with him if he ordered you not to be about on your own—particularly after dark on a bitter winter afternoon."

She could not have intended her sidelong glance to be inflaming, yet it was so. When she looked up at him like that her eyes sloped and her fine red brows gleamed in the light and he was . . . engaged?

"Please don't interfere," she said. "I shall be careful in future."

"Was this a common robbery?"

She bowed her head. "I don't know."

"These were street ruffians who stole your possessions?"

"No."

"What then—or who?"

"Two men. I don't think they were poor. They were well dressed, or the one I saw was well dressed. The other, the one who captured me, was always behind and I did not see him. They didn't steal anything. There was something about the way one of them spoke. A foreign suggestion. I don't know."

He frowned at her. The ugly possibility that her experience was linked to his own concerns loomed larger. "Are you sure they took nothing from you?"

"Quite sure." Holding her lower lip in her teeth, she took off her other glove, rolled the pair together, and tucked them inside her reticule.

"Your hands need to be cleaned."

"They will be cleaned soon enough."

"I insist you tell me all—exactly what occurred, if you please."

"Latimer will return soon. There is not time."

"Begin if you please," he told her. He could take no risks with the task he had been charged to perform.

From a distance, but growing closer, came the rather tuneful sound of Latimer "pom-pomming" his way back.

"Listen to him," Finch said with a smile that was clearly forced. "He is cheerful. I don't expect you to understand such things, but there has been too little cheer in my brother's life of late. He has suffered great strain. I beg you to allow me to deal with this in my own way."

To agree might be the easy way—for himself—but such a course wasn't open to him. "These men spoke to you?"

She glanced to the door and back, and said, "Yes," with urgency. "I have said as much. Please do as I ask."

"What did they say?" He knew he was merciless and disliked having to press her, but he was no stranger to force in many guises. "I have to know."

The patches of color in her pale face grew more vivid. "Will you not heed my wishes, my lord?"

He found he did not care for her formality. How strange, he had lived with such formality all his life. "At least begin. Tell me something."

For an instant she gritted her strong teeth and glared.

A smile came to Ross. "You have a temper, I see. How very charming. I do not care for milksop females."

"Perhaps you prefer *tigers,* my lord."

He grew still and watched her closely, watched and waited.

"Old tigers? Or new ones? There, does that nonsense mean anything to you?" she asked.

His very skin turned cold, but he must remain calm and show no sign of particular concern. "I'm quite fond of tigers—of any age. What connection have they with your attackers?" It was as he had feared. It had to be. Her misfortune was somehow tied to his own affairs.

Without warning her eyes filled with tears. But when he made to go to her, she held out a poor, injured hand in warn-

ing for him to stay away. "I have had too much excitement.
I'm a country person and unused to such things. I shall recover soon enough though. One of them spoke of tigers,
that's all. Nonsense with no meaning at all. Now be silent,
please."

"I should like to talk with you further. Do you have an engagement this evening? Perhaps at ten. Yes, ten."

"I have an engagement with my bed," she said, all snap,
and blushed even more fiercely.

Where was his mind? Of course she must not come so late
at night—alone. He thought quickly. "Quite so. That would
be much too late. But I still ask you to come to me. And
please be certain you are not missed. At eight. Doubtless
that will be time enough for you to arrange to get away—
and for me to do what I must do." Eight o'clock was also unsuitable, yet there seemed no alternative. He must make an
opportunity to question her in private. "Since you live on the
first floor, you should have no difficulty. My own front door
shall be unlocked so you will not be embarrassed by a confrontation with one of my servants. I'll make certain of that.
I'll await you in the red salon. You know the way."

He saw that his meaning came to her slowly. She took a
step backward. "You jest, my lord."

"I rarely jest, and never when I issue an invitation to a
lady."

"A pity. You surely cannot expect me to take such an unsuitable suggestion seriously."

"Forgive me if I am forceful, but I can and I do." *He must.*

"Perhaps we shall speak on another occasion. Latimer is
here."

The door was indeed opening, and the annoying "pom-
pom" became loud.

"Eight this evening, or as soon as possible thereafter. Unless you wish to pursue the subject here and now," Ross
said, not liking himself overmuch. Expediency forced his
hand. "Fear not, your reputation would never be jeopardized
by me."

There was the slightest pause in which he longed to take back the careless words, then she said, "No, I'm sure it wouldn't. How else could such an accomplished flatterer have remained a bachelor?"

§ Chapter 3 §

"*I ache in every joint. This really is too much, entirely too much. There is something afoot here and I cannot be certain what it is, but I shall find out.*

"*I took a short rest. Well, quite a long rest, but I did not anticipate that there would be any developments that might prove an impediment to my design.*

"*If I had no scruples, no integrity, I might stoop to devious means to obtain my ends—and with my peerless intelligence I could devise methods only guessed at by lesser intellects—but integrity dictates that I adhere to the codes of any honorable mortal.*

"*Ahh, but an aching back does let a person down at certain stages. Now to assess what has occurred. Such a lot of fuss and bother. Number 7 is in uproar. Comings. Goings. Squealings. Sighings. Petulant demands for smelling salts and the like.*

"*Lady Hester is beside herself and enjoying a great deal of attention. The cause for this domestic unrest will emerge soon enough, but I have more pressing concerns. The Mores. It is in their apparent intrigues that I must first immerse myself.*

"*I spoke with one of the servants at Number 8 this evening, and I understand Lord Kilrood is in a foul humor. According to the silly woman who talked so freely of her master's affairs, he went to the Mores' place of business in Whitechapel and returned an angry man.*

"*I might have celebrated at the thought of his being with my pigeons, but not if there has been some disagreement. Why, one wonders, did he go to Whitechapel anyway? I had thought all his business dealings with them were accomplished beneath his own roof, or at the very least, at Number 7. There is something I don't know, and that will not do. The servant, Alice, a flighty one who imagines herself a coquette, she informed me that her master had ordered all to retire early in the evening and warned that he would not be pleased if one of them showed so much as a nose. I asked why she had made so bold as to venture forth. She was in the back garden, you see. On her way to a meeting, she said, an important meeting. And there was the wink of the eye, and the sway of the hip. One can imagine the nature of that meeting.*

"*Now why would young Kilrood return from Whitechapel in such sour temper?*

"*Hmm. And what, one might ask, is the reason for Miss Finch More's tragical face and the manner in which she and her brother returned to Number 7? Her nose was all wrinkled as if she were in pain. Really, young women are a puzzle. No matter. My concern is to bring the tragical-faced Miss More together with the sour-humoured Lord Kilrood— and to have them caught so, alone.*

"*Ooh, saving the fortunes of a family can be a heavy burden, especially when the ungrateful wretches will do nothing to help themselves, and when one has to expect them to squander their advantages yet again.*

"And so it goes. I have work to do. It is time to bring my unwilling lovebirds together.

"I have designed the first step. I have a visit to make."

❧ *Chapter 4* ❧

Lady Hester Bingham was beloved by all her "guests." A generous, if garrulous lady, she beamed down from the third floor of Number 7 upon her little brood of resident souls, and took rather too much interest in their affairs.

Actually she had to beam up at Adam Chillworth because he rented the attic for a price that was hinted to be ridiculously low. Adam's abode was referred to as 7C, while Her Ladyship and her nephew, Hunter Lloyd, resided at 7. After all, it was only appropriate that theirs should be the prime address, wasn't it? Lady Hester's choice of the third floor over the first had yet to be explained, but there had been hints of a sentimental reason.

Lady Hester and Hunter occupied two suites of rooms fronted by balconies, that faced each other across Sir Septimus Spivey's grand staircase. Sir Septimus, the architect who designed the house, had allowed his artistic powers full flight at Number 7. The splendid, carved-mahogany staircase stood open through the three main floors of the house.

From each flight there unfolded a fresh vista to elaborate plaster-worked ceilings, soaring pillars, the odd chinoiserie screen, and bronze bases supporting fanciful wooden urns in the shapes of Sir Septimus's favorite animals. Here a huge gold-painted cat-thing with a tail for a handle. There a swan ewer, its neck and beak apparently intended to represent an elongated spout. In another spot, a shiny green armadillo with too many feet. Extravagant velvet drapings, massive wall hangings, and silk coverings embellished the walls. Carpets were of silk in what Finch privately called "amazing combinations of colors."

Unfortunately Number 7 had suffered somewhat from seventy years of continuous and heavy use without renovation. When Finch spoke of the subject to Meg Smiles at 7B they were fondly kind, but the fact was that the splendor of the house was tarnished.

"I wonder what has Lady Hester so upset," Finch whispered to Meg when they met in their host's boudoir in the early evening, after Finch had taken a private moment to clean her wounds and change her clothes. "Old Coot was all dark hints about *things gorn missing*. But everything is old and not particularly valuable." Coot was Lady Hester's aged butler.

"Except for its curiosity," Meg said, her impish smile making her somewhat ordinary face quite pretty.

Finch smiled back and patted the seat beside her on a black-and-gold-striped chaise. "Sibyl isn't coming?" Finch said of Meg's older and more quiet sister.

"She's too tired," Meg said. "This is the day Lady Chattam brings her son. Poor Sibyl says he will never make a pianist at all and that it's probably sinful to take money for trying to teach him, but his mother is convinced he has talent. In fact Sibyl says that Lady Chattam never stops marveling at her dear Teddy's talent, in loud tones, throughout every lesson."

"Poor Sibyl," Finch said of Meg's beautiful but retiring sibling. "I would much rather sew lovely things as you do."

"Thank you," Meg said, but studied her hands in her lap.

On the death of their minister father, the Smiles sisters' male cousin had inherited the house in which they had grown up and almost everything that went with it. Rather than remain as little better than servants in the home that had been their own, Meg and Sibyl took their meager funds and set about making a life for themselves. Sibyl gave piano lessons while Meg, who sewed wonderfully, made gowns for a select group of customers. Unfortunately, Meg was ashamed of her unaccustomed station in life.

"Do you suppose this will take long, Finnie?" Latimer asked, taking out his watch and looking anxious. "Old Coot had a message for me when I got in. I've got an appointment to keep."

Finch didn't recall Latimer getting a message but made no comment. It was quite possible that she'd been too preoccupied with her own great dilemma to notice anyway.

"They're trying to get Mr. Chillworth to come down," Finch said. "I understand Lady Hester felt we should all be present."

"Adam won't come," Meg said. She was the only member of the household who used Adam Chillworth's first name. "If he gets wind of any fuss, he won't even answer his door." She smiled fondly. A kindhearted girl, she alone had broken through Chillworth's reserve. Finch had even seen them quietly chatting from time to time, and Meg had viewed some of his paintings although she would never discuss them.

The door from Lady Hester's bedroom into the boudoir opened, and that lady entered in a flurry of flounced black silk. A tall, striking woman who could not be more than fifty, she created an atmosphere of agitation wherever she went—which wasn't far since she almost never left Number 7. Apparently in extended mourning, one assumed for her husband, she managed to look gloriously noble in her somber but stylish garb.

"Come along, Barstow," she said to her housekeeper, who

ran the house, acted as Lady Hester's personal maid, and generally ruled over all. "Get me seated, if you please. We must decide on a plan at once. This is all most serious and distressing. We are under siege, darlings, under siege. I am anxious to ensure your well-being." She paused, drawing up her considerable and jet-draped bosom. "And your *safety*."

Finch and Meg looked at each other.

Latimer looked at his watch, yet again.

"*Where* is everybody?" Lady Hester asked. She raised her tortoiseshell lorgnette and surveyed the room as if Adam Chillworth and Sibyl might be hiding behind the gold-fringed, black-velvet draperies at the narrow windows. "*Hunter* is not here, either? I told you to be certain he was aware of this meeting, Barstow."

A substantial, gray-haired lady in matching gray uniform, Mrs. Barstow rarely showed emotion. "Mr. Hunter is aware," she said without inflection. "He had to go out."

"*Out?*" Lady Hester said in her full, rounded voice. "He went out after I asked that he be here?"

A large collection of keys rattled on a chain at Mrs. Barstow's waist. At the moment, while she plumped pillows on her mistress's ornate black-lacquer daybed, the metallic noise was like the sound of an agitated prisoner's leg irons. "There, Your Ladyship. You get comfy. Mr. Hunter said he'd be back as soon as he could. We can probably expect him at any moment."

"Sibyl is tired, my lady," Meg said. "Today was Teddy Chattam's day, and you know what that does to her." She smiled, and deep dimples appeared at each corner of her mouth. Her hair was brown, a very shiny brown, and coiled in a loose chignon that gave her a soft appearance.

"Frightful child," Lady Hester said with relish. She did enjoy any gossip her flock brought to her. "What can you expect when he has such a frightful mother? Marjorie Chattam was a silly girl, and she's a silly woman, and that's that."

"You asked to see us," Latimer announced, silencing all. "Coot mentioned some trouble."

The interruption earned him his own, personal stare through the tortoiseshell lorgnette.

Sometimes Latimer missed obvious warning signals. "I have an appointment." He looked at his watch. "So I hope this won't take long."

Oblivious to Lady Hester's astonished stare, Latimer bounced the handsome gold watch in his palm. The timepiece had been Father's gift for his son's twenty-first birthday.

Finch regarded her brother with fond resignation. He would always plow through life only partly aware of those with whom he journeyed. Sometimes she wished for him to meet a strong, capable woman who would love and care for him. On other occasions she was sure no such paragon existed. Her brother did have a sweet side to his nature and could even be playful when diverted from his true passion: things old. And he was certainly an attractive man. With his dark, curly hair and eyes that were almost black, he resembled their mother's side of the family. The ugly red hair, freckles, and pale brown eyes were Finch's legacy from the Mores.

Latimer could charm if he so chose. He had a ready enough smile that gave him a devilish air, and he was tall and strong.

Why didn't Latimer seem to notice that women found him noteworthy? Finch sighed and glanced at Meg, who looked at Latimer, but with more speculation than thwarted adoration.

"It's almost seven-thirty," Latimer said, pulling his dark brows together in a formidable frown. "Look, Finnie, I simply have to get along. You fly the family flag, old thing. I'll be all ears to know what this is about. You can tell me later. Got to go out now. 'Evening, all."

With that he strode from the room, and Finch dared not meet Lady Hester's blue eyes.

"Very well," the lady said. "I might have anticipated that only the most sensible of us would take a serious matter seriously. Although I had expected Hunter to be sure to join us. Is Coot doing as I asked, Barstow?"

"I'm sure he's doing his best, my lady."

Finch attempted to concentrate. Other matters made her efforts useless. The autocratic Lord Kilrood would expect her to creep, like a thief, into his house in half an hour. Alone. He would make certain no member of his household saw her. Then she would go to his red salon so that he might press her for information he had no right to request and which could not possibly be of interest to him.

The man was certainly memorable.

He was stunning, yes, that was the word, stunning.

Of course there was no need for concern about her virtue. Ross, Viscount Kilrood would no more look at Finch More as anything more than a minion to do as he asked, than she would look at him as more than . . . Yes, well, he wouldn't look at her as more than an almost-invisible nothing.

That didn't mean she couldn't wish he would.

Finch smiled a little. She might have lost the man she was to have married to some horrible foreign war, but evidently her own interest in the opposite sex had not died with him. Some might say she should be ashamed. She wasn't. She was realistic enough to know that if she ever had the unlikely good fortune to meet another man who would want to marry her, and whom she would want to marry, she would be delighted. However, she was not foolish enough to think she'd ever have a chance with someone like Lord Kilrood.

Not that she would want him.

Would she?

"You cannot rely on the help these days." Lady Hester reclined on her ornate Chinese daybed, but only for an instant before leaping to her feet once more. She smoothed her skirts and tucked away stray wisps of blond hair.

Startled by the outburst, Finch made a courageous effort to shut out thoughts of their neighbor.

Lady Hester said, "We are under siege, ladies. We have suffered an attack of a most odious kind."

Finch caught Meg's eye, and they exchanged bewildered looks.

"Oh, where is Coot?" Lady Hester marched to the bellpull and yanked three times.

"Are you sure you want him to bring it here?" Barstow inquired mildly. "It is a bit heavy, m'lady."

"Apparently heaviness isn't an impediment to some," Lady Hester declared darkly. "I'm a believer in making sure everyone understands exactly what one is talking about. That's why I want the item in question here. Or what's left of it."

The door to the balcony opened without warning, but it was Hunter Lloyd who entered. He carried, or rather staggered in with, one of the bronze bases, and set it down before his aunt.

"I asked Coot to do that," Lady Hester said.

Immaculate in a dark blue coat and black trousers—although a trifle red in the face—Hunter produced a handkerchief and mopped his brow. "Coot is ninety if he's a day, Aunt. Did you wish to kill the poor man?"

Lady Hester appeared mildly chastened but didn't apologize. "You're late for a very important meeting, Hunter."

"But I'm here now," he said, smiling at Meg and Finch. "Are we waiting for anyone else?"

"Latimer was here but already left," Lady Hester said, scowling. "Adam Chillworth has not deigned to put in an appearance. And Sibyl is too tired."

"Is Sibyl ill?" Hunter asked. "She does too much."

Finch thought Sibyl spent entirely too much time alone and doing nothing more energetic than reading, but would never say as much.

"Sibyl had a taxing day with the lessons," Meg said.

Hunter nodded. "Not a suitable occupation for one with such gentle sensibilities."

"We are here for a *very important meeting*, Hunter," Lady

Hester said. "We have been attacked and must prepare ourselves for further insults upon our persons."

Hunter rested an elbow on the base. "Did you intend to
use this to bar your door?" In a slim, utterly serious face,
only one corner of his mouth twitched the slightest bit.

"Do not be insolent," Lady Hester said. "On occasion you
are far too much like your father, my boy. He was given to
most unsuitable and ill-timed outbursts of so-called *wit*.
How my poor departed sister tolerated that irresponsible
man I shall never know."

The spark in Hunter's green eyes suggested he only contained a retort with difficulty—and in deference to the two
strangers present. He said nothing. He did smile engagingly
at Finch and Meg.

"You may leave us, Barstow," Lady Hester said. "Kindly
go to Coot and make sure he isn't wasting his time in that
too comfortable apartment of his."

Barstow "humphed" and left for the basement with a rustle and a jangle.

So now they were four, Finch thought, and could see by
Her Ladyship's irritated moué that she had hoped for a
larger audience to witness her announcements at this "very
important meeting."

"First I must ask who has been in the house all day," Lady
Hester said, swinging her silk skirts behind her as she turned
to pace toward the fireplace.

"I say, Aunt—"

"You will say nothing at all, Hunter. Nothing at all until I
instruct you to do so, or until you have something useful to
contribute."

If his aunt's curt, overbearing manner concerned Hunter,
he showed no sign. He merely bowed slightly, giving a view
of thick brown hair that waved back from a broad brow.

"Who?" Lady Hester demanded.

Finch gathered a breath, and said, "I'm afraid Latimer and
I have been in Whitechapel all day."

"Whitechapel." Her ladyship's eyes opened wide and she

shook her head. "I cannot imagine what Latimer is thinking of, taking a young woman to such a squalid place."

"I was here," Meg said, rushing her words. Meg disliked seeing another placed in an uncomfortable spot. "Sibyl and I were here."

"Hmm," Lady Hester said, pushing her lips well out and pacing. "Hmm. Well, there was that abominable Teddy Chattam. How old is he now?"

"Eight," Meg said.

"Hmm. Perhaps Mr. Chillworth was also here all day. Go up and insist he come down, Hunter."

"Adam returned late," Meg said. "He has a commission to paint a large portrait, and it will be done at the subject's home."

"What subject?" Lady Hester asked at once, and rudely, Finch thought.

Meg drew a shaky breath. "I don't know. He says he is not permitted to discuss this particular subject, or the painting."

"Fishy, if you ask me," Lady Hester said. "Hunter, dear, regardless of what Meg says, would you please go up and ask Mr. Chillworth to join us?"

With a good-natured nod, Hunter ventured forth on his mission.

Lady Hester seated herself again and produced a black fan, which she fluttered rapidly before her face.

A small Swiss bracket clock chimed the half hour and Finch was reminded of the instruction Lord Kilrood had issued. At eight in the evening, he *expected* her to go to him.

A thrill—an absolutely inappropriate thrill assaulted her. In her stomach. Below her stomach. She felt herself redden, something she did far too readily. This sensation low inside and in her thighs was new, and she didn't know—no, she thought she knew what it meant but perhaps she should not admit as much even to herself.

She enjoyed what she felt.

This must be carnal. But of course, women didn't have carnal reactions. She had read that wisdom in a book given her to explain the more sensitive aspects of a female's place in the world, particularly when it came to marriage.

Well, so much for the wisdom of experts. She, Finch More, obviously did have carnal reactions, and very nice they were, too.

She hadn't felt them for Greville.

Greville. No, she would not think of that dear man tonight. He had been too good to die so young, and she missed his delighted smile whenever he as much as saw her.

Hunter returned—alone. "Retired for the evening. Sends his regrets. Says he'll await bulletins tomorrow. Now, can we get on with this? The hour grows later and these young ladies need to be about their own business."

"Very well," Lady Hester said, drawing herself up to sit very straight. She snapped her fan shut and pointed it at the bronze base. "What do you see?" she asked.

Finch looked at the base. So did Hunter and Meg.

"Well?" her ladyship asked. "Answer me. What do you see?"

"A bronze base? Or I suppose one might call it a plinth," Hunter said, one well-shaped brow raised.

"A plinth," Meg echoed.

Finch said, "Yes."

"And what else?"

After exchanging glances with Meg and Finch, Hunter said, "I don't think we get your drift, aunt."

"You do know your dearly departed great-grandfather"— she looked at Meg and Finch—"*my* grandfather, Sir Septimus Spivey. You do know that he did not design any two of his bronze bases in an identical manner, don't you?"

"Actually not," Hunter said, giving the base in question a closer look. "They're all ugly."

"*Hunter.*"

"Sorry, Aunt. Just a personal opinion, of course."

"These pieces are a triumph of daring. Each one is scribed with symbols that tell stories, some of them quite, well, quite . . . quite . . ."

"Daring?" Hunter suggested.

"Quite," Lady Hester said.

Hunter peered closely at what Finch had noted as intertwined figures engraved on the pieces. She had not examined them since she had little interest, either in bronze or in more modern objects generally.

"I see." Hunter did not sound impressed.

"I hope you do. This one bears the story of a beautiful, wealthy, and pious young woman who visits India and becomes lost in the mountains."

"How?" Finch asked.

"How would I know?" Her ladyship's ire raised her voice. "She just does. And she falls in love with a great, strong beast who takes her to its lair. Of course this is a myth."

"Really?" Hunter said.

"I'm sure the beast is a symbol for a man."

"You were always blessed with acute insight, Aunt."

"Yes, I know. Anyway, he isn't nice and after he's taken advantage of her, he eats her, but not before she's produced a little beast."

Finch didn't trust herself to as much as peek in Hunter's direction. She bowed her head to hide a wide smile.

"No matter if you do not appreciate Indian myth. The whole point is that the stories are about the beasts on top of the bases, and the beast—in this case, beasts, are missing. That's the answer I'm looking for from one of you. The *beasts* are missing when they were there this very morning. Standing on top of that base, or plinth, or whatever. We have been violated, I tell you. We have been the victims of common criminals bent on appropriating the treasures left by my sainted grandfather."

"Great-grandfather was a puffed-up little dictator—or so my father said. Made his wife and daughters' lives hell—"

"That will be quite enough, Hunter. You are a man of the law. A *barrister*, no less. Have you only concern for crimes against strangers and none for outrage upon the person of your own aunt? And if you do not care for me, what about others—innocents—who live beneath our roof and whom I am sworn to protect? What of them? Should they be expected to live in fear while they wait to be attacked in their beds and very possibly murdered?"

Meg squealed.

"Hush," Finch said, and put an arm around her shoulders. "You will be quite safe."

"So you say," Lady Hester told her. "But I am not nearly as convinced."

"Very well, Aunt," Hunter said, all signs of humor gone. "Let us be calm and sensible. Would you kindly explain exactly what has occurred?"

"Very well. That's exactly what I've been trying to do. We have been robbed."

"When? Of what?"

"At sometime since this morning." Lady Hester stood up. "I thought I had made that very clear. And I have demonstrated that the beasts are missing. They were also of bronze, by the way."

"You could have demonstrated that without asking poor old Coot to haul a heavy lump of metal from the library. We could have gone there."

The library was on this floor and, much as she longed to, Finch had never found an excuse to enter.

"Nephew. At some time today while the Misses Smiles, Mrs. Barstow, Coot, and the rest of the household staff—and perhaps some daily help—were alone and helpless in this house, someone entered and stole from us."

"How do you know this happened today?"

"This is the day the library is dusted. One of the daily women worked there this morning. Mrs. Barstow checked her work after she left and everything was in place. Later, when Coot went to fetch my evening brandy—for my nerves—he noticed something was amiss and came directly to me."

"No beasts?" Hunter said.

"No beasts," her ladyship agreed.

"Who would want the things?"

"That is not the point." Lady Hester's annoyance turned her nose red. "The point is that the tigers are gone."

Finch held her breath.

"And they have value," her ladyship continued. "Quite apart from their remarkable realism, their teeth are of ivory, and their eyes of jade."

"Small eyes and small teeth," Hunter pointed out.

Tigers, tigers.

"The old tiger has quite large eyes and teeth. And the young tiger has a ruby in its paw. The ruby had belonged to its dear departed mother. The legend on the base says that's why the young tiger will eat the old tiger. To take possession of what is rightfully his."

§ Chapter 5 §

Ross had bought Number 8 Mayfair Square ten years earlier when he'd decided his future rested in accepting commissions overseas, dangerous commissions few men would undertake but which sated his thirst for adventure. Or they had for some years until he'd started to grow bored with battling the evil men did in pursuit of riches. He had not taken long to discover that greed and jealousy were always at the root of the most heinous crimes committed by men, against men.

Now he continued because, frankly, he wasn't sure what else to do. And he had found a certain peace in undertaking only those commissions that might save innocent lives and pit him against the evil ones.

When he'd begun renovation on the Mayfair Square house he'd expected to marry shortly. He had hoped his wife would travel from their Scottish home to London in time to meet him on each of his returns from overseas. Fate had changed those plans.

He went to the windows in the red salon and looked down

on the flagway. The evening only grew more bitter, and he knew a moment of remorse at the thought of Miss More venturing forth again in such unkind weather.

"There you are, Ross. Shall you mind if I come in for a little while?"

He turned to see Lady Evangeline Trimble, wife of his old friend Sherwood Trimble, entering the salon. "Come along in, Evangeline," he said, but wished she were in her rooms and resting as he'd expected her to be. "But I'll call Zebediah to escort you upstairs. You are still convalescent, my dear, and Sherwood would never forgive me if I didn't make sure you got your rest."

She smiled, but took a seat by the fire and extended her hands. Ross had not fully understood why Sherwood Trimble, a sensible man, and an archaeologist who had seemed married to his work, had married the coquettish Lady Evangeline. Eventually Ross put the entire thing down to Evangeline's being in India with her father at a time when Sherwood was vulnerable. A beautiful, if too-obvious creature, evidently Evangeline met strapping, vital Sherwood, who had been separated from females of his own kind for several years, and dazzled him. Deprivation and lust. That was the only explanation. After all, he was a man even if he did spend most of his days communing with holes in the sand.

It was unfortunate that Lady Evangeline did not engender even a shred of liking in Ross, although he put up an admirable front. "My dear," he said. "I shall ring for Zebediah at once. He has told me he is under strict instructions from Sherwood to make sure your strong will doesn't overcome common sense."

"Oh, please, don't," she said, turning great, gray eyes on him. A white-skinned female with luxuriant hair so black it shone with blue lights, her plump flesh was a deal too much on display for Ross's taste. He was certainly not averse to a succulent female form, but in the wife of a friend, a wife he'd been charged to take under his roof, and to protect during her convalescence after a lingering fever in India, he would as soon deal with a more modest lady.

"Could I have a small glass of Madeira, Ross? I do believe I am improving, but my strength is still disappointing, and I have often found a little Madeira to be a tonic."

Ross gave another glance into the street. No sign of Finch More yet. He tried not to appear hurried when he crossed the room to pour the Madeira. "There," he said, giving her the glass. "Now for Zebediah."

"Oh, fiddle, Zebediah," Evangeline said pettishly. "Sometimes I wish Sherwood had not insisted that great brute accompany me. He is so unbending in every way. Why, I cannot make up my own mind about a thing."

Polite silence was often the better part. Ross decided to avoid comment on Lady Evangeline's companion. Secretly he couldn't understand Sherwood's choice at all. True, Zebediah Swift made an excellent bodyguard, but one could hardly say that it seemed appropriate for a lady to travel with a large and vital male who turned the head of every female he passed. Nor was Zebediah's room—next to Lady Evangeline's at the Trimbles' request—the done thing in Ross's book. Swift and Sherwood had met in India—Ross was not entirely certain how—but Sherwood had sent a letter to England explaining that he had chosen Zebediah to bring Evangeline home because he knew he would not have to worry for his wife's safety.

Surreptitiously, Ross checked the time. After eight. Finch would be looking for the best opportunity to come to him. He poured himself some cognac and quietly considered how he felt about the visitor he expected. His feelings, he immediately decided, were not at all simple. He had known other intelligent women but not, he was almost certain, one as intelligent as this austere redhead. She was certainly not at all his type as a woman. He preferred . . . *softer* women. A ready laugh. A sense that his masculinity was enjoyed, sought out, even. The type of woman who threaded her hands through his arm and looked up at him in anticipation of his next comment. No, Miss More was a deal too acerbic.

But she was appealing. Really, she was a bundle, a rather angular bundle of contradictions. He'd like to know her better, not that there was likely to be an opportunity to do so—unless he decided to go out of his way to make such an opportunity. He'd never had particular difficulty impressing a female or making her want to please him. There would be no difficulty impressing Miss More should he set about doing so. He did find that he anticipated their coming meeting with a degree of pleasure. Now there was a revelation worth pondering.

"You are deep in thought," Lady Evangeline said.

Ross drew in a sharp breath. He would still be deep in thought if she hadn't interrupted him. "Not really. How are you? You are certainly looking well. Blooming, in fact. Almost ready to return to Sherwood?"

"Return to Sherwood?" She stared into her Madeira. "Oh, no, I am not nearly ready for that."

Her tone disquieted Ross, but he decided to let the comment pass. The lady had been under his roof for several weeks, and he grew impatient to be free of her. The timing for a visitor was poor. His current undertaking demanded close attention, and Evangeline's presence could prove inconvenient at any moment.

"Don't you ever grow bored with such a quiet life, Ross?"

His life was anything but quiet. "Not really."

"But music, poetry, *culture*—surely you are a man who enjoys the finer things. Yet you are very much alone, and you never *do* anything."

"I am alone when I choose to be alone." By now he should have been married to Fiona, quite possibly with children, but his former fiancée had grown tired of his repeated quests and had married Ross's older brother instead. Patrick Bruce, Marquis of Wakefield, and his marchioness now had a young son whom Ross had yet to see. He had not returned to Wakefield Place, the family's Scottish estate, or to his own home at Heath's End, in three years. He had no plans to do so in the future.

"India is a harsh place for a woman," Evangeline said. "Especially a woman who enjoys an active social life."

She had not spoken to him about such personal matters until now, and he wondered what had provoked her to do so. "Eventually Sherwood will be finished with his dig, and he'll move on," he told her.

"To another dig." Her voice was flat, and she frowned at the fire.

He wasn't certain how he should respond. "He is a great expert in his field and very highly respected." He really must persuade her to retire. Finch was bound to be here at any moment.

"I know he loves me." Evangeline sounded distant, as if she spoke to herself.

"Of course he does," Ross said with a hearty laugh. "If he didn't, he'd never have married you. Sherwood doesn't make such decisions lightly."

"He doesn't make any decision lightly. He ponders the smallest detail until a person might go quite mad with waiting."

Rather than act as a tonic, the Madeira seemed to be making Lady Evangeline depressed. "I do believe you miss your husband," Ross said. "You are spending too much time alone, and it is making you sad and introspective. I shall write to Sherwood in the morning and suggest he come to visit you." And take her elsewhere.

She turned to him. "I should rather you didn't do that, Ross. I had not intended to burden you with more of our personal problems, but you are a generous, understanding man, and I must beg your further indulgence."

He had to divert her, at least until a more convenient time. "Of course I want to help in any manner I can. We shall talk tomorrow."

The moon had risen and punctured the clouds to send a

clear, pale wash over the street. At least Miss More would find her way easily enough.

Ross contemplated the disturbing experience that young woman had endured earlier. What a terrifying encounter for a gentle creature. His fault, he was almost sure. Her mention of tigers had shaken him—as had been intended. Her attackers knew of his connection to the Mores and had chosen to use her as a messenger, as a means to let him know they had found him and intended to stop him. They must plan to force him into the open, where he might allow urgency to overcome caution.

He could not fail in his mission. And his reasons were humanitarian, not personal; they always had been. He would protect Finch if he could, protect the Mores if he could, but he could not sacrifice the safety of many for the safety of two. The peace of a small nation depended on his success. A legend about tigers, one old and one young, had been passed from generation to generation by those people. Preserving the true interpretation of the legend was part of Ross's task. The weight of his responsibility rested very heavily.

"This separation from Sherwood came at a good time," Lady Evangeline said in a distant voice. She, too, must have troubling concerns. "I'm not sure our marriage would have survived many more months of my being alone in that house in the hills with only servants who didn't understand me for company."

She had said nothing of dissatisfaction in India until this evening, and Sherwood's letters—brief to be sure—had made no mention of any trouble between himself and his wife. "You are not yourself," Ross said. "Sherwood is obviously deeply in love with you and—"

"So you have already said, and I *know* that. And I feel responsible for his happiness. But it would not do for me to return to India very soon. I fear that unless I am much stronger, and have had a significant opportunity to satisfy my hunger for *civilization*, I shall not be a good wife for Sherwood. That would destroy us both."

What Ross did not think he needed was to have the responsibility for a friend's marriage thrust upon him. It was not even as if Sherwood Trimble were *that* close a friend. They had got along well enough at Oxford, both of them being of the studious sort, but then, apart from occasional meetings—most often in faraway places—they had spent very little time together. In fact Sherwood's request that Ross take Evangeline had been a great surprise. He made the assumption that Sherwood didn't have many friends to call upon, so he'd remembered Ross.

"I implore you not to contact Sherwood about this outburst of mine," Lady Evangeline said, her beautiful eyes soulful and pleading. "If I am a burden to you here, I shall set about finding myself apartments elsewhere."

"Oh, not—"

"No, do hear me out. You are too generous. I am sure I could find a very suitable arrangement. It would not, of course, be as agreeable as living here in your beautiful house, but I think I see that I have imposed upon you long enough." She rose, her head bowed. "Of course I have. How selfish of me."

"I absolutely insist that you remain here until it is time for you to return to your husband." What else could he say? A fellow had to be a gentleman, and tossing a man's wife into apartments somewhere—alone but for a male companion—was hardly gentlemanly.

She looked up at him, and he would be less than a man if he failed to notice her considerable charms. Her full mouth was red and moist and a suggestion of dampness clung to her long, curled lashes. Her gray eyes were wide and wonderful. It wasn't difficult to see how old Sherwood might have been swept away, particularly in the middle of all that sand and nothingness.

"Are you quite sure?" she asked in a soft voice. "Only say you aren't, and I shall leave you, Ross. I respect you too highly to overstay my welcome here."

"I am sure," he told her quietly.

With measured step she came to stand in front of him. Such luminous skin. A gown of vivid violet, embroidered with tiny crystal beads, complemented her dark hair, her pale complexion. Cut exceedingly low, the bodice clasped the sides of her breasts but contrived to drape where it settled on their tips. The faintest hint of dusky pink rims peeked out and a fine tracery of blue veins showed in her trembling flesh.

She trembled? With emotion?

This might be dangerous ground.

"You are so kind, Ross." Her voice broke. "Without you I do not think I should have survived when I first arrived. And I'm not sure I should survive even now if you had not convinced me that you care about my welfare. I do thank you from the bottom of my heart."

"The pleasure is mine." How the conventional pleasantries flowed, dash it all.

Her soft smile brought the tears in her eyes trembling onto her bottom lids. She pressed her eyes shut and a single tear coursed each cheek. Pressing a hand flat on each of his upper arms, she sighed and rested her cheek against his shirtfront.

Ross studied the top of her head, her rounded, bare shoulders, her breasts crushed to his chest. He felt their fullness and warmth. And he responded in parts slightly more distant but very sensitive to such events. A man did not always have perfect control over his reactions.

The clock chimed the half hour. Eight-thirty. He had dismissed the servants—informed them that he wished complete privacy, and seen to unlocking the front door himself. A pretty fix it would be if Miss More were to walk in on this scene.

Ross considered that a little more deeply. Perhaps not such a fix after all. It might awaken the cool bluestocking from her emotional coma.

Why should he wish to awaken her in any sense? He had spent years distancing himself from personal interest in any human being. If there should be any hint that he cared for someone, it might make certain others think he had a weakness that could be used against him. Such knowledge could also bring grave danger to the object of his affection.

Evangeline was rubbing his chest beneath his jacket.

A pretty pickle if he was not to embarrass her.

"Sherwood told me you spent too much time working on very secret matters overseas," she said. "But you are here now. Have you decided it is time to give up all that excitement? You have an estate in Scotland, I know, and could certainly find more than enough to do."

He was a very private man. The idea of others discussing his affairs did not sit well with him. "My choice of occupations always pleases me."

"Aha. In other words, do not probe, Evangeline. Forgive me, but I am very fond of you, Ross. How could I not be when you have been so good to me? Your well-being is of interest to me. I'm glad I didn't know you until after all that dangerous business on the Indian border. Such wild, unpredictable people. Sherwood told me so. You are finished with those people, aren't you?"

Her reference to the very business with which he was presently involved disturbed him. "There is nothing to bother your pretty head about." Best make light of things. A husband and wife who were close shared a great deal, so he'd been told. He had hoped for as much between himself and Fiona.

He no longer pined for her, but he regretted the loss of his dream, and he had not managed to forgive Patrick for taking his place with her. Not that Fiona was any the less to blame.

There was no danger of his developing an affection for anyone else at all, but that didn't mean that an idea recently come to him was without merit. The idea concerned Finch More. But there would be no need to explore it further unless appropriate opportunities presented, and unless he decided he needed to take extra steps to protect Finch and Latimer.

"Ross," Lady Evangeline said. "I am cold."

Absently, he patted her back. "You are overwrought. You should retire early—now, in fact. You'll be warm enough once you're in bed."

She grew still.

There, finally she began to realize that touching him was inappropriate. He would not show any sign that he thought so—just allow her to go to her rooms and consider her own behavior. He was certain there would be no repeat of this performance.

"I know you are right," she said, her voice breathy. "Once in bed I am always warm, I assure you."

Did he imagine that she pressed even closer? The skirt of her gown was a filmy nothing and he could feel the outline of her limbs—among other things. He would be strong and fix his mind on higher matters.

Over her head he still had an angle on the front steps and part of the flagway. Finch would come, he knew she would. He had been very definite, and she must have understood the urgency behind such an extraordinary invitation.

"I am so warm in bed," Evangeline said. "So very warm."

"Good."

"So warm I find I cannot bear to wear a thing between the sheets."

He dropped his hand from her back. "Is that so?"

"Oh yes. And you? What do you wear to bed?"

Some might think him vague, or preoccupied in some areas, but he was not a fool. This madam was trying to seduce him. "I am quite attached to long nightshirts myself. The heavier the material, the better. And I insist strings be sewn on my nightcaps to keep them well down over my ears. I simply cannot abide chilled ears. Mrs. Dickens has the knack of sewing them on just so. And she knits my bed socks of natural wool. Some say they cannot bear the smell of uncured wool but for me it brings back sweet memories of my nanny when I was a toddler in Scotland. She knitted socks like that for me, too, and blankets I could hold to my face."

Evangeline had become so silent that Ross had to contain the chuckles that threatened to erupt.

"You will not need any of those tonight," she said.

My, but the female was persistent. "I always need them, or I have bad dreams."

"You mean you still have the blanket, too?"

"Oh, yes. Or rather a scarf now, but I still like to feel it beneath my cheek where I may fully savor the aroma of its oils."

She raised her lovely face, and he saw a mixture of distaste and confusion.

Ross smiled at her and tweaked her cheek as he might a child's. "Run along now, there's a good girl."

"To *my* bed?"

She still hadn't given up. "Absolutely to your bed," Ross said, widening his smile and planting a kiss on her brow. "Off you go."

"To *my* bed?"

He barely contained a groan of frustration. "To *your* bed, dear lady." And with that he turned her around, placed a hand on her well-rounded bottom, and gave a little push.

"I'll see you soon?" she asked over her shoulder.

Ross said, "Soon enough," and wiggled his fingers.

Giggling girlishly she tripped from the room, and he heard her laughter gradually fade as she climbed the stairs.

As soon as he was certain she was well away he went to the front door and opened it a fraction. Even through so narrow a crack a blast of icy air assaulted him. He told himself he was making certain he'd remembered to unlock the door, but recognized the subterfuge while he still stood there. He returned to the red salon and picked up a book.

Nine o'clock.

Nine-thirty.

Ten o'clock.

He had been absolutely convinced she would come to

him. The mention of tigers had convinced him that the assault upon her person had been the result of their—the Mores'—connection to him. They knew nothing of his business with the Sheik of Ranthus, or the danger that threatened the Sheik's son, and heir. Most people on earth didn't even know of the existence of the tiny but fabulously wealthy principality of Ranthus in a pocket of isolated hills just beyond the northernmost border of India. Ross had only learned of it because the Sheik had sent an emissary to find him and bring him to Ranthus, where he was asked to accept a mission that could cost, or save, lives. He was clearly informed that if he agreed, his own future would depend upon his saving the right lives. Should the wrong parties survive, then he would undoubtedly perish with the rest of the just. But there was also a risk that he might save the just and still die at the hands of the enemy.

Ross had accepted the challenge. He would not, however, give up his life easily. He would also not willingly put Latimer and Finch More at risk although it appeared he might already have done so.

Finch might well have had difficulty finding a moment to slip away unseen, but surely by now she should be here.

Ten-thirty.

The allure of Byron's prose would never be clear to him. He flipped pages and read the same lines again and again. He did find the man's escapades abroad of some slight interest, if only because he could not imagine how such dissipated activities could entertain anyone for so long.

Eleven-thirty.

He gave up trying to sit in a relaxed posture before the fire and got up to stand near the window. By leaning forward he could see some of the windows at Number 7. Light showed in the drawing room at 7A, and in the room on the other side of the vestibule. A bedroom, he assumed, although he didn't know whether it belonged to Finch or Latimer.

That light went out.

He pounded a fist into his opposite palm. Finch's bedroom, he'd be bound. And Latimer, who thought only of his work, would be the one still busy in the drawing room, where he also had his desk and his books and an array of interesting objects he brought there to study and prepare for sale.

Finch More had defied him. Despite his very clear instruction, she wasn't coming to see him.

Who did she think she was?

Who did he think *he* was? It was unlike him to consider that his rank entitled him to use others in a harsh or autocratic manner. True, he was bringing the Mores lucrative custom at a time when they were hard-pressed to make their little business a success. Yet they were gentlefolk, and Finch was likely struggling with a quite-natural reluctance to flaunt decorum in the manner he had demanded.

But he needed to talk to her, dammit.

He caught up the cognac decanter and a glass and put out the light.

At the front door he hesitated, wondering if he was giving up too soon. The clock struck another half hour, and he turned the key in the lock. He must find a way to get her alone tomorrow.

Jennings hovered by the fire in Ross's sitting room. The valet's ferocious poking of the coals didn't fool his master. Tufts of salt-and-pepper hair stood up on Jennings's head, evidence that he'd been snoozing in his favorite wing chair. He'd awakened at the approach of Ross's heavy footsteps. A wiry Scotsman and ex-soldier who had been with Ross for years, he was absolutely faithful, and Ross regarded him as a trusted ally.

"Ye're in a tear, m'lord," Jennings said in mild tones. "I happened t'see the Lady Evangeline trippin' down the stairs t'ye early in the evenin'. Upset ye, did she?"

Ross ignored the question as he tended to do when he'd rather not answer.

"Och, she's a bonnie one, that. But no such a one as I'd care t'be my wife. A rovin' eye if ever I saw one."

"Jennings, I hardly think that an appropriate comment about my old friend's wife." True, but not appropriate.

Jennings put aside the poker and went to open the door to the bedchamber. "She's an eye for ye, I tell ye. And I'd like t'know what it is betwixt her and that great Zebediah. *Bodyguard.* Aye, well there's more than one way t'interpret that, isn't there? More than one way t'guard a body, wouldn't—"

"I would rather not pursue this line of thought at all."

"Aye, well that's as may be." In the bedchamber, Jennings went about turning down the counterpane and sheets. Then he threw open a window. "That's no' a lady who'd care t'sleep alone. Mark my words, if she finds her body in need o' guarding and *Zebediah's* out o' favor—which he will be if you give her a stray glance—well then, ye'd better guard your own body unless ye want her t'do it for ye."

Ross smothered a smile and trailed about the bedchamber, shedding his coat and pulling off his neckcloth as he went. "Your imagination will be the end of us both yet," he said. "Now leave me. I want some peace."

"Aye," Jennings said. "As ye wish." But he commenced to gather Ross's discarded clothes and hang them up.

"I'll do that myself when I'm ready," Ross said. His mood slipped lower with each moment. That slip of a female, that skinny, befreckled, bonfire-headed miss could have assisted him this evening. If he had made as much of an impression on her as she had on him, she would have arrived at his home on the dot of eight. On the *dot,* blast her.

Unreasonable, he might be.

His irritation was justified.

He did not care to find himself dwelling on the nature of any female, particularly one who was not at all his type. Most annoying. Most strange.

He pulled off his boots and tossed them into a corner. His breeches followed, and his shirt. "I will see to that, Jennings," he said. "Leave me, please."

"As ye say, m'lord."

Naked, Ross stood before the fire Jennings had kept burning brightly.

His vitals stirred.

Bonfire-headed? Actually her hair was vivid, a most luxurious, rich red. He'd never bedded a particularly slim woman—or should he say, thin. What would it feel like to hold a very slender creature to him? He supposed he would feel some of her bones. Her hipbones, perhaps. And her ribs would be clearly visible? Her breasts small, quite firm—almost hard? It might be interesting to examine the female form without so much extra flesh. It could mean that the female in question would be very lithe, supple, agile. Why, who knew what such a body might be capable of accomplishing? She might move entirely differently from the women he'd known. Slide about him like a silken animal. Here, then there, and then somewhere else again. If she were a particularly passionate creature, well then, on and off and in and out, in the twinkling of an eye, and with him catching her as he could, but enjoying the experience nevertheless. Oh, yes he would enjoy the experience.

And when he subdued the writhing, slippery one he would take her in as many ways as—

"M'lord?"

Ross started. "I thought you'd left, Jennings."

"Evidently," Jennings said.

Ross regarded his man, then glanced down to regard what his man regarded.

"Is that on account o'the cold?" Jennings asked with a pointed gesture. "I'd thought ye chose t'have t'windows open while ye were abed to avoid the likes o' that when ye've no place t'put it. No place convenient, that is, unless Lady Evangeline—"

"Good night, Jennings."

"Aye. Ye'd no be interested in one the likes o'her even if she wasn't married to a friend. But I'd say ye've been wi'out comfort a sight too long, m'lord. D'ye remember that Mrs.—"

"Jennings."

"Mrs. McWorthy. That's it. She lives in St. John's Wood and it'd no' take me but a while t'go—"

"Out," Ross said, doing his best to ignore his highly aroused state while he strode from the bedchamber to the door from his sitting room and flung it open. "Out, now."

Taking his time, Jennings did as he was told, pausing on the threshold to glance once more at the object of Ross's discomfort. "Such a waste," the valet said, before walking away.

❧ Chapter 6 ❧

"Did you hear what I said to you, Finnie?"

Finch felt both tired and flustered. "No, Latimer, I didn't." She'd hardly slept and had then arisen late to find Latimer also still asleep and apparently unconcerned that they were starting their day several hours after their customary time.

"I said I've retained a man to help us in Whitechapel."

Finch put down the triangle of toast she'd been wiggling in front of her face. She had no appetite anyway. They took their meals in what was also their drawing room and office, and she had spent a deal too long there in recent hours. "What can you be talking about? What man?"

"His name is Edwin Oak, and he used to be a museum curator."

This after she'd spent a most disheartening night going over their books. "I'm sorry, Latimer, but I can't understand what you're talking about. You have retained someone to work in Whitechapel? What—"

"There, you see," Latimer said, waving a sausage on the

end of his fork, "you understand perfectly. I do wish you would learn to speak precisely what you actually mean, rather than something that is frequently quite the opposite of your meaning. No matter. This is wonderful, I tell you. A dream. He is most knowledgeable about many areas of great interest to me."

She gave him her full attention. "We cannot take on an employee."

"I have taken him on. He starts this very day. My appointment last evening was with him. He has excellent references. He has even been called upon to go to Windsor and give an opinion on occasion—or he was when he was younger."

"There is something I must say to you," she told him. "I did not go to bed until it started to become light this morning."

Latimer frowned and leaned across the table. "I say, Finnie. Are you ill, old thing? Oh, dash it all, I am a callous brute. You had a shock yesterday, didn't you, and I was so preoccupied with Kilrood's business I didn't react as I should? Was it really awful? Did you hurt yourself when you fell? That's why you were late today." He slapped his brow. "The tiger-thingie. Lady Hester's tiger frightened you."

On any other occasion she might have smiled at his absentmindedness. Not on this occasion. "I am not ill. And the theft of the tiger did not frighten me. I am very tired. And at this moment my concern isn't about what happened to me yesterday, but about what I discerned from our books during the night." During the night when she had also been trying not to think of Lord Kilrood in his red salon, waiting for her to come to him like a good servant.

"Not this morning, Finnie, all right? This morning I feel particularly optimistic. We are going to make a great success of things after all. The time will come when Father will no longer laugh at our efforts, or regret that he allowed me an education, and that you are accomplished so far beyond any woman of his acquaintance."

Finch couldn't look at him. She wanted to cry. For all his brave speeches about not caring if her father had turned his back on them because Latimer wouldn't go into the family business, and Finch had followed her brother—for all of that, Latimer wanted Father to be proud of him.

"Buck up, Finnie! Edwin Oak is going to help me get things into proper order. You won't have to work so hard. You may not think it bothers me that you labor like a man in that warehouse, but it does. With someone knowledgeable to help me decide on purchases and to deal with unpacking and storing properly, you need only—well, it's a big enough job—but cataloging and the books can become your primary task. And you will have some time for yourself."

"And what do you suggest I might do for myself?" she said before she could stop herself.

"Why"—Latimer pursed his lips and spread his hands—"why, whatever young women like to do, I suppose."

"I like to study antiques, especially antique glass. As you know. And I like the excitement of seeing new acquisitions and helping you with them."

"Edwin—"

"Oak," she finished for him. "Yes, now you have Mr. Edwin Oak. Latimer, what I have to tell you is that despite our best efforts and a slight upturn in business, our resources are becoming dangerously low. Even with Lord Kilrood's commissions I fear we must cut back, not take on more ways to spend money. We cannot afford a salary for such a man as you describe. What could you have been thinking of?"

The sausage paused in midair. "We have been so careful. How can it be that . . . How can it be, Finnie?"

"Rent here. Rent in Whitechapel. The items we must purchase to increase our inventory. We pay a little more for our food because Mrs. Barstow provides it, but I do not think it would do for me to intrude in her kitchens. Then there are the simple necessities of living. We absolutely must make more money. I'm hoping Lord Kilrood will decide we have performed well for him. Perhaps once we have received the seven shipments he commissioned he will ask us to attend to more—or decide he would like us to locate other items."

Latimer took a thoughtful bite of his sausage and followed it with a mouthful of strong tea. "I understand your concerns very well. And they mean that I'm doubly glad for Edwin Oak. He requires no salary at all. He is a retired person of independent means and wishes only to find an occupation to interest himself, an occupation that relates to his interests. And his interests are my interests."

She should not be hurt by Latimer's sudden exclusion of her from the passions they had always shared. He had been jubilantly grateful when she had followed him to London. "Even so," she told him, "as I have just told you, unless we can make some extra money somehow, and quickly, we shall not survive."

"Extra money? What can you mean? How can we make extra money? Perhaps we must use a little more of your allowance."

"We already use all of my allowance."

"Can we increase the allotment from my inheritance?"

"We have already increased it. I fear using more unless you wish to risk having to turn to Father and beg for help when—"

"Never." Latimer's expression closed. "I can always find work in an office somewhere."

"No," Finch said. "You know perfectly well that you already work too hard. You also know that you've had one breakdown and—"

"Don't speak of that, please—"

"I speak of it because I must. You will attend to our business and leave other concerns to me. You are the one who is the inspired expert. That will continue to be your part. I must simply manage the money better. Don't worry. Really, Latimer, I know I can make what we have go further."

He smiled again. How readily he smiled, like a child released from a fleeting concern. In his way he was an artist who only wanted to practice his art. Money was of no interest to him except as a means to allow him to pursue his passion.

"What would I do without you, Finnie? If you hadn't come to London I don't think I should still be managing at all."

"I was glad to come."

"I know, I know." He resumed eating. "What exactly was all that about the tiger last night?"

"Lady Hester believes she was robbed of a bronze tiger. Two tigers. A large one with a small one in its mouth."

Latimer grinned. "One of Sir Septimus Spivey's magnificent pieces, no doubt. I had thought all of his were of wood."

Finch said. "I don't know. But I never saw it. She says we must have been broken into—the house, I mean—and that we've been violated and are in danger. But Hunter checked the whole place, and there's no sign of a door or window being forced open. Latimer, I've been thinking about the money thing, and I think—"

"You said we'll manage."

He might not want to hear, but she could not do what she planned without his finding out so she might as well tell him now. "And we will manage. I can always teach. I thought I would ask around and—"

"You hate teaching." His face was utterly serious now.

"Not really. There are schools for young ladies in London, and I could get a job in one of those."

"No."

Finch pushed back from the table and turned sideways. "You are not my father. You are not my guardian. I am nine-and-twenty and a woman in charge of her own fate."

"Women such as you do not command their own fate."

She looked at him. "Women such as me?"

"Gentlewomen."

"I'm a merchant's daughter. A wealthy merchant, true, but I do not delude myself that I am someone special. I expect always to have to support myself and I am not afraid of that. If I want to work in a school, I shall."

"Finch—" A sound stopped Latimer.

As usual Mrs. Barstow had not closed the door when she left, but now it flew wide to admit old Coot. "Found this gentleman loiterin' in the hall," he said, puffing. "Can't imagine how he gained entrance."

Finch might have assumed that Coot had been napping by the basement fire and failed to hear the bell, but she hadn't heard it either. "What gentleman would that be?" she asked.

Pulling his waistcoat over his rotund middle, Coot raised a card close to his bulbous eyes, and said, "Viscount Kilrood. Oh, must be here to see Her Ladyship, not you. Lady Hester won't be up yet." He turned away and started to close the door.

"I'm here to see Latimer and Finch More." Lord Kilrood's voice had more than an edge of annoyance. "I walked in because the fellow from the attic was on his way out and he held the door open for me. Now, if you'll excuse me."

He appeared in the drawing room doorway and surveyed the small table tucked against a wall where Finch and Latimer sat, then the rest of the room with its threadbare greens and golds. The stained oak table didn't escape his notice, nor did the once-green carpet worn to loose gray threads in many places. He had been in the room once before, but on that occasion it had been filled with packing crates and seemed a place of business rather than a domestic scene. Finch felt his disdain and it both embarrassed and angered her.

Coot shrugged his usual disinterest and withdrew.

"You take your meals in here, too?" Lord Kilrood said.

"Would you like tea," Latimer said. "Not very warm now, I'm afraid. Finnie, would you—"

"No, no," Kilrood said. "I've breakfasted, thank you. Hours ago, in fact."

"We do take our meals here," Finch said. She felt pained for her brother. "We also do our clerical work here, and frequently certain other activities related to our business. And this is the room where we take our leisure. Not that we have much leisure, but then, we like to be busy."

Her speech left her small audience silent. Latimer fiddled with a crust of toast, poked it into the grease on his plate. Kilrood's face showed no emotion at all, but he set aside his hat and cane and proceeded to remove his gloves.

"I was disappointed that your shipments were separated," Latimer said, too loudly. "I'd hoped they would all arrive together."

"They will arrive," Kilrood said.

"As you say. The little glass piece that did come is most interesting. I should like to have an opportunity to examine it more closely. I wanted to ask if you know its purpose."

"Glass?" Finch said, unable to hide her curiosity.

Latimer slapped a knee. "I'm sorry, Finnie, I should have thought of making sure you saw it. Fascinating. Egyptian, I should think. Utilizing the technique of pressed color."

"I purchased it as a prime example of early Egyptian glass," Kilrood said, finally finished with the slow removal of his gloves. "I understand it is purely a decorative piece—a tile. But I am no expert on such things."

Finch studied him. His eyes were downcast, and she experienced the sensation that he wasn't pleased to discuss his acquisition, that he wished to be done with the subject at once.

"Time," Latimer said, leaping up from his chair. "I am very late. I must be away. I'm meeting Edwin Oak in Whitechapel, and he doesn't have a key yet. I say, m'lord, I haven't even asked you your business here this morning.

Will you forgive me if I rush away? I've a new man starting work for me."

This time it was Finch who averted her eyes, but she
gathered herself quickly and began to pick up dishes. "Give
me a moment," she said. "I won't be long getting ready to
come with you."

"No need for you to hurry," Latimer said. "I thought I'd
spend the day acquainting Mr. Oak with the place and my
way of doing things. Why don't you rest? You didn't sleep
last night. Yes, yes, I insist you rest today, Finch. Perhaps
you'd care to walk the way with me, Lord Kilrood. It's
quite possible another of your pieces may arrive today."

"Thank you," His Lordship said, "but I think not. I came
to chat with Finch. She mentioned her interest in antique
glass, and since I have quite a collection, I thought she
might enjoy taking a look this afternoon. She may educate
me on some pieces."

Hurrying toward the door, Latimer stopped and turned
back. "Finch?" he said. "You want Finch to look at your
collection?"

"Very much. I've been impressed with her opinions on
some of your offerings. She seems most knowledgeable.
I'm hoping she can help me with one or two items I have
questions about."

Only with resolve did Finch stop herself from gasping.
She did decide to put the plates back on the table while she
collected her wits. He wanted *her* opinions on his collection?

"Well"—Latimer frowned and seemed uncertain how to
proceed—"well, I cannot come with you now because I
have to meet my new man."

"No need for you to come, Latimer," Kilrood said. "Your
sister will be safe. There are women in my house."

"His Lordship means my virginity will not be in danger,"
Finch said, and couldn't believe the words had come from
her mouth. Every inch of her skin bloomed hot.

"Good grief," Latimer said. He took a step toward the door, turned back, and said, "Good grief," again.

He left in a flurry of coattails and could not have seen the faint, enigmatic smile on Kilrood's handsome face.

Finch decided she hated the man. He was so certain of his elevated position in the order of things. How dare he smile because she had made an idiot of herself. She *had* made an idiot of herself, and she'd let him know that his comments of the previous day had upset her.

"Thank you for inviting me, but it won't be convenient for me to see your collection today," Finch said. She would like him to look at her as he must look at women who interested him—as women. She was perverse.

"No, I'm sure it won't be convenient for you to come today. Just as it wasn't convenient for you to keep your appointment with me last evening." He strolled to close the door.

How unfortunate that she had already showed part of her hand. "I did not have an appointment with you."

"But you certainly did. And you obviously recall our conversation. You quote from it very well."

They needed this man's business. Diplomacy had never come easily to her, but she must tame her tongue. "I regret if I was the cause of inconvenience to you. To be honest, I did think you expected me to come, but it wasn't possible, and I have no means of sending messages so I couldn't warn you."

He took a very long time to react and when he did, Finch jumped. Lord Kilrood came to her side, took her by an elbow, and led her to the couch. Without a word he guided her to sit down and took his place beside her—too close beside her.

"Honesty is a quality I admire," he said. "Perhaps we should see if you can be even more honest. Were you afraid to come to me?"

Greville had not been a small man, but neither was he large. And he had been gentle in every word and action. He had never made Finch feel overpowered. Lord Kilrood, through his size alone, dismayed her. His pointed manner of speaking showed that he considered himself superior and justified in asking questions that were too intimate.

Yet she was deeply attracted to the man. He brought out a daring she'd never suspected she had. She would like . . . She would like him to take her in his arms.

Her mind must be growing weak.

"Finch?" He bowed his head to watch her more closely. "Do I frighten you?"

"Of course not." If she jumped up and rushed away, she would put the lie to those brave words. "I am not inclined to such weakness."

Continuing to return his gaze was one of the most difficult feats she'd accomplished. He sought to put her in her place—which he had probably decided was much below his—through outrageous behavior. But then, she had no proof of what he did or didn't think. She did know that she felt a kind of daring, a longing to explore with Lord Kilrood the pleasures of the flesh about which she'd read so much, yet knew so little from actual experience.

"Latimer mentioned that you didn't sleep well last night."

She didn't want to discuss personal matters with him.

And she wanted to be a greater distance from him.

His knee actually brushed against her thigh. His hand that rested on his knee brushed against her thigh.

Heat surfaced in her neck and face again.

"Why was that, Finch? That you didn't sleep, my dear."

My dear? Was he actually trying to soften his naturally harsh manner? If so, why?

"Are you going to ignore me?" He took her chin in his fingers and turned her face up to his. "I shall be deeply wounded if you ignore my obvious charm and absolutely refuse to answer my questions."

She couldn't stop a corner of her mouth from twitching.

He brought his face even closer and smiled. "I see I have chipped that very hard exterior of yours—at least a little."

Finch collected herself. "You say you admire honesty. And I like admiration. So more honesty is in order. I do not understand your sudden interest in me. I didn't understand it yesterday, and I still don't. I cannot imagine why you would care whether or not I sleep well, or ask . . . yes, now that is truly extraordinary. Why would you ask my opinion on your glass collection when you are clearly a connoisseur of everything that matters to you?"

"You really believe that is true? That I am a connoisseur of all I see and desire?" His lips remained parted, and he tilted his head. His thick eyelashes lowered over his eyes a fraction, and he studied her mouth.

Nervously Finch ran the tip of her tongue over her dry lips, and she swallowed. For a second time she experienced a sensation in her limbs and deep within her that could only be of an unsuitable variety in an unmarried woman. There was no other explanation but that despite any negative feelings she had for Lord Kilrood, she was also attracted to him.

What a terrible and terrifying thought.

"I should love to hear what you are thinking," he said.

Finch blinked rapidly. "Nothing of note, I assure you. Don't you have very important matters to attend to?"

He nodded, and said slowly, "Oh, yes," in a deep soft voice that caused her insides to fall away. "Very important. You, Miss More. I have to attend to you."

She could not begin to form a response.

"I may be fairly expert on those items I value, but I still enjoy showing them off to someone who will truly appreciate them, someone who can teach me more. I can be honest, too. When I said I wanted your opinion I lied to a degree. Yes, I want your opinion, but mostly I want to watch your interest and your pleasure when you see what I have collected."

"I have never been . . ." Fie, she'd almost said the most

dreadful thing, that she had never come into the particular notice of a man like Viscount Kilrood.

"What have you never been?" he said. "Asked to see something you like a great deal? By a man? Alone?"

"Yes," she said in a rush, grasping for safer ground. "That is exactly what I meant."

"And what of honesty, dear one?"

Dear one. My dear. Confusion made her head whirl.

"That is not what you meant. Let me see. What might you have meant? You have never been sought after, perhaps?"

"For shame, my lord," she said, a fierce rush of indignation making her bolder. "How cruel a comment to an unmarried lady of my age. In fact I was loved—loved by a man who was lost to me. But you were not to know that. One such as I would not be expected to have been the object of a wonderful man's attention. You certainly would not expect it, and so you sought to wound my feelings."

He stared at her. "I am justly chastised, Finch."

With the long, strong fingers of one hand he touched her hair, touched it and actually pulled an already-loose tendril free. Studying what he did, he threaded strands around his fingers and let them slip through before gathering them again, and again.

Finch could not move. His utter preoccupation stunned her. The very manner in which he studied her hair, as if nothing else existed in the world, was the most amazing experience she had ever had. Why, this morning was a morning of many firsts.

She was breathless, or rather seemed not to need to take a breath. The air was still, but she smelled Lord Kilrood, smelled the fine stuff of his coat, his starched linen, the supple leather that formed his topboots, topboots that fitted solid calves without the slightest room to spare.

"It is not bonfire red," he said at last. "Just the richest red hair I have ever seen."

"And I have the freckles to go with it," she said. There

simply wasn't any air to breathe. Her heart thumped too quickly, but she doubted she could do anything to slow it down—not while His Lordship played with her hair, breathed softly on her brow, and forgot himself enough to run the forefinger of the hand on his knee, back and forth on her thigh.

"I like your freckles. I find them charming."

So, he intended to seduce her with pretty words and inappropriate familiarities. Finch straightened her spine. Fiddle-de-dee, she *liked* the way he made her feel. She would explore that feeling in more depth if she ever had the chance.

"What happened to your lover?"

He had no right to ask. Distressed, she looked at her lap, only to find herself watching the rhythmic motion of his finger on her . . . thigh.

Lord Kilrood had exceedingly interesting thighs. Unlike some gentlemen, his were thighs that filled his breeches more than well without the aid of padding. From the knee up to . . . well, upward, a heavy muscle flexed on top. It flexed quite sharply, in fact and she glanced up to find him watching her. He had watched her watch him. How terribly awful.

"I asked about your lover."

"And you shouldn't have. I was engaged to be married. To Greville Hambro, the son of the local squire where I lived in Cornwall." She had loved Greville for his kindness, his unswerving loyalty and friendship. "He fell in '15. He was such a peaceful man. He never wanted to fight but insisted he must do his duty."

"Waterloo?" Kilrood said. "A victory but a massacre."

She loathed thinking about it. "Yes."

"Five years have passed," Kilrood said. "Are you ready to love again?"

Rather than heat, Finch experienced an icy current through her body. She shivered.

"What does that mean?" Lord Kilrood asked, too politely. "A shudder of longing, perhaps? You shudder at the thought of thrills to come. Why, I do believe you are a passionate woman after all."

She bit back the temptation to ask what he meant by *after all.* "Thank you for stopping to pay your respects, my lord. As soon as more of your shipments arrive, I know Latimer will inform you."

"I'm sure he will." Still he wound her hair in his fingers. "Will you come with me to see my glass, Finch?"

"No. No, thank you. I have a great deal to do today."

"You're going to seek a job as a teacher to young women in one of those unpleasant academies, no doubt."

"You eavesdropped." She scowled at him. "You deliberately stood in the vestibule listening to my conversation with Latimer."

With great concentration he took the loosened lock of her hair and tucked it beneath a braid that circled her crown. "When you look up at me like that—especially when you are curious rather than angry—you are utterly alluring. Any man you were to look upon just so would be bound to feel a, well, a quickening."

When he dropped his hand she patted her own hair and felt flustered. No man had ever spoken to her in such a manner. "I am a plain woman, and I know it. I should be grateful if you would state your business plainly. Flattery has never been inspiring to me. If I can help you in some manner, I will, simply because my brother thinks highly of you."

"Good," he said. "Very good."

He still stroked her thigh. She should chide him again for not announcing his arrival, but listening to a private conversation instead.

He stroked, and stroked—tickled almost.

"I have need of you, Finch."

Her heart stopped. Surely it did.

"There it is again, that intriguing sideways look. That light shade of brown, hmm. I think I should call your eyes, gold. And your eyebrows and lashes. I should like to see those lashes on your cheeks as you sleep."

Finch could not move, speak, breathe, or think.

"Yes, I really need you, my dear. I should understand if you feel you have to continue to live here, but I should vastly prefer to have you beneath my roof at all times."

"Beneath your roof?" Finch said, too bemused to be annoyed by her small, cracking voice.

"Yes. You agree? So much more convenient for both of us. I would make you very comfortable. And there would still be time for you to help Latimer. What do you say?"

He could not possibly be asking what . . . what he was asking. But if he was, well then, he must expect that there must be a great deal more time to be sure they were suited to each other.

What was she thinking? She had lost her mind. The man was making clearly improper suggestions. The sooner she let him know that although his custom was very much desired at More & More, she was not the stuff of ladybirds.

He touched her cheek and smiled. "Come. You look stricken. And I must tell you that I am surprised to learn you are nine-and-twenty. You do not appear a day over two-and-twenty."

"You heard—"

"I did." His smile was so charming. "I admit it, and I do not apologize. Everything about you interests me. If we are to be—close—I should like you to use my given name, if that would please you. Only when that seems comfortable and appropriate to you, of course."

"When we are . . . alone, I suppose?" This was too much, it was incredible. Such things did not happen to Finch More, spinster of the County of Cornwall.

"Oh, certainly then." He bent even closer until Finch felt his breath upon her mouth. "I am delighted you are so enthusiastic. I'm sure we shall have a very—satisfying arrangement. You will benefit greatly, and so shall I."

Was he going to *kiss* her? If she thought so, she should remove herself to a distance at once.

A frown snapped his brows together, and he narrowed his eyes. Then he pressed them shut for an instant.

She almost reached for him. "Are you well, my lord?"

"Ross, remember. I am perfectly well." But small muscles in his jaw tightened. "So, you will come with me now?"

"I . . . I cannot." Not she *would* not, as she should have said.

He frowned once more, this time from annoyance she assumed. "This afternoon then. The sooner we become acquainted with each other's ways, the better—but wait until late in the afternoon, if you don't mind."

"No, not this afternoon, my lord. I—I think it would be best—"

"To wait until this evening. Good idea. I am a man of the night myself. And of course, I already know you perform well in the night also. I do believe this is a match made in heaven. Until tonight then?" He rose, and Finch could not help but notice that now he repeatedly narrowed his eyes.

"You should discuss all of this with Latimer." There, that would put things in quite the right order without her having to sound antagonistic. She had heard that men who felt their manhood had been thwarted could be vindictive.

"Why discuss it with Latimer? This is a matter between the two of us. You and me. Since we now know I overheard a deal of what you and Latimer discussed at breakfast, why be coy? He said you might not take a job as a teacher, and you told him you were mistress of your own fate. Don't you believe that? That you can choose to bestow your skills wherever you choose?"

Now she was hot again. "That would seem to be true, but—"

"Good, then you can certainly choose to come to me. I shall certainly pay you a great deal better than any academy for young ladies."

"Oh. Oh dear, this is dreadful."

He laughed, actually laughed. "I just said we should not be coy. Certainly we should not be coy when discussing payment for services rendered."

"Oooh."

"There, there, my dear." Ross put an arm around her shoulders and squeezed. "We shall not say another word on the matter. I'll look for you around four. Just be certain that you will be worth a great deal to me. My collections have never been catalogued adequately."

Lights danced behind Ross's eyelids. He had waited too long to get back and find the darkness he needed, but he hadn't had one of his crippling headaches in more than a year.

"Please go upstairs and lie down, m'lord," Jennings said, in the low, careful voice he adopted at such times. "Mayhap we can stop the beast before it overtakes ye."

Ross shook his head and immediately regretted doing so. "I shall remain here in the salon. I dislike feeling like an invalid." The heavy curtains had been drawn, and blessed darkness shut out the daggers of light that could impale his eyes.

A cold, wet cloth settled on his brow, and he managed a grateful grimace.

"Ye've a deal too much for one man, m'lord. Too much to do that's a great burden. This is what can happen and ye know it from old. But for the warnings, and they've come t'nothing of late, I'd thought ye were cured. Ye wil'na take measures t'save your strength, considerable though it mebbe."

Ross waved a hand for silence.

"Aye," Jennings whispered. "Aye. I'm here beside ye, though."

Jennings had been beside Ross through many a difficult hour with the raging headaches he'd suffered since his fifteenth year. And the man was right, they had abated considerably.

"Were ye able t'speak t'the young lady?" Jennings asked.

"I made a hash of it. Offended her, of all bloody things. Why is it that a man of the world such as I can become an obtuse buffoon in the company of a simple and decent—and intelligent—woman?" He drew in a harsh breath and waited for a tightening band of pain to release. "I have no such difficulty with the vain creatures I'm accustomed to."

"I think ye answered your own question. Practice is what ye need. More time spent wi' simple, decent, intelligent women. O'course they can also be appealin' t'ye, like the one next door."

"You're taking advantage of my state," Ross said, but he couldn't laugh at his jest. "I never said Miss More was appealing."

"Ye dinna have to. I know ye well enough t'tell she's caught your eye. And I've seen her for myself."

"And how did you manage that?" The tightness ebbed, and he sucked air deep into his lungs. "I have never introduced you to her, and you were not present when she came here with Latimer More."

"I have my ways. Mrs. Barstow—she's Lady Hester's housekeeper and a nice enough body—Mrs. Barstow makes a passable cup o'tea."

"Say no more," Ross told him. "You have ingratiated yourself into our neighbor's household for the purpose of spying. But don't apologize. If only I had done nothing less acceptable. I believe I deeply insulted Miss More. In fact I'm certain that if she were not concerned with protecting their business, I should have been ejected from the house long before I left on my own. Ouch."

"Quiet, quiet," Jennings said. He replaced the cloth on Ross's brow. "I take it ye dinna discover more about the attack on the lady, then."

"No. I'm convinced those men were who we feared they may be, though. I have sent word to Ranthus to discover if the Sheik is in good health. I did not expect any sudden moves on the part of our enemies, but if the sheik were seriously ill, they would be desperate to stop my interference. We must remember that these people have already killed."

"Aye. Greed will make men do vicious things."

"*Mad* things," Ross said. "The devil take them, they want to claim a country. And they'll do anything toward that end. I had hoped all parts of the Sacred Box of Ranthus would arrive quickly. My plan had been to secure it as soon as possible."

"Aye," Jennings said, "but that was before ye drew the villains to ye. If they should lay hands on the box, the kingdom will fall. No doubt ye'd as soon—"

"Have time to think," Ross finished for Jennings. He held up a hand for silence. "We must not grow careless even for a moment, particularly since we do not know how close the enemy may be. Say no more."

"I still wish ye'd left well enough alone," Jennings muttered. "This time the danger's too great."

Ross slitted his eyes a fraction to see his man. "You know I've made such missions my life."

"Ye've made them a way t'avoid your life. Excuse me if I'm blunt, m'lord."

"You are always overly polite when you take liberties, Jennings."

The next wet cloth covered Ross's eyes entirely, ensuring he couldn't easily see Jennings at that moment. No matter. He succumbed to a fresh wave of pain and the sickness that came with it. If he admitted the truth, he had begun to question his own motives for the way he lived, but there could be no question of abandoning what he had given his word to accomplish.

The timing for deep thought was poor.

Damn, but his approach to Finch More had been overbearing and designed to confuse her. There, he'd admitted the truth to himself—not that there was a thing to be done about it. And another, more pressing truth was that he could not afford to become concerned with the tender feelings of a woman. That was a part of his life that would never again hold the power to bring him low.

"I've always had a weak spot for red hair, m'lord," Jennings said. "That one who's caught your eye has the reddest I've seen, I think. Are ye sure she's no' a Scot?"

"She is from—ah—from Cornwall. And Miss More has not caught my eye. My interest in her is of a purely business nature."

"Aye. As ye say. She'd be too thin for your tastes, no doubt."

"I find her slenderness intriguing."

"Intriguing? It's just as well she's no' caught your eye, then."

Ross ignored the impertinence.

A light tap at the door brought an oath to his lips. "Have I no control over my own household," he said. "Do they not know that when they are told to leave me be, they should do as I say?"

He heard Jennings open the door and speak in a low voice.

"Excuse me, m'lord," he said. "I'll come back t'ye soon enough."

The cloth over his eyes grew warm, and he removed it. The headache would not last as similar ones once had. Already he felt the start of a drained, sullen depression that invariably followed the pain.

He must complete the Ranthus business—without causing harm to innocents—and find a new direction for his energies.

"M'lord," Jennings said, entering the salon again, "it's Miss More come t'call. She tells me ye invited her."

A vague thrill of triumph cost Ross dearly since it sent a crushing blow into his temples. He waited an instant for it to pass, gathered his strength, and pushed to his feet. He tossed the cloth onto a pile in a bowl beside his chair and turned to confront his visitor in the gloom.

If he'd been in command of himself earlier, he would have told her he admired her in her gown, which was the color of forest greens. He had not been in command of anything but a desire to get what he wanted as quickly as possible. But the shades of green in her simple gown with its modest muslin chemisette at the neck did suit her. She'd put on a plain bonnet with only a single green feather at one ear to relieve its starkness, and a green shawl.

Ross thoroughly liked the appearance of red-haired Finch More. A study in vibrant contrasts, she pleased him.

"Miss More to see you, m'lord," Jennings said, formally. "Shall I arrange for refreshments?"

"Not for me," Finch said, turning her golden eyes on the old Scotsman and smiling. "I shall not take up much of His Lordship's time."

Jennings's pleased smile was a sight to behold. Dour in the extreme, he rarely responded to anyone, but evidently he was not immune to Miss More's charms.

"That will be all, Jennings," Ross said, and managed a threatening glance as the valet left the room. He wouldn't put it past the man to eavesdrop, or find a way to interrupt. "Come and sit by the fire, Finch. I may call you Finch? It grows ever more cold. Have you no plans to return to your family for Christmas? I imagine the hearths of home must hold some appeal at such times of year."

"No," she said, a deal too quickly. "Latimer and I are very content in London. And there are some weeks yet before Christmas."

"Not so very many." He attempted to control the automatic shudders that overtook him at times such as this. "Do accept my invitation to warm yourself."

She approached the fire, timidly he thought, and sat on the edge of one of his prized Italian armchairs—acquisitions from a French friend who received them in partial payment for helping a certain aristocrat to escape Paris.

"Will you return to Scotland for Christmas, my lord?"

Ross thought, *Touché,* but he was also irritated at her swiftly combative attitude. Unreasonable, perhaps, but he was unaccustomed to women who thought nothing of turning his direct manner of questioning upon himself.

He concentrated on breathing deeply and concealing evidence of the discomfort that still clung inside his head. "I shall not return to Scotland for Christmas."

She removed her gloves carefully, and was also careful to keep her palms hidden. "Well then," she said, "it seems that you and I shall spend a quiet season, although mine will be more quiet than yours. You will enjoy your social obligations, no doubt. And I'm certain a great many people will be delighted to have your company in their homes. Or perhaps you will depart for some other country house?"

The minx was letting him know that she had earned the right—or thought she had earned the right—to be inquisitive because he had been less than circumspect in his questioning of her.

"That is neither here nor there," he said shortly. "I thought you were unable to accept my invitation today."

She raised her thin face. Her eyes glowed in the firelight. "It is dark in here, Lord Kilrood. Do you like the darkness?"

"On occasion." He had no intention of divulging a personal weakness. "I find it calming and an excellent atmosphere in which to think."

"It is calm and quiet." She fell silent, and from the manner in which she held her hands, he knew they continued to hurt.

He was grateful for the period of quiet, but he had worked

too hard on managing his affliction to reveal its effects now. "What made you change your mind about coming here?"

"Exactly how long were you in the vestibule this morning? How much did you hear of our conversation?"

Eventually he might hope that she would answer his questions directly. "I was there for some time. I heard a good deal. There, I am taking your lesson in honesty seriously, you see."

"So you heard that we are in considerable financial difficulty and that we may not survive if we do not find ways to increase our funds."

"I heard that, yes. I regret your distress."

"Please don't bother. We are capable people and shall cope well enough."

She was a barbed creature, prickly and quick to snap. He said nothing.

"You disconcerted me, and I reacted badly. I thought you were announcing designs upon my person. I have the sensibilities to be embarrassed by that since you would, of course, never notice me as a woman at all. Please accept my apologies. I have come to say what I have said, and to impress upon you that Latimer and I value your business."

"Out of necessity."

"You do not make my unenviable position easier, but yes. Out of necessity. Certainly it would seem as if the nature of your acquisitions is very interesting, but to be blunt, we need the money you're paying us. I ask you not to withdraw from More & More because I was foolish enough to misunderstand you."

And a fellow was supposed to feel better because a genteel young woman under dire stress gave him an opportunity to snatch back his undeserved pride? Ross did not like the way she made him feel.

"I have no intention of withdrawing." In fact he had no alternative but to continue on the path he had begun. The shipments were coming via Latimer's efforts and, in addition, Ross had decided that it could be disastrous for all pieces to be in one place, so his plan was to leave some with the Mores. He had had reservations about that decision since yesterday, but until he could devise an alternative it must stand.

Another tide of nausea besieged him. He sat down once more and turned his head away.

He heard the muted rustle of Finch's skirts but could not look at her.

Her hand on his brow shocked him. He did not move or react at all. He did close his eyes. Her hand was cool and steady.

"Is this ailment something you have suffered before?"

"I am not ill."

"No? Have you felt the need to sit in the dark with your eyes closed before?"

"You are persistent and impertinent."

"You have experienced similar attacks. Severe headaches, perhaps?"

Damn her. Damn all women for their ability to make a man want to feel their touch. He knew where that longing could lead.

"Do cool cloths bring you relief?"

"They are comforting."

"I shall ask for more."

"You will do no such thing. I have no further need of them."

"I have had some experience with these things. Will you allow me to try what I've found useful?"

He looked up at her, at her somber, but open expression of concern. He did not deserve any such thing from her, yet he said, "Yes," with enough ill temper to be mildly ashamed.

Quickly she felt through the cloths on the table beside him and selected one. Glancing around, she saw a pitcher of water which Jennings must have been using for the purpose she had in mind and she dampened the cloth before easing his head forward and applying the cloth to the back of his neck. Without hesitation she loosed his neckcloth and collar and pressed the cool compress more firmly to him.

Gently she guided his head to rest against his chair. "Close your eyes."

He did as she requested with a sense that he should not be enjoying her ministrations. "I have no intention of taking business from you and Latimer. Whether or not you are kind to me—much kinder than I deserve—I have committed to use you for my needs. I am a man of my word."

"You are a man of too many words at the present, my lord. You will do better to hold your tongue."

"I—" He closed his mouth, and his eyes, but not without first aiming a glare at her. "You came only to make sure I wouldn't take my custom elsewhere?"

"Why else should I come?" The backs of her fingers settled on his brow.

"I asked you first."

She massaged the tensed muscles in his forehead, repeatedly passing upward between his brows and spreading outward toward his temples. "You mentioned that you might have a job for me. Some work cataloging your collection. But perhaps, in light of my shrewish behavior, you have changed your mind."

At this moment he thought her behavior angelic. Her stroking fingers calmed his churning brain and cooled the feverish fight against pain that only made it more severe. "Are you telling me that you may be interested in my proposal—to employ you?"

"I will not pretend. I need work because I need to augment our living. Latimer was correct when he said I am not fond of teaching. It would seem that an opportunity to work among objects that deeply interest me would be a great benefit and a relief. In light of the fact that I have not had great experience other than the few months I have worked for my brother, I would expect only a little remuneration, of course, but I should do my very best. And when there are questions upon which I need help, I could go to Latimer. And I do believe he might thoroughly approve of my assisting you. He would see that as a suitable thing for me and feel that I was not toiling at something that made me unhappy. I—"

"Hush." He caught one of her wrists and held it until she looked into his eyes. "You have no need to convince me. I assure you that you have a place with me at this very moment. I would pay you all I have just to keep your clever fingers on my brow. You are a magician with those gentle hands of yours."

"Thank you." Moisture filmed her eyes. "I am so embarrassed at my ridiculous assumptions earlier. I am not practiced in the social arts, I'm afraid. I lived a very quiet life with my father, and with Latimer there is no reason to be other than removed from dealing with such situations. But I am nevertheless appalled at my stupidity. You must have found it insulting, and I apologize."

He shook his head and was instantly overwhelmed by the black weight once more. This new circumstance, his conviction that he had taken the Mores into deep danger, disgusted him. The burdens he undertook had begun to make him feel like a drowning man. He *must* find a new passion. Perhaps he should consider leaving London also. Until he'd lost Fiona he'd expected to farm at Heath's End eventually. He could not return to Scotland, but he could buy property elsewhere.

But for now he should at least find some cause for rejoicing in the knowledge that he could keep Finch near him a good deal of the time, near and therefore protected. Jennings would observe her closely when Ross could not.

She resumed stroking, a rhythmic rolling of the pads of her fingers upward. Again and again, never ending, the one finger reaching his hairline as another began between his brows. The insistent pressure lulled him. He began to drift.

Women had their own scent, each one subtly different. Finch More didn't smell of expensive perfume, but rather of whatever simple soap she used to wash, and a suggestion of camomile perhaps. To wash her hair, he wondered? He would very much like to release her hair entirely and see it fall down her back. Her naked back.

His eyes snapped open to find that hers were shut as she concentrated. She frowned a little.

"I'm glad you're going to work with me," he said, making sure he spoke softly enough not to startle her. "We shall do very well."

She looked at him then, and he could not begin to guess her thoughts. Without a pause she massaged his brow, and beneath her hands his pain and tension dissipated. True he could not shake the dark gathering of evil premonition, of fear for her and any who might be caught in the web that had started months ago in a small place so far away. He must act. He must strike before they struck—again.

"Do you have many glass pieces?" she asked.

He managed a smile. "You do have a passion for glass, don't you?"

She sighed, and said, "Yes. I have read a great deal, and my interest only grows. I had hoped to have more chances to study actual specimens when I got here to London, but there hasn't been enough time—or opportunity."

"Then this is a fortuitous day for you as well as for me. Perhaps I have been too modest in my description of my collection. It is quite extensive, and I rather think it will enthrall you. You may also find my library of interest to you."

"You wouldn't mind if I read some of your volumes?"

He could think of nothing more wonderful than sitting, reading, in the company of this woman—and knowing that they were both content. "I shall be delighted to give you access to my library. It isn't used enough." His weakened state had also weakened his mind. Of all things, he was yearning for pretty domesticity.

Finch stood beside his legs, leaning slightly to reach his head. Ross looked from the smooth, pale skin of her neck, to her pointed chin and her mouth that tilted up a little at the corners. While she concentrated on her task, her straight, narrow-bridged nose flared at the nostril. Such a fine, slender face. None of the pouting, rouged roundness to which he was accustomed, and which he was candid enough to admit he could very much enjoy—particularly when the pouting lips were applied to his body.

He contemplated Finch. She focused utterly, breathing gently through slightly parted lips.

Her muslin chemisette was thin and he saw her skin through the stuff of it. High and tight, the bodice of the green gown fitted her small breasts closely, and her skirts fell in close folds to reveal the dip of a narrow waist, the swell of modest hips. She was too thin, but no doubt better food and certain other things could change that.

His eyes were on a level with her breasts.

What would she do if he touched them? There could be a certain wonder in the moment of first exploration between a man and a woman. He had always enjoyed new challenges, and just such a possibility stood before him.

Without particular caution, he closed his hands around her waist.

Her hands stilled on his brow.

"Please don't stop," he said. "I do think you may manage to cure me."

She continued, but more slowly and with less certainty.

Ross spread his fingers wider. He passed his thumbs over the bones at the front of her hips. So little meat on the woman. His instant burst of arousal surprised him. It also sent enough blood pumping through his veins to cause another pounding in his head, and he marshaled himself to be calm.

Finch's efforts grew even slower and more jerky.

Ross smiled privately and repeated his exploration of her hipbones. He desperately wanted to do more, but divined that caution would be of the essence here.

"I do not think you should do that," Finch told him.

He rubbed her spine all the way to the cleft in her bottom. She stopped moving. "I insist that you cease at once."

Ross smoothed the stuff of her gown over her buttocks.

He squeezed a little and reveled in her small cry. It was a cry of surprise, perhaps, but not of dismay.

"Your head must be better," she said, standing straighter.

Parting his thighs, Ross maneuvered her between his legs and used his muscles there to hold her where he wanted her.

"My lord—"

"My head is not better enough. You are caring for a sick man, and your responsibility is to continue until you have cured me."

"Then you had better cease . . . cease, if you please. What would anyone think if they came in and found you . . . thus?"

"We will not be interrupted."

"Oh."

He squeezed the firm flesh he held. "So very nice. But perhaps you don't like it."

Finch planted her hands on his shoulders. "What I do and don't like is of no account. What is appropriate has to be the question, and this is not appropriate."

In other words, she did like it. "Cool my brow."

"Gladly, but you must release me so I may get more water."

"Cool it with your lips. Kiss the pain away."

She hesitated, then resumed work with her hands.

He smiled again, then frowned. "Are you hurting your hands?"

"It is my palms that are injured, not my fingertips. Kindly let me go, my lord."

"Hmm? Oh, this is a technique I learned sometime ago. One creates a strong focus to take one's mind off whatever one doesn't want to think about. How can I dwell on pain in my head when I have perfection in my hands?"

"You are a bad man, and you're taking advantage of my being a plain woman whom you expect to be flattered into submission by your attention."

Ross shook her a little until she met his eyes. "Your looks are—different. I find them delightful. And I should not want your submission under any circumstances other than our mutual desire to enjoy each other."

Her stricken expression reminded him that she was not, could not possibly be a woman of great experience——regardless of her betrothal. "Kiss my brow," he requested for a second time, smiling up at her.

Very slowly she closed her eyes and brought her lips to his forehead. She rested them there, and he felt them part in a gentle kiss. If she had stripped away her clothes before him, he could not have felt more stimulated.

Her body might as well be naked. Beneath the gown there was little restraint. Her belly was flat, her ribs narrow. He paused beneath her breasts, and felt her hold her breath. But she didn't pull away.

The chemisette untucked easily enough, and he had little difficultly unloosing the tapes at the back of her bodice.

"My lord?" A protest? Yet she did not struggle, or cry out for help.

"Ross, don't you think?" He didn't take his gaze from what he did. The bodice parted from her breasts, slipped down at his urging. As he had visualized, she was small and firm, and pointed, the tips of her breasts a pale, faintly apricot hue and puckered where the air caressed them.

She made a sobbing sound and would have covered herself, but he took her wrists to her sides and held them there while he took a nipple carefully into his mouth. If he was not cautious, she would bolt, and this time it really would be the end. He had not intended to go so far, or to go anywhere at all with her, but she bewitched him. That, or his own perversity, bewitched him.

He pulled a little with his mouth and Finch made incoherent sounds, amazed and shocked sounds. Perhaps this Greville had indeed been a paragon and had preserved his future bride in utter virginity. Good for Greville, but better yet for Ross.

He switched his attention to her other breast, and Finch worked her hands free of him. She plucked at his open shirt, pushed her fingers inside to his shoulders. She drove her nails into his muscles.

The sleeves of her gown were tight, but Ross worked them down to her elbows, then removed first one, then the other hand. He held her arms and looked at her body, then at her face, at her wide, bemused eyes. "You are a very desirable creature. Not at all like any other. You are yourself alone, and wonderful."

"This is not right," she told him in shaken tones. "I betray myself by wanting this."

He regarded her seriously. "But you do want it?"

"I do," she said, moving closer until she pressed between his thighs, pressed that part of him that was already engorged and needy of more than the hard, unknowing caress of a woman's thigh.

He was a man of experience. If he could not subjugate his needs to hers, he was a selfish cad. With intense absorption, Ross pulled her face down to his and kissed her mouth. He kissed her with passion that mounted and mounted, despite his resolution to keep at least a part of himself removed from her. And she kissed him back. Not with the practiced technique of those who were accustomed to such things, but with sweet ardor that all but undid him.

Their faces rocked together, and they breathed in unison, and harshly. The hair that he'd thought only a minute ago he'd like to see snaking down her back began to uncoil.

Her sudden harsh little cry, her pulling away, broke his concentration. He held her waist once more and looked questioningly at her.

"I am not myself," she said. "This is not the woman I have ever been."

"You don't think it is the woman you are meant to be?"

"A woman who disports herself with a man she scarcely knows? Is that who I should want to be?"

He only knew that he wanted her and that he believed she wanted him. "I should be the one to be strong for both of us."

"No," she said, showing her teeth. "I know enough to understand that a man finds it more difficult than a woman to withdraw from such moments."

"Because you have wide experience in such things?"

She made fists and for an instant he thought she might hit him. "Because I have a father who is blunt and painfully outspoken. My mother died when I was young and there was no one but he to guide me. He told me what he thought I ought to know."

"An unusual father."

"Yes." Her eyes glazed, and she lowered her lids. Ross felt the fight go out of her.

The decision was his. Stop or proceed, but in any case what he did with this woman here and now would be on his conscience.

Finch leaned toward him. She raised his chin and placed a breast against his mouth. For a second he resisted, but his mouth opened, and he took her in and tasted her—and she was so sweet.

It was so very simple to raise her skirts, to run his hands over her limbs and between where hair sprang, and he felt how moist she was. He sucked in his belly, willing patience, warning himself that he must be strong and remember that for a man to have the best he could have with an inexperienced woman took time, and was worth waiting for.

He stroked her there and her eyes grew even wider before she fell forward and buried her face in his neck.

Wanting to be between her legs himself, to push inside her, all but overwhelmed Ross. He had deprived himself of a woman for too long, yet he'd become bored with spilling himself into vessels that meant nothing to him.

Finch More would be no different. Would she?

"I feel . . . I feel. Ross!"

"Mmm." He smiled the old smile of knowing exactly what he wrought. And when he had her panting and sated, she would be pliant in his hands and willing to do whatever he wanted. Later would come her self-derision, the horror at what she had done. But why should he care? He would be satisfied.

He reached a finger, two fingers deep inside her, and her passage tightened. She raised up onto her toes. Her gown pooled around her hips. He feasted on her lithe body. How could he not have known that there could be such eroticism in firm flesh such as this?

He smoothed his fingers back and forth within her, and rubbed his thumb over the swollen place where her pleasure waited.

She convulsed sooner than he expected, and grasped his hand and pressed him to her as if she feared he might cease before she was complete.

Ross stimulated her with greater insistence. His own sweat ran from his brow and between his shoulder blades. He was afire. While he touched her, he took her free hand and pressed it over his straining rod. She squeezed him convulsively until he panted aloud.

Her release rippled on and on, and he began to loosen his trousers. Stretching her on the carpet before the fire took little effort, and he freed himself with a surge of relief, gave himself up to the power springing forth within his body.

He raised himself over Finch and looked down into her face. She smiled at him, a still-bemused and so-very-vulnerable smile, and she put her arms around his neck to pull him against her.

Braced on his arms, Ross shook his head, shook away the stinging sweat that had run into his eyes.

"Show me what to do," Finch said. "Please."

The voice of a trusting gentlewoman.

He bowed his head. How he needed her, needed her now.

She reached to take hold of him. "Show me, Ross. I want to please you."

She wanted to please him? Because she was full of wonder and thought he *loved* her. She was the type of woman who would think that a man who gave her pleasure, a man of supposed honor who wanted to lie with her, that such a man must be in love with her.

Love and commitment. *"Forever, Ross. I will love you forever."* He heard a voice from the past, a voice he'd thought forgotten.

He rolled heavily onto his back.

"What is it?" Finch asked. "Ross—I mean, my lord, what is it?"

"I am Ross. It is nothing. You are a delight to me. I am glad you are here."

"Then let me please you, too."

"You do please me." Almost roughly he pulled her over him and cradled her head on his shoulder. Stroking her long back, her sides, her breasts, he said, "Rest a while. Then we shall do some work."

§ Chapter 8 §

Frost lay heavy on the grass in the park in Mayfair Square. Finch walked slowly along a gravel path. In summer flowers blazed in beds and children chased each other near their chatting nannies. All that remained of the flowers today were brown and broken stalks, and only a single hardy nanny sat on a bench while her two rosy-faced charges blew clouds of vaporous breath at each other.

She had remained at Number 8 for two hours after . . . Raising her face she felt the sting of cold on her cheeks. Her shawl wasn't adequate to keep her warm, but she could not bear to go home yet.

When he'd taken her to his library to show her where she would work some of the time, Lord Kilrood had treated her with gentle but distant reserve. As if they had not touched each other with such utter intimacy such a short time before. At first she'd felt confused by his behavior, but then she'd seen that he was trying to be polite, that he undoubtedly had not found her desirable enough.

She should be grateful that he had not persisted. At least there was some chance that they could put the debacle of today behind them and carry on in a suitable manner. When—no, if she could forget what had occurred, and how she'd felt, and how much she still longed to be in his arms again, well, then, she should be able to find great satisfaction in working among his beautiful things.

Hunter Lloyd could sometimes be seen taking a turn around this park. Latimer and Finch had seen him from their drawing-room window and speculated that he found it necessary to escape his aunt's reach on occasion. He was a dashing man, and a successful one. All the lodgers at Number 7 had offered theories as to why he remained, sharing a single floor in his aunt's house, but none of them actually knew. Perhaps he was too interested in his work to care about anything else. Or he could be too kind to desert Lady Hester, who had, some said, brought him up and educated him.

Finch completed her second tromp along all four sides of the park and set off for a third. She was going to work for Lord Kilrood. Latimer would be pleased, she was certain, because he would see the development as a sign that the relationship with His Lordship was growing even stronger.

The evening grew dark. She wrapped her shawl about herself more firmly. The remembered images of her encounter with Lord Kilrood made her legs tremble. What would Latimer say if he knew about that? She shook her head. Fool that she was, for a while she had felt not only lost to herself and glad of it, but as if she could love the man, as if he might be able to love her.

When news arrived that Greville had fallen, Father told Finch that she would love again. She had protested that such a thing was unthinkable. Father had meant that she would be capable of loving again, and he was right.

Love. So beautiful when shared, so painful when lost, or unrequited.

A small, sad smile came consciously to her lips. If she

smiled, the world would see a woman who appeared happy. A fine disguise for one who had no wish for pity.

No matter what happened to her she would always believe that to love and be loved was the ideal. Once she'd hoped she could put such thoughts behind her. Now she knew that would be impossible. A part of her would continue to regret what she had lost.

A husband, children—how wonderful to have a family of her own.

If someone caught sight of her from the windows of Number 7, they would be puzzled by her unusual behavior. Widening the smile that almost made her feel better, she hurried from the park and crossed the cobbled street to the flagway before the house. Keeping her eyes from Number 8 was difficult, but she managed to concentrate on looking for her key instead.

There had been no definite arrangements for her to return to Ross—yes, she would think of him as Ross now, but she would not call him by that name for fear someone would overhear and misunderstand. Or worse yet, understand completely.

She was still sorting through her reticule when the door to Number 7 opened and Adam Chillworth looked down upon her.

Mr. Chillworth came and went from the house like a perpetually agitated, but silent giant. Beneath one arm he usually carried sketch pads, while his cheap and battered case of equipment dangled from the long fingers of the other hand.

He rarely spoke unless spoken to, except to Meg Smiles. "Has something occurred, then?" he said to Finch, with his faint north country brogue. "Have you had some trouble, Miss More?"

Mr. Chillworth had been told to use her first name but showed no intention of doing so.

"I'm well, thank you, Mr. Chillworth," Finch said, delighted that she'd chosen today to practice empty smiles. "And you?"

"Well enough. I happened t'look out and see you marchin' around over there in the cold. You'll catch your death in those light clothes. Not at all the sort of thing you make a habit of, is it? Stands to reason some of us might think you had a problem."

"Not at all." She ran up the steps until she arrived beside him. Well over six feet tall, with black curly hair that reached the shoulders of his rough tweed coat, he had dark gray eyes, and wore a perpetual frown. "Latimer has retained a new person to assist him in the warehouse. So I am enjoying a day of leisure. I thought a little air would be good for me."

"Air cold enough to freeze your toenails? Females have strange notions. Come on in and get yourself warm. Meg's set a pot of hot cocoa on the hob for you."

They'd all been watching her. Why would they do such a thing?

She kept on smiling and walked into the vestibule, walked to be confronted by Meg and Sibyl Smiles seated on one of the wide steps of the grand staircase. Whereas Meg was rounded and comfortable, her hair and eyes shiny brown, her blond, turquoise-eyed sister had the delicate features and frame of a more fragile creature. In fact Sibyl was quite lovely, but the transparent quality of her skin made her seem frail. Like Meg, Sibyl was generous and kind and could not bear to behold unhappiness.

Meg had already jumped to her feet. She rushed to clasp Finch's hands. "What is it?" she asked. "Please don't keep us in this awful suspense any longer. What has happened? We are already decided that we will go as a body to deal with—well, with anyone who may have done you harm."

Bemused, Finch could only stare at Meg.

"There, you see?" Meg said, clutching Finch's hands, but turning to look at her sister and Mr. Chillworth. "Look at her. I knew there was something seriously amiss. What do you both say? Shall we go and demand an explanation?"

Mr. Chillworth, withdrawn into his awkward silence again, hovered at the foot of the staircase and studied the carvings with close concentration.

Motionless as a sculpture, and striking in silver-gray, Sibyl's eyes grew larger and larger.

"Oh, *do* say something, one of you," Meg demanded. "Say something. Or I shall go alone. I don't need you because I am not afraid of anyone."

"Go where?" Finch said at last in an agony of curiosity and with an unpleasant premonition that she would not like the answer.

"Have you looked at these carvings, then?" Mr. Chillworth said. "Really looked at them? The faces, Meggie. I wouldn't be surprised if they were likenesses of Lady Hester's family. Very good indeed. Very well done. And flowers. Camellias and roses. Gardenias, perhaps. Thistles, too. Laurel leaves. A baby's face here."

"Really?" Sibyl said. "Oh, that must mean the child died in infancy, don't you think? Poor little soul."

"Sibyl," Meg said, clearly outraged. "Adam? We have to speak to Finch sensibly and decide what to do. Which of us shall begin?"

"I wonder who this is. Hard-faced devil. Arrogant. There he is again, over there. And there. Must have been fond of himself."

"Very well," Meg announced. "Finch, we are aware that Lord Kilrood visited here late this morning, and that he remained with you after Latimer left."

She felt her color rise. "Latimer had to go to meet our new employee. His name is Edwin Oak, and he is very knowledgeable."

"As I said," Meg continued. "Lord Kilrood remained for some time. When he left he was angry."

"You have been watching me very closely—and our visitors."

"I happened to see Lord Kilrood leave. Adam told me he had let His Lordship in when he was going to his commission. That was long before the man left again. A cold, arrogant creature he is, too, Finch. A gentle person like yourself would be no match for such a man."

"He has not invited me to match pugilistic skills with him."

"Sarcasm isn't like you, Miss More," Mr. Chillworth said. "Could it be you're covering up for feeling awkward. Has that man done something to put you low?"

Misery stole Finch's voice. She untied the ribbons on her bonnet and pulled it off. "Since you passed His Lordship when you were on your way out, Mr. Chillworth, how do you know so much about his movements, and mine?"

"I had to come back. But that's neither here nor there."

"Tell her that Mr. Jennings is in the kitchen with Barstow," Sibyl said. "And what you overheard. Go on, Meggie."

"You've already told her," Meg said.

"Not what you overheard."

"Very well." Meg inclined her head. "I heard Jennings say his master was in a mad mood. Those were his words. He said he has suffered from severe headaches since he was a boy. He intimated that they are rare now. Evidently Lord Kilrood had one of these *rare* headaches today, and Jennings suggested that it was probably the result of His Lordship not getting his—his—his—"

"Not gettin' his way with you?" Mr. Chillworth said, covering his own discomfort in further examination of the newel posts and banisters.

"Mr. Chillworth!" Sibyl pressed a hand to her bosom. "Why will men insist upon rushing ahead and making matters sound so very unpleasant? You don't know that's what was meant."

"Ah, but it could have been, and being as it's a man we're talking about, it's quite likely."

"Well," Meg said, her eyes carefully downcast, "as a man yourself, you should know."

"Stop this now," Finch said, appalled at the direction of the conversation. "Lord Kilrood came here to discuss some business with Latimer. He remained after Latimer left. He asked to speak with me about help with cataloging his glass collection. Glass happens to be my deep interest and His Lordship knows this."

"Is that why you went running over there to Number 8 this afternoon?" Mr. Chillworth said. "Looking as if you'd lost a quid and found a tanner."

"Perhaps I *had* lost a pound and found a sixpence," Finch said severely. "Perhaps I was upset by quite a different matter from the one you have manufactured. Now, if you will excuse me, I have work to do. Thank you for your concern, but it is unfounded."

Meg sat herself on a stair again and spread her tangerine-colored skirts. "You went to Number 8. You were there for well over two hours. Then you left and went to the park, where you walked around in the cold and gloom—completely unsuitably dressed—apparently in need of a place where you could be alone to think."

Finch felt perilously close to tears. "You are certainly right about the necessity to look for places to be alone if you live at Number 7 Mayfair Square. Everyone else who lives here has nothing better to do than observe one's movements and invent preposterous stories about one."

"We haven't really invented any stories," Sibyl said. "You do seem awfully touchy, Finch. If all went well at Number 8, well, then, good. We are delighted. How was the glass collection?"

"I didn't see it." Oh, fie, her silly mouth would not wait for considered instructions. "As I've said, I may be doing some work for the viscount. Cataloging. With Mr. Edwin Oak doing much of what I used to do for Latimer, I shall have time on my hands, and I should enjoy a new challenge."

"At Number 8?" Sibyl said, her feathery brows rising.

"*Alone?*" Meg sat farther forward on her stair.

"It's only fair to warn you that we've noticed you aren't the way you were when you left here."

Finch's stomach made a complete revolution and left her feeling sick. "What can you mean? You didn't see me when I left, did you, Mr. Chillworth?"

"I didn't, that's true enough, but I did see you return. You would never knowingly look the way you do now."

"Of course I would. I'm—"

"Disheveled," Meg said, looking most unhappy. "I admit I'm the one who has watched for you all this time. I was worried when you were alone with that man in your sitting room. Then, when I'd gathered the courage to come to you, I was in time to see you leave the house. So I went to the window to wait. When you left Number 8 and went to the park you appeared harassed and your hair was—isn't properly done. Finch, these highborn men think they have the right to force themselves on—"

"Don't," Sibyl said, her distress evident. "Please don't embarrass Finch. If she has been violated she—"

"Stop this," Finch said. "I have not been *violated*." Not really. At least, she doubted one could call what had happened a violation, especially when she had been so willing to participate.

A fresh blast of icy air heralded the exuberant arrival of Latimer with an ancient, white-haired gentleman in tow. Latimer slapped his gloved hands together, surveyed the assembly in the hall, and laughed. "Quite a reception committee, what? My friends, allow me to introduce my new colleague, Mr. Edwin Oak. Mr. Oak, my sister Finch, Meg and Sibyl Smiles, and Mr. Chillworth. All, meet Mr. Oak, an extraordinary authority on Middle and Far Eastern antiquities. Also a gift from the gods to me, my friends. A gem. A—"

"Come, come," Mr. Oak said in a crackly voice. "You will embarrass me. I'm delighted to make the acquaintance of all of you. But I should be on my way. It is time for your suppers."

"You shall do no such thing," Latimer said. "Finch, insist that Mr. Oak stay for supper. Then we must help him with a knotty problem. He had lost his lodgings this very day and has nowhere to return to."

"I told you I shall be comfortable enough at the warehouse for tonight," the gentleman said. "In the morning I intend to visit a relative in Hampstead. He has a beautiful house there and will be glad to have me until I can find another place of my own."

"You cannot sleep in the warehouse," Finch said, horrified. "The night is already very cold and will only become colder."

"Cold is of no concern to me. I don't feel it at all."

"Oh, no," Sibyl said, on her feet now. She turned to Meg. "We could manage in one room and let Mr. Oak have the other bedroom."

"I've an old couch in the attic," Mr. Chillworth said promptly.

The front doorbell silenced them, and Latimer turned to find out the identity of the latest visitor.

Dressed in black relieved only by a glimpse of his collar, Lord Kilrood came into the house to join the crowd gathered at the foot of the stairs. His very blue eyes made a cursory assessment of the group before settling intently on Finch. In one hand he carried a large bouquet of white roses tied with a white ribbon.

"I say, m'lord," Latimer said. "Good to see you. Fortuitous. I'd hoped you might drop around at Whitechapel today. Although it's as well you didn't, I suppose. A shipment arrived, and there was a piece meant for you listed, but it didn't come with the rest. I'll watch for it tomorrow. We're at the mercy of stowadores and dockers. Each extracts their price. The more trips they make to our doors, the more they can bleed from us."

Lord Kilrood's attention had shifted from Finch to Latimer. "You are sure there was only one piece for me?"

"As far as I can see, yes, my lord. If it arrives tomorrow, I will deliver it to you myself."

"Do not concern yourself," His Lordship said. "We'll discuss the matter later."

"Night all," Mr. Chillworth said abruptly. "Perhaps I can escort you ladies upstairs." He spoke to Meg and Sibyl, and surprised Finch by offering each woman an arm. "Come up and knock if you decide you'll stay, Mr. Oak. You'll be welcome."

Evidently Meg and Sibyl were caught equally off guard. They hesitated a little too long before accepting Mr. Chillworth's offer and falling in, one on each side of him.

Finch watched the trio retreat with a sense that she was being abandoned to her doom. However, she was grateful that impetuous Meg hadn't decided to interrogate Lord Kilrood on the spot.

"To what do we owe the pleasure of your visit, my lord?" Latimer asked.

"New business in a way. Your sister did me the honor of accepting a position with me. Naturally she will have plenty of time to do what you need, but since you now have help"—he gave Mr. Oak a cordial nod—"Miss More will have time to spare, and she has told me she would be pleased to assist me in making a full catalogue of my collection."

Finch hardly dared meet Latimer's eyes, but when she did she saw only delight. "Splendid," he said. "Absolutely splendid, Finnie. Mr. Oak knows far more than I do. If he weren't so congenial, I'd be mortified."

"You flatter me," Mr. Oak said, his pale, watery eyes a deal too expressionless for Finch's taste. "You have given me fresh interest, my boy. What use is knowledge if there is no outlet for that knowledge? I am in your debt. But now I should leave you young people, although I should appreciate it if you would walk with me until I can find a cab, Latimer."

"No," Latimer said. "Finnie is right. We cannot allow you to sleep in that warehouse. If you cannot go to your relative tonight, then we shall find a place for you here."

Lord Kilrood raised one brow. "What of your regular lodgings, Mr. Oak?"

The old gentleman explained succinctly, and Finch was grateful he forestalled Latimer, who would doubtless have taken far longer to tell the tale.

"You'll come to me, then," Lord Kilrood said. He had not smiled since he entered Number 7, but he repeatedly looked at Finch as if he attempted to see what was in her mind. "I will have my housekeeper make a room ready for you."

"Are you certain?" Mr. Oak said, so quickly it was impossible for Finch to miss that he was considerably keener to accept this invitation than the ones he had been offered under their roof. Possibly because he was not threatened with "an old couch," or with putting one of the Smiles sisters out of her bed.

Lord Kilrood said, "I insist. I shall take you there myself."

He made a move toward the front door but paused.

In fact, he hovered, all but shuffled his booted feet. The black cloak he wore accentuated his somber expression and his stark handsomeness, neither of which did anything to calm Finch's wildly pounding heart.

Mr. Oak leaned toward Latimer and said something to him very quietly.

"Yes, yes, of course. Can you wait a moment, my lord. I had promised Mr. Oak that I'd give him some small jade game pieces to study. He'd like to take them with him to your house. May we get them?"

"Take your time," His Lordship said. "I'm sure Miss More will entertain me, won't you, Miss More? We, too, have much to discuss."

If Latimer noted anything unusual about his client's attitude toward his sister, he gave no sign. Mr. Oak did pass a cool glance over the man who would give him refuge for the night, then extend that glance to Finch, before following Latimer into 7A as quickly as his thin and rather bent legs would allow.

"So, Finch, your brother appears delighted to learn of your new employment."

"Yes, my lord."

"Please call me Ross. I should consider it a pleasure to hear you use my name."

"It would be inappropriate before others, but if you desire it, then, Ross. I'm glad Latimer doesn't object. And I'm looking forward to trying to be of use to you."

He came closer. "You have already been of use to me."

Finch raised her chin, defiant that he should make such a comment. "I hardly think that was kind—Ross."

His lashes lowered, and he looked away. "Ill put, but not deliberately so. I'm sorry. I came to tell you I'm sorry for my behavior. Unforgivable, but I do hope you will forgive me anyway."

She stared at his white collar, his black neckcloth. The urge to reach for him shook her, and she almost turned away to stop herself. "I don't want to forgive you. I mean, I am not sorry—you should not be sorry. Oh, I am a muddle. We should not speak further of this."

"We should, and we will. After you left I thought at first that I could stamp the incident from my mind. I cannot. We must come to terms with what passed between us."

"If you will not promise to cease discussing the matter, I cannot work for you, and I must make certain that we never see each other."

Without warning Ross pulled a bloom from his bouquet. He stroked the white rose across one of her cheekbones, over her ear, along her jaw, brought it to rest on her lips.

Finch smelled the heady scent of the flower.

"I brought these for you," Ross said. "A peace offering. A tribute. I'd like to see you with white roses in that red hair."

"You must take them away," she said, watching for Latimer's return. "Who would understand such a gift from a man like you to a woman like me?"

"I would," he said simply, and he bent to place a kiss at the corner of her mouth. "Oh, yes, I would." And after another kiss, this on her ear, he straightened, leaving her tingling. He placed the roses in her unresisting arms.

Voices heralded the reappearance of Latimer and Mr. Oak. The latter carried a box made of dry and graying wood as if he'd been charged to protect an infant. Finch could scarcely form a thought, but she nodded at Mr. Oak, and said, "Chess, do you think?"

"We shall see," was his answer. His appraisal of both her and Ross was sharp. "Possibly."

"I say, Finnie," Latimer said. "Flowers from an admirer?"

Fiddle-de-dee on her wretched pale skin and its insistence on fiery blushes.

"See what you've done," Ross said, laughing. "You've quite undone the poor girl. Those are from my hothouse."

Finch wished to disappear at once. The questions were bound to start now.

"I insisted she cut these while we were looking at some statuary. I'm afraid I tired her out so badly, she left them behind. So I have returned them. Come along, Mr. Oak, we shall find you suitable rooms."

Ushering the gentleman before him, he sent Finch a last backward grin. "If Latimer has no objection, I'll expect you tomorrow afternoon. Better yet, for luncheon at, say, noon? We'll discuss how we should proceed—in all matters."

§ *Chapter 9* §

Evangeline did not know how Zebediah Swift had come into her husband's employ. Sherwood didn't discuss such matters with her, but told her instead that she was to rely on the watchful man completely. Following Sherwood's instructions might be more simple if Zebediah ever answered a question directly, and if she were not convinced that he bore her ill will, that he might, in fact, be planning to kill her.

The proximity of his rooms to hers did nothing to relieve her fitful sleep each night. His tendency to arrive unannounced repeatedly shocked her, and sent her hand to the place where she kept a twist of pepper about her as the one form of protection unlikely to be turned against her. Her pistol was too large to conceal on her person and remained within easy reach of her bed.

Zebediah's current visit was in response to her request that he come to her. He stood, his black eyes hard and watchful as ever, beside her writing table. He had made no attempt to ask the reason for her summons.

Evangeline smiled at him and lowered her eyes. She had seen how he looked at her. He desired her but feared Sherwood enough to control his lust. She did not trust the man and wished she could convince her husband that he had chosen a dangerous confidant who might turn against him. She knew better than to question Sherwood Trimble's judgment openly. No, she would do his bidding and console herself with dreams of a glorious future.

"I had expected a discussion with you much earlier," she told Zebediah. "You cannot have failed to note changes in this household. Dangerous changes."

"Why dangerous?"

She overcame her preference to keep distance between them and went to sit in the chair before the brass-banded walnut desk. "Where were you yesterday? And last evening?"

"Attending to my employer's business."

Zebediah was a tall man whom she knew to be extremely strong. His indolent manner disguised an ability to move with great speed. On the crossing to England he had narrowly saved her from being struck by a falling crate. She did not believe anyone else could have saved her, but she didn't deceive herself that he would have done so if he hadn't needed her at the journey's end. He might want her, but she was certain he disliked her, that perhaps he disliked all women.

"Do you have a point, my lady?" He was insolently formal.

She flipped the silver top of a crystal inkwell open and closed, picked up a pen, and twirled it in her fingers. "It would seem to our best advantage to work together rather than independently."

He spread the fingers of his right hand on the surface of the desk, and she felt him bend over her. No doubt he had a fine view down the front of her gown. So be it. In fact, if she could arouse him, so much the better. The more difficult part would be to convince him that she returned his interest, but she would accomplish that if she must.

"You do know that members of this household assume we're lovers, don't you, my lady?"

The pen shot from Evangeline's fingers and rolled across the desk. She glared up at him. "How dare you say such a thing? Why would you risk my writing to Sherwood of your impertinence?"

"Your husband requires you to follow his instructions. Isn't that correct?"

She didn't answer him, but he was right.

"His instructions are also that you follow mine. So enough said of that. But if you don't know we are the talk of the servants, and very possibly Lord Kilrood, then you are a fool, my lady."

Her heart beat far too fast and she felt light-headed. "They all know that Sherwood retained you to protect me."

"They all know that they are supposed to believe that is the entire story."

He never smiled. A full beard and mustache hid much of his face, but she had covertly studied him and noted the narrow bridge of his nose, and his wide, sensual lips. His skin was tanned, and the sun had struck traces of red into his dark hair. But it was his unblinking black eyes that most disturbed her.

Zebediah Swift stared at her now, and she would swear he hated her.

"I didn't ask you here to talk about what the servants may or may not think about us. The person from next door— Miss More—Ross visited her yesterday morning."

"He visited both of them. The brother, too."

"The brother left."

"You must have been up much earlier than usual." His gaze flickered from her face, to her breasts. "Did you have trouble sleeping after you failed to lure the viscount into your bed? A woman such as yourself likes company between the sheets, doesn't she?"

Evangeline willed herself to look at him until he returned his attention to her face. She raised her brows. "You cannot know what may have passed between Lord Kilrood and myself in private."

"I can, and I do, madam. And since you don't, or won't understand that we have to protect our position in this household, I'll remind you that your behavior toward His Lordship only makes more food for gossip. Don't you think Lord Kilrood must be questioning why you should openly invite him into your bed?"

Evangeline swallowed and had difficulty breathing. He mortified her. "You are disgusting. My husband did not retain you to insult me." The words were brave enough, but she heard no conviction in her voice.

"You don't know exactly why your husband and I are colleagues. It isn't necessary for you to know. There is a reason for you and I to be together here. Sherwood gave you instructions to do as I tell you. I suggest you never forget that."

Her fear of him was founded. If only she could speak to Sherwood, reason with him, make him lose faith in Zebediah. "That woman followed Ross here. They were together for a long time. And I heard Jennings tell Cook to prepare lunch for Ross and Miss More today. He said she was coming at noon. I want you to find a way to stop her from coming."

"Why? Do you fear the competition of another woman for His Lordship's favors?"

A detestable creature. Detestable and completely confident—a fearsome combination. Finding a way to reverse the balance of power between them was imperative. "I may not know everything, but I do know that Lord Kilrood's safety concerns Sherwood. He warned that we must be suspicious of anyone who tries to get close to Ross. He said we must discourage any questionable persons."

"And you think the Mores are questionable?"

"I most certainly do. They are much beneath his station, and a friendship between them is suspicious. I know Sherwood would agree."

"Perhaps," Zebediah said, a glint in his eyes. "Perhaps you are absolutely correct. It is also possible that you are right in suggesting that you and I should attempt to be more accommodating to each other. After all, we are alone in our task here. Alone together, hmm?"

Evangeline felt as she might if confronted by an awakening viper. At last Zebediah had made the inevitable move toward a strike. She smiled and dipped her head, and said, "Perhaps."

"Good. I'm glad you agree. Now, can I rely on you to do as I ask and stay away from our host—other than in my company?"

He had sensed that she might have a motive for wanting to be with Ross, a motive he knew nothing about. "I don't have to ask your permission to come and go about as I please." She would grasp any opportunity to be alone with Ross. Sherwood had left her with no doubt that her future depended on her success with the viscount. Success being, in Sherwood's words, *"Make sure he likes you enough to keep you close. Don't press me for my reasons. Trust me, and trust Zebediah Swift. Do as he tells you. So much depends on his victory in London."* She disliked having to consider Zebediah, but she would do what she must.

"If you defy me," Zebediah said, "you may force me to take steps to ensure you behave."

He treated her like a willful child. "How is your friend?" she asked. There, let him ponder that.

"Friend?" He showed no emotion at all.

"Artemis? Yes, I'm sure that's his name. Artemis."

The curl of Zebediah's lip showed strong-looking white teeth, and did nothing to soften his harsh appearance. "Have you been following me? Surely not. You have not the wit or the subtlety."

Another insult. "Only think and you'll know I have no need to follow. Sherwood was kind enough to insist that you purchase a carriage for us, so that Lord Kilrood need not be inconvenienced. The coachman is Artemis. Each time you insist upon accompanying me on a drive—which is on every occasion when I leave this house—well, then, I have heard you mention the man's name. And you insist upon sitting up on the box with him, and I have heard how you speak together in low voices. A man with such a high opinion of himself as you, Zebediah, does not make pleasantries with mere coachmen unless there is a very good reason. He isn't a coachman really, is he?"

"He drives your coach, my lady."

She waved a hand before her face. "Don't try to divert me with such nonsense. He is your ally, and you didn't want me to know. But I do, and I shall be watching both of you. And in case you think your lot would be easier if I were to disappear, I will remind you that without me you will not be able to remain in this house. And if you cannot remain in this house, you cannot watch His Lordship as my husband has commissioned you to do."

"For Lord Kilrood's own health, my lady. And his safety. Do not forget that."

How interesting that he should imagine she needed to be reminded. "I have not forgotten. I'm glad you are also keeping that fact close to your heart." If only she were not so certain that Ross's safety was Zebediah's last concern.

Zebediah straightened, and she thought his sharp features became sharper. His indrawn breath was audible. "Aren't you going to mention our other unexpected arrival, m'lady?"

"Ah, yes." She pushed to the back of her chair and gripped its arms. "Who can he be? Does he have a name, even?"

"Most people do. He is Mr. Edwin Oak."

"Where did he come from? I was unaware of him until I heard him in the hall downstairs. He asked to take supper in his rooms and His Lordship agreed. I did catch a glimpse of him as he went upstairs."

"I'm sure you did," Zebediah said. "Did you note that he carried a small package of some sort?"

At that Evangeline clenched the chair arms beneath her hands. "A package? You're sure?"

"Quite sure. Unfortunately, I was not close enough to see it clearly, but I am inclined to think we should be wary of Mr. Oak."

She had almost forgotten that she must watch for packages—small packages arriving. Those were also Sherwood's instructions. She was to tell Zebediah if she saw anything of the like. "We must get our hands on whatever the man brought into this house last night." Urgency sent her to her feet. "His room must be searched. Did he leave this morning?"

"I've already searched his room."

"When? Are you sure you weren't seen?"

"I wasn't seen."

"You made sure he had left?" Agitation all but overwhelmed Evangeline. Sherwood could be a very angry man if he was crossed. "So much depends upon our not making any mistakes."

"He left at eight. Mr. More met him on the flagway outside, and the two went on their way together."

"Oh." Relief made her giggly. "Thank goodness. Let's go to his room again, and we'll both search. Or rather, I shall search while you keep watch. If someone comes, you must divert them."

"There is no point. I was there at two this morning. I left no cranny unchecked, I assure you. Despite his advanced age and frail appearance, this man may be our pigeon, I believe, my lady. He's certainly a wily one, or I'm very much mistaken."

After weeks of waiting the drama had truly begun. Evangeline thought of what Zebediah had just said and clapped a hand to her cheek. "Two this morning? You were in his room at two this morning? What if he had heard you and raised an alarm?" She spun about and pointed at him. "He had it beneath his pillow. Of course, that's it. You could not have searched there with him sleeping."

"He wasn't sleeping."

Evangeline blinked and sat down again. "Not sleeping?"

"Not in that room—or any other room in this house. I saw him leave this morning, but he was not here during the night."

§ Chapter 10 §

Jennings, expert on such matters, or so he insisted, had decreed that a lady such as Miss Finch More (whatever he meant by that) would be delighted by the unexpected. To that end luncheon was to be served in the conservatory.

A table had been carried out and carefully set. "Set pretty," so Alice, one of the maids had volunteered, without being asked. Ross eyed the table critically and decided he was pleased with the coincidental choice of white roses as a centerpiece. Finch would assume they had been his idea, and he would take whatever help he could get with her.

He checked his watch, and tucked it back into his waistcoat pocket. Already past noon. He had planned that they should have some time for conversation before the meal was served, but that would no longer be possible. He paced.

She might not come.

How did that make him feel?

"Oh, the soufflé, m'lord," Jennings, said, rushing into the conservatory with a bowl of fruit which he set between potted ferns on a stone ledge. "Brandy soufflé, Cook says. She says it would weaken the resolve of a Puritan—turn him into a glutton."

How he would feel if Finch didn't come wasn't really the issue, Ross decided. The true conundrum was, how did he feel about feeling a necessity to ask the question at all?

His only feeling should be one of annoyance. The chit ought to come when he told her to come. She should remember her station—and his.

"Ye're displeased, m'lord? Ye disapprove o' the menu?"

"What? Oh, no." He stared at the fruit cascading from its silver bowl. "Soufflé, you say? She isn't making it now, is she? Good grief, the thing—"

"No, m'lord. Mrs. Hastings only told me what she intended t'serve."

Ross went to the table and studied silver, crystal, and china. He clasped his hands behind his back. "Approve, do we, Jennings? Sort of an indoor picnic, hmm? I expect that was your idea. Very clever."

"An elegant repast in exotic surroundings was my idea, m'lord."

"Hmm." He glanced toward steps leading up to a large salon he rarely used. "Elegant repast, hmm? Yes, indeed." He took out his watch once more.

"Twelve-thirty," Jennings said.

"I can read the time, thank you." And his agitation about Finch More, any agitation about her on his part, made him feel damnably vulnerable, and he didn't like it one bit.

"Ye're no' yourself, m'lord. Perhaps your head—"

"My head is quite wonderful, *thank* you, Jennings."

"Yes, well, if there's nothin' I can do for ye, m'lord, I'll see what I can do elsewhere. Mrs. Hastings has the house in an uproar. Somethin' tells me it's past time ye entertained more. The staff needs t'practice."

"Good enough," Ross said. "Go along, then."

A parakeet chirped in a gilt cage shaped like a miniature pagoda. Ross turned his attention to the bird and poked the tip of a forefinger between the bars. A squawk and a sharp peck were his reward. He jerked his hand away, sucked at a bead of blood on his wounded skin, and eyed the sidling creature.

"Miss Finch More t'see ye, m'lord," Jennings said from behind Ross, who turned to see his valet and guest descending the steps. Evidently Jennings had assumed the duties of the butler today. "I think ye'll be warm enough here, Miss More. But I could bring ye a robe for your knees if ye'd care for one."

"No, thank you," Finch said, nodding at Jennings. "But you're very kind."

Jennings positively bobbed on his toes. "It'd be a pleasure t'make ye more comfortable. A little stool for your feet, maybe?"

"No, thank you."

"Will ye take a seat, then?"

She wore the green again. Perfect. The single feather on her bonnet was . . . tasteful in its simplicity. He had thought he liked more flamboyant, perhaps more *revealing*—or more obvious dress on a woman. He had been wrong. Simplicity that relied more on the intrinsic loveliness of the wearer was the thing. After all, a woman could not be truly lovely if she needed finery to make her so, could she?

Finch had declined Jennings's offer of a chair and stood with her reticule hanging from a wrist and her hands folded together at her waist.

"M'lord?"

Ross frowned and met Jennings's eyes. The insolent fellow raised his bushy eyebrows and grinned knowingly. What did he think? That Ross, who had made clear his self-sufficiency, might be bowled over by a Cornish merchant's plain daughter—a spinster—and decide he relished domestic bliss after all? Hell and damnation, would he never be free of match-making efforts? Despite having married Fiona, his brother continued to remark on his hopes to see Ross married and with offspring. Invitations to boring gatherings, invitations from mamas looking for suitable husbands for their daughters, arrived regularly. And Jennings never allowed a week to pass without he spoke of the benefits of "settling."

"Thank you, Jennings," Ross said. "Let them know we'll be ready for lunch at any time."

Jennings—still grinning—departed with a spry step, leaving Ross and Finch to face each other in silence.

The lead must be taken by him, in all things. "I'm glad you wore the green again, I . . ." No, no, no, he should not refer to yesterday. "Come along in. I'm so glad you could come."

She seemed about to speak, but pressed her lips tight shut instead.

"Mrs. Hastings—my cook—is preparing a delightful lunch for us, so I'm told." Banal chatter had never been one of his afflictions. Why should he be stricken now? "I hope you're hungry."

"Yes."

"I didn't see your Mr. Oak this morning. He left before breakfast. But he seems an agreeable and knowledgeable fellow."

"Good. I don't know him."

"I see." He didn't see at all but he did understand that this was a dashed awkward exchange. "Would you care for something to drink?"

"No, thank you."

Hell and damnation, if only he could take the woman in his arms and hold her close, and make her understand that he was what he was, and he must protect them both from impetuosity. At least, he must protect them from further impetuous interludes.

The bird chirped loudly and repeatedly, and Finch's lips parted a little. She looked at the bird with evident delight.

"Ungrateful little devil," Ross said, sucking his finger again. "Just decided to take a bite out of me."

Finch approached the cage and made soft cooing noises.

"Nasty disposition. Dangerous."

She glanced over her shoulder at him. "Fiddle-de-dee. A great big man like you calling a tiny bird dangerous. He has only his cage to call his own. He must protect it, and himself. No doubt you poked your finger into his home, so he let you know he hadn't invited you. Anyway, it can't hurt that much. Blow on it."

Blow on it? Well, at least he was grateful to the feathered fiend for providing a break in the glacial atmosphere.

"How is your head today, my lord?"

She had the most infuriating way of making a man feel defensive. "My head is perfectly well, thank you, Finch. I would appreciate your remembering to use my first name on occasions such as this."

He was rewarded with another all-seeing stare. She said, "You didn't have to go to the trouble of providing a meal, you know. I'm well aware that there are matters we need to discuss, and I don't only refer to your impulsive offer of employment."

"Is that so. Well—"

"What is his name?"

"Hmm? Oh, the bird? He doesn't have a name."

She gave him the benefit of yet another backward glance. "How strange. Everyone gives names to pets."

"He isn't my pet." Dash, but his finger stung. "You give him a name."

"You should name your own bird."

"I said he isn't mine. He isn't anyone's. Call him something."

"You sound quite pettish, my lord, if you don't mind my saying so. I should think a name suiting his personality would be the thing. Pecker, do you think?"

He looked heavenward to where tall palms brushed the glass ceiling. "By all means." There was no excuse for his behavior—other than some odd onset of uncertainty that definitely had something to do with this female. "Actually the bird is for you. Since you are to spend a deal of time

working here—and, therefore, a good deal of time alone—
you should have company. There. What do you say to that?"

"For me?" She put her nose close to the bars of the cage.
"A gift? Well, I don't know. No, I shouldn't think that would
be appropriate, but thank you."

"Don't let him peck your nose. The bird is yours, miss. It
isn't polite to reject generosity." He was a boor in her company. "What I mean to say is that I obtained, er, Pecker for
you on a whim. Oh, I wanted to please you, and that's the
truth, damn it."

She faced him, one of her bright flushes suffusing her
cheeks.

"There is a very great deal I have to talk to you about,
Finch, but I want you to feel comfortable with me. I want
you to think of me as your friend, as well as your employer."

The gold lashes swept downward.

"What I mean is that we are hardly strangers, are we?" He
pointed at the bird. "When you look at, er, Pecker, you will
recall me. Kindly, I hope."

He saw no sign that he'd made progress in his attempt to
soften her toward him.

"Thank you for the bird, my lord. You are very kind. I
have given recent events a great deal of consideration."

"So have I, I assure you." So had he, indeed, Ross
thought.

She continued to keep her eyelids lowered. "I thought we
might begin by discussing your extraordinary agitation at
my unfortunate experience the other afternoon. In
Whitechapel."

Ross was unaccustomed to blunt women. "We'll speak of
that soon enough. Luncheon will be served momentarily.
Then I thought perhaps a ride in the park. It will be deserted
at this time of day, so we'll have it all to ourselves."

"I don't ride. And it wouldn't be at all suitable even if I
did."

He bit back a retort that he would be the judge of what

was suitable. "You would make a fine horsewoman. You should learn."

A flurry of magenta caught his eye a second before Lady Evangeline stepped lightly down the steps to the conservatory. "There you are, Ross," she said, all charming smiles. "Sorry I'm late, but I didn't realize we were to lunch out here. What a lovely idea. You're always so thoughtful. I've felt a little stronger today, so I made myself useful. All that jumble in your library. Really. *Men.* I shall put it to rights in no time. Oh,"—she saw Finch—"hello. I'm sorry, I didn't notice you hiding there."

Reluctantly, Ross made the introductions and noted Finch's quiet but composed reaction to his houseguest. He appreciated self-assurance. He felt proud of her.

He felt proud of Finch More? Unless he brought his reactions to her under control, his very future could be in jeopardy.

"You're from Number 7, aren't you?" Evangeline asked, and Ross was grateful she was polite rather than condescending to Finch. "There are a great many of you living there, I believe. It must be pleasant to be a member of such a large family."

Ross was aware of Lady Hester's sad little attempts to disguise her need to house paying guests.

"Lady Hester is a very philanthropic lady," Finch said. "She has chosen to champion a number of us. She insists she has no need of such a big home and allows us to live there."

Evangeline looked blank. "But I thought you were lodgers." She averted her eyes. "Difficult for you, but very charitable of Lady Hester."

Her recovery hadn't been quite quick enough. She had intended to make a point of Finch's station in life. Finch's generosity took the sting out of the effort and made Evangeline appear mean.

She placed herself between Finch and Ross. "I suffered a shock in the night," she said. "I've given myself some hours to consider how I should deal with the matter, but I'm still uncertain. I must defer to you. It is on the matter of a man who was in the house last night."

Ross wished Evangeline would go away. Her determination to detract from Finch's presence was transparent now. "Could we speak of this later?" he asked her.

"Why not over lunch, Ross, dearest? An old man was here last night, and he wandered. Really, it was quite terrifying."

"Wandered? Are you talking about Mr. Edwin Oak? White-haired. Thin."

"Yes, yes, that's him. Oh, I'm so grateful you know who it was. But what was he doing here, Ross?"

Poor, poor Finch. "Mr. Oak is employed by Finch's brother. Like Latimer, Mr. Oak is an expert on antiquities. Unfortunately he was without lodgings last night, so he stayed here. You have nothing to fear."

"But I do. He came to my room, Ross, and wanted to come in. He said he was cold and asked me to warm him. One can find oneself in distress because one has been good and kind. Most unfair, but true. Do tell me this Mr. Oak will not be here again."

"Evangeline," Ross said, "Finch and I—"

"I should have made certain this was a good time to speak with you," Finch said. She made a fuss over smoothing her gloves and touching her bonnet. "We can discuss—"

"We will have our discussion as planned," Ross told her. He took her by the arm and ushered her to one of two seats at the table. "Lady Evangeline wasn't aware that I had a guest. Please excuse me while I escort her inside. Your concerns can be addressed at another time, my lady."

Color slashed across Evangeline's cheekbones. He felt sorry for her until she turned and flounced away.

With her back straight and her expression inscrutable, Finch exuded an air of disapproval.

Ross took the seat opposite and discovered to his annoyance that the roses were too high to allow him a clear view of her. "Dashed servants," he said. "Can't trust them to do anything right. They take advantage."

"Of what?"

"Of the fact that I am frequently absent. They become lazy then. And when I return they alternate between trying to run my life and ignoring me."

Rather than the butler, Jennings appeared again and stood aside to watch Alice stagger into the conservatory carrying a heavy silver tureen. She set it on the table and removed the lid. Jennings then amazed Ross by coming forward to ladle a thin but fragrant leek soup.

Alice withdrew.

Jennings took up position at a short distance and stood with his eyes elevated. He should hear about this meddlesome nonsense later.

They ate in silence. Finch didn't affect a small appetite, but quickly finished her bowl of soup.

"Would you like more?" he asked.

"I'd like you to go and make certain Lady Evangeline isn't upset," she responded. "She must have felt foolish when she realized she'd misunderstood about having lunch with you."

"That isn't your affair."

"It's my affair if I caused her embarrassment. These social niceties are of no importance to me, but I understand that they mean a great deal to such a lady."

He swallowed the temptation to tell Finch exactly what he believed Evangeline's motives for appearing had been. "Her Ladyship hasn't been well," he said, instead. "That's why she's in England. She will have returned to her room. I'll speak to her later. I know she'll appreciate your kindness."

"Piffle."

Women were beyond his comprehension; in fact, he wondered why he ever tried to understand them. "What do you mean by that, Finch?"

"I mean that you say one thing and mean another. And most of the time I have no idea what you mean, either by your words, or your actions." Her eyes glittered and appeared suspiciously moist. "I think I should leave."

"You arrived very late, and you have been trying to leave ever since. I suggest you spare at least a little of your sympathies for me. I waited for you. I thought you might not come. And I absolutely insist that we deal with the serious issues that are between us."

"There is nothing between us. You made that very clear after we—" She remembered Jennings and clamped her mouth shut.

"Quite," Ross said, then shook his head. "I mean, not at all. I did not make anything clear which is another reason why we're here. My behavior must have seemed very strange, but you are quite different from the type of women I usually . . . Hmm. Quite different. Jennings, why are we waiting for the next course?"

"Sorry, m'lord!"

"Nothing more for me," Finch said. "Thank you."

"Nothing more, Jennings," Ross said, furious and confused at the same time. He wasn't sure why he was angry. "Leave us, please. Compliments to Mrs. Hastings."

"The soufflé, m'lord?"

One look at Finch's face assured Ross that she wasn't interested in soufflé. "Not now, Jennings."

When they were alone he moved his chair until they sat side by side. "I planned for this to be pleasant."

"You thought bringing me roses and ordering me to appear for lunch would guarantee a *pleasant* experience? I don't wish to dwell on past events, but I shall not . . . well, I am unlikely to have altogether forgotten yesterday."

Ross cleared his throat. He hadn't finished his soup, but he was no longer hungry. "Actually, it never occurred to me that there would be any awkwardness today."

"I find that hard to believe," Finch said. "Yesterday aside, do you mean it never occurred to you that it was a poor idea to bring someone like me into this type of setting? I don't fit here, so awkwardness was inevitable. You blame Lady Evangeline, or Jennings, or your servants—"

"Rather than myself, you mean?"

"Rather than blaming no one at all and putting it down to a well-intentioned thought that was a mistake."

"I hardly think inviting a woman—"

"Inviting a woman to lunch would be perfectly acceptable if that woman was appropriate—appropriate to your station. I'm not, and that's that. Now we should find a place where we absolutely will not be interrupted."

He stared at her.

"There must be somewhere in this great house where we can be alone. If not, then we must go elsewhere. Perhaps drive in your carriage—if you'll forgive my impertinence for suggesting it. You could ask your coachman to drive around until we're finished."

An irreverent burst of humor caused Ross to laugh. "So you want complete privacy to seduce me this time, do you?"

Finch presented a frozen expression—until the corners of her mouth twitched upward and she struggled unsuccessfully to suppress her smile.

"Good," he said. "That's better. What a mature person you are."

"I am indeed," she told him. "Not just mature—aged, and beyond fearing for my virtue, as you should be beyond fearing for yours."

"Hussy," he said, and stood. He offered her his hand, and she took it to allow him to help her to her feet. "You must try to understand that I have not been accustomed to women who treat me with neither coquetry nor respect."

"I don't treat you with disrespect, my lord."

"Ross, remember? We're alone now."

"We are. But we may not be at any moment. What we have to talk about should probably not be overheard."

"Come with me. There is a place where we can be sure of no interruptions. I am the only one who goes there, the only one who has a key. I intended to show you what I keep there, anyway. In fact, you will spend a great deal of time there."

Number 7 was large, but Number 8 was considerably larger. Marble statues stood sentinel duty in an imposing entrance hall. Brocade of deepest green hung the walls above gilded wainscotting. A curving staircase, also gilded, swept to the second floor, where a small but opulent ballroom showcased the musicians' gallery Ross had added. He'd planned it for Fiona, who loved to dance. Originally he'd planned everything in the house with Fiona in mind—and the children he expected them to have.

While he ushered Finch toward his fourth-floor retreat, Ross saw his London home with different eyes. If Finch lived here, would she like . . . Finch didn't live here and never would. What she would or wouldn't like was of no importance. Her safety, and that of her brother, had become his concern. He would do what should be done and try to make certain they came to no harm.

"This is the last flight," he told Finch, touching the back of her arm as she climbed ahead of him. He had brought no one here before, and he hadn't intended to show it to Finch. "My retreat. I keep my collections here. Not large, but I think you'll find at least some specimens of interest to you." He wanted to show her because she was different.

He wanted to share what he loved with Finch.

Not at all. Such a notion was ridiculous. She could hardly catalog a collection without seeing it, that's all.

"When you come here"—he looked at the side of her face, her neck, at the sheen on her red hair—"When you come here alone you will have to use my key."

Yes, he was actually prepared to trust her with the key he alone possessed.

She stepped aside when he approached the only door on this floor that was sealed shut. He let them in and went ahead to throw open the heavy draperies he kept closed to protect his treasures from damaging light.

Finch's slippered feet made the sound of hesitant, then rushed steps behind him. He turned to watch her and couldn't contain a smile at the sight of her bending low to glass-topped cases that framed the room and also made a square in the center of the floor. She frowned over one specimen, moved quickly to another, and another, only to dart back to the first again.

"You're afraid you must make a choice."

She glanced up at him.

"Shall you try to see everything and therefore miss a great deal? Or shall you examine what you can in great detail—and miss a great deal?"

Finch dipped her head and chuckled. "You can see into my mind."

"No, no. I'm suggesting you may feel as I would."

"Then we are at least alike in one way." She bent to a case that contained a small collection of maritime instruments.

"You will have time to see everything, Finch. You are to be the keeper of it all. Other endeavors have made it impossible for me to give the time good cataloging requires, but you will be my deputy."

"Why have you waited so long to find someone for this task?"

Ross approached slowly. He had a sense—no, she held an aura of one removed from reality. Or perhaps it was that in this place they were both removed, although they were together. He found himself controlling even his breath, breathing shallowly and quietly. The silence up here had always pleased him. Each time he returned to London he sought to spend more time on the fourth floor than he had on any previous visit.

"Hah, I might have known you'd have a lodestone."

He grinned with genuine delight. "And you ask why I have waited to find exactly the right person? How many would see a lodestone and think of the first compass?"

"Many qualified people, Ross. It is only by chance that I do. My family were once sailors, and my father has a number of mementos that were passed to him. A lodestone among them. When Latimer and I were children our father discovered us trying to magnetize his horse's tack. We had in our heads that the animal would only ride north and thought that would be great fun."

"And what did your father think?" Ross asked.

"That we needed more productive activities to keep us busy. Latimer spent a great deal of time mucking out loose boxes while I was given extra sewing tasks. I hated sewing and still do."

"And although your family had horses, you don't ride?"

"My father thought it unsuitable." She gave him one of her sidelong glances. How odd that such an evidently innocent habit could have so marked a physical effect on him. "My mother liked to ride. She was severely injured in a fall and suffered ill health ever afterward. She died when I was very young."

"Yes—well." He was uncomfortable. "I'm sure your father wished to protect you."

"I'm sure, too. Ross, we came here to speak in private. I have a good deal on my mind, and I believe you also have concerns."

He found he was unready to let go of the pleasantly familiar mood between them. "May I show you how I have set things up first?"

She raised her shoulders and looked at an archway leading to what had once been a separate room. "If that would please you, it would please me."

Ah, but how delightful it would be if he could expect her always to be so accommodating. "The entire floor can only be reached by the door through which we entered. The other doors have been sealed—for security—but I had the rooms connected to allow easy passage between them from the inside."

They strolled throughout the floor, stopping from time to time to allow Finch to study a piece that caught her eye. As he'd expected, when they reached the area dedicated to glass, she became animated and behaved as if he were not present except as a source of answers to the questions that flowed.

He observed her carefully, gauging her reactions.

"Oh, my," she said, putting her eyes near a case containing conical and cylindrical medicine bottles and some drinking goblets of ribbed glass. "How did you get these? Surely they are by the French workers from Lorraine? It's true that they could trick one into thinking some of what they made was Roman, isn't it?"

"Those are Roman."

Finch gasped. "My lord! How did you come by them?"

"A long story. In fact they were in payment for certain services rendered."

"Amazing."

"I have a considerable number of early Venetian pieces. Very beautiful. And there are some examples of Norman work. Colored window-glass. I think they will excite you."

"I *am* excited. Glass is my deepest interest."

"And also mine," he told her honestly. "You will see that a great deal of space is given to it here."

Finch came to a halt. Ross moved close behind her to see over her shoulder.

"That?" She pointed at a display dedicated to a single square piece of glass. "Is it . . . No, it cannot be Egyptian. And the gem set in it? Surely not a ruby?"

"It is Egyptian and the gem is a ruby." Latimer had spoken of the piece in front of Finch. Perhaps she had been too preoccupied at the time and did not remember.

"I had never hoped to see such things," Finch said. "I knew the Egyptians were very advanced in their techniques—for their time—but I didn't know they made quite such elegant and valuable tiles. Black and gold. Would this actually have been used?"

"No, I should think it was for ornamentation," he said, aware of how the muscles in his jaw tightened.

"Don't you fear for the safety of such a thing?"

He watched her with great care, watched the set of her shoulders, how her hands clenched into fists. "I am the only one who knows of its presence here," he said, but might have added that since it had been brought into England by More & More, Latimer knew Ross had it.

"I know about it now," she said.

How true. "Yes, but you will not discuss what you see with others, will you?"

"No, no, absolutely not." She attempted to see the side of the piece which rested flat since that afforded the most stability. "You may rely upon my faithfulness absolutely."

Her faithfulness? What an odd choice of terms. He had not had great fortune relying on the faithfulness of women. Although his relationship to Finch More was different from any he had experienced with a woman before, which did change things.

She had the most tender, pale neck. And the tendrils of red hair that rested there accentuated the whiteness of her skin. "I hope to rely on you a great deal," he said. "Would you like to see the piece?"

"You mean, *touch* it?"

"Of course. If I intend to trust you with all this, then you will frequently touch things here, won't you?"

"I suppose so." A pulse beat in her throat. She took her reticule from her wrist and set it aside, then removed her bonnet like one in a dream.

Ross forced himself to concentrate on picking up the Ranthus piece—the top of the Sacred Box of Ranthus—and placed it in her hands. She held it with the confident reverence of a connoisseur. He was aware that she was far from being an expert as yet. He had little doubt that she had the potential to become one. He would regard her as his protégée.

"This is the most beautiful thing I've ever held," Finch said. "The color is so deep. And this ruby"—she touched the central stone—"is so large. The patterns in the glass are strange. The threads of yellow are pressed in as one would expect, but not, I think, combed as they usually were. They are more random, and more golden orange. Curved stripes, perhaps."

He waited for her to say, *"Like the stripes of a tiger,"* but she didn't, and he wasn't certain if he was relieved. If she had, he would have waited for her to make a surprised connection to the comments of her attackers, and his task would be to evaluate the sincerity of that surprise. There was no true reason to suspect her of playing a part in the plot against Ranthus, and, therefore, against himself, but he could not take risks.

Finch had turned the piece over. "Backed with gold," she said, studying it from all angles, "and this is a hinge, surely. One half of a hinge. It is meant to fit into something else. This is not a tile."

"Possibly not." She was above suspicion. If she weren't, and if she wished to make sure he had no misgivings about her, she would not show such interest. "Let me replace it for you. You can look at it again on another occasion." Perhaps. In fact, as soon as the rest of the "something else" to which she referred arrived, he must find an untouchable hiding place until it must be produced and returned to Ranthus.

Finch gave up the gorgeous glass and stood back while he put it away. "Now we should have that discussion you spoke of," he said. "I have some questions of my own to ask."

Ross felt her wariness return. He went ahead of her through two more arches to the one area that was furnished for comfort. "Take a seat," he said. Here he had made use of Chinese lacquered pieces. Deep blue silk and even deeper blue velvet pleased and calmed him in the hours he spent locked away from any other human.

The afternoon had grown darker as if a storm might be brewing. He lighted candles, and the fire for which he provided the coals himself.

When flames curled up the chimney, he brushed his hands together and noted that Finch had remained standing. "Come," he said. "Please sit down. As you say, we have a great deal to talk about. I want to hear exactly what was said by those ruffians in Whitechapel."

She stood her ground, spread her feet a little wider even, as if preparing for confrontation. "First I want you to answer a question, my—Ross."

He decided he liked her by firelight. Shadows beneath her eyes and cheekbones made her even more ethereal. He had never thought to be bewitched by a girl with a gamine face and figure, and such a weight of red hair that it appeared too heavy for her slender neck.

"May I ask a question first?" she said, and he realized she was repeating herself.

"Is there a hurry? Could we not sit together and learn a little more about one another?"

"I'd like to know more about you, but I am an honest woman. Sometimes I am too honest for my own good, and I am not so silly that I don't know I may be putting myself in grave danger, not only by saying what I'm about to say—but by being here, alone with you, and without anyone else knowing where I am."

He narrowed his eyes. Surely he misunderstood her. "Are you suggesting that you might come to harm at my hands?"

"I'm suggesting that if you wished to do me harm, this would be the perfect time and place because—unless someone saw us come here, and I don't think they did—I could be missing for many hours without a soul knowing. And when they did begin to search for me, they would never look here."

Amazed, he pushed back his coat and gripped his hips. "Are you actually telling me that you . . . No, I refuse to entertain the notion that you are afraid I may—*murder* you. That is the most preposterous thing a woman has ever said to me."

She had carried her reticule and bonnet with her, and now she used them to gain time to formulate her next comment. She placed the bonnet on a brass table with dragons spiraling its legs, moved the headpiece from one side of the top to the other several times, then set about searching inside her reticule.

"I marvel that you are so calm in my company, miss. Do you not quake in your slippers? How do you think I shall accomplish this horrible deed?"

Apparently she had exhausted the possibilities inside her reticule and she placed it with the bonnet before raising her face, her mutinous face, to look at him. "You, sir, could hit me on the head. You could produce a pistol and shoot me, or a knife and stab me." Color began to rise in her cheeks, and her eyes were overbright. She searched about her. "Why, you could lock me in that trunk until there was no air for me to breathe. You could even put your hands around my throat and, and—and strangle me." Her voice soared upward to a squeak and faded completely.

Ross felt the faintest beginnings of a blasted headache. "You are mad. You are completely mad. But, then, perhaps you aren't. Perhaps I am this crazed killer you think I am."

"That I think you could, just possibly be," she corrected him, "or that it now occurs to me you *might* be. That is quite different from my being certain."

He stepped toward her.

Finch retreated.

"Could I know *why* you would concoct such a theory?"

"I haven't. At least"—she went backward a little more—"at least I don't think I have. But I believe in examining all potential outcomes. There is no doubt that your persistent attention to me demands an explanation. I do not understand it at all."

What he felt now wasn't difficult to identify. He was enraged, and while he was enraged, he was also aroused. A dangerous, quite possibly disastrous combination. "Well, Finch, I applaud your ability to inflame a man. I am so inflamed that I might do any, or all of the dastardly things you have suggested."

"You asked me, and I told you—about those things." Her voice was still high and still weak. "And given the fact that I can think of no reason why you should choose to do business with More & More in the first place, or to show such interest in either Latimer or me, or to react as you did when those horrible men accosted me, or to offer me a position—especially dealing with such valuable items, or bring me roses or invite me to lunch, or give me a pretty bird—or, or, oh, I cannot speak of the other."

He pushed his hands into his pockets, the better to control what he did with them. "Please don't stop now. Finish telling me the reasons for your suspicions about my almost assuredly deplorable character."

"I don't know why you forced yourself to do what you did yesterday when it must have been abhorrent to you." She bowed her head. "There, I have said it."

Ross gave up attempting to control his rage. What had felt for a moment like ice running in his veins was rapidly turning to burning, pumping heat. "That is it! *All*, my dear Finch. It is time you were taught a lesson in prudence with that errant tongue of yours. And in the wisdom of caution when in the company of someone much larger, much stronger, and almost assuredly much more capable of *violence* than you."

He closed his hands around her throat.

§ Chapter 11 §

Finch closed her eyes and considered death.

If she died now, at least she would leave this world as a woman of a little more experience than she had feared would be the case. She was not completely inexperienced. In fact she was a woman who had tasted the purest of physical excitement at the hands . . . at the hands about to squeeze out her life.

"Don't you think you ought to scream? And kick me?"

Exactly, she thought, *why don't I kick and scream?* Because she wasn't afraid of this man. But she could scream if she wanted to. She hadn't done so in many years, not since childhood, but one never forgot how to do those things.

She opened her mouth to scream, but stopped. "I have never admired weak women, and I will not become one." The truth was that she felt completely calm. Was that because she was ready to meet her Maker?

No, she definitely was not ready, but then, she didn't believe she'd be doing that today.

"You don't think a little hysteria is warranted when you're about to be strangled, miss?"

She raised her eyelids and looked into his eyes. There was no doubt that she had angered him, but she had been declared insightful into people's natures on many occasions, and she saw into Ross, Lord Kilrood's nature now. He was a man of deep, controlled passions, not a violent one, and he had no intention of killing her. Certainly he considered that she needed to be taught a lesson (how very like a spoiled male person), but his hands held her so lightly she could move away—if she wanted to. She didn't want to move away. She wanted his entire attention focused on her, and while he laced his hands around her neck, she certainly had all of his attention.

Why, she was manipulative. How very strange when she had never considered such a thing of herself before.

"I asked you a question," he said. He had the bluest eyes.

Finch drew a quick breath, and said, "I have never admired weak women given to hysterical outbursts and lack of self-control. I refuse to be such a woman."

"Even if you're being strangled?" he asked.

She grimaced a little. "That was very theatrical of me, wasn't it? Those suggestions I made? You pressed me, though, so I said what came into my head. I always did have a theatrical bent, or so Latimer likes to remind me when he doesn't want to take me seriously."

"Latimer is a sensible man. But you have known me how long? Two months, perhaps?"

"I do not really know you at all, do I?"

"Oh, I think you do. You know I will not hurt you, and that requires that you have divined certain things about my character."

She divined that she was playing a dangerous game. There was definitely an excited glitter in Ross's eyes and a flush in his cheeks. She had excited his temper, and even she knew that a man whose sensibilities were inflamed was a dangerous animal.

"I've changed my mind," she told him. "I do know you, and I know I have incited you. You are aroused by my little drama. But you won't hurt me. You are only holding me as you are to frighten me because you're angry that I should suggest you might stoop to such things. Really, men can be very pettish, can't they?"

"Pettish, miss? I do believe that's the second time you have used that word relating to me. Females are pettish, my girl. That is not a description applied to men."

Finch made sure the smile she felt inside didn't show. "Men take offense very easily, you know." She frowned and allowed her gaze to rest on his mouth. She did like Ross's mouth. It was a firmly set mouth, but she knew how it could alternate between hard, determined pressure, and the gentlest of touches. "I have just realized something very important."

"Please don't keep me in suspense."

She glanced at his eyes again. "You have a very sarcastic turn of phrase, my lord. But no matter. I have just formed a monumental thought about men. In fact this is a truth which could very well set the world of thinking women on its ear.

"First, do not forget that I am unimpressed by your overbearing ways, and such things as being threatened by you."

"Duly noted." He appeared . . . deeply engrossed in her. Fascinated by her, in fact. Finch smothered another smile. She liked the idea of being able to hold the man's attention so firmly.

"As I have already said, men take offense very easily. And I've just realized something absolutely revolutionary. Men frequently tell women how weak they are. They have always told us such things. But the only reason, or reasons, women allow them to get away with such nonsense is because it is annoying to have large people sulking about the place."

Ross shook her lightly. "Would you care to elaborate on this revolutionary theory of yours?"

"Men have a need to place women in poor light, to insist that the female is weak and prone to all manner of petty whims, when the truth is that by such talk and actions the male is distracting attention from his own inadequacies. Why, that is *exactly* what it's all about. And if strong-minded women—"

"Such as yourself," he interrupted.

"If strong-minded women would refuse to play men's annoying games, the male would be forced to acknowledge his own weaknesses and *do* something about them. Consider, please, what can the challenge be in subduing someone whom God made smaller and weaker—in any manner at all? Except for attempting to subdue the mind you consider could be a threat. Aha, now there is a titillating thought for an intelligent female. To pit one's mind against that of a man for the pleasure of proving him no more intelligent than oneself—if *as* intelligent."

He looked . . . hawkish? Closely watchful. Finch felt a thrill within her and gave herself up to that thrill. A wonderful feeling. "There is another reason men provoke situations where they feel they are justified in exerting their superior strength over women."

"I am breathless with anticipation." Always slow, his speech had become even slower, even more deliberate—and even more exhilarating to her.

She prepared herself to make an outrageous suggestion, but one she was convinced was a breakthrough in logic. "Violence, even the suggestion of violence, excites men. It arouses their—sexuality." She dropped her own voice to a whisper for the last word. *Sexuality.* Surely Papa had thought the word, but he had certainly never spoken it aloud.

"I believe you are informing a man who holds you by the throat that he is a weak and terribly flawed being. You are telling him that in all ways but those that are basically physical, you are superior to him."

"Not exactly, only that you would never treat another man as you treat women. Or as you have treated me. You are overbearing and arrogant. You expect that I shall defer to you in all things. Because you are—by an accident of birth—considered more important than I, and because God gave you a larger, stronger body than he gave me."

He listened intently and when she'd finished, said, "You are wrong, of course. And you are misguided in testing my patience so. But I conclude that you must be little different from some men in some ways. You enjoy extreme danger. To be alone in the company of a man, and to goad that man into the arousal you so blithely mention, is foolhardy in the extreme."

"Perhaps. But would you gain particular satisfaction from disposing of someone who is such an inferior specimen to yourself?"

"This is ridiculous." He dropped his hands. "We both know I have no intention of harming you. There was a moment when I should dearly have enjoyed hearing you beg for mercy, but I doubt you have sufficient wit to do so. You need to be protected from yourself."

Finch smiled. It was so simple to manipulate the male.

"Now *that*," he said, with a very hard edge in his voice, "was unwise."

"I have no idea what you mean."

"That triumphant smirk of yours. You have won nothing, Finch, except what I have allowed you to win. If I wished to, I could have my way with you in any manner I chose, and within moments."

She swallowed, and fiddled with the chemisette that folded softly over her bosom. "You don't frighten me. No, and you will not frighten me again. I have proved what I have long considered true—that men are inferior. Oh, don't misunderstand me, I consider them exceedingly necessary, enjoyable even. You have certainly brought me pleasure even if I should never have enjoyed such pleasure because I am a spinster who should—according to our world—preserve her virginity."

He looked at her as if there were no one else alive but the two of them. "As far as I am concerned, your virginity is intact, Finch."

"A boring thought," she said. "And what is such a thing's importance, I ask you? If men think nothing of losing their virginity as soon as they may, why should the rules be different for women?"

"Because they *are!*" He snapped out the words, and a thunderous darkness crept over his features. "God made you weaker for a reason."

"That reason being that he understood the nature of men completely, and knew there must be superior people— women—whom they could subjugate in order to help them develop egos like hot-air balloons."

"By the gods, you are impertinent, and imprudent."

"But I am making you think, aren't I?"

Very deliberately he removed his coat and loosened his neckcloth. "You bemuse me. You are a very bemusing subject."

"Subject?"

"Specimen."

"A specimen?"

He rolled up the sleeves of his shirt. His forearms were heavily muscled and bore a coat of dark hairs. "I think of, and refer to all new acquisitions as specimens." He moved so quickly and surprisingly that she had no opportunity to evade him. Without a sign of strain, Ross picked her up and cradled her in his arms while he walked into the next room. He set Finch down on a long, carved ebony table that might almost have been an altar since it was too high for any but the tallest of people to sit at and eat.

"I insist you allow me down from here. This is mortifying."

"Not at all. This is where I examine all of my new acquisitions. Better for the back to be more upright."

"I am not a specimen to be examined. And I am *not* your acquisition. Kindly let me down."

His own smile could easily be classified as a smirk. "I consider you the most fascinating specimen ever to grace this room. And I have decided to acquire you. To that end I shall undertake a most careful, a most thorough examination."

What did he mean, he *intended to acquire her*? She grew cold and then hot, by turns. Surely he didn't intend to . . . He might. Right here on this bench. "What are you doing?" Genuine alarm struck fear to her heart. If she were to examine her emotions, she was afraid she might find that even stronger than fear, was the drive to feel again what he had made her feel such a short time ago. She had vowed never to be in a similar position with him. Yet she had followed him willingly through this house—and she'd submitted to being completely alone with him. *And* she had goaded him, used suggestive language even.

In the charged silence Ross removed his waistcoat, then his neckcloth, and, finally, his shirt.

"You should be the one on this bench," Finch said, breathless. "Some of the farm laborers at home have great, strapping bodies like yours, but I doubt there are many gentlemen of higher birth who can boast such splendid torsos." There. Again she let him know how he attracted her.

He slipped his hands beneath her knees, whirled her around, and stretched her out on the bench. "Women are not supposed to look at men and have lascivious thoughts. Why, the entire order of things would spin out of control if women were allowed to go about sizing up the, er, physical assets of the male, and deciding their own fate based on what they did or didn't like about a certain man."

"Is that so?" She attempted to sit up, only to be deposited on her back again. "Then why have you just taken off your clothes?"

"Some of my clothes."

"Why have you taken off some of your clothes if you don't wish me to *size you up?* I put it to you that you are more than satisfied with your own body and that you *like* to have women admire it. But I don't see why that should mean that I have to be kept here like this."

"Because, my dear, sharp-tongued one, although I may

not be the kind of violent man you suggested I could be, I am most definitely *sexual*. And you are correct in your theory about danger, excitement, and the potential for sexual arousal to follow. I am very much aroused, Finch. And I have concluded that you are also aroused and will be quite happy with what I have in mind for us. You want to be with me—as a woman, a passionate woman."

Finch noted Ross's honesty, and her own answering thrill, but she was not a reckless noddycock, and her interests had become entirely self-focused. "Why do I have to lie here on this bench?"

He shrugged his great, tanned shoulders. "We both have scientific minds. We're going to conduct an experiment. I shall examine you—for the sake of science only, of course—and I shall watch for any reaction you may have to the male body. Conventional wisdom suggests that there is no such thing as true arousal in the female."

"How will you know if I am aroused?"

"I have a simple little test I can run to find out. You have no need to worry. Now lie still and relax."

Ross removed his topboots and went immediately to unbuttoning and taking off his breeches.

"This is amazing." She would neither swoon, nor hide her eyes. "You are every bit as theatrical as I am. You are setting a stage for great drama. But, Ross, if I am to work for you, don't you think such familiarity on a personal level may make it difficult to maintain our professionalism?"

"Are you afraid you may not be able to contain yourself—that you may be moved to ravage me on the spot," he said. "Fear not. Allow me to lead the proceedings. You may examine me as soon as I have examined you. We may both learn a great deal.

"There is a risk. It would be a simple matter for you to become besotted with me. You might also find yourself begging me to remain on the table. One cannot begin to imagine how much time could be spent in such pursuits. I certainly think that if this experiment goes well, we should regard it

as only the first of many, and I will charge you to maintain
meticulous notes of our findings. To justify the time used,
that is."

If he was joking, he did so with a remarkably serious
countenance. "What kind of scientist works with no clothes
on?"

"An innovative one who is anxious to ensure the absolute
integrity of his experiments. There are two of us involved.
I've told you I have my own small test to discover if you are
aroused. It's only fair that I give you an opportunity to return the favor. If I were dressed, it wouldn't necessarily be
impossible to assess the level of my arousal. But undressed
there will be no question."

Finch stared at the high ceiling with its molded cherubs
cavorting, leading each other by draped scarves held in their
pudgy hands. Her heart would be more glad if she could
convince herself that what she did wasn't wrong. It was
wrong, but she would do it anyway. She would grab this little oasis of sensual pleasure in the middle of her dull life and
plan to hold it close, to revisit it in her mind during the years
to come.

"Stand up," Ross said—or rather, ordered. "Here, take my
hand and I will help you."

She closed her eyes and wound her fingers tightly together on her stomach.

"Come, come now, Finch. Up you get."

She squeezed her eyes more tightly shut and shook her
head from side to side.

He kissed her forehead.

Finch sucked her bottom lip between her teeth. His cool
mouth worked a wicked magic on her resolve. Another kiss,
and another. He kissed her face again, and again, until he
pressed his mouth to hers, and she let out a sigh. He took her
face in his big, gentle hands, and kissed her long and deeply.
She could not keep still a moment longer. To run her hand
up his arm and across his shoulder was such pleasure. To let
him open her mouth wide with his own was such pleasure.

To have him hold her face and make no attempt to touch her anywhere else was . . . it was such pleasant torture.

He pulled off her slippers.

His right hand settled on top of her feet and he held them together.

"Ross!" Rubbing the soles of her feet, he made her attempt to squirm away from him.

Soon enough he moved on to her ankles, moved upward, stroking, stroking, and lifting her skirts as he did so.

And still he kissed her.

Finch pointed her toes, closed her eyes again. Upward to her knees, around to the sensitive skin beneath, down the back of a leg to her ankle.

Her body tingled.

"You have long legs," he said. "Long, lovely legs." And when he returned to her knee, he didn't stop there but continued up her thigh, past the top of her stockings to the bare skin above.

Finch's eyes flew open. "I promised myself we should not become close again. I thought we would be careful to do nothing that might make our working together difficult."

"So did I." He kissed beneath her chin, nuzzled her head to one side so that he could press his lips to her neck. "Yes. So did I. Not possible. You smell so sweet, and feel so sweet."

He stripped away first one, then the other stocking. His fingers, lightly playing along each of her inner thighs, was exquisite agony. Finch could bear it no longer. "Stop that." She drew up her knees and attempted to bat him away. Her efforts gained her nothing since he only captured her two hands in one of his and took her fingers to his mouth so that he might kiss each one and draw it into his mouth.

When he made as if to lift her, Finch clung to his neck, but he did not carry her away as she expected. Rather he stood her on the table, held her by her waist, and looked up into her face.

Not a whisper of a smile softened his features. "Take off your clothes. I want to look at you."

She blushed instantly, an intense, raw hot flush. "I couldn't."

"Of course you can. You dress yourself, don't you?"

"Yes."

"And you undress yourself again when you wish to change or go to bed?"

"Yes."

"Good. Then I repeat, take off your clothes for me."

She should refuse again, but she didn't want to. And she wouldn't.

"Turn," he said. "I will help with the tapes." He turned and loosened the back of her dress.

Air slipped across her skin.

Ross gripped her elbows and he kissed the line of her spine to her waist. Her knees weakened and she crossed her arms to press her hands on top of his.

He held her there a while, his breath hot at her waist. Then he rotated her to face him once more.

Finch looked down into his upturned face. Candlelight cast a sheen over his body. Happenings behind the door of the marital chamber were a mystery to her. She had never considered that there might be times such as these. The small book she had been given to help her prepare for the marriage that was never to be had alluded only to being submissive to one's husband. One should not, it had exhorted, ever remove one's clothes for "the act," nor, under any circumstances, find any pleasure in "the act." To find pleasure was a sign of weak moral character in a woman.

"I have a weak moral character," she said aloud, but to herself.

Ross gave a barking laugh. "What? *You?* Why would you say such a thing?"

"It isn't seemly for a female to enjoy such times as these."

"Rot," he said with vehemence. "You are a woman of intense passion, and you are perfect as you are."

Looking at him, at the length of him, she contracted in inner places until she ached with longing to touch him. She rolled her shoulders forward and pulled off the tight sleeves of her gown. The bodice followed automatically. The pale green chemisette fluttered to the floor like a large butterfly.

Ross stepped back, and his slight smile fixed. As quickly as she could, Finch stepped out of her dress and took off her chemise.

And she stood before him on the table. Naked.

Ross studied her from head to foot, and a great breath expanded his chest.

Finch's skin prickled. She longed, a desperate, forbidden longing.

Ross spanned her hips, dug his fingertips into the soft flesh of her bottom. Finch's legs wobbled, and she locked her knees. "I'm nine-and-twenty," she told him. "A shameless elderly spinster. And I revel in being with you like this. I could not bear to have refused you, because that would have been refusing myself, and I think that foolish. What is to become of me?"

"Because you are honest? Because you have allowed yourself to be free with me? I shall protect you, and your reputation, that's what is to become of you."

But he would not do so by becoming her husband, Finch thought with regret. And she did still long to be married. If that was unreasonable, then so be it, but she had actually decided that she never wished to be without this man. And that would be her burden, to live out her life knowing there was a man who breathed the air she breathed and whom she longed to have as her husband, as the father of her children, but who could never be so because they had been born in different worlds.

His mouth, settling over her navel, shocked her. He wrapped his arms around her body and held her stomach to his face—and he moaned a little. "Lie down again, Finch. Please."

Obediently she dropped to her knees. His male part was

engorged. It stood out from his body, large and distended. Gossip she'd overhead among certain young ladies in Cornwall had suggested a man's private parts were ugly in the extreme, laughable, in fact. Finch did not find them so. She would like to cradle them in her hands, to kiss them. But, of course, she would do no such thing for fear of shocking Ross.

"On your back," he said, smiling again. "I have decided that nine-and-twenty is a perfect age in a woman. Possibly only to be exceeded by thirty and the years to follow."

She could not seem to accomplish his request but wobbled each time she attempted to maneuver herself onto her back. He had undone her composure entirely.

Without a word, Ross assisted her. He stretched her out on the table and stood with his belly pressed to the hard, carved wood while he studied her face. "All wonderment," he told her. "How beautiful you are. Golden-eyed girl. Innocence and desire. You are a heady creature."

She could not forget that she lay before him completely revealed, and she attempted to cover herself with her arms.

Ross gently put her hands at her sides. "We have not been taught to be comfortable in our bodies. A misfortune. You have a body that should be looked upon—by me." He brushed fallen locks of her hair away from her face and outlined each feature. When he outlined her mouth, he became even more intent, and he kissed her again, and Finch felt how he reined in his ardor. Control cost him dearly now, but it thrilled her that he fought to restrain himself.

With scrupulous attention, he began touching her. He remained silent for so long that Finch began to shift restlessly. He caressed every part of her. Nothing was left untouched. His passing fingers explored her shoulders, her arms. His hands surrounded her waist and he grunted. "Very small," he said. "I have never thought to care much for a woman made as you are, but then, I never had the good fortune to meet you before, did I? Your belly is taut and falls back hard between your hipbones. Does it please you for me to touch you here?" He pressed a finger into her navel.

She gasped. "Yes, yes, touch me there."

He removed his finger and bent to use his tongue instead. Heat flared the length of her, and she pressed her abdomen upward, the better to feel him.

"Most interesting," he said when he paused for breath. "Is there no part of you that will not respond to my touch?"

"I don't think so. Is that wrong?"

"It is the most right thing I have ever encountered. Your Greville . . . he did not—well—did he?"

She turned her face from him. To think of Greville now was both painful and unsuitable. She had recovered from the loss of him, but a part of her heart would always be his. "Greville and I were younger and very traditional. He wanted more than we shared, but he never pushed me. In the end we should have done very well together, but we were not given the treasure of time to explore each other in more detail. Oh, Ross, I don't think I could bear that again."

He had centered on her breasts and he cupped each one in a hand, weighed the flesh, ran his thumbs back and forth over her nipples until the sensation undid her. Her legs twisted helplessly. She caught him by the hair at the back of his head and urged him closer. "Don't stop. Please don't stop, Ross."

He didn't reply, but he did kiss her breasts. Even though she knew she was a stick of a woman, he made her feel voluptuous. "They are very small," she said at last, panting from the exhilaration he made her feel. "I'm sorry."

"Sorry?" He raised his face and glared at her. "They are the sweetest of breasts. They respond to my every touch, and I would not want them any way else. Look at your nipples."

Reluctantly, she did so and blushed afresh at their puckered, pointed condition. Ross took a nipple into his mouth again and she watched him pull at it, gently, repeatedly, letting it pop from his mouth, only to capture it again. He abandoned the nipple to trail wet kisses in circles around each breast, stopping just short of the center and refusing to allow her to force his open mouth to settle where she wanted it most.

He kissed the space between her breasts, ran more kisses down to her stomach, and below. He buried his face in the hair at the apex of her legs. His tongue darted out to surround the aroused flesh where she now knew the ultimate sensation lay. But as quickly he withdrew and proceeded to plant kisses down the length of her legs, to her feet. Once there, he raised each one and kissed the instep while she giggled and tried to pull free.

She knew she would never be able to let him go from her heart. But she had decided that she would not easily let him go anyway. He might consider that marriage was not for him, but he had not met Finch More before. She was a tenacious woman when she really wanted something or someone.

Finch wanted Ross, Lord Kilrood.

She wanted him to marry her, and she wanted to bear his children.

She also wanted to conduct many examinations such as the one presently under way.

Without warning he lifted and turned her to lie on her face. "What are you doing?" she asked, rising up to rest her weight on her elbows.

"Further study. I find the lines of my acquisition quite beyond compare. In fact they are all but perfect."

"What makes them less than perfect?" Finch asked, but with a giggle in her voice.

Ross slid a hand and forearm beneath her chest and supported her breasts. The instant burning low inside her shocked Finch. Shocked and thrilled her. She wriggled a little, moving her breast within his hand.

"You will undo me if you keep that up," he told her. "Then we shall have to start our experiment all over again."

Promptly Finch swung her upper body from side to side,

brushing her taut nipples and the straining flesh of her breasts back and forth against his arm.

"In other words you want me to start over again, miss?"

"In other words I would not consider it a disaster if you had to do so. Ross, I ache. I burn."

"So do I, my love. Please do as I guide you to do. You will bring us both great pleasure."

She rested her brow on her crossed arms and waited. The pads of Ross's fingers were slightly rough, but still they delighted her. To work with his hands—as Ross clearly had—was good for a man's soul.

Could he possibly feel the intensity which she enjoyed now?

Ross smoothed her spine and brought his hands to rest on her bottom. There he touched lightly, then squeezed almost roughly. "I shall have bruises," she told him.

His response was to settle his mouth on one cheek, to pull a little skin through his teeth, and to suck. Every touch was a needle pulling a heated thread beneath her skin.

He moved and she saw his shadow fall over her, over the table. His skin and flesh touched hers, touched hers where his hip and thigh settled. He sat beside her and began to rub her back.

Finch gave an uneven and blissful sigh. And then she cried out and jerked from the table. He had smoothed her back from waist to shoulder, and on the return path, made a flurry of brushing strokes over the sides of her breasts. She could not lie still.

The shadow shifted again, and he put his head beside hers to whisper into her ear, "Be still, or I shall tie you to this table and have my way with you until you are too exhausted to move."

She did not tell him she thought she might like that very much.

Again and again he repeated the wonderfully wicked massage of her back—with its butterfly-wing seduction of her breasts—and caused the deep, tugging response within her.

Ross remained beside her, but turned her onto her back and stretched her arms above her head. He held them there while he looked down into her face, then kissed her deeply, passionately, and continued to kiss her when she writhed, rolled from side to side.

He raised his head to look at her, and he smiled. His eyes narrowed and the smile was carnal. "You were made for this, Finch." Her hair had completely escaped its coiffeur and fallen about her shoulders. What he could gather, he draped over one breast, then he used his tongue to find her nipple and nibble lightly. "Your hair smells of camomile. And now your breast smells of camomile, too."

Releasing her arms, he framed the undersides of her breasts and pushed them upward, and smothered them with kisses until Finch moaned and begged for release without being certain what release she asked for.

When Ross left her, she was bereft and searched about for him, but he returned soon enough and stood beside her once more. "It's your turn to ask for what you want."

A blush was unsuitable now, but she blushed anyway. "I want—I don't know what I want except for you not to leave me. My skin grows cold when you leave me."

"I thought you might say that." He held a lacy, black silk shawl aloft. "A suitable cover for such tender skin, don't you think?"

She thought it looked ominous and strange. "I suppose so."

"I know so. See how it warms you." Tassels decorated the corners, and Ross used one of these tassels to make a feathery path around her navel.

Finch jumped and giggled.

"Be still, or I shall not be able to warm you adequately," he said, with a quite devilish grin.

Next he stroked the soft, silken tassel along a groin and Finch all but leaped from the table. She gasped and made a grab for the instrument of torture. "You are wicked, my lord."

"No, it is Ross who is wicked. Tell me to stop, and I will." Her other groin received the same treatment, and again Finch squirmed.

"You don't like it."

"I didn't say that," she told him, fighting down chuckles. "Demon. That is what you are."

He pushed aside her hair and used the tip of the tassel like the end of a paintbrush, to stipple her sensitive flesh, and her nipples. To stop herself from grabbing his wrist, she clutched the edges of the table instead.

"Good girl," Ross said, and he spread the gossamer fine shawl over her. "Like a silk net in which I have caught a most enticing fist." He pulled his "net" tight over her, bent to poke his tongue through strategic holes in the mesh. "Most enticing. Why I think one could do almost anything one wished to do through this net—with stimulating effects."

"You enjoy taunting."

"I enjoy teasing," he said. "Teasing with a view to increasing pleasure. Yours and mine."

"You planned this, didn't you?"

He stroked her while he frowned in concentration. "No, in fact I did not plan it. But it has become very clear to me that whenever I am with you—and I intend to be with you very often—particularly intriguing possibilities will come to mind."

"Then we shall have to keep our distance." Drawn tight, the silken threads inflamed her.

He glanced at her face, grinned, and kissed her mouth so slowly she felt melded to him. "We shall do no such thing, dear Finch. Such harmony of mind and body is a rare thing and I, for one, will not easily relinquish it. Mmm, how delicious you look. And what magical moments I foresee." Next he bent over her breasts and drew first one, then the other nipple through the shawl and into his mouth while Finch was unable to keep her back on the table.

"Relax a moment," he said when he paused for breath. "But allow me to make you more comfortable if you please."

Making her "more comfortable," consisted of placing a plump cushion beneath her hips, and ignoring her pleas that he remove the thing at once.

"I shall not remove it. No, no, the pillow is most necessary. Allow me to show you why."

With unerring authority, he pulled her far enough down the table to allow her knees to rest at the edge and the rest of her legs to dangle. He spread her thighs and tucked the shawl between. "Stimulating, you see. The silken fibers, I mean. They will heighten your pleasure, and your pleasure is mine, dear lady."

"Ross, I really don't think—"

"I do," he said. And before there was another instant for her to protest, he placed himself between her knees, used her breasts as anchors for his hands, and set about making a moist path through the shawl to her most private parts. And he flipped his hard, strong tongue back and forth while Finch's mouth fell open. Horror and ecstasy made a strange mix.

"This is absolutely wrong," she managed to tell him. "I cannot imagine how we have gone from discussing your collection, to . . . well, I just can't imagine, that's all. But . . . Oh, Ross."

"Mmm. Let yourself go. It is happening because it is meant to happen. I don't entirely understand either, but we shall find out. Later."

"I am falling apart. Losing myself."

"To me. Which is exactly as it should be."

For this moment, a small voice told her. In a short while he would be about his own business again and she would be left to ponder, and worry about her total weakness in his company.

"Now hush and let me do my work."

Ross did his work. Oh, he did it very well. Once more his clever tongue made its way past the shawl to the fiery place that, already prepared, flared with response and sent her jackknifing to sit up and pluck, ineffectually, at his black hair. But he kept his head buried between her legs and continued to stimulate her while waves of intense pleasure racked her.

Slowly the sensation receded and she looked down at his head, so dark against her skin where the shawl had worked away. Muscles stood out in his wide, sweat-filmed shoulders. The black hair on his chest shone moistly.

She was lost, abandoned, and had no wish to be found, not yet.

The deepest of breaths failed to calm her trembling. "Now it is your turn," she told him. "You shall lie down as I have, and submit to minute examination. You shall become my specimen."

With glittering eyes he glanced up at her, and he laughed. "That is an examination that must await another day. I am a fair man and will make certain you have your rightful turn, but I am also only a man, and I can bear only so much restraint. I fear I must make this charming experience mine alone to control."

With agile grace he leaped up behind her and lifted her to stand with her back to him. The shawl he draped about her shoulders. "To keep you warm," he said, with laughter in his voice. And he set about stroking her again, stroking and weighing, and testing, and touching until she feared she might fall, and she reached back to grasp him. His body was instantly flattened to hers and she felt every dip and rise—especially the rise of that part of him that fascinated her most.

Without warning he delved between her thighs, delved into the hair that covered her genitals. "Aroused," he announced. "I told you my test was very simple. You are moist and ready, dear Finch. But I must be very certain that you understand what I want to do. We have played, sweet girl, and I would like to play some more, but a more serious game."

He rotated her to face him and they stood, toe-to-toe, their naked bodies pressed together.

"Finch," he said, his voice hoarse, "I would like to join with you. Do you understand."

"I am not a child, nor even a very young woman. I understand."

He averted his face. "No. No." He made to put her from him but she clung to him. "You are not a woman to be taken lightly. And I am not a man to take a woman such as you lightly. The bond such moments form will always be there, Finch. No matter what happened between us in future, you and I would always recall that we had known each other."

He was an honest man. He was not a man who used sincerity as a weapon to weaken her. "If I turned from you now, you would not be the only one to feel an emptiness. I should feel it, too."

Ross searched her face. "What exactly are you saying to me?"

She swallowed, and swallowed again. Her mouth had never been so dry. She pushed him from her a scant few inches and studied his body. "I find you so pleasing." She took his manhood in a hand and ducked her head to hide a smile when she heard his sharply drawn breath. "As I suspected. Aroused. You see, I have a simple test, too. I wish to *know* you, Ross. What follows, follows. I am not a child, and the decisions I make are not a child's decisions."

Capturing her face in hands that were not entirely steady, he closed his eyes and kissed her yet again. She would never forget his kisses, or cease to long for them.

Then, with his eyes wide open once more, he caught her by the waist and hoisted her high. "Wrap your legs around my waist."

She stared down into his face. "We shall fall."

"Then we shall fall together but I shall make sure you do

not hurt yourself. Do as I tell you." Slowly he lowered her and while he did so she slid her legs around him and crossed her ankles behind his waist.

The rigid tip of him sought to enter her body. As if guided by some force she did not know, it probed there and she felt her way open in response. It opened and ached, and let her know that without a part of him, this part of her would be incomplete.

"You are absolutely certain," he whispered against her neck.

"Oh, please." She rubbed her cheek against his and licked the contours of his ear—and Ross shuddered openly. "Come into me, Ross."

"So I shall."

Her heart thundered, and even the candles did little to push back darkness that collected at the edges of her vision, heated darkness.

With one hand Ross raised her hips. With the other he contrived to guide himself past the opening into her body. "You are very tight. Relax. Sometimes the first time isn't without discomfort for a woman, but it will get better."

"I want to feel you."

Their sweat mingled.

From somewhere in the connecting rooms came the sound of a hard object falling.

Finch and Ross grew instantly still. She pressed her face into the crook of his neck and listened.

Whatever it was slid, clattering as it went.

Ross grasped her tightly to him and called out, "Is there someone there? Who are you?"

Another sound came, a scraping.

"Speak up, damn you, or I'll shoot," Ross cried. "I'm sorry," he told Finch quietly, swinging her away from him and depositing her on the floor. He leaped lightly down beside her and caught up his breeches. "Announce yourself, I say."

Bewildered, Finch fumbled with her clothes. She ignored

her chemise but managed to struggle into her gown. With great effort she reached back to tie the tapes at the back of her neck, then at her waist. The rest must wait.

"I see you," Ross roared. "Don't move or your life is forfeit." Fury twisted his features. He stopped only to button his breeches at his waist before catching up his jacket and taking a knife from a hidden pocket in the lining. To Finch he said, "Remain here and hide," and he said it very quietly. "Go back into the sitting room and get into that trunk you spoke of."

He was a man who expected to be obeyed.

The instant he passed through an alcove into the next room, she gave him only seconds before she followed, catching up a heavy candlestick as she went.

"Stand where you are, I tell you," Ross shouted. "Don't move a muscle. I have men at the door."

Finch knew he had no such thing, but prayed his bluff would work. There was much going on about them that needed explanation, and this might be the start of revelation.

"Oh, hell and *damnation*," Ross yelled from a distance in front of her. "Damn your hide for the villain you are. You shall suffer for this."

His yells continued for several seconds, together with loud crashing sounds.

Finch forgot caution and followed at a full run. She didn't have far to go before she saw what had happened to Ross. He lay sprawled through an alcove, half of his body in the room he'd been leaving, half of his body in the room he'd been about to enter. And beneath him was something large and glinting.

He moved with evident pain, rolled to one side, and saw Finch approach. "I fell over the damned—fell over the thing, dash it all." He got slowly to his feet. "It was placed across the doorway to make sure the blackguard got away while I was incapacitated."

"Oh, Ross," Finch said, stepping around the object in question. "Are you really hurt?"

"I am very probably mortally wounded. But, more important, that villain has escaped. There will be no catching him now, whoever he is." He got to his feet and limped to take up a branch of lighted candles. Those he held aloft.

Finch went to his side and slipped an arm around his waist. "Lean on me," she told him, looking down at the fallen obstacle.

She held her breath, and heard Ross say, "I'm damned."

"Quite." She tried to right the thing, but it was too heavy. "A bronze tiger, with a cub in its mouth."

❧ Chapter 12 ❧

"I know apologies are inadequate but they are all I have to offer. I deeply regret that you have been forced to witness such . . . abandon.

"The young of this generation are a disgrace. They are irresponsible, self-serving, base, carnal, oh, my dear friends, there are not words to fully express either the depth of my embarrassment, or my desire to make amends to you.

"I would have spared you such an exhibition, but I must be completely honest with you—I had not the slightest notion that those two would toss everything aside. I mean I had no notion that they would defy convention so completely.

"My mortification knows no bounds. Of course you trusted me to spare you any discomforting little details, and I have failed you, but I must ask you to forgive me and to understand what happened.

"Naturally I know that you know what happened. What I mean is that I feel it is my duty to explain how it came about *that we—you and I—had no choice but to be present for the, ah, events.*

"You see, usually I would have avoided the entire, tawdry interlude, but I was trapped. Yes, I got myself into a corner from which I couldn't gracefully escape. So there I was, you see, caught. Not that I could actually leave at all anyway— you see. So much has occurred that I did not expect. I simply must put my natural genteel squeamishness behind me, don a brave front, and hope for the strength to deal with occurrences beyond my control.

"But as I was telling you, I couldn't have left because I had to attempt to get important clarification of certain happenings. Imperative clarification. Yes, friends, that is why I had to remain, to obtain imperative clarification. Only I obtained no such thing. All that has come of my selflessness and sacrifice is—well, you know what we were forced to standby and suffer through, but apart from that I myself gained only further reasons for concern.

"Now it will be necessary to keep an eye on all this tiger silliness. Oh, I know it may be all a foolish design to distract me from my only goal, but it could just have bearing on what has been happening. And I must confide in you that I had no idea we would be drawn into this intrigue. One cannot help but think that if those involved would attend to business and avoid wasting time on pointless play, then the issue would be quickly solved.

"Whatever happens, I must get things moving as I have planned, or who knows how long it will take to reclaim Number 7.

"I do have a suggestion that should ease your way. If there should be—and I shudder at the thought—but if there should be a repeat of the disgraceful performance we have just seen—well, don't look!"

§ Chapter 13 §

Hunter Lloyd opened the door to Number 7 before Ross had a chance to ring the bell. "Heard you coming," Hunter said. "Thought you might be Latimer. Hoped, should I say."

Ross had only met Hunter on a few occasions—mostly in passing outside Number 7 and Number 8. But from those brief encounters he'd gained a sense that given an opportunity he'd like the man.

"Glad to see you, of course, Lord Kilrood," Hunter said. He nodded at Finch. "Come on in, please."

He turned from them and went to hover in the doorway to Latimer and Finch's apartments. "No one seemed to know where you were Finch. Were you in Whitechapel? Did the runner deliver the message I sent?"

Finch said, "No," and sounded confused. "Why did you send a runner to Whitechapel?"

"We're hoping to get Latimer. But who can begin to guess how long that will take? Or if the message will arrive at all?"

"What is it?" Finch said, starting forward. "Is it my father? Is something wrong?"

"No, no, no," Hunter said. He had very green, very expressive eyes, and at the moment they registered distress. "I'm sorry to alarm you. I'm afraid there has been trouble, though. Someone got into the house. And into your apartment. The confounding thing is that they had to have done it after you had left, but they weren't noticed, or heard."

Sudden shrieking could be heard from an upper floor. "Lady Hester," Hunter remarked, sounding apologetic. "My aunt's sensibilities are somewhat tender. She will just have learned of the intrusion."

"When was it discovered?" Ross asked. Finch had left his side and was putting the shabby drawing room to rights while she evidently searched for missing items.

"Adam Chillworth is forever coming and going. Quiet chap. Doesn't say much but sees a good deal. He noticed the Mores' door was open when it should have been closed and went to check. This is what he found. He's upstairs with the Smiles sisters now. They're upset, naturally."

"*When* will something be done about the lawlessness in this city?" Finch demanded, snatching a pewter jug from the floor and replacing it on a sideboard. "The watchmen are useless."

"They are afraid and justly so," Hunter said. "If you saw the collection of riffraff I see daily in the courts, you would understand that any sensible man would keep out of their way."

"But we seem to have no recourse for things like this."

"Your recourse is to take steps to guard what you value."

Finch stopped hurriedly picking things up and searching for anything that might be missing. "What steps should we take? The doors are kept locked. This is a fine neighborhood."

Hunter met Ross's eyes. "I should say that whoever got in did so with a single thought in mind. There was something specific he wanted. Does anything appear to have been stolen?" He looked at Finch.

"Nothing, yet," she told him, glancing around and stopping to retrieve an armload of pillows. "Such carelessness. Throwing things this way and that."

"What of the doors?" Ross asked. "Forced, I suppose."

"Not so," Hunter said. "Not forced this time, or on the first occasion. When the tiger was taken."

Ross felt uneasy. Jennings had instructions to bring the tiger in half an hour, by which time Ross had expected to have time to pave the way for its return through a quiet conversation with Lady Hester. "He got in through a window, then?" he asked.

"He got in through the door he unlocked," Hunter said. "The key to each tenant's rooms also unlocks the front door."

Ross thought about that. "In other words, any one of you can unlock any door within the house?"

Hunter smiled a little. "My aunt is a very kind woman. She is not always possessed of deep analytical ability."

"*Deep* . . . well, yes I see." Sometimes prudence was invaluable. "So there are a number of keys that would unlock the front door, and this one?"

"Afraid so."

"Then we'll just have to request that all parties produce their keys, won't we?"

Hunter nodded.

"Finch," Ross said. "Leave it alone for now, my dear. You'll tire yourself out and achieve nothing. Let's go and speak with Lady Hester. Jennings will be here shortly."

Finch smacked her palms together and blew at strands of escaped hair. Hunter cleared his throat, and Ross caught his eye. Drat, but he would have to be more careful of what he said. The man's expression was politely curious, and it was also knowing. The odd "dear," and any proprietary attitude toward a woman could be very telling to a man with sharp wits about him.

"Perhaps you'll join us," Ross said to Hunter. "Finch and I have rather a shocking event to reveal. Shocking, but we think, enlightening."

Promptly Hunter led the way to the third floor, where he tapped on a door. Almost at once a gray-haired woman's annoyed face appeared. Upon seeing Hunter, she smiled, and said, "Your aunt's in a rare state, Mr. Hunter. She feels we are beset on all sides."

"My aunt is justified in her concerns, Barstow," Hunter said. "Would you tell her I'm here, and that Viscount Kilrood from Number 8 has come to call."

The door opened wide and the woman ushered them into a well-appointed boudoir presided over by a particularly beautiful, carved Chinese daybed. "Her Ladyship is resting in her bedchamber," Mrs. Barstow said. "I'll inform her you are here."

With a hand at Finch's waist, Ross guided her ahead of him to a black-and-gold-striped chaise—and caught Hunter's eye once more. Hell and damnation, he must be cautious for her sake.

Another door into the room was thrown open and a statuesque blond woman dressed entirely in black entered. She closed her eyes repeatedly, as if under enormous strain, but her *toilette* was impeccable. The black-velvet robe she wore over a black gros de naples gown had not been obtained for a bagatelle, and the rope of jet beads that rested on her admirable bosom was interspersed with diamonds. There were also diamonds at her ears and on her fingers.

"My dear Viscount Kilrood," she said, offering him a hand and accomplishing a fine curtsy at the same time, "I am honored that you should think to visit in my hour of need."

"Lord Kilrood didn't—"

"Not at all," Ross said, smiling and shaking his head at Hunter. "We neighbors must stick together when we're under attack, hmm?"

"Under *attack*?" She righted herself with remarkable

agility. "Is there a mob in the streets? Oh, say it isn't so. Barstow? Fetch my salts."

"No mob, m'lady," Ross said hastily. "I referred to this disgraceful episode here at Number 7 with someone feeling free to enter where they have no right to be."

"Quite, quite." Lady Hester gestured with her tortoise-shell lorgnette. "And it isn't the first time. Someone got in and stole my grandfather's prized tiger, y'know. Sir Septimus was an architect, and a collector of magnificent artifacts."

"So I've recently been told," Ross said, glancing at Finch, who had lost even more color from her face. "The first thing we must do is make sure each tenant, and each applicable member of the staff, knows the exact whereabouts of his or her key. Then I suggest you set about making sure there are different keys for the front door from those that fit the apartments."

Lady Hester sighed hugely. "I'm sure you're right. Barstow, inform the tenants that I shall wish to see their keys before the day is out."

"Yes, my lady," Barstow said, keeping her eyes lowered.

Hunter produced a key ring from his pocket and selected a key. "Mine is present and correct."

"So's mine," Barstow said, holding up a key on the chain at her waist. "And Her Ladyship's. I keep it for her."

Finch felt about in her reticule.

They waited.

She opened the little velvet bag wide and removed a bevy of items, including shells and buttons. These she set in her lap. Finally she upended the entire thing and sorted among its contents.

"It's not here," she said, scrabbling more anxiously. "How can that be when I used it only . . . I didn't!" She raised her face and looked with horror, first at Ross, then at Hunter. "I haven't used my key for several days. I've either been with Latimer, or someone has opened the door just as I arrived. Where can it be?" She repeated her search. Two red spots formed high on her cheeks. "It is gone, I tell you. I don't have my key."

"Whitechapel, perhaps," Ross suggested. "Since it is clearly time to divulge all that has occurred, you can explain exactly what happened there, too. It's possible one of those ruffians stole your key."

She blanched and made no attempt to return her possessions to her reticule.

"What's all this?" Lady Hester asked. "Finch, my dear, has someone hurt you? Why haven't you told me about this? You know I make it my business to look after each and every one of you."

"You are too kind, and I would not think of adding to your burdens," Finch said.

"Finch," Ross said gently. "I think it's time you shared all the details of what occurred when you were on your way to meet with Latimer that day. Try not to miss a word. Hunter, you will find this interesting, and you may have an idea as to how we should deal with matters."

Hunter frowned, but he nodded and tossed the tails of his jacket aside so that he might take a seat on the chaise with Finch. "Come along, Finch. You know you are among friends. Tell us what has happened to you."

"It cannot have anything to do with this." She sent Ross a reproachful glance. "I was the victim of some ne'er-do-wells in Whitechapel, that's all. But I escaped unharmed. Or rather they ran off."

"Not quite unharmed," Ross told her, deliberately mild. "Your clothes were muddy and torn, and your hands bleeding. And, in case you have forgotten, you were most upset."

Finch had avoided a complete discussion of the encounter in Whitechapel, but this time Ross intended to get to the bottom of the event.

"As you have said, I was on my way to the warehouse," Finch said. "I heard someone call my name. It happened several times. Then a man grabbed me from behind and bundled me through a hole in a fence and into a yard behind some buildings. A most unpleasant and filthy place."

"My dear," Lady Hester said in a whisper, "how perfectly dreadful."

Barstow had pressed her hands over her mouth, and her eyes were huge and horrified.

"It was unpleasant, but it was soon over," Finch said.

Ross felt a swell of pride. She was a magnificent girl. He cleared his throat, then recalled that at least his thoughts could not be seen or heard by others. He did feel proud of her, dash it all. He felt that, and a great deal more. He felt protective and possessive toward her.

Good God.

"Finch," Hunter said. He had by now turned completely sideways on the chaise to face her. "Please carry on."

She became quaintly pink. "There isn't much more. He put his hand over my mouth and pushed me into that yard. It was getting dark, so I couldn't see very much."

"You were walking through Whitechapel in the dark?" Mrs. Barstow said. *"Alone?"*

Finch, who despite her best efforts, appeared disheveled, said, "I had an errand to do, and it wasn't completely dark."

"Don't interrupt," Lady Hester said to Barstow. "Carry on, if you please, Finch."

"I struggled. And I kicked. And then I . . ." She pushed her lips out and looked to the side. "I bit the man's hand. It was over my mouth, you see."

"Awful," Lady Hester said.

Ross felt murderous.

"Then another person came. A very tall man in a cloak. He billowed from the darkness, and I thought him like a large bat in a top hat. But if he hadn't come, I should have been considerably more hurt. The first man threw me down, but the second caught me before I hit the ground. Only then he pushed me down anyway. But it wasn't as hard as it would have been, I'm certain of that."

"Good Lord," Hunter said. "And you didn't tell us until now?"

"What could you have done?" Finch asked, raising her face. "Just this day our home has been broken into, and we have all agreed that the law can do nothing. What could anyone have done about two ruffians long gone into the night? At least they didn't kill me."

"Don't," Ross said, unable to stop himself. Self-conscious, he added, "You will frighten Lady Hester." But he caught yet another glance from Hunter and guessed that the man saw beyond any subterfuge to the truth; Ross cared what happened to Finch More.

"They took everything out of my reticule and . . ." Finch bobbed to her feet. "They hit my back and threw my things down and they fell in the mud. No doubt that's where my key is."

Ross breathed in through his nose and shook his head before saying, "That's when they *took* your key, you mean. And so the puzzle of how they entered is solved. It was those same creatures who accosted you, and they secured the key with this very deed in mind."

"Is that all that happened?" Hunter asked, and stood up. A kind man, Ross noted. The barrister's quiet voice held genuine concern.

"Except for their silly message."

At last, Ross thought. This was what he had to hear in its entirety. He had to be sure he wasn't imagining that there was a connection between incidents here and his quest on behalf of the Sheik of Ranthus.

"One of the men. The tall one, I think—although I didn't see how large the other was. But one man said that the time would soon be coming. He said an old tiger would be gone and a new tiger would come. And he said—and this sounded so horrible in that place—he said the young tiger would eat the old one. Or I think he said, its predecessor. He said we all have a purpose, and once we've served our purpose we aren't needed anymore. He told me I'd served my purpose, but I might be spared if I kept quiet, or something like that. I honestly thought it was just a made-up piece of nonsense to frighten me. And I still do. Even if they wanted to get the key to rob us, all of the rest of it makes no sense."

"Doesn't it?" Ross said, aware that he must make her wary without revealing too much. "Perhaps we don't understand the sense it makes. But if you consider a little more carefully, Finch, you will realize that those men knew your name, and evidently knew where you live. They still do." And their cryptic message had been intended for him. They must have known he was with Latimer and that Finch was on her way to the same place.

"Oh, my lord," Lady Hester said, shivering markedly and dropping to sit on the edge of her daybed. "You have turned me cold all over. You mean there are villains out there. Villains with a key to this house and who are very probably set on murdering us?"

"Why should they be?" Barstow said loudly. "Why us? They're thieves, nothing more. They must have been watching Latimer and Finch. That's how they knew Finch's name. Then they found an opportunity to get her alone and steal her key. They know where she lives because they have a nasty piece of business they do, probably over and over with different people. I expect they chose Finch and Latimer because Latimer deals in all those strange foreign things. We should have a watchman on the door. A big fellow, we should get. And then there won't be any more trouble, you'll see."

"Barstow's right," Lady Hester said.

Ross went to Finch's side. "I don't think Mrs. Barstow's right, do you, Finch?"

"No," she said, looking up at him. "No, I don't. I think there's something much more sinister going on. And I doubt any watchman will be clever enough to stop whoever is intent on mischief here."

Steps sounded lower down in the house and began to rise

up the stairs. Heavy footsteps. And there were excited voices. One was unmistakable as belonging to Jennings.

Ross prepared himself for the outcry to come.

Lady Hester's butler backed into the boudoir, uttering gasping orders to Jennings, who supported the other side of his burden. He had, very sensibly, wrapped the thing in sacking—no doubt to make certain he drew as little attention as possible getting to Number 7.

"Careful, careful," the butler said. "You'll knock something down."

"Aye," Jennings said, scarcely breathing hard. "I suggest we put it down where it is. I've no doubt it'll be moved soon enough, anyway."

"Quite," Hunter said, and for an instant Ross thought the man might laugh, and he liked him even more. A sense of the ridiculous could often save a difficult moment, or so Ross had always believed.

Lady Hester stood up, raised her lorgnette, and studied the large object now ensconced on her Aubusson carpet. *"What,"* she said, pointing, "is that?"

"Excuse me, my lady," Coot said. His hair stood on end and his full face was red. "I think I'd better return to my duties."

No fool, Coot, Ross decided. The man knew when trouble loomed.

Once the butler had retired, Ross said, "Better reveal the evidence, Jennings. The sooner, the better."

"That depends on your point of view, I shouldna' wonder, m'lord," Jennings's dour expression became even more dour. He whipped off the sacking with the air of a magician revealing the most prized part of his performance, and announced, "The evidence."

"Oh!" Lady Hester's mouth remained in the shape of that single word, and she sat down again, this time with an audible thud.

"Well, I'm dashed," Hunter said. "Good old, Great-grandfather's ugly tiger returns to its cage. Well, I'm . . . Well, yes, there it is, then."

"It is not," Lady Hester declared, "an *ugly* tiger. Perhaps you do not know what a famed man Sir Septimus Spivey was in his time. Or how much he sacrificed for the good of this family."

"Really, Aunt," Hunter said, his ears turning somewhat red, "I'm sure we need not bore the rest of our company with family stories."

"Bore? Bore? That man was a saint. He lived to a hundred and two. Did you know that?"

"Yes," Hunter said quietly.

"Do you know *why*?"

"Yes," Hunter said. "Because he died before he reached a hundred and three."

Lady Hester's outrage brought her back as straight as one of the daybed posts. She pursed her mouth and breathed in loudly through her nose before saying, "My grandfather managed, through sheer strength of will, to live to one hundred and two because he didn't dare die until he'd tried to make sure his silly family didn't manage to lose this beautiful house. This beautiful house that he designed himself, and supervised the building of himself. He was a renowned architect, Hunter. An architect who obtained commissions from the Crown for which he was *knighted*. He accomplished a great deal. But his silly wife, and his silly daughters—*and* their silly husbands, weren't worth a jot, I tell you. Not a jot."

Hunter got up from the chaise. He coughed into a fist and gave a sheepish smile in all directions. "Our family has always been—or so I understand—fiercely passionate on the subject of, ah, *family*."

"Do not make excuses for me, my boy," Lady Hester said. "My poor grandfather couldn't die in peace when he needed to because his ridiculous family couldn't be trusted not to lose everything he'd worked for. Everything he'd accomplished."

Ross, who searched without success for some means to rescue Hunter, admired the man for not pointing out that Lady Hester's own relatives were the "ridiculous family" to whom she referred.

"Now," she said, "with that unpleasantness behind us, let us discover how our beautiful tiger was recovered. No doubt the wretched thieves found it too heavy and abandoned it."

Finch looked at Ross and raised her eyebrows.

"Not exactly," he said. "I should be happy to explain how the piece was found, and where." A man could be forgiven for the occasional small embellishment of the truth. He would not be at all happy.

"You know about this, Viscount Kilrood?"

"I do indeed, my lady." His shins still stung from their cruel impact with the metal beast. "It was in my house."

The lady's blank stare suggested she either had not heard or did not understand him.

"I say." Hunter recovered faster than the rest of the company. "In *your* house, Lord Kilrood?"

"Yes." And placed there, he had no doubt, as another message to him. He was to understand how vulnerable he was, and how easy his foes would find it to reach him personally if they wished.

"But"—Lady Hester frowned, and her eyes lost focus—"how could such a thing occur without your knowing? And why?"

The reason was a subject he would not discuss, here or elsewhere. "I do have a theory." He had to offer an excuse that would ensure their prudence, without striking fear into them. He had reached a troublesome conclusion: the foes of the throne of Ranthus had made a mistake. His task must be to use it to his advantage—if he could. In showing him that they had both found him, and that he wasn't safe anywhere, they had also alerted him. He had no doubt that they hoped he would attempt to hurry his task. They were waiting for him to have all the parts of the Sacred Box of Ranthus in his possession. Then they would strike against him directly. But they had made a very poor calculation, for his only defense was now obvious. The pieces of the box must be kept separate, and he must never be in possession of them all.

"My lord?" Hunter said.

Ross looked around at the faces that watched him with anticipation and realized he'd been lost in thought. A theory? He needed inspiration. "We are dealing with inept villains. Thieves." It could be a nuisance to be surrounded by amateur sleuths, but at least if they were busy detecting, they would doubtless pay little attention to his own comings and goings. "For whatever reason they have decided there is treasure to be found at Number 7."

"Then why did they leave that thing"——Hunter indicated the tiger——"at your house?"

"They didn't know where to hide it in a hurry." Ross improvised. "They thought it would not be noticed among my collection——which is where I found it."

He could not avoid Finch's troubled eyes. She knew the truth, that every effort had been made to make certain the tiger was noticed.

"So they also have keys to your house," Hunter said, discomforting Ross with his intensely watchful air.

"So it would seem." And that was where he was completely confounded. "We must conduct an investigation, Jennings. The keys to Number 8 must also be accounted for. And new locks installed."

"Aye, m'lord," Jennings said, and Ross did not at all care for his valet's tone. It warned him that his man had theories of his own. In the past, Jennings had been known to take rather too much initiative.

Lady Hester's sudden shriek brought a collective gasp of alarm.

"What is it, my lady?" Barstow asked, rushing to bend over her mistress. "This is too much for a delicate lady. We can't all stay awake day and night waiting to be attacked, or robbed——or worse." Her meaningful glance around was proof that Ross had failed to bring all, if any, of these people any comfort.

"Oh, do stop fussing, Barstow." Lady Hester flapped at her companion as if she were an annoying pet. "I am not delicate, I am shocked. Where are your eyes? All of you? The ruby is gone. Oh, they knew what they were doing. They didn't want the tiger, that's why they deposited it at Number 8. For all we know, they took it directly there to those *deserted* rooms of yours, Lord Kilrood, so that they could remove my precious ruby from the tiger in comfort."

Ross could not openly dispute Lady Hester's theory. He smiled politely.

"Have you forgotten, Aunt?" Hunter said.

"Be silent for once, Hunter."

"You *have* forgotten. It was only glass. My mother told me her father—your father—sold the real thing to raise money."

Outrage turned Lady Hester's attractive face stony. "No such thing," she said. "Perdita fabricated the most extraordinary stories. Even as a small child. I'll thank you never to mention such nonsense again."

Hunter's face became expressionless. "My mother was a sensible woman, Aunt," he said, in a tone harsh enough to bring color to Lady Hester's neck. She held her tongue.

There was a light tap at the door, and Barstow went to admit a small but elderly maid.

"What is it, Pearl?" Lady Hester said, very loudly, and Ross guessed she was glad of the interruption.

"There's a person come to see Miss Finch. A most disreputable person. I closed him outside the front door to wait. Says he was sent by an old gentleman."

Finch rose at once. She swept aside Hunter's protests that, under present circumstances, she should not deal with strangers, and hurried from the room. Ross said, "Look after things here, will you," to Hunter, and was close behind her. "Be calm," he told her, keeping his voice down. "Every step we take must be considered." He wanted, desperately, to remove both Finch and Latimer from harm's way.

Coot stood guard over the front door as if he expected an army to break in at any moment. Finch hurried past him to take a look at her visitor.

The "disreputable" person was a ragged boy of about sixteen whose clothes had probably been old when he obtained them—when he was considerably shorter. Bony wrists and ankles protruded. He held a cloth cap in his red-knuckled hands, revealing a head of thick, sandy-colored curls.

"Who are you, please?" Finch asked.

"That don't matter." The boy's dark brown eyes were troubled. "Well, I'm Hayden. But it don't matter."

"Why not step inside, Hayden," Ross said. "You look cold. Coot, perhaps we could find Hayden something hot to drink."

Without a word, but exuding disapproval, Coot departed for the kitchens.

Hayden stepped gingerly just inside the door, but kept his eye on the outside as if ensuring he could make a speedy getaway if necessary. "You're Miss Finch," he said, darting a glance at her. "I knows 'cause I sees you go to the warehouse opposite where I lives."

"I see," Finch said. "Yes, I believe I've seen you, too."

"Our 'ouse ain't much," the boy said defensively. "Leastwise, not anymore. Our mum says it used to be a grand one."

Ross knew the dwellings the boy referred to, and they could never have been grand, but there was a pathetic need for pride in Hayden's voice. "I'm sure you're right," Ross said. "Is there somewhere we could sit down, Finch?" He hated to ask her to admit an urchin who might possibly bring small, crawling visitors with him, but it didn't seem kind to keep the thin creature, who was little more than a child, standing in the hall. Anyway, the boy was ragged but not particularly dirty.

"Of course," she said at once. "Come into our rooms, Hayden. Coot will know to find you there."

With evident reluctance, Hayden followed Finch into the Mores' drawing room. He refused to sit down but did draw close to the fire.

Coot arrived shortly with a cup of strong, steaming tea in hand. "This'll warm you, my lad," he said, all gruff and formidable, but Ross noted that the old man had also brought a thick piece of bread spread liberally with butter, and a wedge of cheese.

The boy eyed the food hungrily, but took it from Coot and slipped it into a pocket. No doubt there were other mouths at home to share the prize. Hayden did sip the tea with evident pleasure while his nose, blue from the cold, gradually faded to chapped red.

Still frowning, Coot retired again, muttering as he went.

Hayden held the cup in both hands. He wore woolen gloves with the fingers cut out. "I seen you before," he said to Finch.

"So you told me," she said.

"It's bitter outside," he told her. "That old gent what works for the other one. Your brother, I think. The old gent give me a sovereign to come to you. I ain't never 'ad one of them before."

Ross deliberately stood aside and allowed Finch to conduct proceedings since he had a notion the boy would feel easier with her.

"Finish your tea," she said kindly. "I have some biscuits you might like." With that she took a biscuit barrel from the sideboard and opened it. "Gingersnaps. My brother's favorite."

"Well," Hayden looked at her, "if you're sure."

The boy was rough, but not without manners.

Promptly Finch removed a large biscuit and pressed it into Hayden's hands. Then she found a piece of clean cloth and wrapped up the rest of what was in the barrel. "Pop these in your pocket for the journey home." She must be anxious to know why her visitor had been sent yet she had the self-control not to hurry him.

"Thank you," Hayden said. He dipped his biscuit in the tea and ate hungrily. "The old gent said he don't dare leave the warehouse. Says he's got to watch things. 'E told me to say you wasn't to go there. 'E said you'd understand."

Finch turned to Ross. She pressed her fingers together before her, and fear stretched the skin of her face tightly over the bones. "I don't understand," she said. "What can it mean?"

"Keep calm," Ross said, not feeling particularly calm himself. "I'll go and see what's happened."

"'E sent this." Hayden pulled up his coat and fished a crumpled wad of paper from a trouser pocket. "The old gent is a goodun. 'E likes to sound angry, but 'e ain't. I can feel it."

Finch took what was a sheet of paper wrapped around another sheet of paper and something hard. As she unwrapped the first piece, a small gold key on a chain fashioned from small rubies fell into her hand. While Ross controlled the urge to snatch the key to the Sacred Box of Ranthus, Finch began studying a written note, and Ross did his best to remain patient. The thought that a lad, and a stranger to boot, had been entrusted with part of a treasure that spelled life or death for so many turned his heart cold.

"From Mr. Edwin Oak," Finch said at last. "Dear Miss More, I exhort you to remain calm. Any display of emotion can only waste valuable energy that will be needed to deal with the unforeseen disaster that has occurred." She looked up at Ross. "Disaster? Oh, Ross, what can have happened?"

He smoothed her arm and did not remind her that in light of what had already occurred in recent days, further drama should be expected. "Finish reading."

"I got to go back," Hayden said abruptly. "Me mum'll be lookin' for me."

"Perhaps there needs to be a message sent back," Ross said to Finch.

"No," she told him. "Mr. Oak writes that I should not attempt to contact him or go to Whitechapel. He will come to me."

"'E said there wouldn't be no letter to go back," Hayden said.

Ross found another sovereign in his pocket and gave it to the boy, whose eyes became startled, so amazed was he at his good fortune. He turned the coin over and over in his palm, and said, "The old gent already paid me," but with regret in his voice.

"Mr. Oak paid you to come here," Ross said. "Now I must pay you for the return journey. Off you go before you worry your poor mother out of her mind."

Hayden took a final look at his newfound wealth before stuffing it deep into a pocket. He gulped the last of his tea and stood winding his cap once more as if uncertain how to go about taking his leave.

"Thank you, Hayden," Finch said. Ross noted how her hands shook. "I'll look for you when I'm next in Whitechapel."

The boy bobbed his head repeatedly, backed away into the hall, then turned and raced from the house.

"In a great hurry to share news of his fortune, no doubt," Ross said, but he kept his eyes on Finch's face. "What else does Mr. Oak write?"

She raised the paper again. "I am afraid we may have difficult times ahead, but be assured that I shall help in any way I can. Give the key to Viscount Kilrood. It belongs to him. Latimer passed it to me at great risk to himself. It might also be prudent for you to ask Viscount Kilrood's opinion on what I enclose—this from your brother—since I rather think His Lordship may be a man of considerable intelligence and resourcefulness."

Ross wondered how Mr. Oak could have come to such large conclusions from such a short acquaintance, but made no comment.

Finch smoothed out the second piece of paper. This had been folded very small and thick.

Finch quickly read whatever Latimer had written to her.

"Oh, Ross, no. No!" She spun away from him and made her way to the nearest chair. "What shall I do?"

He would not be short with her. He was schooled to deal with intrigue. She was most definitely not prepared for such things. "Should you care to share what Latimer says?"

Without a word, she held out the note. When he took it, she also offered up the key, and he accepted it with as much nonchalance as he could muster.

"Finnie," he read aloud. "Now, do *not* panic. All will eventually be well but first we may have to tolerate some difficult times. I have to go away for a period. I'm not sure how long. I am instructed to warn you against raising any alarm since, if you do so, things will not go well for me. I don't know how long I shall be gone. You should go about your business—this I've been told to tell you. And do not try to find me. Finnie, do as he says you must, or I shall not be returned."

§ *Chapter 14* §

Men were impossible.

Overbearing, unreasonable, pompous—*rattles*. There, that's what Ross, Viscount Kilrood had driven her to. Wild words.

He actually expected her to follow his instructions and remain there. As if he owned her, or at the very least, had some right to judge what was, or was not, suitable for her.

Finch stood as close to the lace curtains at her drawing-room windows as was possible if she were to avoid being seen from outside. There he went. An imposing figure exuding an air of purpose. Ross strode from Number 7 without looking back.

He didn't look back because it never crossed his arrogant mind that she might defy him. Well, he was about to learn that just as all men were not created equal, there were women who could not be judged by the standards of other women. No doubt His Lordship was accustomed to simpering, whimpering, cooing, fluttering, fawning females who could scarcely wait for him to exert his male mastery over them. He had obviously not suspected for one instant that Finch More was mistress of her own fate and, as of tonight, a woman with a mission she would not shirk. She would go in search of her dear brother, and no man should stop her—not even the man who threatened to haunt her, waking and sleeping, for the rest of her life.

Ross passed out of sight, probably on his way to Number 8, and to summon his carriage.

Finch had no carriage, but she did have money enough to pay for a cab. Mr. Chillworth had been appointed by Ross—with Hunter's approval—to take the first watch in the hall. As Latimer's note had instructed, no mention had been made of his sudden absence. Ross's suggestion that Hunter and Mr. Chillworth take turns watching for intruders had supposedly been only to foil potential burglars. With Mr. Chillworth in place, and, Finch supposed, Ross's own conviction that she would do as she was told, he'd said he must go to Number 8 and attend to its security.

He had lied to Hunter and Mr. Chillworth. Oh, he might pause at Number 8 to post a lookout, but he'd be off to Whitechapel a moment later. He would be discreet, but he would be no more able to do nothing than she was.

She must get out and find a cab.

Climbing from a window was out of the question.

"Mr. Chillworth?" Without being quite sure of her intentions, Finch opened the door and confronted their trusty protector. "Mr. Chillworth, did you see my . . . oh."

In the dim light of the hall, shadows clung to Mr. Chillworth's sleeping features. Slumped in a chair that had been positioned to face the front door, fatigue showed in every line of his tall body. One arm hung down, the long fingers of the hand almost trailing on the floor. The only sound Finch heard was the tick, tick, tick of a small clock on a marble-topped table, and Mr. Chillworth's deep breathing.

What had she been about to ask him?

Fiddle-de-dee, no matter for goodness sake. She must

close the door to the apartment very quietly so that no one should suspect she was gone, at least not yet. Then her task was to get out of the house without being seen. Now.

The first was easily accomplished. Mr. Chillworth did not as much as stir. But in her haste she had left without a cloak or even the lightest of mantles, and her dress was not particularly warm.

On her toes she sped past the bottom of the great staircase, glancing at the carved figures on her way. As evening approached, drawing darkness with it, the wooden faces seemed ominous.

Behind the foot of the stairs, a door opened into a passageway that led to what had once been a room intended for family and staff to use on their way to the mews behind Mayfair Square. Some household staff members usually lived in rooms above the stables that formed the single row of mews buildings. In fact Number 7 was the only address in the square that did not have servants housed in the mews.

Finch found her way to the cloakroom she'd remembered and noticed with relief that several items of outerwear had been discarded there. She caught up a nondescript hooded black cape and pulled it on, wrinkling her nose at the musty odor. At least she would be warmer. Unfortunately, she did not find gloves.

Praying that no one would see her, she let herself out and sped, head down inside the big hood, to a gate into the mews.

Once outside, she stood against the garden wall and watched what little activity there was. Farther along the mews a groom led a horse into its stable. Hooves clapped the cobbles loudly, and the animal snorted and blew into the cold air.

When man and horse disappeared, all was still.

Finch sank deeper into the place where the gateposts offered some concealment.

She didn't know what to do.

All her brave thoughts had spurred her to act, but she had not considered what such an act might be. Not really, other than to hire a cab. Both Latimer and Mr. Oak had warned her not to try making a search, yet to go back inside the house would be to give in and admit helplessness.

"I am not foolhardy," she told herself, and took heart from the steady sound of her voice. "I cannot go alone to Whitechapel, particularly in the dark. But I cannot abandon you to chance, Latimer. I cannot."

"Miss More?"

Finch jumped so badly her back ached. And then she saw, of all people, Mr. Oak, who must have approached without her seeing him because she had been so deep in thought. "Hello," she said, breathless. "I did not see you coming."

"Forgive me," he said, doffing his hat. "I did note that you seemed preoccupied. Perfectly understandable in the circumstances. When I discovered you were not at home I gave up finding you and decided to approach Number 8 by this route—since it seems more suitable that I should gain entrance through the kitchens. I fear I have not made contact with my relative in Hampstead and must ask the viscount's indulgence for another night."

Finch's thoughts tumbled about. "You awakened Mr. Chillworth in the hall? Oh, dear. That means he knows I've left, and he'll raise an alarm about that."

Mr. Oak leaned on his cane. He said, "No, no, er, Mr. Chillworth did not awaken. But that is of no importance to us when we have such desperate matters to attend."

"Did you see Latimer taken?"

"Er, no. Not exactly. That is, I heard a degree of commotion in the office and went to investigate. It sounded quite violent."

Finch gasped and clapped a hand over her mouth.

"Forgive me for being blunt. Anyway, as you see, I am an old man and hardly fit for fisticuffs or the like, so I hid outside. Evidently your brother, a highly logical man, assumed I must be nearby for he spoke very loudly and those are the things I wrote to you. He shouted that his sister would come after him and another voice, a very rough and unpleasant voice, informed him that he'd better hurry up and write a note to leave for you. He was told to warn you to stay away because if you tried to find him, he would likely never be returned."

She would not cry, she would not.

"Latimer said he had this very day received something of great importance. He said he had sent it to Lord Kilrood and must be allowed to make certain it had arrived. I knew he referred to the key I had the boy bring you, but I also knew it had not been sent, because Latimer intended to deliver it himself. I believed he was secretly telling me to get the key to Lord Kilrood for him. And so he was."

Finch shook and knew that the shaking was only in small part because she was chilled. "How can you be sure of his intention? Did you speak to him direct?"

"We did not speak. He was taken away, and I found the note to you on the desk. But in the lock of the desk drawer, a lock that takes a much larger key of course, I found the beautiful gold key that arrived from the docks today—complete with the ruby chain. An audacious and clever move by your brother in hopes that I would notice, while the hiding place was so obvious his captors might *not* notice. And they didn't."

Finch waited, wishing she could hurry each of the elderly gentleman's carefully enunciated words.

"So, I wrote the note and sent it off."

"And you told Hayden—the boy—"

"I am acquainted with Hayden."

"You told him you could not leave the warehouse."

"Not until I made sure there was nothing addressed to His Lordship in the next delivery. We had been told there would be one late in the afternoon, you see. And, although I may be wrong, I am disposed to wonder if there is some connection between Lord Kilrood's shipments and this trouble that has occurred. Given Latimer's great concern over the key, you understand?"

"I do understand. Lord Kilrood has his key now."

"I know that. But my concern, as you would expect, is for Latimer's rescue. All haste must be employed. That was a desperate man, and—"

Finch cried out. She couldn't stop herself.

"Hush, hush," Mr. Oak said rather sharply, surveying the area around them. "Nothing is to be gained from hysterics. Allow yourself to be guided by one a great deal older and wiser in the ways of the world."

So, even Mr. Oak thought they should disregard Latimer's request that they take no action. "I'm going to hire a cab and go directly to Whitechapel," she announced.

"To accomplish what?"

She opened her mouth, then frowned and felt her shoulders droop.

"Exactly. You have no plan. Plans are essential. They are the basis for all successful enterprises. Will you allow me to suggest a plan?"

"Of course," Finch said. She did not especially care for Mr. Oak, but she was alone and he her only apparent ally to hand.

"Thank you." He inclined his head in regal fashion. "I know Latimer holds Lord Kilrood in high esteem. Having spent even a short while with the gentleman, I share your brother's opinion. I believe you should go to him and request his help."

Finch's shoulders drooped even lower. "He has gone off on his own. I don't know where. But clearly he does not expect me to take any part in trying to find my brother. Oh, it is most annoying."

"Hmm. Young men can be reckless. Their problems often spring from forgetting that they are mortal and—if I may say so—forgetting that women possess a certain wisdom of their own that may even prove somewhat useful on occasion."

Given the number of qualifications attached to the faint compliment, Finch didn't feel grateful, but she said, "Thank you for that," anyway.

"Not at all. So, take my advice and follow Lord Kilrood.

Inform him that, given the identity of the missing man, you must insist on being present for the search. And refuse to be separated from His Lordship. Stay with him at all costs because I believe he will not rest until he has found Latimer."

Finch wanted, even more than she had realized she wanted, to be with Ross. But he did not want her. "Even if I agreed with you, Mr. Oak, I have no idea where Lord Kilrood may be now—other than on his way to Whitechapel. I think it might be unwise to follow him there alone. I could add to the already extremely serious situation. Oh! If only I could speak with my father. He . . . no, I should like to have my father with me because he is a good and solid man, but he would not be cautious, I fear. He would probably manage to make such an uproar that he'd absolutely assure Latimer's permanent removal from us."

"That is the other reason I wanted to find you," Mr. Oak said.

Finch stared at him. "Because of my father? My father is here?"

"Oh, no." He gave a dry little chuckle. "Because I know where Lord Kilrood is and that he is not, as yet, on his way to Whitechapel. I think he has a plan in mind, and it may not include Whitechapel at all. But you will find that out from him, won't you?"

The man spoke in riddles. "Do go on," she said, with a sense that by the time he got to whatever point he intended to make, there would be no hope of accomplishing any help for poor Latimer at all.

"You do know of Lady Evangeline Trimble, I suppose?" Mr. Oak said. "Mr. Sherwood Trimble's wife who is in residence at Number 8 while she convalesces?"

"We met briefly."

"A rather flashy creature."

"I'm sure her husband likes her as she is, which is what matters, Mr. Oak."

If the gentleman were chastened, he hid the fact. "And then there is Zebediah?"

Finch frowned. "I'm afraid I do not know any Zebediah."

"He is Lady Evangeline's companion."

"*He?* Surely you are mistaken. A lady doesn't have a man as a companion."

"This lady does. Zebediah accompanied Lady Evangeline from India so that she could convalesce in Lord Kilrood's house. Lord Kilrood being a friend of her husband. Anyway, that is incidental to the fact that I believe Lord Kilrood regards Zebediah Swift with distrust. A huge, obviously strong, and darkly ominous fellow who says little and moves about like the shadow of a shadow. Most disturbing."

Finch's heart made a little leap. "I should certainly find such a person disturbing."

"Yes, well, I happen to know that Lord Kilrood, on getting back to Number 8 from being with you, heard from his valet, Jennings, that there had been an altercation between Lady Evangeline and this Zebediah. They argued about Zebediah's inattention to his mistress. This occurred shortly before His Lordship's return, and Jennings said there were hints in the conversation that suggested Lady Evangeline did not trust this Zebediah. Apparently Zebediah was to take off for the stables. Jennings thought he intended to take the carriage somewhere. That would be the one that was obtained for Lady Evangeline's visit. According to Lady Evangeline's comments, Zebediah and the coachman are rather better acquainted than would be expected."

"But haven't they already left?"

"Oh, no, in fact Zebediah will not have arrived yet."

Logic had always been one of Finch's strong points. The logic of how and when these events of Mr. Oak's occurred escaped her.

"Now, Miss More," he said, "I have reason to believe that Viscount Kilrood intends to investigate what is afoot there."

"After ordering me to remain in my rooms because he was going to find Latimer? How perfectly disgusting of him."

"Perhaps not, my dear. Perhaps there is something here

that is about to be revealed that will prove of great interest to us all."

Finch restrained herself from asking how Mr. Oak came to know so much about so many things, and how he was so informed about the movements of people who lived in a house where he had, as yet, spent only one night. "So what are you suggesting?" she asked him.

"I suggest that you follow my directions with great care. If you slip behind the stables and count the doors until you come to the one for Number 8, you will be able to get inside and hide. Perhaps among the feed or whatever. Then you will be in a position to overhear anything that is said. I believe that Lord Kilrood may also be somewhere about, but I cannot be sure. I do not think he will reveal himself to Zebediah."

Finch thought about that.

"So, off with you, my dear. At once. If possible, you must be in position before the others arrive."

"But what if this is nothing at all to do with what has happened to Latimer? I will have wasted time."

"What choice do you have? At least this venture holds possibilities."

"According to you."

Mr. Oak's nose rose skyward. "I, my dear young lady, am a man of considerable intelligence. And intuition. My intuition has saved many a day, I assure you."

She hesitated a moment longer. "You're right. I have no other ideas. I shall do as you suggest." And hope Ross didn't discover how she'd defied him. *And* hope she was not wasting valuable time and putting Latimer into even deeper jeopardy.

Mr. Oak was correct. If Ross intended to follow this Zebediah at such a difficult time as this, then His Lordship must consider that the man had something to do with Latimer's disappearance.

She left the cover of the doorway and started across the cobbles, then remembered Mr. Oak and turned back. "Thank you for caring . . ." She looked in every direction but saw no sign of him. No doubt he had hurried through the gate into the gardens behind Number 8.

The first drops of rain began to fall. Finch checked about to plan her route, then lowered her head and went as fast as she could to the end of the mews, where she did as Mr. Oak had suggested and made her way behind the terraced, stone building. Next she dutifully counted until she reached what must be the property belonging to Number 8. Sure enough there was a door there.

Finch slapped her hands against her skirts. She was a noddycock. It would be locked. Why had superior Mr. Oak failed to consider that?

She tried the handle. It turned. Holding her breath, she pushed the door inward a few inches, then a few more, and listened. Not a sound reached her save the snuffling and pawing of animals.

Very quickly Finch went inside and closed the door again. Finding a hiding place wouldn't be difficult. She was confronted with a veritable wall of hay. Unfortunately, she feared that such a mass might make it difficult to hear well, and impossible to see. She went to a spot against a wall where some of the bales had been removed from the top. Cautiously she worked a space open at the bottom, and crawled inside. She wiggled forward, inch by inch, burrowing as she went. Dust clogged her nose, and she closed her eyes against the pricking stalks. When she was entirely inside she feared she might choke, but at last she reached a forefinger into open space on the other side and felt cool air seep against her face.

Then she stopped and listened. Still nothing but the horses.

Pulling a stalk here, and a stalk there, she gradually fashioned a screened peephole. Not that she could make out anything clearly in the space beyond, nothing other than hazy shapes, but if, as was to be expected, whoever came brought a lamp, then she would have a perfect vantage point.

She hadn't long to wait.

Bearing the light she'd expected, a stocky fellow in a long, many-caped cloak and an old-fashioned tricorn hat came scuffing into the stable. She couldn't see him as well as she might have liked, but he appeared neither young nor old. Perhaps in his forties if he had lived a hard life. He set his lamp on the floor and pulled forward a crate which he used as a seat. From a pocket he produced a flask, from which he commenced to drink long gulps, between each of which he wiped his mouth on the back of a sleeve and belched.

Finch wrinkled her nose. An unsavory type, but she should remember that he did not know he was observed and, therefore, had a right to his choice of behavior.

She was wasting precious time here. There was no reason to connect this man to her brother's misfortune.

The straw to Finch's right, near her ankles, moved.

She held absolutely still. It could not move. It must not move. What if it all toppled? She might be discovered. Although she'd probably die from smothering first.

It moved again. Rather it bulged toward her. At the level of her hip this time.

She squinted to see the man on the crate more clearly. A swarthy, sullen fellow, he continued to drink, clearly oblivious to any other presence.

Once more the hay pressed against her—her shoulder. As if something were moving forward from the back to the front of the stacked fodder.

Something moving forward as she had. *Someone.*

Her heart stopped. Yes, it did, it stopped beating.

She rested her forehead on her folded hands and uttered every calming word she could think of—to herself, of course. Someone was burrowing into the wall of hay in exactly the same manner as she had, and from the feel of it, not very far away.

Ross. Of course it had to be Ross.

"Bloody bastards," the man with the flask announced suddenly. "Think they got the upper hand over the likes of us. We're goin' to show 'em. We're goin' to get it all. We'll be the masters, and they'll beg us to let them live at all." He chuckled, chuckled on and on. Finch decided he was assuming an accent not his own.

The stable door swung open again, this time to admit an immense person, immense in height. He wore a cloak but no hat and slammed the door shut behind him as if he didn't care who might or might not take notice of his arrival.

"Nice of you to come," the first man said. "Far be it from me to call you away from your cozy place between the lady's round thighs, but sometimes we has to put other things ahead of these little comforts, we does."

In her prickly hole, Finch blushed at the coarse language. The thought of Ross, so close by and hearing what she heard only made her more embarrassed.

"You called for me, Artemis. And I came. Where I may or may not have been is no affair of yours."

"So you say, Zebediah, me old love. But I shouldn't mind a turn at that pretty-scented package, I can tell you. Me rod's beginnin' to think me 'ead's forgot it, if you know what I mean. And every time I tell it 'ow you're in there ruttin' with a prime piece, it jumps around and starts talkin' about revolution and the like."

"Think with your cock, do you, Artemis? I always had my suspicions that might be the case."

Finch had never heard the terms these people used, but she understood that they were lewd and sexual. Her stomach flipped and left her feeling deeply sick, and shaky.

Warmth reached her through the hay. Warmth from the body that lay beside her with only inches of straw separating them. Ross had told her to remain in her rooms, and he was a man who expected his wishes to be followed. She closed her eyes. Never had she been so trapped, or in the company of more dreadful people. To think that one of them actually lived in Ross's house. At least he now knew that all was definitely not as it should be with this Zebediah, or with the man, Artemis—a fearsome, posturing creature indeed.

Artemis stood up, but barely reached his fellow's shoulders and sat down again. "Save your clever mouth for others," he said. "I'll get me turn soon enough. I told you I expected it, and she'll like what I've got to offer, I can tell you. After all, we both know she ain't no better than she ought to be."

"I am weary, Artemis, and I have no hope of rest for many hours. If you have nothing else to tell me, I'd as soon leave you with your fantasies."

"*Fantasies?* Bloody hifalutin talk. What I'm goin' to 'ave with Lady Evangeline won't be no bloody fantasy. It'll be real, and she'll know it. I've been through too much, and 'ad too little reward—for too long. I done me part now, and I expect me just desserts."

"By no means have you completed your part. It will be over when I judge it to be over. Meanwhile you will do nothing, *nothing* to jeopardize our position. You will do nothing, and say nothing. And if I discover that you have made a move that could spell disaster, I will ensure you make a journey that will take you to your *just deserts.*"

Finch knew a fear so intense it rivaled what she had felt in the yard in Whitechapel. These were dangerous men about dangerous business.

It would be better if Ross never found out she was there. Perhaps if she could be very, very still, he wouldn't discover her.

"You're goin' to be glad you've got someone with a brain workin' with you," Artemis said. "I've made sure we gets a move on with business."

Finch peered to see the scene in the stable as clearly as possible.

The big man, Zebediah, stared down at his cohort and his features were unreadable. He said, "Go on," and his dark eyes seemed to sink into shadowed holes in his face.

The faintest pressure against Finch's right side suddenly

increased. Panicked, she tentatively reached out with her left hand, but remembered that there was almost no room for movement on that side. If Ross continued to encroach upon her, she must surely be discovered soon.

"I'm tired out with the waitin'," Artemis said. "That hoity-toity bastard's got to get a move on before I lose me mind."

"You haven't gone against my instructions, have you?" Zebediah's silken tones froze Finch's heart. "You know patience is our most prized ally."

Artemis drank deeply from his flask and offered it to Zebediah, who waved it aside.

Another shift to Finch's right.

Something solid touched her leg . . .

Then there was utter stillness in the hay. She listened, and knew Ross listened, too. Unlike Finch, he would not know the identity of his comrade in the hay. At that moment he would be recoiling at the knowledge of another's presence.

"Artemis?" Zebediah caught his cohort by the neck of his cloak and hauled him to his feet. With one hand he shook the smaller man hard enough to dislodge his hat from his head. "What have you done?"

"You ought to be grateful, you ought. Nuthin' was goin' right. All your subtlety wasn't doin' nuthin', but I put that right."

The faintest rustling sound preceded another touch, this one by a hand on Finch's face. Only with incredible control did she stop herself from screaming.

There was no escape. But, if only for his own reasons, Ross would not reveal her presence. He would wait until they were alone to drag her out. She grimaced at the thought of his ire.

His fingers followed the line of her cheek, and her neck before stopping atop her shoulder. And his hand stopped on top of her shoulder and squeezed, and she could swear it was a warning, a warning to remain silent and still.

She felt a subtle relaxing, the faintest swell of relief. He was with her. Ross was with her, and he gave her courage.

"You have disobeyed me," Zebediah said. "You have done the one thing you were warned would never be tolerated. You have gone against my orders."

"What made you the boss, then? Just because you talk fancy, and you're bigger'n me? Hogswill, I says to that."

Ross's hand traveled on, traveled downward to her waist and rested there.

Could he know it was she? Finch frowned. Of course, he couldn't. Why . . . She snapped her lips together. Men were so predictable and never, ever to be trusted.

"My patience begins to wear thin, Artemis. Perhaps I should send a message to those who pay for our services."

A distant boom sounded.

Thunder. Not that Finch cared what the weather chose to do at this point. Why, oh why hadn't she set out to find Latimer? Why had she listened to Mr. Oak? If she were on her way to Whitechapel, she wouldn't be here feeling betrayed. *Betrayed.* Oh, really, she must be losing her senses.

"You wouldn't send no message," Artemis said. "If you do, I'll say as how you haven't tried to get things done and over. Those people you're talkin' about want us to make sure their *interests* is safe."

"Have you forgotten that you've already made one vast mistake?" Zebediah said. "You actually stole that tiger— that huge thing, when you should have known that what we sought must be so much smaller, so much less obvious."

"'Ow was I t'know? It's all about tigers, ain't it? Old tigers and younguns? I 'eard you tell the girl that foolishness, remember. 'Ow was I t'know there'd be something else like that at Number 7? I can't be blamed for thinkin' that was it."

"Well, if you had taken the time to ask me, I'd have told you it wasn't *it,* you fool. I warned you to enter only the Mores' rooms. You came very close to wrecking our plans."

"But I didn't, did I? I was right to take a good look around just in case. If you plays your cards right, I might share this beauty with you." He held out a hand and Finch saw a red gem in his palm. "Now, what do you say about my makin' a *mistake?*"

Zebediah took the jewel and turned it over. "Thank you for you generosity, *fool*, but I've never been fond of red glass."

Artemis made a growling sound and snatched back the glass "ruby" he'd taken from Lady Hester's tiger. "We'll see about that," he said. "You're goin' to be grateful you've got me to rely on. I've got things movin' proper, and we'll get what we want and be out of 'ere in no time."

They had been the ones to attack her. They had stolen her key.

Ross began to rub Finch's back, lightly, soothingly.

Inch by inch Finch turned her head to the side. Eyes glinted, eyes that could only belong to Ross, Lord Kilrood. Very faintly she could make out his features. How could she not. His face had become as familiar as her own.

He patted her back and his eyes narrowed. As if he had smiled at her.

He knew her, too. He was trying to calm her, to comfort her.

Perhaps she shouldn't be angry with him after all.

"That is enough," Zebediah said. "Our instructions are absolute. We do nothing that might be able to be traced back to us—and to our employers. The success of the mission depends on absolute secrecy."

"Well, what I done is secret enough for anyone. I snitched that Latimer More."

Finch dropped her head into her hands.

Ross slid his hand around her waist and held her. Ross had unwittingly followed her example and hidden in the hay. Would he leap out and shake the whereabouts of Latimer from these people?

Zebediah had remained still and silent for a long time.

"You utter *fool*," he said at last and, with a great shove, sent Artemis sprawling.

Horses nickered and fussed in their stalls.

A crackle of lightning increased the animals' agitation, and they pawed the floor and whinnied.

"Where is he?" Zebediah said. "If you've harmed him, I'll—"

"You'd better not threaten me 'ad you? I'm the only one what knows where 'e is. 'Urt me, and you might not get 'im back. Then what, Your Lordship?"

"I asked where you've secured Latimer More. And if you've hurt hm."

"And I've decided not to tell you. If you'd treated me with the respect I deserve, and been suitably grateful for me havin' made sure we're finally going to get somewhere, well then, the situation would 'ave been different, wouldn't it?"

Zebediah's big hands opened and closed at his sides. "The people we work for do not regard one man's life as particularly important. Have you forgotten that? If they discover that there is any doubt about our obtaining and keeping what they want us to obtain, they may just decide to dispose of us."

"What is it, then? Go on, we're equal now. You got information, and I got information. Tell me what it is we've got to nick. Tell me exactly. Not like what you said about lookin' for it at the Mores'. *Anythin' unusual. Remember the bloody riddle.* Tell me straight. Then I'll tell you where the gent is."

Zebediah's face, by nature devoid of emotion, showed an inner struggle. "I can tell you that thanks to Lord Kilrood, this thing we seek has been dismantled and is coming to England in pieces."

"I already suspected that," Artemis said, his mouth curling. "What I pinched was a mistake, but I ain't sorry. And I'll tell you that I lifted More to let Kilrood know he's not safe. We can get to 'im anytime we want to, that's what I want 'im to think about. It'll make 'im jumpy, and that'll make 'im 'urry, and that can make a man careless. Even if it don't make 'im careless, 'e'll still 'urry, and that's what we wants most. Get what we come for and go into 'iding till we're told what to do next."

Ross had some part in the plans these men spoke of. It was because of him that Latimer had been taken.

"But, thanks to Kilrood, we need Latimer More in place," Zebediah said through his teeth. "The shipments are to be delivered to him. Seven pieces. So far we know of only one having arrived. How do you imagine His Lordship will finally have everything we want—so that we can *take* it from him—if you don't put this *dupe* back where he's supposed to be?"

"Tell me what it is, then, this tiger thing? Don't ask me no more questions, just answer me that."

Zebediah shook his head. "I only know there are seven parts. Gold and glass I was told. And quite small. But a large precious gem is involved."

"Gold and gems, eh?" Artemis said. "Worth a pretty penny, I'll wager. Why not take it for ourselves and forget about them foreign beggars?"

Finch didn't care about tigers, and jewels, and gold. She only cared about Latimer. Zebediah had called him Ross's dupe!

"You really don't understand, do you, Artemis? You are a little man, with little ideas, and you do not understand. When you agreed to this undertaking, you took a grave risk. You cannot fail. Do you understand now? Our employers will not accept failure. If we do not accomplish what they want—for *any* reason—they will find us. Hiding is out of the question. Escape is out of the question."

Artemis tipped his flask slowly and let the drink pour down his throat before he belched again, and said, "So what do we do?"

Finch held totally still. *Please let the man say where he had Latimer,* she thought.

"We make an arrangement with the old man. Not in person, of course. He must never know who we are. He'll be the go-between. Latimer More shall write to him, telling him that each time something arrives for Kilrood—"

"'E gives it to us instead," Artemis said, jubilant at the idea.

"No, rat brain, remember that Kilrood already has one piece. Oak *tells* us and we count. When the last piece arrives, we get Kilrood and make him give us everything."

And you must let Latimer go, Finch wanted to shout. She would make certain that Ross showed no opposition to giving these creatures what they wanted just as quickly as he could.

"Then we kill 'im, right?" Artemis said with relish.

"If necessary."

"No choice if we don't want no one coming after us. We slit Kilrood's throat, and More's."

To stop her cry, Finch bit her wrist.

"The old man, too, I suppose." Zebediah sounded bored.

"And More's sister," Artemis said. "She'll be less trouble dead than alive."

§ Chapter 15 §

How, Ross wondered, was it possible to be both elated and infuriated? At the same time? For the same reason?

"Thank you, but I can do it myself," Finch told him, ignoring his proffered hand and scrambling up from the dust-laden stable floor. She picked straw from her hair, and brushed at her clothing. The cape she wore was execrable; black, shiny from wear, and rubbed thin in places.

Finch More was the opposite of any other woman of his acquaintance. She cared nothing for fashion, although this evening she had managed to exceed any previous sartorial disaster.

Yet his blood ran hard at the sight of her. She excited emotions too strong to be ignored, or swept aside as the product of either typical male response to the female, or an echo of his need to unleash anger.

To discover her here, to know she had heard everything Zebediah Swift and the coachman said, that she now knew he, Ross, was deeply involved in a clandestine affair, infuriated him.

To discover her here when he had not expected to see her, to be witness to her brave determination, her fiery spirit, and her independence, caused quite a different response. He admired, and desired her.

And his choice of a time for this discovery could not be more inappropriate.

"I am not afraid of you."

He inclined his head. "I beg your pardon?" Would she never say what might be expected?

"I am *not* afraid of you," Finch repeated. "I am afraid of certain other things—although not for myself—but I will not allow you to divert me from my responsibilities. All of my responsibilities are to my brother, whom, according to those two despicable creatures who just left, you *duped*."

Oh, he had not expected her to miss that comment, not at all. And, naturally, she hadn't disappointed him. "I doubt the fellow even knew the meaning of the word."

"I suggest he knew it very well." She removed the cloak and shook it, not that she was likely to improve the monstrosity, regardless of her efforts. "That man, Zebediah, is educated. A person of intelligence, albeit misguided. You cultivated Latimer, and our business, for your own ends."

"I thought customers always used businesses for their own ends. It's hardly—"

"Do not play with me, my lord." For an instant Ross thought her eyes glittered with something other than anger, but she quickly looked away. "You have involved us in a dangerous situation. Perhaps you did not intend for us to be at risk, but you must have known the possibility existed. You cared nothing for our safety. After all, we are expendable strangers."

He made to take the cloak, but she swept it from his reach. "This is not the time for you to be difficult with me, Finch. We have a common goal—to secure Latimer's safe return.

And I insist on pointing out that you and I can hardly be considered strangers."

She rewarded him with a view of her back. "You are not a gentleman," she said, her voice muffled. "If you were, you would never resort to mentioning such things at such a time. I agree that Latimer is our first concern. He is *our* only concern. We have to plan carefully, to move very carefully. Please begin by explaining exactly the nature of your connection to those people. And who are these unpleasant persons they work for? What is it that has caused such disregard for the lives of the innocent? What is your part in all of this?"

If he'd anticipated that she'd discover his mission, or at least the fact that he was involved in a mission, he'd have been prepared for her questions. As it was he disciplined himself to take plenty of time before answering. She would, of course, learn nothing of the truth. For the sake of her own skin—and his. There were more people than she could imagine whom he must protect.

"Kindly don't attempt to deflect me, or lie to me—lie to me again, I should say. I will have the truth, Ross, or I shall go to someone official and request their help."

He grew cold inside. The sensation was familiar and strangely comforting. This was the reality of it all. He could not allow any interference. "You will go to no one. Tell no one. You will speak of the matter only to me, and then you will chose to do so only when there is no danger of your being overheard. Is that clear?"

She stopped her ineffectual batting at the cape.

"Not a difficult question, Finch. Do you fully understand that I will not tolerate your interference in my affairs?"

"You are threatening me," she said quietly. "How could I have made the foolish mistake of trusting you? You are a dangerous man."

If he must tolerate her fear of him to ensure her silence, so be it. "I am a determined man. I will do what I must do. But I will also protect you."

"I do not need your protection." She whirled to face him, the color in her cheeks high. "I need your assistance for practical reasons. If that were not so, I should wish never to . . . I should wish never to set eyes on you again."

He would grasp at that hesitation. He would chose to believe it meant she did not speak the whole truth. "I shall hope I can change your opinion of me, but perhaps, at least for now, it will be best if you understand that I can be a hard man when the stakes are high. They have never been higher than at this time."

"You think you have to remind me? Latimer is, who knows where, and possibly suffering greatly."

"Those are not the stakes to which I refer." The words were spoken. Regret followed instantly. It wasn't like him to be so imprudent or careless with what he said. "That is not to say that I am not concerned with Latimer's speedy release."

She contrived to erase all expression from her face—except for the desperate light in her eyes. "Very well. You have made yourself clear. So be it. To get what I must get, I shall assist you in dealing with your own concerns."

"No such thing, my girl. You will do as you're told this time and remain in a safe place."

"I am no relation of yours to be put in her place," she said. "I demand an open discussion with you. Now. I have questions to ask of you. More questions. And I expect answers. So far you have explained nothing that helps me decide what to do next. I can go to Hunter—"

"Do so," he said, with an icy threat he made no attempt to keep from his voice, "and you will never see Latimer again. Alive."

Her right hand went to her mouth. He saw her throat jerk several times and detested what expediency demanded he do. She was a spirited, but vulnerable creature, and he took no pleasure in frightening her.

"Finch, please be guided by me."

"You dare to ask that of me after all you have done to us?"

"I have not wittingly done anything to you."

"You knew that this—this, whatever you are about is a dangerous matter, yet you used us to obtain your ends. And you did not care that we might suffer greatly."

He wanted to touch her. There was no doubt that she would rebuff any such attempt. "I did not know you would suffer greatly. I had no idea that—" No, he must not allow emotion to make him careless. "Unforseen circumstances have made my task much more difficult. I beg your indulgence and ask you to trust me. I will secure Latimer's release." Please, God, let him do so without any injury to that innocent man.

She took in a breath and expelled it in shaky bursts. The cape she swung about her shoulders and fastened at the neck. "What are these *pieces,* these things being shipped to you? What do they mean? Who wants them?"

"I cannot tell you that."

"Why? You expect me to put my trust in you. Trust me in return."

She was so difficult to resist, to deny. "I cannot tell you these things, Finch. The knowledge would place you in grave danger."

"Even *greater* danger, do you mean?"

Ross shook his head. "You will not believe anything I say about this matter, so I won't say anything."

Without thinking, Ross pulled a remnant of straw from her rich hair. Finch brushed his hand aside without looking at him. "When those men left, they said they were on their way to some sort of establishment," she said. "I do not understand all they expected to find there, but they will take time about their drinking and their decisions on how to proceed. We must use that time to advantage."

She spoke as if they were to work as partners, as equals. That could not be allowed, but he would inform her of that with considerable care. "I suggest we return to Number 8. The house will be quiet, and we shall make our way to my rooms, where I will instruct Jennings to keep watch and ensure our privacy." Zebediah and Artemis had expressed their intention to go to a house of ill repute—one known for its base and excessive performances for the edification of paying guests. It was cheap. Cheap liquor and cheap entertainment designed for customers for whom no act was too low, too debauched. The clientele was of a common type.

Finch pulled her hood low over her face and tucked back frayed ribbons of satin lining. "We should go separately perhaps?" she suggested. "I can enter by the tradesmen's door."

"We shall both enter from the mews. Together. Since those we seek to avoid are absent, we have nothing to fear."

She allowed him to guide her out of the back door, but once outside she stopped. "What of Lady Evangeline? What do you think of her part in this?"

"In honesty I don't know. She may be involved, but I tend to think not. Sherwood was never a close friend, but he is a man of a certain class, and I think a man of integrity. He is certainly very intelligent and absorbed in his work. No, I don't think Sherwood is involved. Therefore, I am disposed to believe that Zebediah managed to ingratiate himself with the Sherwoods. It is quite possible that he was acquainted with them and that when he heard how Lady Evangeline was to come to me for convalescence, he convinced Sherwood that the dangers of the journey to England—for a woman alone and ill—were so great that she should have a bodyguard. Men such as Sherwood—academics, scientists—sometimes lack a certain worldliness." He wished Evangeline had not shown herself willing to be an unfaithful wife.

Finch carried on walking in silence until they were safely inside the back gate to Number 8. "I take it we are to speak with Mr. Oak first?"

"Later. After you and I have made things clear between us. Then I shall see you home and go to speak with him at the warehouse."

"He isn't at the warehouse. He's here. At your house. He spoke to me just before I entered the stable. Then he continued on to come here. Evidently he has been unable to contact his relative in Hampstead."

Ross was puzzled. "He left this morning without making any mention of intending to return. And I certainly didn't see him this evening."

"He only returned recently. It is perfectly possible that he went to his rooms without your seeing him."

Was it indeed? Ross thought. He became irritated at the thought of his home being invaded by enemies and strangers.

He let Finch and himself into the neat kitchen gardens inside the high brick wall and led her along a path lined with naked pea and bean trellises, to the back door. They passed through the kitchens with no more than polite greetings from the servants busy preparing dinner, and went on their way to higher regions of the house.

"They will chatter," Finch said when they were out of earshot of the staff. "They will wonder why we are entering the house, together, from an unexpected direction."

"You are my curator, the keeper of my valuable collection. Should any questions arise, that will be the answer and it is enough. I think it wisest if we go to my rooms rather than the study or the library. Less likelihood of interruption."

She glanced at him, squared her shoulders, and followed the direction he indicated.

"Let us seek out Mr. Oak at once, please," she said. "If we still need discussion between the two of us, it should come afterward. And I think the study or library will be perfectly appropriate, thank you."

In other words, she was afraid to be alone with him in his rooms. He disguised a grim smile. She was foolish to think she would be any more safe from him elsewhere. Best to keep his thoughts to himself and capitulate without argument. Turning in the opposite direction from his own rooms, he carried on up another narrow flight of stairs. Keeping his voice down, he said, "I believe this was the room he was given. He will have returned here, I'm sure." And he knocked.

Several knocks later he gave up and tried the handle. The door opened, and they were confronted with an empty room.

"I thought he intended to stay here," Finch said. "He said he would impose on you for another night. But he must have decided to find alternate lodgings."

Ross looked to the fireplace, where a fire burned brightly—and at a tray of uneaten food on a table nearby. A napkin rested on the seat of a chair and a book lay open on top. "No, I don't think he has found another place. We have simply come while he has chosen to be elsewhere for a few minutes. We shall wait for him."

Standing on opposite sides of the room, they did wait. For half an hour. Since there was still no sign of Mr. Oak, Ross decided to inquire as to his whereabouts. He rang for a servant and sent him in search of Jennings and to ask about Mr. Oak. The valet quickly returned a message revealing that he had seen Mr. Oak go out only half an hour earlier. No, he had not summoned a cab as far as Jennings had seen.

"Half an hour?" Finch said when they were alone again. "We were here then."

"He must already have been downstairs."

"But we did not pass him."

Ross considered that. "No," he said slowly, "No, we didn't pass him. Evidently he was somewhere else. It isn't difficult to miss someone in so large a house—particularly if he wishes to be missed."

"Why should he?"

Ross shrugged. "He is an old man. It's possible he is frightened by the violence he has witnessed, and at the prospect of becoming part of any violence. He may also be embarrassed by his need to seek refuge here again tonight."

"I believe he has returned to Whitechapel, and I intend to follow him there. He must be warned that he will be approached by Zebediah and Artemis. He must understand that great responsibility rests with him. I do not think he is a man who will shirk that responsibility."

There was no time to succumb to desperation at the possibility that his task might become almost impossible to control. There was also no time to indulge doubts of any kind. To remain absolutely effective, he might have to show Finch a side of him normally reserved for those who needed to learn the nature of a formidable adversary. He would, at any cost, govern every aspect of what was happening.

"Come with me to my rooms, please," he said to Finch. "I need to speak with Jennings."

"We have delayed long enough. We shall lose the advantage of a little extra time if we do not leave now. Or rather, if I do not leave now. I must find a cab. Or perhaps Jennings would summon one for me."

There were certain things women had in common. One was that they were manipulative. He had no doubt that she wanted him with her, and that she expected him to relent and accompany her.

"First we go to my rooms and make sure we are clear about the course we shall take."

"That is a waste—"

"That is what I insist upon." Holding her elbow, he walked with her to the corridor that opened into his apartments.

There she balked and planted her feet. "I told you I should prefer any conversation between us to take place elsewhere."

"And you spoke of not wanting to waste time," he reminded her. "My rooms are closest."

He saw how she struggled with her instincts, how she wanted to continue to argue. And he knew the moment when she gave up and let him guide her onward.

Jennings leaped up the instant they entered the sitting room. "I've been expecting ye, m'lord." When he looked at Finch he showed no emotion other than deference. "Good evenin' t'ye, Miss More."

"Are you certain you saw Mr. Oak leave?" she asked.

"Aye, miss. Quite certain."

Finch cast a significant glance at Jennings, then at Ross. She did not expect that Ross's man would be taken into their confidence.

"Jennings and I go back a very long way," Ross said evenly. "We have shared more than most men will ever share. He is my trustworthy right hand."

Jennings rolled up onto his toes and jiggled. He assumed an expressionless countenance.

When Finch had digested this information, she said, "Mr. Oak has certainly gone to Whitechapel. He has started the search there in his own fashion. And he is awaiting your shipments."

"Perhaps," Ross told her. "I shall not give that theory any credence until I have interviewed the man."

To his discomfort, Finch tried to smother a sob. She swung away from him, and he saw her back shake.

Immediately he strode toward her, but when he set a hand on her shoulder, she flung away. "Do not touch me, please. I am finding it difficult to maintain any dignity at all. Consider my feelings, if you can. I don't know for sure that Latimer isn't already lying murdered. I have no guarantees that he was not cruelly killed by that monster, Artemis. But until I am forced to give up finding him alive, I will search for Latimer. And that search must begin now."

He could not argue with her on this.

"Jennings," she said, "could I prevail on you to procure me a cab?"

Jennings, his gaunt face troubled, looked to Ross, who nodded. "Capital idea, Jennings. Except, rather than a cab, why not get a cart and nag. We would be less conspicuous traveling so in those parts. Make sure the cart appears to be used for some sort of suitable trade. And see to providing us with clothing that will not draw attention to us."

"My clothing will do nicely," Finch said.

Ross was surprised at her ready acceptance of his directions.

He rather thought she spoke close to the truth about her clothing, but he said, "You need something old enough and darker in color. The green gown is of too good a quality and too noticeable. We will have to make sure your face remains covered. And your hair."

"I'll return as soon as I can," Jennings said, letting himself out of the sitting room.

"Do you know whom Zebediah and Artemis work for?" Finch asked at once.

"I might have some vague notions," Ross told her, distorting the truth a little.

"Share your vague notions with me."

She was a caustic miss and not to be fobbed off easily. "Zebediah is using Sherwood Trimble for his own ends. I also believe the man is very dangerous. He may be the one who has caused great concern to a friend of mine who has good reason to want his claws pulled so he may do no more damage." He spoke of his friend, the Sheik of Ranthus, who was desperately trying to retain his power over Ranthus in order to pass it to his son, as that power had been passed from father to son for generations.

"Claws," she said. "Are we alluding to tigers again?"

"That was purely a figure of speech."

"How can you allow this Zebediah to remain in your home when you know he plots against you?"

Until tonight he had only suspected the man's involvement. "Better he should remain here where I have some hope of keeping an eye on him, than in any other place."

"How could you have employed the coachman, though? I really cannot understand all this. It is most suspicious."

Despite understanding her distress and her confusion, he recognized that she questioned his motives in all this and did not like her suggestions. "Do you think I may be playing a less-than-honest part in all of this, Finch?"

She tilted her head to one side, and firelight turned her red hair a brilliant hue. "I am unsure what I think." Her pale skin was luminous, her eyes so dark, they appeared black. "We have been taken advantage of by you—my brother and I. How can you expect me to consider you a man above reproach?"

"You seemed able to consider me a great many things, all of them *intimately* acceptable, on earlier occasions."

She raised her chin and clasped her hands beneath her breasts.

He lowered his gaze to that level. "I used to think the better endowed the woman, the more sexually desirable she was. You have changed my mind. I find your small, extremely sensitive breasts irresistible. In fact I should like to touch them now. May I?"

"You are outrageous," she told him, blushing, and crossing her arms. "You seek to confuse me with your audacity. But I am a mature woman, and I am able to tolerate your nonsense without losing my head, my lord."

"Are you?" Very deliberately, he shot a hand around her neck and jerked her against him. "Oh, please don't insist on keeping your head, Finch. I find you irresistible when you give in to passion."

"You make fun of me. To do so at such a time is unforgivable."

She was right, of course, but he wasn't making fun of her, and there were times when a man could be no more than . . . a man. He kissed her swiftly, covered her mouth before she had time to collect herself.

The gauze chemisette was no deterrent to his finding a way to her skin. He held her shoulders firmly and drew her even more tightly against him. The force of his mouth on hers tipped her head backward, and she filled her fingers with his sleeves to find her balance.

He parted her lips and pressed his tongue inside, and knew he didn't want to stop. There was an instant when he recognized that in Finch he had met a woman with the power to do what he'd sworn would never again be done—to interfere with his levelheaded reason.

Her mouth was sweet. Her lips were sweet, and pliant.

And her soft breath mingled with his. Small cries came from her, but her tongue met his and reached, just as his reached. Such passion was rare in the genteel woman, or, as in Finch's case, the gently bred and sheltered woman. He knew a good deal of the Mores' story from Latimer. Finch's decision to break away from her father and come to live in London with Latimer had taken great courage, and it was her first act of defiance against a very structured life.

Her eyes were closed. Her auburn lashes flickered against pale cheeks. Some might consider her mouth too large, too wide. Ross found it exactly right for his purposes.

She made a different sound, and she let go of his sleeves to place her fists between them and push. Her resistance might as well have been that of a bird. He simply held her more firmly and kissed her more insistently.

Removing his mouth from hers, he nipped at the lobe of an ear, and continued to nip his way down her throat.

"Stop it." She sounded desperate. "Jennings will return. We shall be found like this."

"Jennings never enters without announcing himself," Ross said, so aroused he could scarcely think. "You smell so sweet, love. Let me touch you."

"No! Please. How can you think of such things now?"

"Why not? We have to wait for our cart, after all. Why shouldn't we amuse ourselves?"

"Oh, this is insupportable. *Amuse* ourselves? That is all our times have ever been to you, of course. I was foolish to think they might mean something more."

Women were always so serious. They always looked for such deep meaning. They did not know how to find the simple, unfettered pleasures that could be between a man and a woman attracted to each other. He smoothed aside the chemisette and revealed the tops of her breasts. They swelled gently but provocatively at the low neck of her gown. "Mm," he said, "how very lovely."

Finch stepped backward, but he followed her. Ross followed her until her back met the door. Then he took her head

in his hands and searched her face. "You are the most unusual of women," he told her. "There is nothing in you that
is at all like any other woman I have known. You are a
charming puzzle and I . . . I delight in being with you."
What, in God's name, had he almost said? He would not
allow himself to consider such foolishly careless speech.

She dropped her hands and pressed them against the door.
Surely she could have no idea how desirable she was with
her fire red hair escaping and her moist mouth begging to be
kissed again—and her barely covered breasts rising and
falling with each breath. He rested his hands at her waist and
massaged her there, running his thumbs back and forth over
her ribs. With his fingers he could reach the beginning flare
of her buttocks.

"Tell me you want me," he said. "Tell me you will let me
bring you here and make love to you once this night's work
is done."

She didn't answer him.

Ross bowed over her breasts and kissed them softly, insistently, repeatedly. He curled his tongue just beneath the
neck of her gown and over a nipple—and smiled to himself
when he felt her sag. So sensitive to every touch on eroge-
nous flesh, this little one. Such a delight to a man who relished passion in a woman. Not for him a passive female.

"Jennings will come." She panted, and plucked at his hair.
"Oh, do stop, Ross. Be strong for both of us."

He guided one of her hands between his legs. "You think
I can be strong, dear Finch. Come now, I am only human. I
should not mind if you squeezed me there."

Her fingers closed convulsively on him, and he contrived
to bare her breasts. The tight bodice clung beneath, pushing
them upward so that her nipples tilted. He braced his legs
apart, straddled her hips, and trapped her hand between
them.

Opening his mouth wide, he took in as much of a breast
as he could and sucked until she made a keening cry. Her

grip on him was painful, a milking pressure that closed with rhythmic desperation.

They were desperate. They had something between them that would not fade away. Ross was certain he was right.

He pulled up her skirts and smoothed her skin above her stockings. Her rounded buttocks were flexed hard, her stomach contracted flat, and when he hooked two fingers deep into the hair between her legs, he met slick moisture.

Finch cried out afresh, and with abandon.

She released him and her hands banged against the door. She arched her back, thrusting her breasts at him, rolling her head away.

He breathed hard and suffered the throbbing in his rod, the hardness in his balls. She would learn all that she must do—but in good time and not now. For now he would satisfy himself in other ways while he remembered how she looked right now.

"Ross." She moaned and tossed her head from side to side. "Oh, please, Ross."

He heard footsteps on the stairs, but knew she did not. He hurried, applied firm strokes between the lips that sheltered her vagina, then made hard little circles just inside with the end of his thumb.

A second, another, and she began to slide downward. He held her in place but did not stop his ministrations. Even when she bucked uncontrollably and grasped his wrist as if trying to hold him still against her, he kept moving until he felt the spasms of pleasure fade.

With one arm around her waist, and whispering gentle words in her ear, he pulled her skirts down again and eased her bodice over her breasts. With as much finesse as possible, he rearranged the chemisette. Then he smoothed back her hair and tucked escaped pieces into place.

She trembled, and clung to him, and he hugged her close, raining light kisses on every inch of her face. "You are so lovely," he told her. "Such a joy to me."

"I am a woman beyond redemption, I fear," she said,

laughing weakly. "But I'm not sure I want to be redeemed. What do you say to that?"

"I say you are wise and mature, and that I am a lucky man to be the recipient of your fall from grace."

Her smile slipped away, and she walked unsteadily to his dark green brocade couch, where she subsided and made an obvious attempt to collect herself.

Just in time for a knock at the door, and Jennings' voice calling, "Your conveyance will be here shortly, m'lord. I've the items ye asked for."

Ross opened the door and took a pile of clothing from Jennings's arms. He didn't meet his valet's eyes and had no doubt the man, who was nothing if not excessively observant, would recognize signs that there had been some intimacy here recently.

"Thank you, Jennings," he said. "How long for the cart?"

Jennings put a finger to his mouth and looked about. He dropped his voice to say, "Five minutes at the most. I haven't seen either Her Ladyship or Zebediah. We wouldn't want them to overhear anything."

His own voice equally low, Ross said, "Zebediah and Artemis have gone to a tavern they referred to as the Cock and Jugs. I imagine they intend to spend some time there."

Jennings looked him straight in the eye. "It's no' a tavern. It's a—"

"I know what it is," Ross said, keeping his voice down. "I'm to Whitechapel now. If I fail to find any trace of Latimer More, I shall be forced to follow our friends and hope they lead me to him."

"You'll no' go alone, m'lord. Ye'll need me t'back ye up."

Ross smiled slightly. "Sounds like an appealing mission, does it," he said. "Really, Jennings, you surprise me. A churchgoing man like yourself."

A haughty expression didn't quite draw attention from Jennings' twitching lips. "Ye can say what ye will. We've a pact. If there's ought t'worry about, then where ye go, I go.

But sure I'll no' be far away from ye this night. Ye don't really intend t'take the girl wi' ye?"

Ross pulled the door to behind him. "I think it will be the better part if I do. She's a headstrong creature and will never submit to being left behind. Can you hide yourself in the back of the cart?"

Jennings frowned, but said, "Aye, o'course I can."

"Then do it. I'll change and make sure the young lady changes also." Without waiting for further comment he turned from Jennings.

Once back in his sitting room, he made himself concentrate on what must be done. His actions with her had been impetuous—again—but he would not chastise himself. He couldn't resist her, dammit.

Shortly he was dressed in rough wool breeches and coat, with cheap linen and no neckcloth. A ragged coat didn't fit his shoulders but would be warm enough, and he wrapped a gray-wool muffler around his neck before donning a shapeless black hat that shaded his face. Jennings had even thought to provide worn boots with holes in each sole. No doubt the cold would enjoy creeping inside.

Finch took a little longer to emerge from his bedroom where he'd sent her to change. As she'd left, their eyes had met, and their unspoken message to each other was that there was unfinished business between them. Still he was grateful that he did not have to see her change. If she'd been naked before him now, he might never have disciplined himself to leave.

Her garb was also gray. A shapeless, gray gown that hung so loose she seemed even thinner inside its folds. The bodice laced, and she'd done her best to pull it tight, but still it gaped. A black shawl, worn on her head with the ends tossed over her shoulders, showed too much of her brilliant hair and Ross pulled the drab headdress lower over her face. He looked down the front of the gown, at her pointed breasts, and raised his eyes to find her watching him. She drew the shawl about her chest, crossed it, and tied it behind her.

Ross didn't comment.

"To Whitechapel, then," she said.

"To Whitechapel. Jennings will be hiding in the back of the cart. I tell you this so you will have more courage. We are veterans of some very dangerous encounters."

If she was comforted, she disguised that comfort well.

"Are we ready?" he asked her.

Finch tarried. "Do you know the whereabouts of the place where those men went?"

"I know it."

"Why are we not going after them, to try to overhear them? We should follow them, shouldn't we?"

He didn't want to as much as consider taking Finch to that place. "I think we should first check the warehouse to make sure Latimer isn't imprisoned somewhere there."

"Yes," she said. "I had thought of that. They could have stopped him from making any noise and put him in a crate, couldn't they?"

"Possibly. But I don't think it likely. They will know we'll think of that. But we'll check anyway. Finding Mr. Oak is a priority. Do you know exactly where this relative of his in Hampstead lives?"

"I know nothing about him, really. I met him when you met him. Latimer said he had the best of references. He even did work for the King at Windsor."

"Yes, yes, well I should be very relieved to get to him and warn him of our unpleasant friends' plans for him. Finch, will you consider waiting here, please."

"No."

He had to try. "I know you are desperate to find Latimer. So am I. I am very concerned for his safety. I am also concerned for yours. If you remain here I can move faster, and—"

"No."

"As I was saying. I can move faster if I don't have to worry about your safety."

"You don't have to worry about me. I can look after myself. If I couldn't, I should be in dire trouble, shouldn't I?" Finch pulled on a pair of ancient wool gloves with holes in the fingertips. She studied them as if fascinated.

"Why must you look after yourself, Finch? Why must you insist upon undertaking unsuitable missions?"

"Because I am alone." She avoided his eyes. "My brother gives my life purpose, but he will make his own way in the world. I pray he will be safely returned and make his own way. Find a good wife. I, on the other hand, am destined to the lot of a woman without a man. No doubt I shall eventually be forced to teach, and like it. For now I shall relish my opportunity to sample independence."

Ross considered what she said. "You are not alone," he said, and closed his mouth deliberately. He must guard himself from saying anything he would later regret.

"Because *you* are with me?"

He did not think she was a woman who sought declarations, who sought to entrap a man. "Certainly I am with you. You shall not be alone. And soon your brother will be returned to you." There, an innocent enough remark, yet one guaranteed to reassure her.

She looked at his eyes. "We should go. But will you answer me this? When you said you found me a puzzle—did you almost say—You said you delighted in being with me, but you hesitated before that. What was it that you almost said?"

He had not been discreet enough. She was, after all, only a woman. Delightful, rare, beguiling, and bewitching, but only a woman nevertheless. And she had noticed that fatal little hesitation. He would have to remedy that.

"What did you almost say, Ross?"

He chuckled. "What did you think I almost said?" He disliked treating her lightly.

She stared at him a while longer, then lowered her eyes

and went to open the door. "I really can't imagine," she told him. "We'd best hurry."

He had almost said he loved her, hadn't he?

§ *Chapter 16* §

Leaving Ross and Jennings to secure the doors, Finch emerged into stinging rain and hurried to climb onto the cart. If Latimer was in the warehouse, he was too well hidden to be found by even the most ardent searchers.

The nag was a sorry creature. Watching its sagging back and the breath it sighed into the frigid air, she felt guilty for pressing the beast into service on such a cold, damp night.

"So now we must go to that place," she said to Ross when he leaped up beside her and took the reins. "The place those men spoke of. We could have gone after them sooner, but we did have to search the warehouse, didn't we?"

"They have the advantage of us," Ross said, glancing around as they felt the cart sag, and heard Jennings burrow beneath heaps of empty sacks. "When Artemis took your brother, he snatched a winning card, and he knows it. I am puzzled, though. If Artemis told Latimer to write to you, why didn't he mention the fact to Zebediah? Surely he would have congratulated himself on his brilliance in making sure you stayed out of their way. And he is like so many men of small intellect, he craves praise."

"Och, he dinna tell Mr. More t'write the note a'tall, d'ye think?" Jennings muffled voice came from immediately behind Finch." That's as plain as plain t'me."

While they'd made their way to Whitechapel, Ross had told Jennings what had transpired in the stables.

"Latimer did write to me," Finch said, desperate to cling to what knowledge she had of Latimer's whereabouts. "Mr. Oak found the note and sent it to us. He wrote a note of his own to explain."

"I've already told Jennings as much," Ross said. He continued to sit huddled in the darkness. Rain sparkled as it ran from the brim of his hat. His face was obscured. "But you voice my own conclusions, Jennings. I confess I am as anxious to find our Mr. Oak as those two villains. One wonders what caliber of forger he is."

Finch turned sideways on the hard seat. "What can you mean? The coachman admitted to abducting Latimer. Mr. Oak is an old man working for us to fill his time. Why would you suggest he is a forger?"

"You say you met him when I met him. From what Latimer said that night, he didn't know the man, either. He appeared here and offered his services."

"He had references."

"Hmm."

The old black shawl was sodden, as was the gray dress. Water ran down Finch's back. "You think Mr. Oak may also be a part of this scheme?"

"I think I should have you study Latimer's so-called note very closely."

"But—" It had been Latimer's writing, hadn't it?

Ross looked at her and uttered a low curse. "You're soaked. I'm taking you home now."

"No." She put distance between them, then jumped down from the cart. "I shall not return without my brother." With that she hurried to the opposite side of the alley.

"Get back here," Ross called.

She ignored him. She had no idea where to go, where to look on her own, and her only plan was to make him take her with him. He must not take her home. At least he would be able to find those men.

"Finch! I told you to get back here. You are wasting valuable time."

"You speak of suspecting Mr. Oak," she told him. "Yet it is you who are the mystery—"

"*Keep* your voice down," Ross said, his tone strained with urgency. "And come with me. That is an order."

A window slammed open above Finch's head and another voice joined their fray. " 'Ere, 'ere, what's all the noise? This is a respectful neighborhood, this is. You bugger off and take your row-bargy with you."

"Why don't ye bring yourself down for a wee bit o' a chat," Jennings said from the back of the cart, his tone silky. "Ye can discuss who it is that's a blight on this *respectable* neighborhood."

The window closed with enough force to make the glass rattle in its frame. At least it *had* glass—many windows in the area did not.

Ross left his seat and bore down on Finch. "Run, and you'll wish you hadn't," he said, and she visualized his strong teeth clamped together.

"I'm not going to run," she told him. "But neither am I going to be intimidated by a man to whom I owe no allegiance." A man who was part of—if not the entire reason for—the disastrous events that had befallen Latimer and Finch More.

"All right, you have my full attention." He stood over her, the rain beating the brim of his hat and pouring down to add to her already miserable condition. "What is it you think I know? What do you think I can do? What knowledge do you think I have that you don't have? You don't know where to look for Latimer. Why should you think I do?"

"We are both aware that you are hiding something." She

could scarcely breathe for the tightness in her throat. His angry features appalled her. "I didn't imagine that I listened to a conversation between a man who discussed you and your very important part in a dangerous scheme. You know about that scheme, and I want you to tell me. Not because I would ordinarily have any right to know, but because I believe you have *used* Latimer and me, and now Latimer has been taken away and may never be returned. I want to know just exactly how desperate our position is, and if you will not help me, I must seek help elsewhere."

"You are overwrought. I order you to be calm."

"Oh, you are insupportable." The querulous sound of her voice mortified Finch. She pressed her lips together and seized Ross by the lapels of his ill-fitting coat. "Like all men—and women—you must accept responsibility for your deeds. And it is not within your power to order me to do anything."

Ross closed his hands on her wrists but didn't attempt to remove her hands. He brought his face close to hers. "These are dangerous times," he said, his voice low and earnest. "The world is larger, much larger, than this little world of London that seems so big to you. And larger than the even smaller world inhabited by Latimer and Finch More. Beyond your life and experience, out there, far away, there are other worlds, other cultures that are and have been in existence long enough to make this petty civilization of ours childish and without accomplishments. Do you understand?"

He treated *her* like a child. "I am well aware of the wonderful legacies of societies that are many generations older than ours."

"You are aware of their pieces of glass, their statues, their gewgaws, but you are *not* cognizant of their sophistication. And you have no knowledge of their cultures or creeds today. How could you? You are a sheltered woman from a tiny Cornish town."

His overbearing arrogance incensed her. "And as such, I

am beneath notice and my concerns are irrelevant. How dare you." Her palm and flattened fingers met his cheek with a sound like a frozen branch snapping.

Finch dropped her arms to her sides and stared up at him.

"You also don't know," he said, so very quietly, "that there are dangers so great that you cannot imagine how terrible they are. And you have never been forced to face a choice between saving your own life, or saving the lives of thousands. I never intended to draw you into such a desperate situation, but it has happened, and I have no choice but to carry on and do the best I can."

She rubbed her eyes. The moisture there wasn't all from the rain.

"I will protect you, Finch. And I will try to protect Latimer."

Expecting him to brush her away, Finch settled her hand on his face.

He stood still, moved not a muscle, said not a word.

"I've never hit anyone before. I'm sorry. I'm not myself."

"Do you believe I will take care of you?"

"I believe you want to. But I'm not sure you'll be able to. You are not even certain of all the people who may be involved in this matter."

"True. But you shall not be harmed."

"I hit you, and you are concerning yourself with caring for me." And with every hour she spent in his company, Finch became more enmeshed with him. Enmeshed with a man who could not be further from her reach, nor more unsuitable even if he were of her own class. She removed her hand.

"Jennings and I will deliver you back to Mayfair Square now. I shall carry on and see what I can learn."

He swung her back and forth between sweet joy, and exasperation. "You think you can soften me with a few pretty words. As I have already said, I will not go home without Latimer. We, you and I, and Jennings, will follow those men."

"You have forgotten that *those men* have also threatened your own life. I cannot take you near them."

"I am not afraid for myself." She would not argue that point further. "But I do dislike the idea of going on alone, so I beg you to take me where I must go. But if you'd rather not be further involved after that, you may leave me, and I'll manage well enough on my own."

To her humiliation, he tilted his face up to the pouring rain and laughed. He laughed, and now she could see those strong, white teeth gleam.

"Why are you laughing?"

He didn't hear her, or at least, gave no sign of having heard.

A hand came down on her shoulder and she spun around. The boy, Hayden, stood there bareheaded and wearing his thin coat. "They came 'ere, y'know. Two men what went in over there. The big one was in charge. 'E pushed the other one around. Nasty-like."

"What can you be talking about?" Ross said. "And where did you come from?"

"I saw you come, see, so I watched t'make sure no one touched the cart."

"You have my thanks." Ross still sounded skeptical. "Why didn't I see you approach? Was the person who shouted from the window a relative of yours?"

Hayden hesitated before saying, "No. I lives next door to 'im. You gets used to movin' about real careful 'ere, movin' careful, and keepin' your eyes open. And it don't do to let people 'ear what you've got to say."

"If you say so," Ross told him. "What did you mean about two men? You saw two men here?"

"I 'eard what you and the lady was sayin' about two gents. I reckon you been searchin' the warehouse for 'em, only you ain't found 'em because they're gone already. I didn't ought to put my nose in. Could be dangerous. But you been kind t'me."

The rain grew even heavier, and Ross stood with his back

to the wind as if trying to shield Finch from the weather. "This is damnable," he said. "How can you be sure the two men you saw were known to us in any way?"

"I 'eard you say, Artemis. Funny name, that. The very big gent. The tall one. 'E called the other one, Artemis. All nasty-like."

"For you to hear so much, they must have been shouting in the street," Ross said with a meaningful glance at Finch. "One would have expected them to be more cautious."

Her attention had wandered for a moment to the houses behind them. Certainly Hayden didn't live next door on the one side because that was another warehouse. On the other side stood a house missing glass in almost all its night black windows. Boards had been nailed across the door—one assumed, to discourage vandals or other intruders.

So where exactly did Hayden live, Finch wondered?

Hayden sniffed and swiped his streaming hair away from his eyes. "They wasn't shoutin' in the street. I went in there after them, didn't I? I thought I ought to since they was strangers—or I thought they was strangers—and the gent what owns the place wasn't there, just the old gent."

"Mr. Oak?" Alarmed, Finch looked over her shoulder at the warehouse. "Mr. Oak was there?"

"Oh, yes. 'E was watchin' the other two, just like me. And 'e didn't see me, neither. Them blokes reckoned they was goin' to be real rich once they got the better of some important gent. 'E was goin' to get some packages and when he 'ad them all, they'd take them from 'im and some friend of theirs would claim the throne. That's what that Artemis said. 'E's only going to wear gold and precious gems and silks and satins then. And 'e's goin' to have an 'arem with different women for every night. Several of 'em for each night. 'E's goin' to pick 'em out and they're goin' to fight each other to be chosen. 'E said they'll all line up naked in front of 'im beggin' to be chosen and then they'll—"

"We don't need more details, Hayden. In fact I have quite a clear picture."

Hayden was clearly not finished with his explanation. "'E said 'e'd take 'em two at a time to 'is tent. That's when 'e didn't take three. And—"

"Thank you, Hayden. Artemis and his friend left."

"Oh, yes. Goin' to a place called the Cock and Jugs, they was."

"How long ago was that?"

"Not long before you came."

Finch shivered. "We might have walked in on them."

"They will have to be confronted soon enough," Ross said. "But not with you present, Finch. I take it Mr. Oak left quite quickly after the others, Hayden?"

"Yeah. That was funny, that was. 'E came out, all quiet-like, after they was in the cab. Did I say they came in a cab? And then, just as cool as you please, 'e climbs on the back of the cab and hangs on, and off they go. So wherever they are, 'e's probably there, too."

"I told you he was a good and trustworthy man," Finch said. "He is attempting to follow them on his own. An old, frail man all alone. We must go to his aid at once."

"Mister," Hayden said. "Do you think you could use a boy like me? I'm a 'ard worker, and I follows directions. I could run errands and do all manner of things. I learns very fast. I'd be useful to you. If you're goin' to this place tonight, I could come along and watch over the cart while you're inside. Make sure no one takes off with it."

"Well, I suppose—"

"Och, the boy's got a good head on his shoulders," Jennings remarked from the cart in question. "And he looks strong t'me. The kind of lad who won't shirk any duty. We can put him in charge o' everything that'll need watchin', if ye get my meanin', m'lord."

Ross's thin smile puzzled Finch. He nodded briefly at Hayden and motioned for him to go to the cart. Then he took Finch by the arm and directed her firmly in the same direction. "Up front with you, Hayden," he called. "I'm going to put Miss Finch in the back. She'll be more protected from the weather there."

And she found herself dumped, without ceremony, into the cart, where Jennings promptly piled pieces of coarse sacking over her. He took them from the bottom of the stacks so they were dry.

"Now," Ross said, "we shall proceed to find the Cock and Jugs. A sordid establishment by all accounts. I believe it's in the region of Elephant and Castle."

"We must make sure we are not recognized," Finch said. "Not recognized by Artemis and Zebediah."

"Most certainly. Jennings, you know what to do."

What happened next was so quickly accomplished Finch had no time to call out. A piece of cloth was pressed between her teeth and tied behind her head. She punched and kicked, but to no avail. Jennings captured her hands and tied her wrists together in front of her. Next he secured her ankles. He tipped her sideways onto the sacks again, and she felt something soft put beneath her head.

"Sorry, miss," Jennings said. "But it's for your own good. Ye're a lassie and gentle and where we're goin' is no place for the likes of you. Make your way easy and lie still, or ye'll hurt your fair skin."

She mumbled against the gag, but they weren't listening to her. Already Jennings had begun to cover her once more—including her head this time.

"Now, Hayden," she heard Ross say. "When we arrive at our destination, you will remain here and watch over *everything*. Do I make myself clear?"

"Yes, m'lord." Hayden sounded well pleased with his newfound importance. So much for trying to buy loyalty with gingersnaps.

"If you do well, I shall take you into my employ and you shall have a regular wage. But everything depends upon this evening, mind you."

"*Yes,* m'lord."

Finch seethed. These men could not abide to allow a

woman any part in putting matters to rights. And when they had accomplished their ends—if they accomplished their ends—they would expect her to applaud them. No doubt they would even settle in to watch some of the performances, lowly though they might be.

And all in the name of finding poor, dear Latimer.

Well, they should not get away with it, no indeed. They had not bargained for Finch's ingenuity. Inducing Hayden's pity would be a simple enough task. He would release her. Later, she'd have to think of a way to save his newfound position with Ross.

First she would scrutinize the way of things carefully. Then she would devise a daring plan to attach herself to the villains and follow them until they led her to Latimer.

She wasn't fond of clowns, but she would manage to endure them for as long as she must. In the stables Artemis had made reference to "bold contortions by rare bits of talent." Finch had never seen a contortionist, and thought she might be quite interested in such an act.

§ Chapter 17 §

"This is appalling. Abominable.

"I am, as I have always been, a determined optimist. Regardless of the odds, I never give up. I believe I shall triumph in the end, in all things, despite being forced to rely on the services of complete nincompoops.

"My visions are beyond reproach. I am gifted with extraordinary powers of foresight.

"I am NEVER wrong.

"But despite the gift, the treasure, the inspiration that I lavish upon those who are my responsibility, everything that can go awry is going awry.

"It is true that I see some slight signs that I may at least hope to see the Mores removed from Number 7, but even that success is by no means assured. As to the rest, well, how can I proceed even to think about that as long as this nonsense with Latimer More persists, and Lord Kilrood fails to see that he should marry the More girl at once and take her to live at Number 8? Inviting Latimer to join them, of course.

If Latimer should ever find his way back to Mayfair Square, that is.

"And now, to my utter mortification, I must issue a warning. It is my duty to do so, and I have never shirked my duty. Something . . . Gadzooks, you are mature enough for me to speak plainly. I shall lay matters before you exactly as they are. You will be horrified, perhaps even disgusted, but that will help you understand my urgent desire to bring about a satisfactory conclusion to the dilemma.

"Plain talk then.

"I have been present in a certain place where certain things occur. These, hmm, things are designed to produce certain reactions in those present. I absolutely disapprove of these things.

"There, I can't speak more plainly than that, can I?

"Now I must get to my warning. I will not mince words because in the days to come I must take heart from knowing that I have done everything in my power to protect the interests of all concerned here.

"The warning: Do you remember when I warned you that there might be times when it would be better if you didn't look? At whatever?

"I knew you would.

"All of you who intend to hide your eyes, please do so now."

❧ Chapter 18 ❧

"I have a plan, Jennings," Ross said. "It bears considerable risks, but we must act, and soon, or I fear Latimer More will no longer be with us."

"I've had the same thought, m'lord," Jennings said. "Artemis canna let More go for fear o' bein' identified and brought t'justice."

Ross regretted that Finch, no doubt exceedingly uncomfortable in the back of the cart, would also hear what was said about her brother, but there was no choice. Hayden now kept watch over her while Jennings sat beside Ross on the rough seat.

Rain continued to fall, more heavily if that were possible. A miserable company they were, and with no relief in sight.

"You were saying, m'lord?" Jennings said.

"Yes, yes. As long as Artemis thinks he can force my hand with his captive—and I believe he plans to use him to make me hand over the Sacred Box—he'll likely keep him alive. One other thing is clear. Although I am certain Artemis was known to Zebediah before they came to London, I don't believe he's aware of the whole story. Zebediah is, and he's chosen to keep the other man in ignorance. And for that I am presently grateful. Zebediah will play his cards with care. He will not reveal details of—"

Ross caught Jennings's glance toward the back of the cart and nodded. Finch made no attempt to struggle, no doubt because she was straining to hear every word.

"Well," Jennings said, inclining his head toward their unwilling passenger. "I'm glad we can be sure of Mr. More's current safety."

"Yes indeed." Ross gave thanks, as he often did, for Jennings's natural attention to human detail. "What neither man will consider—since they assume I am oblivious to their schemes—is that they will never get what they want. But regardless of that, we cannot wait to bring Latimer back."

The aged piece of horseflesh that pulled the cart toiled gamely enough through the deserted streets of Elephant and Castle. The establishment they sought could not be far now.

"Hayden," Ross said, raising his voice. "You know what you are to do?"

"Yes, Your Lordship," the boy said, sounding as if he'd lost some enthusiasm for his newfound post. "I, er, takes care of the cart, and the lady."

"Just so. And if there is any untoward occurrence, such as evidence of impending violence, you are to set off for Number 8 Mayfair Square at once. By then you will have—hmm—disposed of Miss More's impediments to freedom, and—"

"Im—what?" Hayden said.

"Untie the lady," Ross said, glowering into the sodden darkness. Jennings had been right when he said they could speak in front of the boy because he wouldn't understand much of what he heard. "At the right time."

"Over there, m'lord," Jennings said. "Left at the corner. Fish Terrace."

Ross followed his valet's directions and drew the cart to a

halt on one side of a triangle of dwellings turned to vaguely glimmering black by the storm. In the center of the triangle, raucous laughter issuing even through closed doors, stood a building that was much older than the houses that surrounded it.

"A tavern," Ross said. "I understand that's what it's supposed to be." To casual revelers the Cock and Jugs would appear to be just that.

"Aye," Jennings said, "and from what I've heard they do a fair job o' pretendin' it's nothin' more. In parts o' the place. We'd best get on."

Ross smiled. Jennings showed considerable enthusiasm for this task. "Very well. This is the plan. We seek out Zebediah and Artemis."

"M'lord?" Jennings jerked to look at Ross. "Not directly, o'course."

"Not at first. We will do our best to get close enough to overhear anything that is said. If they see us, we pretend we've been drinking—as they will have been—and we go to them as surprised fellows caught in similar circumstances. Here we are, disguised so that we will arouse no particular notice, and what do we find? *Friends.* Ah well, the best we can do is propose that we enjoy the evening together and make a pact to ensure no one else knows we have been here. I will not tell Lady Evangeline, or Sherwood—if Zebediah and his mistress's coachman hold my secret, too."

"But, what will ye find out from them if we're—"

"Together?" Ross said, leaping down to the street. "Nothing. But we watch for an opportunity to get Zebediah on his own and we take him captive. Fair enough, I should say. Artemis needs Zebediah. We need Latimer. We will be glad to make an exchange."

Hayden wrenched the cloth from Finch's mouth but she continued to cough and pretend she might vomit at any moment.

"Miss," Hayden whispered desperately, "miss, you'll lose

me job for me. Someone'll 'ear you. Say somethin', miss. Are you dyin'?"

"Untie me," she said, struggling against Jennings's very efficient bonds. "Now."

"I can't," Hayden all but wailed. "I'll lose me job, I tells you."

"You'll lose your job if you don't do what His Lordship told you to do and let me go at once. This is what he meant by the right time." Oh, please let Hayden be uncertain enough of himself to do as she asked.

"'E said . . ." Hayden paused. He had bent over Finch to see her as clearly as the dim night allowed. "'E said I was to take you to that place if I 'ad to."

Her heart thumped. "If there should be fighting here," she said. "There isn't. His Lordship told you to untie me when the time was right. He meant after he'd gone."

"Why?"

Fiddle-de-dee. She must not falter. What Ross proposed was too dangerous. If he failed, he would almost certainly guarantee she'd never see Latimer again. "Because he wishes to test your ability to follow his instructions. Hurry up, Hayden. I don't want you to fail."

"No. 'E don't want me to do nothin' unless there's trouble."

The boy wasn't to be fooled. Finch turned her face into the sacks.

"Miss," Hayden said, his voice troubled. "You was kind to me. But so was the gent. I don't like to 'urt you, miss, but I'd better do what 'e said."

Finch couldn't hold back the tears a moment longer. She tried to muffle the sound in the rough sacks, but fear and frustration, and exhaustion, drove the sobs from her in great bursts.

She felt Hayden's hesitant pats on her shoulder, heard him talk to her but didn't make out the words.

Her wrists parted seconds before she registered that she was being freed. She hiccuped and raised her face to see.

Mumbling fiercely to himself, Hayden labored over the knots at her ankles, but at last they fell away.

"Oh, thank you, thank you," she said. "Now, Hayden, I don't want you to worry. Please remain here."

"Where are you goin'?"

"Into that place, of course. You heard those two rattles talking. They think they can go in there with some ridiculous ruse and secure the release of my brother."

"You can't go in there, miss. 'Is Lordship would 'ave me guts for garters if I let you go in there."

"Not at all." She must be inventive, inventive very quickly or she'd be too late to stop disaster. Even should Ross and Jennings succeed in capturing Zebediah, Finch could not be confident enough that Artemis would release Latimer in exchange. More likely the fiend would run away. "I shall explain that I was unscrupulous. First I pretended I was dying so that you would unleash me, then I persuaded you that my brother's life depends upon my stopping His Lordship's foolishness."

"Well, I don't know about that."

Finch gambled that he would not try to put his hands upon her and stood up. "Trust me, please." She climbed awkwardly over the side of the cart and dropped to the ground. "Remain here, and I promise all will go well for you." Just let Ross try to punish a kind boy for being too sensitive to ignore her pleas.

She left him without further instruction and sped over slick cobbles toward the inn. She certainly had not known this would be an *inn*. Water rushed in rivulets between the stones underfoot. The sibilant gushing could be heard despite the disgraceful din from inside the building. A sign hung, creaking, from a metal bracket outside. A large, painted black fowl who bore a grin, surely, and held a big jug in each clawed foot. Feet that were held up in the most unlikely fashion.

At the doorway she paused and drew back. Surely only minutes had passed since Ross and Jennings left the cart.

Whatever happened, she must stop the noddycocks before it was too late.

The rain had served one purpose. She appeared a disreputable ragamuffin and should pass as beneath the notice of even a most coarse band. The shawl dripped. She pulled it off, wrung as much water as possible from the cheap wool, and draped it to completely obscure her hair and much of her face. Then she set her jaw and pushed open the door.

Heat, body heat and that from a great fireplace, engulfed and all but choked her. Instantly her wet clothing gave off a faint steam, and she felt sick at the discomfort of it all.

The room was of good size. Overhead beams were so low that tall men bent over to walk about. Filthy, clumped sawdust covered the floors.

Patrons crowded about every table, laughing loudly, raising tankards to allow some brew to pour down their throats—such as did not pour down their chins instead.

Finch stood just inside the door. She had never beheld such extraordinary behavior. There did not appear to be a sober soul in the room. Men and women both slammed tankards on tables awash with drink. They drank and mauled each other between doing so. Finch saw how many of the women wore clothing that was in disarray and showed off quantities of flesh intended to be hidden.

A man with a red and bloated face guffawed, showing broken and discolored teeth, and pushed his hand inside the sagging bodice of his companion's gown. The female, obviously delighted, made no complaint when her breasts were revealed for all to see.

Finch's legs weakened, and she felt shaky with humiliation for the drunken creature who screamed with pleasure as the man sloshed beer on her chest and yelled for help licking it off.

Where were Ross and Jennings? Finch averted her eyes from the spectacle and searched the room. She was in danger here, but she would risk her very life for Latimer. The first familiar face she saw was that of the coachman,

Artemis, and that only briefly before he followed a much taller man—Zebediah, no doubt—through a door into another room.

She wished she could retreat, but poor Latimer was detained somewhere, and helpless. There could be no turning back now.

Ross. Ashamed as she was to admit her need, she knew that with him beside her she would find courage.

As if guided by her thoughts, he rose from a table, with Jennings at his side, and made his way toward the other room, ducking his head, and swinging his broad shoulders as he went through the crowd.

Summoning her courage, Finch hurried after him, evading grabbing hands on the way. She reached the door just as it closed behind Ross and Jennings. Hardly able to catch a single breath, she turned the handle and slipped into a darkened room with what appeared to be groups of chairs clustered close together and all facing the same direction—away from Finch.

Clutching her shawl to her neck she closed the door behind her and tried to focus on the scene before her. Lights flickered on a platform where figures moved. The company in the chairs were neither noisy nor silent. Their voices came in rising and falling eruptions of sounds foreign to Finch's ears. They seemed to sigh, and moan, and gasp—sometimes to beg.

"You little fool, Finch." Ross's voice, close to her ear, and his punishing grip on her arm, startled her so much that she almost fainted. "You will ruin everything. *Everything.* What are you doing here?"

She couldn't gather her wits enough to answer him.

"Sit down," a man shouted nearby. "And shut your mouth."

Instantly Ross twisted Finch against him and held her face to his chest. He bent his head over her. "We cannot risk any more attention." He half dragged her to one of several curtained alcoves that flanked the platform on either side.

He checked one and a man's angry growl exploded. Lifting filmy drapes to see into the next box, Ross swung Finch into almost-total darkness, and onto a small, plush couch. He dropped to sit beside her. Still holding her arm so hard it hurt, he clamped her face against his coat once more. "Now I have to get you away, and we may lose our chance to obtain Latimer's release."

Finch pushed her hands between them until she could grasp the lapels of his coat and force a little breathing space and enough room to return his whispered anger. "I don't want to be here. This is a dreadful place. I came to save *you*. And to save Latimer. Where is Jennings? Tell me he isn't already speaking to those men."

"You are wrongheaded, miss. I owe you no explanations."

"You do if you want my cooperation. I could reveal your presence with one shout. And I will if you go ahead with this. You cannot know you will succeed, and if you fail, you will sacrifice Latimer, not save him."

"Drat you." He gripped the hair at the nape of her neck through the shawl and she sucked in a breath. "Wait till I catch that little brat, Hayden. Useless creature."

"I pretended to be dying. He did what any decent human would do—he released me—and I escaped. He is a good boy, and you would do well to retain his services."

"Hmm." Ross seemed determined to crush her face against him. "I doubt I should ever agree with you there. When I say we move, you allow yourself to be guided."

"I go nowhere unless I wish to go. I heard your plans, and they are foolhardy, my lord."

"'Ere," someone from outside the curtains said, "keep it down in there."

Ross tipped her face up to his. "We must wait until we are forgotten in all this." With that, he brought his mouth down on hers. The kiss was not gentle. He kissed her with force, although not with cruelty. And his embrace grew more protective than fierce. Gradually his breathing became louder, and he moved his lips over hers with an ardor she didn't miss. Even while she fought with the panic in her heart, his mouth, his tongue, thrilled her. Every fresh angle drew an answering tug in her belly and in other places for which she had no name except that she knew they were her womanly places and they throbbed.

He pulled her head back and looked down into her face. Even in the near dark, with light flickering on the scene outside, she saw the passionate glint in his eyes. He spread a hand over her throat and studied her. When he looked at her mouth, his own lips parted, and he slowly bent to kiss her again, even more deeply and insistently.

When he paused for breath, she whispered, "Why didn't you include me in your plans? Latimer is my brother. And I have a mind. I will not be excluded anymore. Wherever you go and whatever you do that is of grave importance to us, I will be there with you."

Muscles in his jaw flickered, and he narrowed his eyes. "You do not feel danger even when it's looking at you," he said softly. "As soon as I can remove you to safety, it shall be done. And don't consider making a fuss, or you will surely rue the decision."

Finch made a violent movement and succeeded in turning herself to face forward. For Ross to have reversed her position would only have brought further complaints from other patrons.

He placed his mouth against her ear. "Close your eyes. At once."

She didn't look away. She couldn't. Whereas she and Ross were veiled away in their recess, light directed on the platform spilled over the gathered company. Men and women sat together, close together, some with their clothing undone, or even removed, while they engaged in lewd exploration of each other. There were groups of men on their own who concentrated on the stage, when they weren't watching other members of the audience. And there were occasional well-dressed women who sat, mostly by twos, fluttering fans before their faces and leaning together to murmur. From time to time a man or woman would pass among the patrons bearing tankards and smaller glasses. These they delivered to patrons—until they were pulled into grasping hands and absorbed into the writhing mass.

Ross's arms remained firmly around her. She glanced at him and saw how he attempted to search the room. Looking for Artemis and Zebediah, no doubt. She caught sight of a man who looked like Jennings. He was alone and also searching the room.

Suddenly, as if this were a church rather than a den of evil, a basket on a long pole was passed by a woman who wore a white robe that fell open to reveal her voluptuous nakedness beneath. She thrust the basket in front of each member of the audience and didn't remove it until she considered enough money had been deposited.

Finch blushed at the sight of the woman, and shuddered at the way she laughed when hands reached to fondle her.

"And now, ladies and gentlemen," a woman announced from the platform, "Rudy and Flame will lead you to even more titillating places. This is another opportunity to say you've studied with the best. They call this: The Wedding Night. Encourage them. Show them how they inspire you." She laughed boisterously and backed slowly away while she beckoned to a tall, muscular man in a dark jacket and trousers, who appeared no more than eighteen or nineteen, and a woman some years older whose black hair reached her waist on top of a prim pink gown suitable for a young female at her coming-out ball.

"I told you not to look," Ross said, attempting to put his head in front of hers.

She ducked and shifted to the front of her seat.

"This is wrong," he told her.

"For me, but not for you?" she said. The throbbing surprised her this time. She murmured, "Oh," and crossed her arms tightly.

The woman, Flame, had uttered a small shriek and attempted to run from her suitor, but he contrived to catch the hem of her gown and cause her to fall forward. Promptly "Rudy" snagged a portion of the front of the skirt and pulled it through the woman's legs. He held her neck and turned her to face the audience while he tightened his hold on the folds of muslin, grinding them into her most sensitive folds of flesh. The woman first spread her legs and sent up shrieks of excitement, then pressed her thighs together and jerked her hips to the hollering cries of the audience.

Finch's face grew hot. Her body grew hot. She was reacting to this crude exhibition? As the creature disported herself for all to see, she, Finch More, spinster of Cornwall, grew damp between her own legs, and her heart thudded, and her breasts ached.

"Very well," Ross said, and bared enough of her shoulder to sink his teeth lightly into her flesh. "Since you will not be guided. Since you choose to design your behavior to fit the situation, then I must assist you. We will be nothing more than another amorous couple seeking *inspiration.*"

She felt his teeth, and his warm breath on her skin, but she could not take her attention from what she saw. The man swung the woman around by her skirt, his face assuming a dark threat while she threw her arms wide and began to jerk against the pressure. Finch had no doubt that she knew what the creature was feeling, and she pressed her own legs tightly together.

"Mmm," Ross murmured. His hand slipped upward beneath Finch's skirt.

Breathing through her mouth, she glanced at him and attempted to push his hand away, but she didn't try hard, or for long. The effort was pointless. He found his way past the tops of her stockings to the place that pulsed. And he contrived to kiss her again, groaning a little while he thrust his tongue into her mouth in time to the rubbing motions between her legs.

Finch's bottom came off her chair. She drove her fingers into Ross's hair and gave herself up to a wave of desperate desire for more of the wonderful sensations he brought to a peak.

Wrong, a small voice in her brain said. *Wrong, wrong—a disgusting thing.* But she still wanted this, and could not have stopped it.

Ripples of hot, sweet sensation burst into her, and she moved her hips helplessly. Ross gathered her tightly while he worked over her, worked until she slumped in his arms.

He held her like that, and she heard his harsh breathing, felt the tension in his body, and knew he, too, was incredibly aroused. Could she—could she do whatever he needed her to do—*here.*

Flame called aloud to her "lover." "Take me," she implored. "Make me your slave forever."

Still behind her, Rudy pulled her elbows back and reached to rend her gown apart from neck to waist, revealing a pair of large, round breasts that brought a gasp from every man in the room. The woman's waist was small, and, as the gown opened further, her flat stomach came into view, then the black hair at the apex of her legs. Rudy threw her to the floor and began stripping away his own clothes. A magnificent body emerged. Every muscle showed clearly. The hair on his chest and belly was as dark as the curly hair on his head and when his male part sprang free and erect, it was the women watchers who sent up whoops.

Ross's hand, plunging inside the gaping bodice of Finch's gown, distracted her. "Your breasts are more lovely than hers," he said quietly. "More sensitive. Pointed. They drive me to distraction."

"Ross," she said, "not here."

"Why not?" he said, his tone slumberous, amorous. "We are secluded. But what you see out there excites you. And what I see here excites me." He untied the lace at the neck and pulled it slowly through the holes that held it.

"No," Finch said weakly.

"Yes," was her reward. "What do you think of Rudy? Quite the man, hmm?"

"He is . . . well, he certainly is, isn't he?" And at that moment the man in question pulled his "bride's" skirts over her head, covering her face but showing the rest of her body to all. While she struggled he pinched and sucked, and took advantage of her inability to use her hands. Bending her backward over a chair, he placed his mouth in such a manner as to finally make Finch hide her eyes. The yells about her sent fear into her soul.

Air slipped over her skin and she looked down, tried in vain to clasp her bodice to her chest. She tried in vain because Ross firmly parted it and cupped her breasts in his hands while he kissed them. He kissed, and trailed his tongue in ever-diminishing circles until she panted for him to take their centers into his mouth, but each time he drew close he darted his tongue out in the briefest, most inflaming lick, then withdrew to start again.

Finch rocked from side to side and cleared her brain enough to plan her own method of torture. A hand, insinuated between his hard and muscular thighs achieved her ends. He moaned and paused in his wicked little game.

A roar went up from the crowd and Finch looked to the platform once more, just in time to see the two performers, both completely naked now, join their bodies. Rudy held Flame in an amazing backbend. Her hands were flattened on the floor behind her, her body a perfect arch, and Rudy was slowly pushing himself in and out of her.

Finch's own hips moved of their own accord. "I am wicked," she murmured, so hot she would like to stand undressed in the rain outside. Squeezing Ross with convulsive fervor, she took breaths that drew in no air and rocked her head from side to side. "This cannot be right."

He took her hand and put it inside his trousers until she held his heated, quickened flesh. "This is not for you, my dear girl, but you are a passionate creature and will always respond with passion. You delight me. But this is not where I would choose to spend such intimate moments with you."

She could not tear her attention from the act performed for all to see.

And that was when Ross gave her what she'd wanted. He covered a nipple and flipped his tongue back and forth until she forgot to caress him and arched her back instead. He laughed deep in his throat and gave her the attention she craved until she felt once more the ripple of release, this time taking her by surprise because it happened without his stimulation.

"My God," he said. "You are unique. I've never known a woman like you."

The "wedding night," was over. The naked bride and groom took their bows while men obviously hired for the purpose stopped patrons from climbing onto the platform. Eventually, Rudy and Flame gave in to cries of approval and leaped from the stage to disport themselves with one drunken lecher after another.

Finch clumsily rethreaded the lace of her gown. "I don't understand," she said, every word faint and uncertain. "I couldn't . . . What will you think of me. I am horrified."

"Then we should both be horrified. We gave in to base excitement. You in your innocence, me in—well, in whatever. But I could not resist touching you, Finch, enjoying you."

"I don't wish to speak of this further." With her shawl firmly in place again, Finch attempted to collect herself. "Your idea for approaching Zebediah and Artemis was not without merit, but it was shortsighted, and I have a better idea."

His superior smile might be infuriating, but it was expected.

"Listen carefully, Ross, and tell me if I am not correct. If you go to them and carry out your abduction—and actually succeed in that abduction—your hand will be revealed. They will know you have discovered their identities and their part in this desperate game you play. You should keep yourself above suspicion if you are to continue to act efficiently."

He frowned. "Go on."

She felt a small curl of triumph. "If something should go wrong with your attempt to take Zebediah, you will have lost your chance—Latimer's last chance. In fact I believe that Artemis might well decide to abandon Zebediah to you, do away with Latimer, then escape. No, you must continue to let them believe you do not know about them. I, on the other hand, am unlikely even to be recognized by them. Dressed as I am, and if I pull the shawl over my hair, I could go to them and say I've been sent by Lady Evangeline to warn them you're on your way and they should escape at once."

"No such thing."

"Listen to me. They will likely leave together and—"

"You will do no such thing. Do I make myself plain?"

"You do an excellent job of being overbearing. But I insist you hear me out."

"M'lord?" It was Jennings, whispering from the other side of the curtains. "Forgive me for interrupting, m'lord."

Finch checked to be certain she was decently covered.

"What is it," Ross said. "Get in here, man, before you draw attention to yourself."

Jennings promptly entered the alcove. "They're over there. See. Zebediah's staring at nothing I can see, and Artemis has a woman on his—er—lap."

"I see them."

"Jennings," Finch said, leaning across Ross. "I wish to go to them and tell them I bring a warning from Lady Evangeline."

"And I have told you that is out of the question," Ross said.

Desperate, Finch searched for a solution. "We will do it this way. I go to them with my message. They will rush to escape. You lie in wait and capture them both. Then you refuse to release them until they give you Latimer. Really, it is the only answer."

"It is out of the question," Ross said.

"No, it isn't, and I will do it. I must try." She got to her feet.

"Och," Jennings said with quiet vehemence. "Will ye look at that? If I didna' see it, I wouldna' believe it."

Finch craned her neck to see what he referred to. "What?"

"Dash it all," Ross muttered. "Where did he come from?"

He, was Mr. Edwin Oak. Bemused, Finch stared at the old man with his white hair and bent back, his crooked legs. She stared at him where he stood before Zebediah and Artemis in deep conversation and behaving as if he didn't see the woman who sat astride Artemis's lap.

Zebediah leaped to his feet and hauled up Artemis, depositing the woman on the floor. Mr. Oak continued to gesture and speak earnestly. Then he stood back and smoothed his hair.

In less than a heartbeat, Zebediah and Artemis clambered to the platform and dashed to a door at the back of the building. They disappeared into the darkness beyond.

Ross made to run after them, but Jennings caught his sleeve. "Hold, m'lord. Ye'll no' catch them out there in the dark and with them already away. It's that crooked-backed one we've t'speak with and quickly."

With Finch firmly placed behind him, Ross swept the curtains aside and cut a path through the riffraff to the place where Mr. Oak stood, looking at Jennings and Ross as if he'd known they were there all the time.

"How are you come here?" Ross asked urgently. "And why? What did you say to those two to make them rush away like that?"

"Why," Mr. Oak said—he leaned to see Finch and his features registered the deepest disapproval, "why, I listened to a certain conversation those two ruffians had earlier. In the mews, you know. So I decided to follow."

"And you went to the warehouse," Ross said. "Yes, so Hayden said, of course."

"Of course," Mr. Oak said, apparently unperturbed. "What they said in the stables, they repeated in Whitechapel.

And now I have told them I shall gladly become their partner. For which they have shown great enthusiasm."

"And run away," Ross said.

"Lookin' like angry trolls," Jennings added.

Mr. Oak raised his thin nose. "It is highly unsuitable to have Miss More here. Latimer would be horrified."

"Latimer will never know," Ross said.

Mr. Oak shook his head.

"What did they say when you told them you would be their partner and help them?" Ross asked.

"They said it was just as well since they'd kill me if I said otherwise. Charming fellows."

"So why did they rush out?" Ross said.

"Aye," Jennings said. "As if their lives depended on it."

Mr. Oak shrugged. "I told them that Viscount Kilrood expected to receive certain outstanding shipments at his home tonight—*all* of those outstanding shipments, in fact, and that I understood he intended to leave the country with them at once."

❧ Chapter 19 ❧

"You looked, didn't you? Even though I warned you . . . you looked.

"No, no, I'm not surprised by your denial. I am accustomed to disappointment. Those few of us who are above it all cannot expect honor from lesser beings.

"Matters have taken a desperate turn. If I had but known, even guessed, the intrigues I was about to confront, I should have taken more aggressive action at the outset. But I accept exactly what must be done now. There can be no question of leaving any of these people to make decisions for themselves. Oh, they will assume they are in control, but mine will be the mastermind.

"What I intend may be dangerous. It could even prove deadly. But I have never shrunk from the bold stroke. Now, lest you think me selfish or callous, I point out that I have decided, against my natural reservations, to help one who may not be deserving of my attention. Some of you will think I only do this because it will serve my own ends. You must *make up your own minds on that. I am certainly no stranger to mean-spirited criticism.*

"As you will have noted, the stakes have become incredibly high for some of these irritating people. Yet again I am forced to make allowances for the desires and designs of others. What could have been at least relatively simple, will be unbelievably complicated.

"Bear with me, as I always bear with you.

"It is pointless to deny it, you know. You did look."

❧ *Chapter* 20 ❧

There was no getting the nag to increase her speed above an amble. Perhaps he should be grateful, Ross thought. Their arrival in Mayfair Square would only mean confronting the next phase in the disaster this night had already been. With one notable exception.

"I'm sorry the laddie was too afraid t'wait for us," Jennings said.

Ross puffed up his cheeks and let the air escape slowly. He was grateful the rain had slowed to a thin drizzle, but they were all thoroughly wet and cold, and he longed for a fire and a glass of brandy—and some peace.

"Hayden's a good boy," Finch said. "He's young, and no match for someone much older and more devious. Like me. I wish we had gone after him."

Was he the only one strong enough to avoid this mewling nonsense? Ross wondered. "You seem to forget that we would not have known where to look," he said brusquely. "And it was his choice to run away."

"He would go back to Whitechapel," Finch said, her voice empty. "To that dreadful, cheerless place where he lives behind boarded windows, and—"

"Quite." He did not need to be told what he already knew.

"Mr. Oak's a queer one," Jennings said. He'd insisted on taking a place in the back of the cart so that Finch could sit beside Ross. "One minute he hasna' a place t'go, the next he's runnin' off for a cab t'this relative in Hampstead."

"His interference bears study." In truth Ross was merely grateful that Edwin Oak had not lingered as one more complication he had to deal with—at least not immediately. "I intend to question him and find out why he took such a course. Who knows whether our plan would have been successful, but he unwittingly made sure we had no chance even to try. We'll forget Mr. Oak for now. We have more urgent concerns. I must decide how to deal with our two friends. One can only guess at their confusion when they do not find me at home and preparing to leave the country. Until we arrive at the house, I can only attempt to ready myself for all possible situations."

He cast a covert glance at Finch, who stared straight ahead. The memory of what had happened at the Cock and Jugs wouldn't be easily forgotten by either of them, he rather thought. No doubt his actions had been wrong, but they had been willingly enough received. And reciprocated. She turned her head slightly in his direction. Faint light caught her eyelashes. He looked at her mouth in profile. He could still feel how it had felt on his, taste how it had tasted.

Dash it all. He urged the horse on. Finch More was a difficulty he couldn't afford. Nor did he want to. That was a road he'd walked once, and it was behind him now. He was a stronger, better man for having learned the fickleness of the female. The knowledge had trained him to be faithful to higher causes.

"Artemis won't dare t'show his face, d'ye think, m'lord?"

"No, but I anticipate encountering Zebediah Swift, who will be careful enough—at least at first—since he hopes to get his hands on what doesn't belong to him." He pulled the horse up. This must be dealt with at once. "Finch, may I rely upon you to say nothing of what you've seen or heard tonight? To anyone?"

She looked up at him, her eyes unreadable. "If you have to ask me that question, then it is pointless for me to give you an answer."

Females. They were so abysmally sensitive. "Men understand these things," he told her. "The necessity to make themselves and their requirements plain."

"Your *requirements.*" She gave a short laugh. "Yes, men do make their requirements plain, don't they? Very well. You may be certain that I would never do anything to harm you, or what is important to you."

"Yes, well . . . Thank you." Why did a woman have to make a man feel so dashed *small*?

"I am very afraid for Latimer."

As was he. "Leave his welfare in my hands. I intend to make his release my highest priority."

"I can't do that."

"Hmm? I'm sorry. What did you say?"

"Please carry on to Mayfair Square, Your Lordship. I am anxious to see if those men will approach you with a proposition. Surely they intend to offer Latimer in exchange for this treasure they seek."

He flicked the reins and encouraged the mare to move, and used the diversion to quiet his mounting anger at the obstacle Finch represented. He was unaccustomed to interference, or to any personal responsibility. Long ago he'd decided that a man such as he could only be weakened by attachments his enemies could use against him.

He'd wavered. Yes, he must admit to himself that Finch, her candor and intelligence, her very difference from any woman he'd known, her bravery, her wit, her honesty . . . her passion, had . . . *Dash it all.* He'd suffered a minor brush with boredom, a period of questioning what he'd chosen to do with his life. Instinct had caused him to trifle with what it might be like to return to the conventional, to allow himself to make a woman more than a pleasant interlude. Finch had been convenient, nothing more.

If he'd needed affirmation that he was meant to be alone, tonight had given him that affirmation.

"I shall return you to Number 7 where you will go directly to your rooms and remain there until I send word. That will be when I decide what is to be done next."

"I'm afraid that won't do."

Ross heard Jennings clear his throat and recognized the attempted warning against outbursts of rage. "You, Miss More, will do as you're *told.* Do I make myself clear?" Some warnings were pointless.

She didn't answer him.

"Well? Do you understand me?"

"I understand that you are a rude, arrogant man who expects servile obedience from those he considers beneath his notice. But as we have already seen, you have most definitely noticed me, *my lord,* so I know you really do expect me to have opinions. To disagree with you, even. And I do disagree. I have absolutely no intention of going quietly to my room and leaving my brother's welfare in your care."

"Finch!"

"Don't shout at me. You are an angry man. An angry man cannot be in complete control of himself, and that is unacceptable at a time such as this."

He formulated a response, discarded it, clamped his mouth shut, then felt his frustrations ignite. "Very well, I will not shout," he told her softly. "I will tell you, in a most reasonable manner, that you are going *home.*"

"To your home," she said, all serene assurance. He saw how she raised her sharp little nose. "From now until I see my brother's face again I will not be parted from you."

"Hellfire, will you *think,* woman?" Only with the greatest restraint did he stop himself from pulling the cart to a halt again. "You cannot remain with me. Only imagine the ruination that would bring upon you."

"I don't care about that." Even the set of her shoulders was stubborn. "Fiddle-de-dee to that, I say."

"I'm sure such a curse will save the day. Have you forgotten our present circumstances? Our clothes? You suggest we enter my home—openly—in this manner?"

"I don't care—"

"*Don't* repeat that, if you please."

"Very well. Help me think of an excuse. For our clothes and the cart."

"Well—" Oh, no, she should not exert her will over his. "Out of the question."

"We were set upon by robbers who stole our clothes and left theirs. And they took the carriage you hired for the evening, leaving this cart instead."

Jennings made a sound that was definitely intended to disguise laughter.

"I will not go home," Finch said. "So, if you do not like my explanation, you'd best think of your own."

"Out of the question."

"If you attempt to make me go to Number 7, I will scream and tear these wonderful clothes, and accuse you of all manner of heinous crimes against my person."

"I'm dashed." Ross allowed the cart to roll to a stop. "I do believe you're quite capable of such duplicity."

"Absolutely."

"You are manipulative."

"Very."

"And without shame."

"In this instance." She hunched inside the poor, damp shawl and shivered.

At this moment he could not summon pity for her sorry state. "You will not reconsider?"

"No."

He raised his face to the sky and sighed. "One cannot reason with a woman," he said, more to himself than to her. "If you were a man, we would come to a sensible resolution. There would be no emotion, no manipulation with emotion designed to make one fellow feel he should humor the other."

"A lot of posturing and no honesty," she said, her tone damnably neutral. "And a decision reached by the man with the loudest voice, no doubt. We go on together, my lord."

"May I offer a suggestion?" Jennings said tentatively enough to save him from his master's wrath. "Just an idea."

"No," Ross told him, but evenly enough. "*I* will decide how to proceed."

He waited, certain Finch would make another waspish remark. If she did he would take her to Number 7 regardless and leave her on the front steps if necessary.

She didn't say a word.

Not that he could have left her anyway.

"Very well." He clucked, and they set off once more. "This is what we will do. And before you inform me that my story is too fantastic to be considered as other than a fabrication, I agree with you. But you leave me no choice. I shall simply be forced to bluster my way through."

"*We* shall be forced to bluster our way through," Finch said. "Jennings and I will support whatever you decide. You will not be alone."

"No? That makes me feel so much more confident."

Now she would tell him he was sarcastic, and he would call the whole thing off.

She didn't comment.

Hell's teeth, she is an irritating creature. "We have been to a fancy-dress ball. The invitation came at the last minute and rather than disturb the entire household, I engaged Jennings's assistance. He devised these clever costumes."

"Och," Jennings said, "I'd ha' done a good deal better than—"

"This is my excuse. Kindly don't interrupt. Why did Finch come with me? Because I was requested to bring a lady, and I had no time to find another."

"Flattering," Finch said.

"The best that can be done," he said, not without satisfaction. "Jennings chaperoned."

"*Chaperoned?*" Jennings's voice rose to a squeak.

"We must be resourceful."

"There will be questions about Latimer," Finch pointed out. "Possibly not tonight because everyone at Number 7 will be asleep. But tomorrow they will want answers."

"We are almost there," Ross said. "First we ready ourselves for whatever greets us. Leave the explanations about Latimer's whereabouts to me."

"But—"

"Will you be guided, *miss*? For once, if nothing more?"

She averted her face, but blessedly didn't argue further.

"I'm glad we're finally in agreement."

Did she sniff?

Probably took a chill. Who could be surprised?

She bowed her head, and her back shook.

Dash it all. This was exactly the point he must never let himself forget. Females did not need the protection of males for nothing. They were fragile, unsuited to emotional or physical stress.

Trying to forget that Jennings would be observing his actions, he settled a hand between Finch's shoulders and patted her awkwardly. "You've been through too much," he said, and added before he could stop himself, "My fault, I'm afraid. I drew you and Latimer into all this."

She shifted on the seat, turned toward him with her head still bowed, and leaned against his shoulder. "I'm all right, thank you."

After all, a little sympathy didn't cost a man a thing, didn't detract one whit from his superior strength and control. "There, there," he said, using his free arm to wrap her against him. "We'll make sure everything is settled to our satisfaction."

When Mayfair Square was reached, Ross knew the rush of excitement he always felt when a challenge was in the air.

This situation was bizarre, but he was versatile. That's why he was still alive.

"Allow me to be our voice," he said when they stopped in front of the house. "Where did you obtain this poor animal, Jennings?"

"Dinna concern yoursel', m'lord. Take the young lady in, and I'll follow soon enough."

With a nod, Ross jumped down and went around to lift Finch to the street. She felt insubstantial in his hands. The urge to embrace her flooded him. He schooled himself to hold her shoulders and give her a quick, firm squeeze. "We shall do well enough," he told her heartily. "Please trust me to take the lead."

She nodded and moved away from him as if she would go up the steps alone. He promptly captured her hand and threaded it beneath his arm. "We go together," he told her. "We have been to a ball, remember."

"Oh yes. They're bound to believe us."

"Whether they do or not doesn't really matter. This is a game we're playing. A dangerous game where the strongest and most innovative will win. We will win."

He hadn't expected the door to be opened by Bessinger. The butler had long ago relegated inconvenient duties—such as greeting his master on any late-night returns—to a more junior member of the staff. Tonight Bessinger's small, dark eyes were bright with interest, and he showed every sign of being very much awake. He stood back to allow Ross and Finch to enter, made to take the cloak Ross wasn't wearing, but recovered quickly and crossed his hands instead.

"All quiet, is it, Bessinger?" Ross asked. "Sorry to keep you up late."

"It wouldn't be easy to sleep with so much coming and going, my lord," the man said. His full head of light hair was in the habit of springing free of its owner's efforts to tame it flat. "In fact, if you don't mind my being so bold, there are one or two matters I should like to discuss at your earliest convenience."

God preserve *his* patience, Ross thought. He was besieged on all sides. This domestic scene was entirely too onerous. "We'll make time for that very soon." He fixed his attention ahead, ushered Finch into the red salon, and stopped. Zebediah, a glass of Madeira in hand, sat before the fire in Ross's favorite wing chair. The man got to his feet when he saw Finch and Ross.

Ross shut the door and faced his visitor. "Trouble, Swift? Is Lady Evangeline not well?"

Zebediah's response was a brooding stare.

"Ah, just so." Ross took Finch's soaked shawl and dropped it in a heap on the hearth before embarking on his prepared explanation for what could not possibly have a reasonable explanation.

If Zebediah found the story unbelievable, he hid his skepticism well. He nodded politely from time to time, and when Ross finished got up and went to the tray of decanters. "May I offer you a glass of your own brandy? To warm you? And perhaps a little sherry for the lady?"

Despite a temptation to refuse, Ross said, "Yes, on both counts, thank you." The man had unexpectedly perfect manners, and he was a handsome devil. "To what do I owe the honor of your company at this hour?"

Zebediah stared at him. No trace of humor touched his commanding features. "Actually it was not you I expected." He appeared uncomfortable. "I hesitate to burden you with my concerns, but Lady Evangeline left to visit a lady who she learned has returned from Egypt. Apparently they were acquainted there. But she went hours ago, and she has not returned. I am concerned for her health, but I have no idea where I might find her. She insisted she is feeling constrained by my close attention to her welfare and would not say the name and address of her acquaintance."

"I see." Ross frowned. "Very disturbing indeed."

That this was a story constructed for much the same reason as he, Ross, had been forced to spin his piece of foolishness, there was no doubt. Zebediah had changed his clothes and was returned to his usual impeccable appearance, but less than an hour previous he had run from the Cock and Jugs dressed in a manner guaranteed to draw little attention in that crude place.

The sound of the front door opening again was a merciful diversion. A raised female voice in the hall animated Zebediah. "There she is," he said, with an admirably convincing show of relief. "Perhaps if you would impress upon her that it is unwise for her to venture forth for such long periods while her health is so uncertain . . . Well, perhaps she would listen to you, Lord Kilrood."

Ross doubted that, and didn't care about the lady one way or the other.

She entered the room, and he could not collect himself quickly enough not to stare.

"Bessinger tells me you are just returned, Ross." She settled her extraordinary eyes on Finch and frowned in a most unbecoming manner. "Miss More? Whatever can you be doing here? And dressed like that?"

"I'll leave Zebediah to explain that to you later," Ross said, the epitome of a jovial familiar delighted to see a friend. "But what of you, my dear Evangeline? I do believe you look flustered."

She tossed her head, and a plume of white ostrich feathers fluttered over the crown of a lilac-satin evening toque. "Flustered? Not a bit of it. I am exhilarated by finally being out among society again. The play was quite wonderful."

Ross felt Zebediah watching him for reaction to this rather different story about Evangeline's excursion.

"Do sit down, my dear," Ross said. "A glass of something, perhaps?"

She flipped a hand before her face in dismissal. "I avoid strong drink. Bad for the complexion." Her eyes went to Finch, who held what was probably a rare glass of sherry. "I'm not sure it affects freckles adversely, but it certainly may. If I were you, Miss More, I would certainly be careful. Although it's rather too late for that, isn't it?"

Ross was relieved to see that Finch's response to Evangeline's barb was an amused smile.

"Well," Evangeline said. "Yes, well." She swayed a little, and Ross's attention was drawn to her feet. Beneath the hem of the lilac-satin cloak she wore wrapped tightly about her, a pair of satin slippers showed. One lilac. One green . . .

She sighed, and tilted her head to one side.

Interesting.

Finally Evangeline sat down, carefully draping the cloak over her knees but apparently having no idea that her slippers didn't match.

More sound came from the hall, and Artemis lumbered in with a pile of hatboxes in his arms.

Visiting an old friend. An evening at the theater. And a shopping trip. How, one wondered, could all of these be accomplished simultaneously?

Artemis hovered, not settling in the room—he'd better not, the presumptuous cur—nor doing as he should, by leaving forthwith. He glowered about from one to the other of them. Or rather he glowered at Zebediah and Ross, and leered at Evangeline and Finch, more so at Evangeline.

Zebediah commenced to hum, an unlikely development.

Evangeline patted at rather disheveled curls that escaped the toque and revealed what did not look at all like the sleeve of a gown. It appeared, in fact, to belong to a night rail.

Ross glanced at the hem of her cloak and caught sight of what was definitely the bottom of an item of night attire. He'd wager a good deal that the lady had been roused from bed, made to get rapidly into outer clothes, and sent forth in the carriage with orders to return when Ross arrived. The probable reason might well have been to give Artemis an excuse to insinuate his unpleasant self upon the scene.

"What play did you see?" Ross asked Evangeline.

The lady's expression was at first blank, then agitated.

She looked to Zebediah, and said, "I am always so bad about titles."

"*A Midsummer Night's Dream* perhaps?" Ross suggested, ever helpful.

Evangeline pointed a finger at him, and said, "Of course. How could I have forgotten?"

Artemis coughed and shuffled his dusty boots on Ross's rose-and-gold Aubusson carpet. "Ah," he said. "Itchy feet, if you don't mind my mentioning them, m'lord. Regular plague they are, itchy feet."

Ross saw Finch wrinkle her nose and imagined her considering the distasteful prospect of the coachman's feet.

"And I don't mean the way you've got itchy feet," Artemis said, grinning and showing his yellow teeth. "I understands you've got a different kind altogether. The kind that makes you want to take long journeys?"

"Really?" Ross said. "Was that at the Haymarket Theatre, Evangeline?"

Another blank stare was his reward. He expected Zebediah to step in, but the man remained silent.

"That was it," Evangeline said. "At the Haymarket. The Haymarket, wasn't it, coachman?"

"Ah, Haymarket," Artemis agreed.

Ross decided not to point out that the Haymarket was currently closed for refurbishment and that *A Midsummer Night's Dream* was not playing anywhere in London at the moment.

"There's people as dream of faraway places all the time, I'm told," Artemis said. "Reckon you must be one of those, m'lord."

"Shouldn't you like your coachman to leave your packages with Bessinger, Evangeline?" Ross asked. "I'll be happy to ring for him."

"In a hurry, are we?" Artemis said, sounding belligerent. "Perhaps there's some *packages* I could take out to Bessinger for you, too. Didn't I hear about you getting important packages?"

The fellow was a veritable master of subtlety. "No, you didn't."

"Didn't I 'ear them talking about your *trunks*, m'lord?" Artemis asked. "Leaving to go somewhere, are we?"

Ross didn't answer the man.

"I'd be glad to take 'em to the ship for you. You are taking a ship, aren't you?"

"Oh, will you be silent?" Evangeline all but shouted before turning to Finch. "Surely it's time you returned to your home. How very unsuitable for you to be here like this."

Finch stood up at once.

Taking advantage of her reaction to Evangeline might be convenient. After all, he'd wanted her to leave. "I escorted Miss More to a ball," he heard himself say, well aware of how outrageous his statement was. "She is awaiting the return of her brother." He would not allow her to be belittled—by anyone.

"A *ball*," Evangeline said. "Why—"

"I expect that was to control 'is lordship's wanderlust till it was time for 'im to go to the ship," Artemis said. "Keepin' 'imself occupied till 'e got what 'e'd been waitin' for. What 'e intends to take with him?"

Ross glanced at Zebediah, who in turn studied the floor. One might almost feel sorry for the man's embarrassment at his buffoon of a partner.

"I'm afraid I don't understand you," Ross said to Artemis. "Ship? What ship? I have no intention of taking any ship."

Artemis winked hugely. "Oh, you can keep your little secret if you want to. All I intended was to offer some 'elp."

"Yes, well, very nice of you. Perhaps you should get along home. The hour grows very late." Since there were no servants' quarters available at Number 8, Zebediah had arranged for the man to live elsewhere. "And I insist you go to your bed, Evangeline. If you suffer a relapse, Sherwood will never forgive me."

"Have you heard from Sherwood?" Evangeline asked sharply.

The question was unexpected. "Should I expect to?" Ross said.

Evangeline stood up. She tossed her head, but the glitter in her eyes suggested tears. "I simply asked you a question. I assume Sherwood keeps in contact with *you*. Why not share any news of my husband with me?"

He had not heard from Sherwood Trimble since a few weeks after Evangeline arrived. "Surely he has written to you."

In a whirl of lavender satin, Evangeline turned to Ross. She breathed loudly. "You just don't know, do you? You don't understand. Despite all the hints I've given you, you will not heed the signs, you poor, foolish man."

Zebediah took several steps toward her.

Artemis dumped his packages on a fine marquetry table.

"Oh, my lady," Finch said, going to the other woman, who surprised Ross by patting Finch's hand and pushing her quite gently away.

Evangeline looked only at Ross. "You do not see when a heart is broken and yearning. And you do not begin to hear the warning that may only be hinted at. You are hardheaded, and when you reap the benefit of your blindness you will still wonder what has happened—even though you were given opportunities—"

Artemis made an amazing move. He took Evangeline's hand and slapped it down on top of his left arm. He held it there and led her toward the door with a parody of formal, toe-pointing steps. "You'll excuse us, I'm sure," he said in artificially nasal tones. "Her Ladyship ain't herself. If Mr. Swift would 'elp, we'll escort her to her rooms."

Zebediah shot forward and took Artemis's place. He said, "Come along, Your Ladyship. You have done too much with this outing of yours. I should have insisted you not go. Come, we must get you upstairs at once."

"I shall write to Sherwood in the morning," Ross said. "And ask him to come to at least visit you. He would be most concerned if he knew how you are."

"He would *not*," Evangeline said, and the tears broke free. She allowed Zebediah to urge her toward the vestibule. "And I don't care. I do not want to hear from him again. Not *ever*. And I'm *never* going back to India."

❧ Chapter 21 ❧

When she was too tired, and too frantic to wait a second longer for Ross to speak, Finch said, "What are we to do? How can we force their hand without endangering Latimer any further?"

Ross had shed his rough coat and wore a gray shirt of some cheap cloth tucked into black-wool trousers. Despite the poor manner of dress, he stood tall and straight and exuded confidence even if he did appear preoccupied.

"Lady Evangeline, Ross. She was so upset."

"Upset and a great puzzle," he said thoughtfully. "I have decisions to make there. What is her part in all this? I rather think I have just seen a clever act intended to win my attention—and my carelessness. But we shall see."

The buttons were missing from his shirtsleeves, and he rolled the cuffs back over strong-looking forearms where fine, dark hair grew. His hands were large, his fingers long.

Even the smallest detail about him captivated Finch. She

looked away and said, "Artemis was trying to get you to speak of getting your shipments and going away."

"Really?" She received an impatient stare. "Did you think I hadn't noted that? The man's a fool."

"I knew you had. I was merely reiterating the fact. Why didn't he ask you for what he wants? Why didn't he say he's got Latimer?"

"I'm not sure." He screwed up his eyes. "I'd thought they would all feel powerful enough to lay out exactly what they wanted and why they thought I would give it to them. They might even have used your presence to press their advantage. There are many who think a man will be swayed by a woman's tears. That they didn't mention Latimer makes me wonder about the exact lay of the land."

Finch pressed a hand into her stomach and willed the flopping inside to stop. "If they've . . . If they've done something awful to him, they might not be able to hand him over. Perhaps that's the reason."

Ross's response was, "Where the hell is Jennings? Someone has to be in Whitechapel in case there's a delivery."

"Delivery of what, exactly?" she asked, not really expecting an answer. "Will you please tell me what it is that is worth my brother's life?"

"So that I can risk their capturing you and making you talk?" He strode to her and braced a hand on the mantel to lean over in a threatening stance.

"Your business is all you care about," she told him, holding back tears. "You would sacrifice anything to get what you want, wouldn't you? You'd let my brother die, wouldn't you?"

He was silent so long that Finch could no longer be strong. She put her face in her hands and took great breaths through her mouth. She had her answer. "He is gentle," she said. Tears wetted her fingers. "Not weak. Oh, no, not weak at all. He had the courage to stand up to our father and tell him he would not give up his dreams in order to go into the family business. Father is a hard man. But it isn't important anymore. Only Latimer matters to me now."

"He matters to me, too," Ross said, his voice low. "I will try to make you understand."

"You don't have to. You don't owe me an explanation. We wanted your trade, and we sought it. You didn't intend for any of this to happen."

"Please don't cry, Finch. Please. I can't bear it."

She folded her arms over her stomach and rocked. "Forgive me. I'm usually stronger than this."

"You aren't usually terrified for your brother's life."

His gentleness, and the despair she heard in his words, only made it more difficult to stem the tears.

He touched the side of her face, and she caught her breath. Then he stroked her hair softly. "You have a good mind, Finch. You will have gathered that I am awaiting something that is very valuable in itself, and that it is arriving in parts. My concern becomes that it should all be here by now, not that I intend to allow all of the pieces to be in one place at the same time—particularly not if they are with me. The instant that were to happen, and they—and whoever they work for—found out, my life would be forfeit."

"My brother—"

"For *God's* sake. Don't you think I already suffer thinking that Latimer is in dire danger because of a matter that is no affair of his? Do you think it was my intent to drag him into danger?"

She stood up, careful to step back as she did so and put some distance between them. "I am trying to think well of you. I've said as much. And I must take responsibility for our decision to do business with you. But when you asked Latimer to deal with these matters for you, you were aware of the risks. You knew that it was possible he might suffer— and that I might suffer. I believe everything you have done"—she marshaled all her strength to finish—"everything you have done with Latimer, and with me, has been some part of your master plan to gain the ends you seek. We could not know the risks, could we?"

His features darkened. He looked over his shoulder as if to be certain the door was tightly closed. "Keep your voice down," he said. "If you thought me so vicious, why have you found it so pleasant to enter into our lovemaking?"

She blushed furiously but made no attempt to hide the fact. "I do not think you a bad man."

"Thank you for that, I suppose."

"Let me finish, please. I do not think you a bad man. I do think you are a single-minded one, and you will do what you must to fulfil the promises—the contracts into which you have entered. I am not the type of woman you would seek out. Please do not protest. We both know that is true."

He seized her so abruptly, she lost her footing and threw her arms around him to stop herself from falling.

"You are driving me mad," he said through his teeth. "No, you are not the type of woman I have sought out in the past. My loss. But perhaps I have never met a woman like you. In fact I know that to be true. It is also true that I was not looking for one. I would have if I'd known the excitement—and the deep comfort—one such as you can bring."

She stared up at him, but tears clogged her throat, and she couldn't speak.

Slowly, as if he feared some violent drive within him, he brought his mouth down to hers, and as he did so his eyes squeezed tightly shut. The kiss made her shudder. He kissed her with anger, yet with restraint, and then with all the energy he could no longer hold back. Finch spread her fingers on his back and felt hard muscle contract there. He overpowered her, and she willingly gave herself up to his strength.

He raised his face and stared down at her, his eyes dark and frightening. But then he kissed her again, drew her up to him with such force that only her toes touched the floor. She felt the struggle within him.

"No," she managed to say, turning her face from him.

"No. You don't want this. You don't want to need me in any way. You fear that I may make you vulnerable when you have sworn to need no one."

He grew so still that he stopped her heart. When she dared look at him, her throat felt so tight she could not breathe at all.

"You see into my mind," he said. "Into my heart. Perhaps at another time, in another place . . . We cannot always have what we want. And sometimes what we want is seductive only because it is unattainable."

His words hurt her, but she would not show him how much.

"Truthfully I don't think there is another woman like you, Finch. But we are cursed by the worst timing in the world. I will attempt to tell you some of what is happening without giving you enough information to endanger you.

"These valuable shipments I await are the sign of royal entitlement. They are as significant as a coronation crown. When the pieces are assembled, they form a certain treasure that is brought forth on the occasion of a royal death in a distant principality. They are produced by the heir to the throne, and the people take it as a sign of from the gods that all is well. A great ceremony is held, and this object—in the hands of the successor—strikes confidence into the hearts of the people. Should it not be present, well then, they would be adrift. They would riot. The country would be cast into civil war and thousands would die. If, on the other hand, the sacred sign should appear in the possession of another, the people would likely take that as a sign that the throne had been passed, in the name of the gods, to that man.

"There is a man, an evil, power-hungry man, who seeks to acquire this thing and claim the throne. The present royal leader employed me to dismantle and remove the item from harm's way and to return it at his death—which is imminent. The ruler is seriously ill."

Fascinated, Finch drank in every word. "But if this place

is far, how will you get this—this *thing* there at the right time?"

"There is a period of mourning. Then the successor decides when to call for the great ceremony and claim the throne. He will not do so until I arrive."

"Who is the evil man?"

"If I knew that, I would hunt him down. He has managed to keep his identity a secret. I do believe Zebediah, with his fool, Artemis, acts on behalf of the would-be pretender."

Thrones, and sacred signs, and evil plots to overthrow kingdoms? These were not the stuff of a simple Cornishwoman's life. "The man who hired you? This king? He knows who this man is. Why didn't he tell you?"

"He doesn't know." Ross rubbed the space between his dark eyebrows and winced as if he might be in pain. "A faithful servant brought him the information."

"Does your head hurt, Ross? Should you prefer less light?"

He dropped his hand from his forehead. "No. Thank you."

She did not believe him. "Perhaps you'd like to sit down? You must be tired."

His slight smile pleased rather than offended her. "You are dear, my Finch. Very dear. Kind little bird trying to take care of an ill-tempered tiger."

She was dear? She was *his* Finch? How confused he might make a less sensible woman. "If I were you, I might not have likened myself to a tiger, do you think?" Before he could respond, she continued, "What if the story wasn't true?"

"You are relentless, miss. The servant who told the story was shot by someone who escaped afterward. The murder was committed just as the servant was about to reveal the identity of the enemy."

"You have told me so much," Finch said, wiggling still-damp toes inside her slippers. "Why not—"

"I have also not told you a great many things. I am certain that even our *friends* do not know what it is that they seek.

If they did, they would not have brought that ridiculous tiger here."

"Zebediah knew it was not the right thing. And he said it was in seven parts. And that it had something to do with tigers. I know the tiger thing is true because of the way you reacted after I was attacked and they gave me that strange message."

"He does not know what those seven parts construct. I would wager my life on that."

"So you will wait until you have all of them, then you will take them somewhere to wait for the right moment to return to . . . to whatever this place is." And she would never see him again. Or if he did return to Mayfair Square, there would be no reason for them to be together again.

"That is the plan."

"I see." She made a poor attempt at a smile, gave up, and bowed her head. "Why did you ask me to work for you in this house?"

He was silent a while. Then he said, "For two reasons. The first was that I wanted to keep my eye on you and Latimer, and I thought having you here would help me do so. Secondly, I wanted you near me."

She blinked. Wretched tears gathered in her eyes again, but she would not shame herself afresh by letting him see them.

"I wanted you near me because I . . . I knew I was attracted to you."

"I see." No doubt he was attracted to a great many women, but he had chosen never to be bound to one. "I was attracted to you, also. And I have enjoyed being close to you. I am very aware of what a jaded female that makes me, but I have no regrets." Except that he did not, could not love her, while she already loved him so very much. She shouldn't love him. He had brought nothing but trouble.

"You could never be jaded."

A firm knock on the door sent Finch leaping away from Ross, who frowned and shook a finger at her. "I might think you were ashamed to be with me, miss," he said, then, "Come."

Bessinger entered. "It's almost two in the morning, my lord."

"Yes." Ross turned questioningly toward the butler. "Your point, Bessinger?"

"We have a *caller*. A Mr. Adam Chillworth, who says he's from Number 7 and looking for you and Miss More."

"You know Mr. Chillworth is from Number 7," Ross said, pleasantly enough. "Kindly show him in."

More haggard than ever, Mr. Chillworth came into the room. He offered a sheepish smile. His head was bare, and he ran his fingers through long, rumpled dark curls. "Excuse the hour," he said formally, making a bow that amazed Finch since she'd never seen him do such a thing before. "I hope you don't mind my coming to you with a question, Your Lordship."

Finch wrinkled her nose in puzzlement.

"Not at all," Ross said, and Finch couldn't bring herself to look at him.

"Yes, well," Mr. Chillworth began, "I understand you have some very fine paintings in your collection."

"True," Ross said.

"Yes, well." Mr. Chillworth looked at Finch. He stuck his head forward on his neck as if trying to see her more clearly without getting closer. But he gave up the effort and took several steps toward her. "I was wondering if you might consider showing some of them to me."

Finch ached for him. The excuse for being here was bizarre, yet what else might he have said, other than to demand an accounting of what Finch was doing there, alone, in the company of a man to whom she was not related?

"I'd be delighted," Ross said, and she blessed him for his kind, reasonable tone. He gave no sign of recognizing the ridiculous nature of both the visit and the request.

"Good evening to you, Miss More," Mr. Chillworth said, growing even closer. He really did have wonderful eyes.

They were a dark gray color and deep-set. It was little wonder that Meg found so many excuses to spend time with him.

"Good evening, Mr. Chillworth," Finch said.

"Are you well?"

"Quite well, thank you."

He gave her a significant stare. "Nothing has occurred which you would like to tell me about? Nothing that I should resolve?"

In other words, was she here against her will? "There's nothing, Mr. Chillworth. But I thank you for your concern."

"You must be tired."

"Not especially."

He attempted to put himself where Ross could not see his face. Then Mr. Chillworth raised his well-shaped brows and gave her a meaningful stare. "I'm sure His Lordship will be pleased to let me take you home."

"Oh, it's not late," Finch said with an airy wave. "And I do have to stay here, at least presently."

Mr. Chillworth looked stricken. He dropped his voice. "Where is Latimer?"

Ross walked to stand where he could see Mr. Chillworth. "Latimer had to travel north to buy some items he felt he couldn't pass up. We're hoping he'll be back shortly."

"Miss More can wait in her own bed," Mr. Chillworth said, and immediately turned a dull red. "I mean she can return to her home to wait for her brother. Much more suitable. I will be glad to take her there."

Another knock on the door saved Finch from dredging up more excuses to remain.

Bessinger merely poked his head around the door this time. "Miss Meg Smiles. Will you see her, my lord?"

"Send her in." Ross grinned openly.

Wearing a gown and cape made of wool the color of bright oranges, a gown Finch knew Meg had sewn for herself, she slipped quickly into the room and hurried to Mr. Chillworth's side. Her pretty face was quite pale but with bright spots high on her cheeks. Her brown eyes were as shiny as her hair. She gave Finch a small, worried smile.

"Hello, Meg," Finch said. "You know His Lordship?"

"We've met. I hope you will forgive the intrusion, my lord, but I thought I should pop over and see if there was anything I could do to help."

Finch almost groaned aloud.

"With what, Miss Smiles?" Ross asked.

She shrugged, holding her shoulders at her ears and pushing out her pretty mouth. "Ooh, with whatever, I suppose. We've been neighbors a very long time, and I've been remiss. I should have paid a call a long time ago but, well, sometimes we get busy and allow simple courtesies to slip. I'm sure you understand what I mean."

"Hmm. Simple courtesies slip. Yes."

"So, since we all seem to have decided on a late night, I decided to remedy the omission." She smiled at him, charmingly, Finch thought. "And here I am."

"Here you are."

"Is there anything?"

Ross's attention flickered away momentarily, then back to Meg's face. "Is there anything, Miss Smiles?"

"That I could do to help. Like keep Finch company on her way home?"

Mr. Chillworth looked at Meg.

Ross looked at Meg.

Meg blinked rapidly and swayed a little from foot to foot.

"Thank you, Meg," Finch said, her heart full at the thought that these people who had been strangers such a short time ago had come to care so for her. They cared enough to risk embarrassment in order to help her. "Latimer is to return here, and I am to wait for him."

Meg moved closer to Mr. Chillworth, who held the lapels of his coat and frowned mightily, and said, "In Mr. More's absence I think it appropriate for me to point out that it isn't suitable for you to be here, Miss More. I know I need not explain why."

"Come home with us, Finch," Meg said, abandoning any attempt at subterfuge. "Sibyl and I have been so worried. We've all been worried. We've watched for you from Number 7 for hours. Then, when we saw you come in that horrid cart, we were relieved, but beside ourselves at the same time. What has happened to you? Your clothes?"

Finch glanced at Ross, prepared to stop him from reiterating their preposterous story. He drew his brows down and shook his head slightly. She paused—expecting him to suggest that she go with them, perhaps? When he didn't, Finch said, "All I can say is that you need not worry about me. I am quite safe." She was safe, except from herself, she decided. "Please go home and tell the rest that I am here because I must be here, and I will return just as soon as I can."

"But, Finch," Meg said, a desperate light in her eyes, "you *are* at risk. Your reputation is at risk. We cannot leave without you, can we, Adam?"

"Absolutely not."

The next arrival didn't knock. Jennings came into the red salon, his worried expression out of keeping with his usual calm demeanor. He went to Ross, and Finch actually saw a silent message pass between them. Ross lowered his head and Jennings spoke into his ear. Glancing up, Ross's eyes settled on nothing until he looked at Finch.

She swallowed and felt fevered. He might also be trying to include her in his private exchange with Jennings.

A moment, and he looked at his valet, then rested a hand on his arm, clearly staying him. Finch barely restrained herself from asking if there was news of Latimer.

"Mr. Chillworth," Ross said, "and Miss Smiles. Thank you for coming, and for showing such concern for Miss More. Since you have no responsibility for her, I'm sure she understands how generous you are. However you have no need to be frightened for her. You may know that Miss More is now employed by me and quite accustomed to this household. Latimer and I are by way of being business associates. He is to return here. Shortly, we hope. Miss More will come to Number 7 with him. Also, there is another lady in residence here—in case the question of a chaperone concerns you."

His words were pleasant, but he spoke in a manner that made it clear there would be no further discussion.

Meg set her jaw so firmly that Finch feared she might continue to argue, but Mr. Chillworth took her by the arm and set off for the door. Once there he turned to Finch, and said, "We are close by."

They left, with Meg trotting to keep up with her companion's long strides. She craned her neck to see Finch until there was no further possibility of doing so.

At last the front door slammed and Finch pressed her hands to her cheeks. "What has happened, Jennings? Please don't keep it from me. It's Latimer, isn't it? You've found something out?"

"Bring him in, Jennings," Ross said. "Be quick, man. We don't want them to know he's here."

Jennings went not to the vestibule, but to a door in the corner of the room. Finch had never seen it used before. He opened it and disappeared into darkness beyond.

She clutched her hands together in an agony of anticipation. "Is he injured? Is he ill?"

"Oh, Finch!" Ross set his teeth and reached a hand toward her. "Forgive me. Of course you thought—"

"Here he is, m'lord," Jennings said.

Wearing a coat with a bulging hem that touched the floor, and bleeding from a wound on his brow, Hayden stumbled into the room.

§ Chapter 22 §

"You're wearing one green and one pink slipper," Zebediah said.

Evangeline pulled her cloak and night rail free of her feet. "Hold the candle nearer." When he did so, she told him, "Lavender, not pink." She was beyond shame at such an insignificant piece of nonsense. Her very future hovered on the brink of ruin—if not slightly beyond the brink—and she must act now or accept whatever disaster swept her into its claws.

The heavy evening cloak made her overheated, but her alternative was to remove it and conduct this conversation in her nightclothes. No doubt Zebediah would enjoy that. She did take off the toque and toss it aside.

"Your friend, Artemis, is an odious man," she said, rapidly formulating how she should guide this exchange. She would guide it, and she must do so unerringly or her future would almost certainly become one of utter misery and suffering—if she were allowed to live at all.

"We are not here to discuss Artemis." Zebediah spared her the briefest of steady glances with his dark, dark eyes and went to stand to one side of a window in the attic storeroom to which he'd lead her without explanation.

"What are you watching for?" she asked him. "And why did you bring me here?"

"Do not worry yourself about my watchfulness. A habit, nothing more. I must always be aware of anyone who might come or go from this house and tonight there have been a good many visitors. As to my reason for bringing you here? We are under scrutiny. The household staff expects us to be together in your rooms. To that end I brought you here where we may be certain they will not try to find, and overhear us. There are no servant quarters at this side of the attic, and what is stored in this room has probably been forgotten. We are completely alone. Before we leave, you will have a clear understanding of how you will behave in the future."

Evangeline's stomach made an unpleasant revolution, and her spine prickled. *Alone.* And since Artemis had been dispatched by Zebediah the moment they'd left the red salon, and no other person had seen them come up here, she was at this enigmatic man's mercy.

"I thought your reason for being here in London, in this house, was to protect Lord Kilrood from some awful threat. Sherwood told me that was why I must help you to find and keep a place here."

"You should always believe what your husband tells you."

She was being treated like a fool. "Of course I should, and I do. This is a discussion between two adults. You are here to protect Lord Kilrood?"

"Indeed I am."

"Then what is that creature Artemis about? What of his behavior this evening? Arriving and rushing me out into the night without even giving me time to dress. Then returning so that I was forced to make up a story that I doubt His Lordship believed. And proceeding to make such foolish remarks about *packages,* and taking a ship somewhere. How does this help protect the viscount?"

"Are you so very interested in protecting the viscount? Or are you not much more concerned with engaging that gentleman's interest in you because you think that—even as his mistress—you would enjoy a more exciting life than you do in India?"

"How dare you." She blessed the weak light given off by the single candle Zebediah had lighted. She did not want him to see her too clearly. "You know I am here on my husband's behalf to assist him in being of service to his dear friend, Viscount Kilrood."

"To assist Sherwood in being of assistance to His Lordship, or to be of assistance to His Lordship yourself?"

The man was relentless. Evangeline would not give him the satisfaction of seeing how much he offended her. Or frightened her. She took a sheet that had draped a large, leather chair, shook the dust from the sheet, wiped the chair perfunctorily, and sat down. She dropped the sheet and pulled a small footstool toward her. With her crossed heels firmly planted on this minor comfort, she laced her fingers together and resolved to wait in silence until Zebediah grew weary enough to, she hoped, become less than circumspect.

"Comfortable?" he asked.

"Quite, thank you. But I should appreciate your making haste with whatever you have to say. I'd like to go to my bed. You have not answered my question about that fool, Artemis."

"Nor do I intend to do so. There are things it is better you not know. Safer. For you."

She felt again the prickling along her spine. "It isn't for you to decide what I should or should not know. I think I must contact Sherwood and inform him of these developments." As she spoke the words, they were meant only as a threat to Zebediah. But now that she thought about it, perhaps if Sherwood saw her as attempting to help him, he might decide he should treat her more kindly.

"And what will you write to Sherwood? That you have openly tried to inveigle yourself into Lord Kilrood's good graces—his *intimate* graces? And that you have stated for all to hear that you have no intention of returning to your husband in India? I doubt he would take either of those announcements particularly well."

If she remained calm, she could manage to turn his unpleasantness against him. Sherwood did not treat her well. In fact, since only a few days after their marriage she had been at a loss to understand why he had wanted to marry her at all. His abuses were rarely physical, although they had been on occasion. Sherwood was more a master of the cruel verbal cuts designed to ruin her will, and her confidence.

"You are very thoughtful," Zebediah said, his deep voice soft enough to put her on her guard. "Do share your deepest thoughts with me. After all, your concerns are my concerns. Your welfare is my concern. I should like to know if there is anything I need to deal with for you."

He was a sly man. "Nothing, thank you. Except that I am saddened that you do not trust me. We are both on the same side, Zebediah."

She raised her face to see him, but he stood in front of the window, and what light came in that way, together with the flickering candlelight that was also behind him, cast his face in absolute shadow. His silhouette seemed to fill the little storeroom.

"I'm glad to know we are both on the same side," he said. "Although I should not have thought that was a matter in need of confirmation."

When Sherwood had told her his plan, Evangeline's first thought had been that he was in some sort of trouble—financial trouble—and needed to ingratiate himself with the wealthy Viscount Kilrood, to pave the way for asking his assistance. She no longer believed that. It was far more likely that Zebediah Swift, who might well be a man of considerable influence upon Sherwood, had persuaded him to assist in entering Ross's home for some reason quite different from the one he'd given Evangeline's husband. Why, he might even intend to commit some crime against Ross for which Sherwood—and even Evangeline—might later be blamed.

If Zebediah did have another agenda, she was likely to become a helpless victim swept away, perhaps disposed of, when she was no longer necessary to the man's plot. But if he did truly want to protect Ross from some danger, then her own salvation rested on being able to convince Zebediah to trust her, and to reveal his true intentions. In either event, she must concentrate on winning Zebediah over.

"So silent, my lady? I was sure you had weighty matters on your mind. Will you not share them with me?"

She would play a bold game tonight. It might be her only opportunity to do so. "Come closer, Zebediah. Please. I pretend I am a strong, confident woman. It isn't entirely so." It wasn't, Evangeline thought, so at all—not when she feared for her life. "Please come." She held up her hands, knowing he could see her relatively clearly.

He waited so long she became certain he would ignore her request. Then he came toward her and took her hands in his. His hands were large and cool. He gripped her fingers lightly.

"Thank you," she said. "It is difficult to be cast adrift with strangers. As it is, I was my widowed father's only child— a solitary child—and he was more than grateful when Sherwood asked for my hand. I am quite alone apart from Sherwood, and he is not here to put my fears to rest." Quite alone. Her father was in Egypt yet again and unreachable. She doubted she would see him, or hear from him, for a very long time, and in any case he would never help her cross her husband.

Zebediah increased the pressure on her hands a little. "You said this evening that you would not return to India. I take it you meant that you will not return to Sherwood?"

She must tread carefully here. "I am not well, Zebediah. Please do not question me about this now. The subject embarrasses me. But I intend to seek a doctor's care tomorrow. I have decided the climate in India is probably dangerous for me. If the doctor concurs, I must ask Sherwood to consider returning to England to live."

Zebediah's thumbs, passing back and forth over her fingers, sent a shock that didn't stop on its way to her toes. "We both know Sherwood will never give up India," he said.

She felt a trifle breathless, and the reaction shocked her. "Then I must request that he agree to allow me to take up permanent residence here. Of course I shall hope that he will visit me as often as he can." And provide her with a home and set her up suitably. After all, his own reputation mattered to him, and it would not look well if he forced a sickly wife to fade away in a country to which she was unsuited.

"When do you intend to put these requests to your husband?"

What did she hear in his voice, Evangeline wondered? Some personal interest that troubled him deeply, or merely preoccupation. "I'm not certain."

And what if Zebediah were actually interested in her?

She was becoming light-brained from so much stress and confusion. So what if the man was interested in her? She hated him and was convinced he had used Sherwood. He didn't want to admit to the meaning of Artemis's foolish comments because they would be revealing. No, she and Sherwood were Zebediah's pawns, and it was up to her to make sure of a satisfactory outcome to a potential debacle.

"May I suggest that you make no attempt to contact Sherwood directly until after my task here is complete? Of course, I will be happy to request a doctor's visit for you."

"Thank you." She thought fast. His touch grew warmer by the second, and her arms tingled. And her belly. "Will you please trust me, Zebediah? Will you tell me what you truly intend here? I am, after all, your ally. Oh, I have not been permitted to share the details of what is afoot, but perhaps if I was, I could be more helpful."

"You are helpful because you allow me to remain in this house."

Another thought occurred to her. If she could learn exactly what Zebediah intended, and if it was, as she suspected, to bring Ross down rather than to protect him—from whatever—then perhaps she could be instrumental in saving Ross. If such a wonderful thing were to happen, then Ross would know she was his friend and would undoubtedly offer to be her protector in London while Sherwood was in India. And she would win Sherwood's admiration for saving the day. Then surely, since he didn't really like having a wife at all (and he had a mistress of many years standing to deal with his physical needs), he would be delighted to agree to support Evangeline in London.

She began to feel hopeful, and excited.

"What are you thinking?"

Zebediah had moved silently closer and stood over her, looking down. She glanced up and jumped. Faint, flickering candlelight played over his intent features. The light filled shadows around his eyes and beneath his cheekbones. The beard and mustache covered much of his lower face, but she could still make out the sensual curve of his mouth, and the glint of his teeth where his lips were slightly parted.

His next move startled her completely. He took her hands to his mouth and kissed her fingers, each one, slowly.

Breath caught in Evangeline's chest, and she dared not move.

When he had finished, he looked down at her and she saw where muscles in his face jerked. The man was far from unattractive. Rather he was alluring in a dangerous, almost-animal manner. Beneath his coldness she felt passion, and her body flamed.

Evangeline shifted a little in the chair. So much the better if she could find him—interesting. That would make any overture she must offer, or accept from him, so much less objectionable, not, of course, that she would in any manner jeopardize her respectability.

"Sherwood is a fortunate man," he said in a voice even deeper than she had ever heard him use before. "You are a beautiful, desirable woman. He may be a fool to allow you out of his sight."

This was a departure from his usual, openly sexual manner toward her—when he wasn't observed, naturally. "Thank you." She ought to remove her hands but found that her desire to leave them in his was too great.

She would turn the tables on him. "What are you thinking, Zebediah?"

"That I should like to kiss you," he said without hesitation.

Not a single word would take form for Evangeline. If she did open her mouth, she might say something she would forever regret, and she might also lose her newfound plans for the near future.

He released her, but only for long enough to grasp her by the waist and lift her to her feet. He was such a tall, broad man that he entirely eclipsed the window. She bent her neck, and promptly found herself pressed firmly against him. He took off the cloak and let it fall, then held her by the waist again.

"Look at me, Evangeline."

It was the first time he had used so familiar a form of address. "I cannot see you," she said, and swallowed. "This is inappropriate. I am a married woman."

"Do you love your husband?"

She found breathing ever more difficult. "I am married to Sherwood Trimble. We both know that it would be inappropriate for me to answer your questions more directly."

"Unless you wanted to," he said. He didn't attempt to touch her other than where he held her by the waist.

She could only be commended for sacrificing herself and allowing him to think she was enamored of him. Her one reason would be to make him trust her enough to become careless. Then she would be able to serve Sherwood and Ross the better.

"I don't ask you to abandon yourself to me entirely. Not yet."

Her heart felt fluttery. And other parts of her swelled, grew moist, ached. Sherwood never made her feel this way. He came to her from his bedchamber in the middle of the night, lifted her gown to . . . to perform his husbandly duties which didn't seem to bring him more than fleeting, groaning, sweating relief. And quickly afterward he left again. When he was gone she invariably cried and wished he would never come again.

"Evangeline. This would be our secret—this small comfort we might bring each other."

Small comfort. Evangeline trembled all over. "I don't understand you."

"Will you allow me to kiss you?"

She did not, must not trust him. But if it would ease her way, she would do as he asked. Raising her face, she saw the gleam of candlelight in his eyes and let out a small cry. But then she closed her own eyes, rose to her toes, and offered him her mouth.

His kiss was not as she had expected. There was restrained ardor, finesse, a deeply arousing play of his lips over hers. Evangeline had not known these before, and she leaned against him to give herself up to the sensation. When she opened her mouth and wrapped her arms around his neck, his hands finally moved. He covered her bottom and pressed her hips against him. The solid feel of his reaction to her swept away any shred of remaining reserve. She kissed him with abandon, and sobbed aloud when he bent her backward to explore her breasts with his tongue and teeth through the sheer lawn of her night rail.

Panting, covering the damp fabric where his mouth had been with his hands, he stood straight. "I will stand by my word. I will not ask you more than you are willing to give."

Her mind refused to clear. Dimly she thought about the man. These were not the scruples of an opportunist. Perhaps his goals were the same as Sherwood's after all. But now there were more tangled concerns. What she felt for him, and was certain he felt for her, might be a purely physical attraction—an approaching obsession, even. It was there and likely to force them together again. The next time he might not be able to summon up these fine principles she'd never guessed he had. What then?

"What if I don't want you to stand by your word? What if I want you? Really want you?"

He groaned and began kissing her again. She would not return to India. She would live in London where there was no reason to suppose she should live the life of a nun.

Zebediah grew still. He placed his mouth beside her ear, and said, "Be silent. Not a sound. There's someone outside the door."

Evangeline was instantly rigid. She clutched him to her and was grateful for his return of the pressure. A faint, scratching sound ensued.

"Mice," she said, horrified, gripping him even tighter. "I cannot abide them."

His response was to swing her up into his arms. But seconds later he set her down in the chair again. "Stay there."

She feared he would leave her alone, but he went to the door and returned at once to bend over the candle and unfold a piece of paper. "Pushed under the door," he said shortly.

Evangeline's hands went to her throat. "Someone knows we're here? Oh, what shall we do? What if they were listening to what we said?"

"Calm yourself. I must read this." He scanned whatever had been written, folded the paper, and pushed it into a pocket. "You must return to your rooms at once and put on appropriate clothing. We are going out."

"Out?" She rose to her feet. "At this hour?"

"Do as I ask you, please. I'll explain on the way. I'll get the coach."

"But where are we going?"

He sighed and took out the paper again. He opened it, and read, "Come to me at Piccadilly. Bring Lady Evangeline with you . . ." Pausing, he picked up her cloak. "You will want to dress suitably. Dark clothing that will draw no particularly attention."

"But . . . Tell me what else it says. Who wrote it? Why would we go now?"

"Because we must. It says, "Wait until I arrive, no matter how long that may be. And it's signed, Sherwood Trimble.""

❧ Chapter 23 ❧

The boy's coat stretched over his bulging body and hung as if weighted. His thin neck protruded from a collar that was much too large. Also protruding from that collar was the head of a small and exceedingly scruffy dog.

"Let's have you sitting down, my boy," Ross said, and he tried to take Hayden by the arm.

"I gotta go quick. I just come to give you somethin'." He held the dog in place and tugged at his coat.

"You will do as His Lordship tells you," Finch said, her voice high with tension. "Sit *down* at once. And stop strangling that dear little dog."

Hayden only clutched the animal harder. "She's my dog."

"I didn't say she wasn't," Finch told him. She hurried to slip a hand beneath Hayden's arm and half led, half dragged him to sit in the chair she'd vacated near the fire.

"It's a wee bit o' a smelly thing, miss," Jennings said, sounding apologetic as if he were responsible for the odor. "The boy's in need o' care, but ye're no' t'trouble yoursel' about it. Tell His Lordship what ye came for, laddie, and I'll clean your head before ye go."

"I'll deal with this, Jennings," Finch said. "I'll just need warm water and some cloths, please. And something for the dog to drink."

"I 'ad to let Finch go, milord," Hayden said, his expression fearful. "She was sick, so I 'ad to untie her."

Ross did his best to smile at the boy. A headache had begun some time ago, but he was determined not to allow the pain to overwhelm him. "I understand your dilemma," he said. "Don't give it another thought. What was it you had to tell me?"

"Not until that wound has been cleaned," Finch said, placing herself in front of Hayden and planting her feet apart. "He should be put to bed, and since I won't leave until . . . A bed must be found for him here."

The woman could be both inappropriate and dashed annoying.

"I'll go for the water then," Jennings said, and slipped quickly away.

"Rat deserting the ship," Ross muttered, just in time to be confronted with Bessinger yet again. "What is it this time, man?" Little wonder he had a headache.

Bessinger managed the feat of looking disgusted and bored at the same time. "*Visitors*, my lord. Lady Hester Bingham and Mr. Hunter Lloyd from Number 7." The butler noticed Hayden, and his mouth dropped open.

"Thank you, Bessinger," Ross said, preparing to say he wasn't receiving. Unfortunately, Lady Hester swept into the salon, black taffeta rustling, jet beads clicking, Hunter Lloyd at her heel.

Bessinger rolled his eyes and retreated.

"Lord Kilrood," Lady Hester said without preamble, "are you aware that you are guilty of holding a single woman against her will?"

"Aunt," Hunter said.

"I will handle this, Hunter. Well, my lord, what have you to say for yourself?"

"This is a zoo," Ross said, "a bloody zoo."

"You don't understand, Lady Hester." Finch came forward, and when she stood in front of Ross, she cast him a withering glance over her shoulder. "I am not being held against my will. I already told Meg Smiles and Mr. Chillworth as much. I am here to wait for Latimer's return and—and because I have promised I will help His Lordship with a particularly difficult and unexpected development."

Looking most appealing in black considering the extremely late hour, Lady Hester ignored Ross now and concentrated on Finch. "I have heard all this nonsense about waiting for Latimer, and I want you to know that I don't believe a word of it." Her Ladyship spared Ross an accusing glance. "This man is clearly a fornicator."

"I say, Aunt, isn't that a bit strong?" Hunter said. "His Lordship isn't married, anyway."

"As far as we know. He has bewitched a simple country girl. No doubt he has ravished her, heaped blame and shame upon her—"

"I say, Aunt—"

"Don't interrupt me again, Hunter. Now she is so bewildered, and possibly bewitched by the devil—"

"*Aunt.*"

"As I was saying. No doubt her head has been quite turned by the attentions of a—well—a handsome, powerful man with whom she believes herself to be in love." She struck a haughty pose fraught with disapproval. "Stuff and nonsense. You should be ashamed of yourself, my lord." To underscore the import of her words, she produced a gold lorgnette with which she pointed at him before using it to examine Finch more closely. "You look dreadful, my dear."

Hunter showed signs of a struggle with laughter, and Ross raised a brow at the man. "My aunt is very fond of Finch," he said, grinning. "We all are. She's had Number 7 in an uproar, I can tell you. A fellow couldn't get any sleep if he wanted to."

"Sorry to hear that," Ross said. If he tried to get Finch to go home with these two, she would never forgive him. And he didn't want her to go, dash it.

"Very well." Finch's tone suggested she was about to reveal something momentous. "I am forced to expose the rest of what is happening here tonight—or should I say, this morning? It's true that I am waiting for my brother. It is *not* true that Viscount Kilrood has, well, he hasn't done anything to force me to stay."

"Thank you for saying that," Ross told her.

She inclined her head regally as if she were not dressed in peasant rags. "This is Hayden," she said, standing aside so that the visitors could see the boy huddled by the fire.

Lady Hester clapped a hand over her mouth and showed signs of swooning.

"The poor boy was sent here from Scotland all on his own," Finch said.

Hayden, who hadn't uttered a word since the arrival of Ross's latest visitors said, "I were sent?"

"Hush, now, Hayden," Finch said. "You're not up to saying anything more. He has been kept in quite dreadful conditions, Lady Hester. Deprived—" The dog's abrupt, soprano bark made her wince. "You can see the child barely speaks English, or not the sort of English we understand."

" 'Ere," Hayden said. "Wha—"

"Silence!" Finch's sudden order clearly shocked her as much as it did the "refugee" from Scotland. She gathered herself. "He is exhausted. But I'm sure you see that all this puts His Lordship in a dither."

"Dither" was not a term Ross had ever expected to hear used in reference to himself, but he knew better than to complain—yet.

Lady Hester's expression grew penetrating. She looked at Hayden, then at Ross. "Why should the boy be here with you?"

"He has nowhere else to go," Finch said. "So Viscount Kilrood was forced to accept him. He will care for him, of course, but a woman's touch is needed."

Ross wished he were anywhere but in this room. Fighting hand-to-hand in the dark with knife-wielding assassins was something he understood. The warfare he confronted here was beyond his comprehension.

Lady Hester had turned first a paler shade, then quite pink. She fumbled until she managed to put her lorgnette away. "I cannot imagine what you mean, Finch."

"Hunter," Finch said, "I do think you should take Lady Hester home. It's very late, and this is too much for her. His Lordship will not shirk his responsibilities. A room is being made ready for the child. And until someone can be retained to attend to easing his way into a life to which he has never been accustomed, well naturally I agreed to stay and take care of him."

"I see," Lady Hester said (which Ross sincerely hoped she did). "And I must say, my lord, that I am shocked. But it is not for me to judge such things. The young do foolish things and clearly you are very young in spirit." (She didn't understand, but how could she?)

Ross considered pleading his innocence, but the thought of continuing this scene longer was a worse evil. "Good night to you, then," he said, bowing.

"Are you coming, Finch?" Lady Hester said.

"Of course not. I've just explained that I am needed here."

Her Ladyship showed signs of arguing. Instead, she shook her head and made a stately exit.

Hunter followed but paused at the door, and said in low tones, "Incredible. I thought I'd seen everything, but that was a hash that may break all records." With another grin, and a tap of his cane to his brow, he left, closing the door behind him.

"I'm damned," Ross said.

"Not in front of the boy," Finch told him promptly.

By God she treated him like a husband. He was momentarily confused at the thought.

"As soon as I clean the wound, a room must be found for him, and clean clothes. And he needs food. And his little dog—what is the dog's name, Hayden?"

"Oswin."

"Oswin?" Finch said. "What a very unusual name for a dog."

"I 'eard a gent call another gent that once. 'E said it wasn't a name 'e'd like to 'ave. Then the other gent laughed, and said, 'Friends of the gods, I am? You should a known. I'm a blessing. That's what Oswin means.' They laughed then, and the first one says, 'Blessed you are indeed. More endowed than any I've seen.' Somethin' like that. So when I saw Oswin, I called 'er that. Because she blessed me, see. She's the best dog in the world. When I 'ave to go away, she's always waitin' for me when I get back. She never runs away." The animal's eyes resembled shiny, oversize black currants, and they were turned adoringly up at her master.

If Ross had been inclined to chuckle, a glance at the tears that welled in Finch's eyes would have stopped him.

"I didn't come to cause no more trouble," Hayden said. "I come to bring you what's yours."

"You are not to talk until you've been bathed and fed," Finch said. "Oswin, too."

Hayden shrank back in the chair. "Bathed? I don't need no one to bathe me."

"Why does your coat look like that? Take it off."

The boy all but curled himself up in the chair. "I don't want to."

"He's got other clothes on underneath, haven't you?" Ross asked kindly.

Hayden nodded. The dog stuck out a pink tongue and licked his chin. "I'm movin' on, see. Stoppin' to see you and thank you for what you did for me, and movin' on."

"So you have your possessions with you? You're wearing all the clothes you have? And what you own is about you?"

Without meeting Ross's eyes, Hayden said, "Yes."

Finch looked stricken. She went to Hayden and knelt beside him. "I'm sorry. I only made up that story about why you're here for my own benefit. I needed an excuse to stay. Where is your mother? I thought you might be alone in Whitechapel, but surely you have a mother and father somewhere."

"Not as I know. Not a father, anyway. Me mum's dead. I stayed in the 'ouse after she died because no one bothered me there most of the time. But I can look after myself. I 'ave since I was ten. I'm fifteen now." He sounded proud, and Ross supposed he ought to be proud of surviving alone in a city like London.

Jennings came in with a basin of water, which he gave to Finch. She put it on the floor and went efficiently to work cleaning Hayden's wound.

Oswin-the-blessed wiggled and barked, the smallest, most pathetic excuse for a bark Ross had ever heard.

"Let me have Oswin," Finch said. "She needs to run around and have something to eat and drink."

Ross wasn't at all sure the running around idea was good, but he held his peace. Hayden reluctantly allowed Finch to take the creature, who, when completely revealed, resembled a mostly terrier with an unlikely tail that waved like a flag as the dog trotted about the room sniffing in a manner that unnerved Ross.

"She needs to do 'er business," Hayden said in matter-of-fact tones, at which Jennings swept her up and went through the door leading to a small passage and into the walled garden at the back of the house.

"Now," Ross said, watching Finch wash a very nasty gash just above Hayden's right eyebrow. "I don't want to put pressure on you, my boy, but I know you have something on your mind."

"He will not be allowed to leave, will he, Ross?" Finch asked. "Promise me you will find a bed and make sure he is not sent forth alone. Latimer is absentminded, but he is kind. I know he will help me find a way to give Hayden a home."

It was she who was kind. How was it that no other man had already stepped into poor old Greville's shoes with her? "He shall stay here until a suitable place is found for him."

"I'm not stayin'," Hayden said. "They takes boys like me and puts 'em in 'omes. I don't want to go into no 'ome."

"Neither shall you," Ross heard himself say with a sense of amazement. "I have given my word to Finch, and I never go back on my word. We will help you. How's that? We will not take your future out of your hands, but we will guide you."

"Thank you, Ross," Finch said, and her luminously grateful expression shamed him. She returned to gently removing dried blood and rinsing her cloth frequently. "You are tired. We are all tired. You will sleep well in a lovely, comfortable, clean bed. And have some good meals. Then we will talk about the future."

"But now we could talk about what you came to tell me?" Ross said with hope.

Wincing and clenching his teeth, Hayden closed his eyes, and Ross feared he might have some time to wait for his answer.

Jennings, with a satisfied countenance, returned with Oswin and set the creature down to continue her exploration of Ross's priceless rugs and furniture.

Hayden pulled a wad of dirty rag from his pocket, unwrapped it, and took out a crust of bread. This he crumbled onto the carpet and Oswin fell upon it, growling and snuffling as she devoured it all. When she finished—seconds later—not a speck remained.

"I went back to get me things," Hayden said. "I knew you was angry with me, and I didn't know if you would come after me, so I thought I'd better scarper."

"You have no need to fear Ross," Finch said.

He said, "No," without being certain what he might do to anyone at this point. His patience had worn close to nothing.

"I gets ready to go, see, when I 'ears footsteps in the alley. It's quiet there at that time, so I looks out and there's a cove, one of them from the docks I reckoned, goin' toward your warehouse, Miss Finch. So I slips out into the alley and runs along in the shadows until I can get across to 'ide against a wall and watch."

Ross grew alert. The boy had something to say, and it might be of importance.

"They comes in the night to make deliveries sometimes. Miss Finch's brother works late, and they knows they may get a coin or two for their trouble then. Anyways, I watched, and this man goes to the door and knocks. It opens, and I can't see who it is in there, but I know it can't be the mister because 'e's gone, ain't he? Then I thinks of the things what you said you was waitin' for, and I told meself someone else might be tryin' to get 'em."

The boy had a mind. "Go on," Ross told him quietly, anxious not to frighten him into silence again.

"The man from the docks says 'e's got some little pieces for Mr. More, and 'e 'olds out what looks like squares wrapped in oilcloth and tied with 'eavy twine. They 'ad labels on 'em. I saw 'em."

Ross's breath stuck in his throat. "Yes?"

"'Ands come out from inside. 'Ands in gloves. They was like claws. They grabbed, and I think the docker didn't like what 'e saw—or felt—because 'e drew back just a bit, and that's when I ran at 'im. I ran and pulled those bundles out of 'is 'ands. And 'e yells, ''Ere, 'ere, watcha think you're doin' then?' And that's when somethin' 'it me 'ard, and I went down on the stones with the bundles underneath me."

"Oh, Hayden," Finch said. "Please don't make him go on, Ross. He's had a dreadful shock." There was more in her expression. She stared up at him with desperation in her eyes. Tonight her freckles stood out on her pale skin, and her hair had dried to appear even more red. "I am so frightened."

He knew she spoke of her fear for Latimer. "Of course

you are." Telling her not to worry would be futile. "We must pray for some sign of how to proceed, and soon."

"I thought I was a goner," Hayden said. "I thought the docker would run and leave me to whoever it was what set on me, and 'e might 'ave, but he fell over me and there was a fight. Only I didn't stay to see what 'appened. I come straight 'ere. I'm not bad, Your Lordship. Nor unreliable. I brought you these."

He opened his coat, revealing more than one pair of ancient trousers worn at the same time and several garments knitted of rough wool and put on top of each other. Around his middle was tied a thick skein of mufflers.

The lining of the coat was torn. Hayden sank a hand and arm inside and scrabbled around until he produced what he'd promised, a bundle wrapped in oilskin and tied with twine—and with a label attached. Another followed, and another, and another. His heart pounding, Ross watched and said, "Make sure we cannot be interrupted, Jennings."

A bolt on the inside of the door shot home.

"There," Hayden said, with his treasures in his lap.

Ross took up a package, turned his back on the company and used his knife to cut the twine. He unrolled the oilcloth until he came to what seemed an interminable length of black velvet wound around and around. At last he could discard it, only to be confronted by black silk. He'd expected each protective covering because he'd done the wrapping himself, but still he all but tore the silk away, and then he couldn't speak for the awe he felt at what he held in his hands. He had seen it before, of course, but on that occasion his haste had been so great he had not taken time to admire the exquisite treasure that were the parts of the Sacred Box of Ranthus.

The glass with its waved patterns of black and gold shimmered. Stripes of a tiger. Backing the glass was a thick layer of solid gold that deepened the colors of the glass. The pieces would have to be welded together by a master, a master who could be completely trusted.

"Thank you, Hayden," he said, looking significantly at Jennings, who pressed his lips together and nodded. "You have done a service far beyond any you can imagine, and one day I shall be able to explain it all to you. Four," he said to Jennings, and shook his head slightly when he saw that the other man was about to mention that the piece in Ross's collection made five.

"Then there's the key," Finch said from behind him. "Doesn't that count as a piece?"

Ross closed his eyes for an instant. "Yes. How could I have forgotten?"

"So you have five. Only two more to come."

"Yes." Only one more.

"I couldn't 'elp it," Hayden said catching up Oswin and stuffing her back inside his coat as if he planned to bolt. "I dropped one, and I was too scared to go back for it."

§ Chapter 24 §

"The next time my ne'er-do-well relations get themselves into trouble, let them sink, say I. If I had not given my word to achieve what must be achieved on this occasion, I would leave them to founder at once. But I did give my word, and therefore shall complete this wretched task, no matter how long it may take.

"Connections in high places, and shrewd powers of deduction are most useful. Naturally I now know a great deal more than you do about everything that is afoot here. And most unsavory it is. Unsavory and fantastic.

"I shall overcome all obstacles, but this will not be easy. For a lesser person it would be impossible, but again I must give you some warnings and hope your principles will keep you from defying me—again.

"Ahead lie events I intend to guide and mold as only I would be able to guide and mold them. But some unfortunate, even some possibly terrible incidents are inevitable.

The course of this odyssey convinces me that all of these are bound to be part of what is to come.

"I, because of my obligations, cannot absent myself. In fact I'm sure I shall wish to be in more than one place at a time, so great will be the pressure upon my services.

"No such necessities face you.

"Bear in mind the embarrassment brought about by your prior salacious indiscretions, and avoid any repetition.

"The time will come for us to examine the degree of my success—and yours. I have a task with which to entrust you, but more of that at a less crucial moment."

§ Chapter 25 §

In a voluminous white cotton nightshirt, his face scrubbed, his damp curls partially slicked down, Hayden appeared younger, and thinner than ever. Roused by Bessinger, Mrs. Hastings had taken charge of household arrangements. After showing the expected disapproval of the situation, that lady had provided "the poor little thing" with a red woolen night-cap and a patchwork quilt she'd sewn herself and put away for, "well, just put away."

Tucked into a narrow bed in what had been a nursery during the tenure of the former owners, Hayden had discarded the nightcap. Drooping eyelids, which he forcibly popped open when he remembered, showed how exhausted he was. He'd insisted his possessions be left on a commode near the bed, and he'd refused to be parted from Oswin who, it had been decided, must also be bathed.

"'E won't let you do it," Hayden said, unconsciously smoothing the brightly-colored squares in Mrs. Hastings's quilt. Candlelight turned the boy's fair skin to pale gold.

Oswin sat atop Hayden's pile of clothing, her ears snapping up and down as she watched the comings and goings.

Jennings and Bessinger (Mrs. Hastings having been sent to bed by Ross before he left) each carried large jugs of steaming water into the room. Two jugs were emptied into an enamel bath set on a worn blanket before the fire.

"We'll need at least as much cold water," Bessinger said. Evidently his curiosity had overcome a natural tendency to indolence, and he had outdone himself helping with Hayden. "Run along and get some, Jennings."

Jennings set down his jugs and favored the butler with a stare only a man utterly confident of his position could muster. "You're right, Bessinger. We need cold water," he said, and went to look down upon Hayden. "Why not sleep, laddie? We'll take good care o' your wee dog."

"She's afraid of anyone but me," Hayden said. "She doesn't need no bath. I'll 'old 'er on top of me so she don't touch the bed."

Finch didn't point out the faultiness of his logic. Grumbling, Bessinger went for cold water.

An hour or so and the winter dawn would make its first struggling attempts to appear. Finch went to the dormer window and scraped at frosty whorls that had formed on the insides of leaded panes. The tips of her fingers were instantly ice-cold. Ross had been away too long to have done as he'd promised and confined his activities to a search of the alley in Whitechapel. She feared he had gone into the warehouse, where she could not be sure what he might find, or what, or who might be waiting for him. Finch had wanted to go with him, but he'd finally persuaded her that he could move more swiftly alone.

Her feelings for him only became sharper and easier to interpret. Even the idea of something happening to him was unbearable.

She tried to peer down toward the Square, but the rooflines below the window obscured what faint view there might be. With the fire crackling behind her and Jack Frost's paintings on the windows, she was reminded that Christmas was not so very far away. Please, oh please, let Latimer be safe and returned to her soon, she thought. Perhaps she should try to persuade him to attempt a reconciliation with Father by going home to celebrate the season.

"Very well." Bessinger came back into the room. "Cold water. Put the animal into the bath, if you please, Jennings."

"Not until we've tested the temperature," Jennings said. "Ye'll scald the wee scrap."

Bessinger's response was unintelligible.

If Latimer were alive and well, he would have found a way home by now, or a message about him would have come from those dreadful men. A demand. The silence was unbearable. He must be dead.

Finch pressed her brow to a freezing pane. Perhaps Ross had found something out. Or could he be entirely concerned with his precious shipments and this sacred thing as revered as a coronation crown? Could she expect him to spare any concern for a man he hardly knew and whom he'd only cultivated so that he could use his services?

Sounds of sloshing water filled the air.

"Och, not too much, man," Jennings said loudly. "Ye'll make it cold."

"Bathing dogs is not, and never has been, part of my duties, Jennings."

"No more is it mine," Jennings responded. "But we've t'be able to adapt to special circumstances. That water's too deep."

"Then do something about it," Bessinger said, his temper obviously beyond short. "I've carried a tub. Carried water. Carried more water. Spent an entire night away from my bed. Enough, I say. Enough."

"I'll do it," Finch said, turning from the window. "Go to your beds, both of you. Oswin needs to become accustomed to her surroundings, and all this noise will not help."

"Accustomed to her surroundings?" Bessinger said, amazement dripping from every word. "I hardly think that is the case."

"She don't want no bath," Hayden said, in a voice that suggested he'd dozed for a spell. "She wants to sleep."

"Run along wi' ye, Bessinger," Jennings told the butler. "I'll attend t'matters here."

"It isn't your place to tell me my duties."

"Bessinger," Finch said, deliberately sweet, "I think it would be best if I took over here. After all, caring for the young is women's work. I'm sure you agree. But thank you for all you've done."

"Yes, well"—Bessinger shot his white cuffs and tugged on his waistcoat—"yes, I'm always glad to serve, Miss More. Kindly summon me if you have further need of me."

The instant he left, Jennings set about testing the water in the bath, but Finch went to him and touched his shoulder. He straightened and stood still, his stance as military as always, and said, "Yes, miss?"

"Hayden has been through too much. He needs to be quiet and calm. Please let me be alone with him."

"Aye," Jennings said after a moment's hesitation. "Are ye all right yoursel'?"

She smiled at him. "I've been better. These are difficult times, but I can do nothing but wait." She considered before saying, "Do you not think we should have tried to force Zebediah and Artemis's hand in all this? They know where Latimer is."

"If we believe him, Artemis knows." Jennings rolled onto his heels, then to his toes. "I'm not sure Zebediah does. But His Lordship's a rare man, miss. Highly trained and with superb timing. If he chose not t'press them at this point, it's because he thinks it would be more dangerous if he did. Trust his instincts. I have for years and if he hadna' been right on all the important occasions, we'd no' be here tonight—neither o' us."

"But he doesn't say what he's thinking. He doesn't include anyone. I don't know what he's thinking, or if he's thinking anything at all about Latimer."

Jennings surprised her by patting her back. "I've known

Viscount Kilrood for a number o' years. I'm speakin' out o' turn, but a man must be honest when another's happiness is involved."

Finch could scarce breathe for wanting to hear what Jennings was about to say.

"I've never seen him the way he is now." He pressed his lips together and turned to leave.

Frustrated, Finch ran to stop him. "What does that mean? In what way?"

Firelight leaped over the sloping ceilings, and walls hung with daisy-covered paper. The atmosphere was cozy and warm, but Finch felt cold in the midst of it all.

Just as she thought Jennings would refuse to say more, he looked directly into her face, and said, "Be patient w' him. He's plenty o' reason t'mistrust his instincts in these matters, but he'll find his way to the answer, and I trust it'll be the right one. Let him lead ye, miss. He's more decisions t'make than most men. Good night, miss."

She knew she wouldn't get further wisdom out of the valet. "Good night, Jennings." She let him go.

"Very well," she said to Hayden with false cheer. "Now I shall wash Oswin and make her smell as sweet as a flower. Then, when she is dry, she shall sleep with you."

"Mmm," was Hayden's response.

The instant Finch attempted to pick up Oswin, the creature wiggled, slipped out of her grasp and leaped upon her master.

Finch expected Hayden to wake at once, but he gathered up his pet and rolled over without really stirring.

She considered giving up on her task, then contemplated having to admit defeat and discarded the idea.

Bending at the waist, she sneaked to the very side of the bed and scratched the top of Oswin's head. The gradual extrication of the animal was accomplished, and Finch hurried to the tub. As long as she succeeded in making the mangy fur smell of Mrs. Hastings's rosemary soap, all would be well.

Oswin liked water.

After attempting to drink fast enough to ensure she didn't

have to get wet at all, she set about exploring what was obviously a new and pleasing experience. Each time Finch got her hands on the dog, she quickly rubbed in some soap.

The door clicked shut, and Finch turned.

"Don't let that thing go," Ross said. "It'll be all over the room."

She drew back at his harsh tone. "You were gone so long. I worried about you." If she were not so tired, she'd be more careful what she said. She was very tired.

The candles had burned low. Standing inside the door, still wearing his heavy cloak, Ross's face was more shadow than light. He was a withdrawn presence, she thought, a cold and angry presence. He braced a shoulder on the wall and bowed his head.

Oswin fought for attention, her wet, and now-soapy body slipping from Finch's fingers each time she tried to catch her.

"Did you find what you were—"

"Don't concern yourself with such things," Ross said, raising his face enough for her to see muscles tense in his jaw. "And don't ask about Latimer. If I knew anything, I should have told you at once."

"Yes." She bent low over the tub and did her best to continue. The work would have been simpler if she were not viewing it through a hazy film of tears she couldn't blink away.

"Oh, for God's sake," Ross said. "Let me do that."

She didn't dare look at him, but she heard his cloak swish, and he dropped to his knees beside her, rolling up his shirtsleeves as he did so. He'd removed his coat.

He was definitely angry. Hostility made an invisible barrier between them, and it weakened what resolve remained to Finch. She sat on the floor and covered her face. What had happened to the woman who would not be weak?

He captured Oswin in one large hand and scrubbed her efficiently with the fingers of the other. And the dog let her tongue hang out while she positively grinned at the man. Ungrateful hound.

"Did Mrs. Hastings prepare a room for you?"

"Yes."

"I suggest you go there. Good night."

What had she done to make him so unpleasant, so rude? "I will remain to help with Oswin. Then I am to sleep in the room next to this. I understand it was once the nurse's room. I want to be there in case Hayden awakens in the night."

"The lad is fifteen, not an infant. He doesn't need a nurse."

"We all need to know someone cares about us." Once more she entered dangerous territory, but she didn't give a fig anymore. "It is a sorry and misguided person who thinks they don't need love."

Ross washed the dog more slowly, began to rinse off the soap. He didn't answer Finch.

"The dog likes you," she said for want of something else to say. "I might almost think you had been around animals before."

He lifted the dog from the bath and wrapped her in a towel. "I was surrounded by animals most of my life. I grew up on a large estate, and we had many dogs."

His life before this. He had made little mention of it until now. "In Scotland?" she said.

"Yes." His handling of Oswin was firm but gentle and earned him looks of panting adoration. Formerly dusty gray fur proved to be white and soft. "She needs to be well dried." Accordingly Hayden's companion was rubbed until her coat stood out in a pale, silky cloud. Then Ross handed her to Finch, but not before murmuring soft sounds and stroking her quivering body—and taking her to his face, where he rested his cheek against her for an instant.

He didn't want to show kindness because he thought it might be mistaken for weakness. The result was a disgruntled, grudging manner that did not suit him.

"Very well." The dog was plunked in Finch's lap. "Do what you will with her. But I must sleep, and so must you. There is much to be accomplished. I think we can expect momentous things tomorrow."

He would never know how much she longed to press him to explain. He would do so in his own time.

Holding the dog, Finch got to her feet.

Ross caught up his coat and cloak, and strode from the room without as much as a good night.

Annoyance stole away her tears. She lifted Hayden's covers and slipped Oswin into the boy's arms. They curled together like the tired young animals they were, and Finch withdrew to the nurse's room. Little larger than a closet, the bed all but filled the space, but looked inviting enough.

Grateful to strip off the dreadful clothing Jennings had supplied, Finch threw it up and put it in a corner. Her own clothes had been brought to the room. She wished she had something more substantial than her chemise to wear to bed, but it would have to do.

Cold crept into her flesh. She opened the door an inch in case Hayden should cry out, then she slid between icy sheets. The fire Bessinger had lit in the black grate had burned low, and there was no scuttle of coal to replenish the puny blaze.

The escapades in Elephant and Castle had left her chilled and achy—and overwhelmed with memories of what had happened to her there.

She longed for what she couldn't have. Ross, Viscount Kilrood. Fool that she was. A Cornish merchant's daughter mooning over a viscount who put his missions ahead of all. Not that she could ever be more to him than a . . . a what? She turned her face into the pillow. If her heart was to be broken, she had only herself to blame. Her foolish infatuation with a man far beyond her station had caused her to behave badly, had made her lie and devise outrageous excuses for being with him. Little wonder he was angry. She had insinuated herself into his life, into his home, and was proving a liability.

She curled up. No, he had brought her into his home first. And he'd told her he'd done so because he was attracted to her and wanted her near him.

Father had warned her about men who took advantage of inexperienced women.

Ross wasn't an opportunist, and if he wanted to find a woman to please him, he could have his pick of many more fascinating candidates than Finch More.

Oh, if only her brain would be still and allow her to sleep.

There was a single knock on the door.

Ross. It had to be. So he had returned, just as she'd wished he would, yet she should not risk what could happen if she allowed him to come to her.

She heard the creak of the door opening wider and held her breath.

"Finch" Ross whispered in the darkness. "Are you awake?"

A wise woman wouldn't answer. She said, "Yes."

"This room is cheerless. I shall have words with Bessinger in the morning." His footsteps retreated, and returned shortly. Coal rattled into the fireplace. "This is inappropriate. You will become ill. You have been wet for hours, and now you are cold. I shall summon a doctor to examine you in the morning."

"No," Finch said into her pillow. She should not enjoy his concern for her so much. "I am very strong. But thank you for your kindness, and for building up the fire."

"You have none of your things," he said, sweeping aside her gratitude. "I brought you some."

She heard him strike a match and saw the flare of candle flame.

"Finch, I will leave these things for you. They have never been worn, and I should like you to have them. They have been wasted for too long. There are gowns, too. If it pleases you, I would have you take them. Perhaps your friend, Meg, could make any necessary alterations."

If she remained still and didn't say anything, perhaps she could get through this without further disaster.

"Finch? There is a warm—er—night rail. It is before the fire. Put it on as soon as I leave, will you?"

"I wonder where Latimer is tonight." There, she had said it. "I wonder if he's wet and cold. Or if he's dead," she finished quietly. Let him be angry. He couldn't expect her to forget that her brother was missing.

The side of the bed sank. Ross had sat beside her. The pressure of his hand on her hair, stroking, stilled her heart, her blood.

"They will move soon," he said.

"Zebediah and Artemis?"

"Yes. I am convinced we will hear soon. And there is another issue I have not mentioned. The tiger from Number 7. Haven't you wondered why it was brought into this house?"

"Artemis thought it was what he sought."

Ross shook his head. "I repeat, why bring it here? And who brought it here? Neither man mentioned its disposal."

If only she were not so tired, Finch thought, she might think more clearly. "Perhaps when it was discovered that Artemis had stolen the wrong thing, they thought to put blame for the theft on you."

"Perhaps, but not particularly likely since it would make no sense. They would know I'd take it back direct, and that little plan would turn to nothing."

"What then?" Her eyes felt dry and sore.

Ross picked up a poker to stir the fire and did so for long enough to prove his concentration was elsewhere. "As a warning to me, I wonder? To let me know I am vulnerable within my own home?"

"Because they want to frighten you?"

He cast her a considering look. "I do not tend to become frightened. Not for myself. Your presumption may be partly correct, though, but I wonder if there may not be some other hand at work—a benevolent hand with a reason to wish me well."

Finch wrapped her arms around her knees and frowned. "I suppose that could be, although I can't imagine who your benefactor is." She could not hold back another attempt to hasten him in the search for Latimer. "Why must we wait for Artemis and Zebediah to contact you? Why not press them now?"

"The advantage lies in forcing them to move. But I cannot do as you suggest, anyway."

He was convinced that all the decisions were his to make. "Why?"

"I must do as instinct guides. Whatever happened to Hayden had something to do with them. Instinct assures me that is the case. Zebediah isn't here. Artemis has lodgings nearby, and he is also missing."

"You were searching for them. That's why you were gone so long." She pressed her eyes tight shut. "You should not have risked going alone."

His chuckle startled her, angered her. "Why laugh?" She turned over and sat up, pulling the sheets to her chin. "Is it a joke when someone lets you know they are concerned about you? Is it always the better part for a man to deny fear, or pain—and to avoid saying a simple *thank you,* even if they can't return someone's affection?"

She stopped and pressed the sheet to her mouth. Even a fool would understand what she was saying. This man was no fool, but she was. She had made certain he would keep his distance.

She heard the breath he exhaled. Long and deep, and she could not look away from his face.

"You know what my life is," he said quietly. "You know I have chosen a certain road."

"Yes."

"Yes." Gently he took one of her hands and kissed her fingers. "Yes, you know, but you don't know. You know I am involved in something that has put your brother, and very possibly yourself, in danger. I have told you something of why this danger exists and what is at stake elsewhere. But you don't know my struggles, or why I . . . You don't know everything about me."

"I wish I knew more about you." And she knew she would stay here in this small, cheerless room and listen to him for as long as he cared to speak. She would have him hold her hand in his until there was no more air to breathe. She would gladly watch his face in the almost dark until death claimed her.

She was lost to the most precious and the most destructive need.

"I should let you sleep," Ross said, standing abruptly. "Here, this is warm now. Put it on." He took a pale garment from before the fire and pressed it upon her.

Many yards of soft stuff that smelled of lavender.

"Please don't leave me." Every word she spoke bore her further into a place where she was bound to find despair. "I can't sleep. I feel I shall never sleep again."

"I understand," he said, and she thought he meant it. "But it would be better if I was strong for both of us."

Finch stroked the night rail. "Have you ever felt you would rather not be strong? Perhaps that you would like to give yourself up to needing someone else?"

"Oh, yes, I have done that."

Blood pulsed at her temples. Why couldn't she not stop herself from taking step after step, from revealing how important he was to her? Why did she have to ask, "Have you ever loved?"

He turned his back. "Change into the gown."

Scrambling, she put her feet on the bare wooden floor, discarded her chemise, and struggled into the most luxurious garment ever to touch her skin. It slipped over her like a breeze on a warm day.

"Loss first strips, then hardens us," Ross said. "You and I have both lost in different ways. That boy in there has lost more than either of us could have imagined at his age. Does it fit?"

He disoriented her momentarily. "Oh, the night rail. Yes. Short, but I am too tall. It's a beautiful thing. Thank you. Hayden has suffered more than any child should ever suffer, but he's strong. And he isn't angry as so many would be."

"You are not too tall. I like your height. Get into bed. I will look in on you later."

"When you lose someone you love you can decide never to

risk the same thing again. Or you can decide love was wonderful, and you should not deny yourself the chance of another love. You may not have another chance, but at least you can hope."

"Do you hope?"

Finch climbed back into the bed but didn't lie down. "I hope to be loved again."

"The boy came here because he didn't want me to think he could not be trusted."

"He admires you, Ross."

"He is needy of respect."

"He is needy of love."

"Perhaps." He faced her again, but she could see nothing of his features. "The things I brought here for you, that gown. They belonged to a woman who was to have been my wife."

She rolled in her lips and waited.

"Because of this life I chose, she married my brother instead. I bought this house for her."

He must be able to see her quite clearly. She wished she could hide the blow she felt at his words. She couldn't. "And you loved her very much?"

"Yes."

"You still do."

"I did for a long time." He averted his face, and his profile was a sharp silhouette. "Then I was able to make my work what I loved. Or at least what claimed so much of me that there was no longer room for anything else."

"And that's the only life you want now?" As she always had, she spoke her thoughts.

"I don't know. But I do know that if someone were to get too close to me, they would be in danger. They could be used as a weapon to force my hand in certain circumstances."

"As Latimer is being used? He isn't close to you, except as someone you do business with. You can't isolate yourself from everyone. And if someone chooses to be close to you, and you want them to be, then it is up to both parties to accept the hazards and try to guard against them."

"Some hazards cannot be guarded against."

"Just accepted then? Wouldn't it be better to snatch the joy, the passion of what one might have—for as long as it could be—than never to have it at all?"

"Finch, what are you asking me?"

Tears sprang into her eyes again, and she blinked, felt them run warm on her cheeks.

"Don't," he said, and she realized he was looking at her once more. "I hate myself for allowing this to happen."

Finch couldn't speak.

He took off his coat and his neckcloth, then sat in a chair to pull off his boots. When he stood again, and came toward her, she wiped at the tears, but more replaced them.

"This is the hardest of nights," he said. "For both of us. And perhaps the best of nights, too. What remains of it. If you agree we shall hold each other at least until the light wakes this house."

Finch nodded, then rested her brow on her knees. Dry sobs hurt her throat. This was the way it would be. This was the start of the next, and the greatest loss of her life. He had told her that he knew she loved him, and that he might be able to love her, too, but that he would never give up his commitment to danger.

Ross moved her to the wall, stretched out on the bed, and pulled her on top of him. Very carefully he settled her, settled her face on his shoulder and held her in his arms.

Once more he stroked her hair. "We shall go through this terrible time together. I give you my word that I will do all in my power to return your brother to you."

"Thank you."

"Now sleep. You are safe."

And if she did as he told her without another word, then there might never be another moment when she had the courage to tell him all that was in her heart. "I believe you will keep me safe. But my safety will mean nothing if you aren't safe, too."

His hand came to rest on her back. "I want to tell you not to care about me. I can't."

"It would be useless." And she grasped the shred of hope he offered. "The time for that is gone."

"Yes," he said. He lifted his head from the pillow and nudged her brow until she looked at him. "The time for that is gone, isn't it? We cannot be as we were before we met. But I cannot tell you that I know what lies ahead, or what I should do."

"Because you can't give up this path, this dangerous life you live?"

"Could you spend your days and nights tied to a man and never knowing when you were saying good-bye? Or for how long? A man for whom there would always be one more dangerous foe to face?"

She knew she was reckless, but she said, "Better that than to go on my way and be certain I had said good-bye."

"Ah, Finch," he said, bringing his mouth slowly toward hers.

His kiss was soft before he let his head fall back to the pillow and held her with such force that she felt his desperation. Framing her face with his hands, he kissed her deeply, urgently.

When he broke from her, he kept her where she was, on top of him, with his jaw against her temple. "Sleep now." His voice was unsteady. "Soon it will all begin."

And she accepted that he knew he was right. "Yes. But first I must tell you that I—"

"No," he said, pressing a thumb over her lips. "It's best that you don't."

She said no more, and neither did he.

Ross slept first. Finch listened to his breathing and settled a hand over his heart. "Wherever I go I shall feel you, my love," she murmured. "I shall feel the beat of your heart as if it were my own. I love you."

§ *Chapter 26* §

Evangeline followed Zebediah up a flight of stairs at the Piccadilly address Sherwood had sent. She tapped Zebediah's back, and said, "Did he say when he arrived? I didn't know he intended to come to London."

"Hush."

"This is not the sort of place where one takes rooms. Who owns it, do you suppose?"

"*Hush.*"

"All right," she whispered, "but why must we be quiet if these are my husband's lodgings and he summoned us here? And why didn't you ring the bell?"

"The letter instructed us to come in and not to make any noise."

They had checked rooms on the ground floor, but, despite a lamp burning in one, there had been no sign of Sherwood.

"Perhaps we took too long getting here and he has left," Evangeline said. "He may have gone to Mayfair Square in search of us."

"I think not."

Zebediah had taken some time to find Artemis. The man had returned to his lodgings a good deal after Zebediah arrived there. They drove the coach into the mews behind Mayfair Square so that there would be less likelihood of being noticed by those in the house. Evangeline had been waiting for them.

A sound behind them sent her hand to her breast, and she whirled around, but it was only Artemis who came after them with an exaggerated attempt at caution and silence. With one finger to his pursed lips, and much shushing, he climbed the stairs, managing to bump the wall, then the banisters on alternate steps.

Zebediah frowned heavily, but carried on to the next floor.

Only one room was furnished, a bedroom where a few remnants of a fire still glowed in the grate.

Artemis, in a hoarse voice, said, "I don't like this, I can tell you. I say we get away while the gettin's good."

"Hold your tongue," Zebediah told him. "I'm going to light a candle."

He did so, and an austere room was revealed. A heavy mahogany bed, its mattress exceedingly high, dominated the space.

"Look," Evangeline said, hurrying to a bureau of some other dark wood and inlaid with brass medallions. "These are Sherwood's." She picked up his initialed, silver-backed hairbrushes and her attention went at once to a small leather valise open beside them. Sherwood always carried his important papers in it. "He must be here. He would never leave this behind."

Zebediah didn't answer. She turned to see him at the side of the bed farthest from her. "Damnation," he said, the word hissing through his teeth. "What has happened here?"

"I tell you I don't like it 'ere," Artemis said. "Mr. Trimble'll contact us again tomorrow. 'E's probably gone to find 'imself a bit of fun. Oh, excusin' my careless tongue, m'lady."

She detested the man.

"He hasn't gone anywhere. Lady Evangeline, I would suggest you wait for us below."

The feeling seeped out of Evangeline's limbs. Rather than retreat, she took tottering steps toward Zebediah, and said, "What is it?"

He shook his head. "Don't come any closer. Artemis, can you explain this?"

"Me?" The coachman shrugged. "'Ow should I know. Explain what?"

Evangeline made her legs move and flew to the end of the bed. She edged around until she could see what Zebediah saw.

She screamed, and kept on screaming until a hard hand clamped over her face. His breath laced with liquor, Artemis brought his mouth close to her cheek and said, "Shut your mouth, you silly bitch. You'll 'ave people comin' t'see what's what."

Evangeline shook so violently her knees sagged, and earned her the horror of the coachman's arm around her, his hand splayed over her breast and squeezing as he held her up. She struggled but could not break free.

Partly beneath the bed, Sherwood lay sprawled on the floor. His head lolled to one side, and his open eyes stared the empty gaze of the dead.

Evangeline's next scream made it to her throat, where it threatened to choke her. She looked at Sherwood's neck, and a thin, livid line there.

"Strangled with twine," Zebediah said.

"I reckon 'e had visitors from Ranthus. Who else would kill 'im except someone what wanted that box."

Evangeline struggled some more.

"Who do you have in mind?" Zebediah asked Artemis.

"Well, you know." Artemis jerked Evangeline's bottom against him. "I've got somethin' for you, *m'lady*."

"Let her go," Zebediah said. "There's no point—"

"There's point all right," Artemis said, interrupting. "You've 'ad your turn. Now it's mine."

"We've other matters to attend to. Go to the carriage and keep watch. I'll see what there is to be found here and follow as quickly as I can. We must decide how to proceed."

Evangeline closed her eyes, but opened them again when Artemis surprised her by doing as Zebediah ordered and releasing her. He released her and gave her a hard shove at the same time, sending her to her hands and knees.

"We'll just 'ave to finish the job on our own without Mr. High-and-Mighty Trimble. Whoever it is who's payin' won't care if we're the ones what brings 'em what they want."

"You forget that we don't know who that is," Zebediah said quietly. He pulled a sheet from the bed and draped it over Sherwood's body. "Unless I can find some clue among his papers, we'll have our work cut out for us, won't we?"

"What do you mean?" Evangeline said. She felt faint. "You worked for Sherwood."

"Yes," Zebediah said, his voice still low, "but Sherwood worked for someone else, and since your husband is—well, now we'll have to complete this business ourselves. Go, Artemis. We mustn't waste any more time."

The coachman clumped from the room, apparently abandoning all efforts at caution.

A great trembling overtook Evangeline. Her teeth chattered, and she shook so badly her muscles hurt. Fear swelled, and she began to cry, softly at first, then in great dragging gulps that erupted in hiccups she couldn't control. Sherwood had been a cruel man, but she didn't wish him such a horrible death.

"Evangeline," Zebediah said, "please calm yourself. I must make haste, and I need your help."

Dimly she realized that he had used her first name again. Was she now to lose all dignity?

"Come. Look through some of these papers and see if

there is anything that refers to something called Ranthus, or to a precious box."

He took her by the elbow and helped her to her feet. "We will remove everything from his valise."

"I assure you there is nothing to find."

Evangeline whirled around to see Artemis back in the doorway. In front of him he held the man from next door, Finch's brother, Latimer.

"But do go ahead and look," Artemis said in a cultured accent. "Perhaps this one can assist you." His downturned smile and altered carriage showed his satisfaction at revealing himself as something other than a slovenly coachman.

Pale and unshaven, Latimer More was thrust into the room.

The door slammed shut, and a key turned in the lock.

❧ Chapter 27 ❧

Out of the gray early-morning sky, snow began to fly at the window. Finch watched fat flakes meet the panes. The fire still burned, and she realized that Ross had added more coals during the scant time she had slept. She hadn't felt him move, or move her, to do so.

He slept, his uncompromising features robbed of their sharp contours. As dark as his hair, and with the same hints of red, beard growth shadowed his jaw. When he'd returned from building the fire he must have discarded his shirt before gathering her to him again. There was no softness to his body. Where her hand rested on his shoulder, unyielding muscle covered bone. Where her face pressed his chest, smooth dark hair flared over solid flesh.

Very soon the house would fully awake. In some parts servants would already be moving about. She raised her head to glance at the door. Ross had closed it. If Hayden cried out, would she hear him?

"You need more sleep."

Finch closed her fingers on his shoulder and glanced at him. "So do you, my lord." He watched her through heavy, slitted eyelids, his usually brilliant stare warm and drowsy. Finch said, "I must go to Hayden."

"That won't be necessary." Low, and slow with its soft Scottish burr, his voice rumbled in his chest. "Jennings took the duty. He put a cot in the boy's room, and he'll remain with him."

Finch attempted to rise, but Ross urged her firmly right back where she'd been. He used his free hand to stroke her face and hair and to ensure any attempt to leave him would be beyond her strength—her strength of will.

"The servants will be abroad," she said.

"Not up here. Not this morning. Don't think about that. You and I are here together. Everything else has been taken care of. And there is nothing to be done about the rest—the other—until we are contacted."

"You have thought of everything."

"It is all very well for a woman to be strong. I like that in you. But you are a woman, and you need protection. Unless you refuse me, I shall give you that protection."

He puzzled her, but she wasn't ready to ask him to explain. "It's snowing. I hope . . . I hope Latimer is somewhere safe and warm."

"As do I," he said. "There are things I do not know about what has happened. Things I would not have expected. But I am as certain as I can be that our friends will not be able to wait much longer to make their move."

She breathed deeply, felt her breasts expand against his body, and a burst of heavy tension that heated her and started sensations she had felt before with Ross. "You made up the fire." She must stop herself from dwelling on how he made her feel, and how much she wanted to feel that way.

"The room grew cold. I didn't want you to wake."

"Thank you."

He tangled his fingers in her hair. "So red. I never saw

hair as red as yours This night has been unique for me, Finch."

She arched her back to see his face. "Because there is so much to worry about?"

He smiled and shook his head. "A night when I lay with a woman and held her in my arms—nothing more. I think you understand me."

"Yes." And she blushed. "You are kind to be concerned for me. I don't think I should have slept at all if I'd been alone with my fears."

All humor fled his face. He narrowed his eyes to study her. "Yes, I'm sure. I should leave you now. You will sleep now that it's light outside."

She wanted to beg him to stay, but knew she must not.

He set her from him and sat on the edge of the bed.

Lying on her side, Finch yearned to touch his long, sleek back. She yearned to wrap herself over that back and throw her arms around his neck, and kiss every inch of his skin she could reach.

He bent forward to rest his elbows on his knees and brace his head in his hands. He appeared to look into the fire.

Finch held herself motionless, afraid to breathe too loudly in case she interrupted his thoughts.

"I don't want to leave you," he said, very quietly.

Her stomach tightened, and her skin flushed. She must not say anything, not yet.

"I should have gone as soon as you slept, but I couldn't. You are troubled, and I should not burden you with my concerns, but I feel your strength. And I feel—I hope I am not mistaken—that my welfare matters to you."

His welfare mattered to her? "Yes, it does. You have decisions to make, Ross. We both know what I mean. I feel it in my heart that you are not decided about your future. Until you are, nothing in your life will be clear to you."

"Always so reasoned," he said, running his fingers through his thick curls. "Do you know why I didn't leave you to sleep?"

"No," she told him honestly.

"Because I am a selfish man. I have been through blackness of the soul in recent days. Confusion. The part of me that is a soldier, a pursuer of quests, a righter of wrongs, has stayed true and firm to its responsibilities. The part of me I thought I had forever quelled—the thing they call heart, whatever that may be—and emotion, and physical need for the softness of a woman, and for the knowledge that she is the only woman I want because I am the center of her life as she is of mine—that part has demanded that I pay it attention."

He stood and went to toss more coals on the fire. These he stirred with a poker before returning to the side of the bed. "So there it is. I am not the man I was. I am divided."

"And you wish you could regain your former iron will? Your total dedication to your causes?"

"Do I?"

She knew he didn't expect an answer.

He inclined his head to gaze at her. His frowned pained her. There was a struggle within him and he must surely want to push any thoughts of wanting her far from him.

"Throughout my life alone, I have known that there was no one I could or would turn to. Men like me avoid attachments that might be used against them, but I have told you that before." Still looking at her, he sat on the bed once more and smoothed her hair away from her face. "Miss Freckles. What have you done to me?"

Finch smiled a little and caught his hand. He laced their fingers together.

"I want to tell you why I didn't leave before. Selfishness. And infatuation with something I have never known before. A sensation I have never known."

When he paused she was afraid he might not continue. He pulled his hand away and turned to sit with his back to her again. Then he was silent for what felt like a very long time.

"She is here," he said, as if Finch were not there at all. "Here where you can hold her, feel her. In the blackest hour, this hour when you fear that you have failed so many and you will never heal from that failure, still you can reach out and hold her."

She held her breath. Raising a hand, she almost caressed his back, but stopped herself. He spoke what was in the deepest parts of him, and she heard grief tinged with a hope he thought he did not deserve.

"I am besieged. I must wait surrounded by a sort of silence that roars out its danger, and I am, indeed, besieged. But when I look at you, when I touch you, the darkness I feel, the subtle desire for it all to end no matter how, slips away beneath my wanting you.

"In the midst of the madness, the despair, there is you, dear Finch."

She quivered from the sheer force of wanting to pull him into her arms. He was a man, a strong, strong man who had seen more of the world than she would ever know enough about to summon up in dreams, yet he had no peace.

"I am frightening you. I will leave now. Do not concern—"

"You do not frighten me, Viscount Kilrood—except when you let me know that you have not heard what I have told you. Be it clumsily so, I have told you that from the day we met, although I could not have guessed how much it would be true, my life has felt changed. Now it is changed."

"I have no right to do anything but work to return your brother to you, then embark on attempting to finish this commission. I am wrong to allow you anywhere near what is happening here."

She turned her face into the pillow to hide a smile.

Ross rubbed the side of her neck with the backs of his fingers. "What? What is so funny?"

Peeking out at him, she said, "Allow me here? You poor, beleaguered man, I have forced myself upon you. I would not leave. Have you forgotten that?"

Her neck had become fascinating to him. He watched the

progress of his fingers there. "I could have put you out if necessary."

"Oh, surely. You could have carried me to the flagway and set me down."

"No, I couldn't. I could carry you, Finch, but not away from me, damn it. I could not do that."

"Come to me, then," she said, holding her arms out to him. "Come and lie with me until you have to go. Rest as long as you can."

A muscle in his cheek flexed. The lines on either side of his mouth deepened, and he watched her with disturbing intensity.

"Only if you want to, of course," she said, abashed lest he disliked her suggestion. "I know I am forward, but I am concerned for your strength."

"There is nothing wrong with my strength," he said. "I am a very strong man, and a man of considerable appetites. True, I have learned to temper those appetites, but I am, after all, only a man. I have already given in to the power of my attraction to you. I should not have done so."

"There has been no harm done." Her heart thudded so hard she felt breathless.

"I doubt that is true. After this night it is unlikely that anyone will not come to certain conclusions about our relationship."

"That we have been together like man and wife, you mean?"

He tipped his head back.

"What have I said to annoy you?"

"Annoy me? You don't annoy me, you intrigue and captivate me. I have never met another woman like you, and I shall never meet one like you again."

Knowing she was daring, Finch settled a hand on his thigh. The muscles there jerked so hard she gasped. Ross clamped a hand over hers until she met his eyes.

Slowly he bent over her and supported his weight on an

elbow. "Do you know what will happen if I lie with you to *rest*?"

She rolled her head from side to side, but she thought she did know.

"We may very well be together like man and wife."

Finch nodded, and everything within her raced.

"That could be a disaster, don't you think?"

She shook her head, no, again.

"No? We have spent wonderful times together, you and I. We have explored each other as we should not have. My fault, not yours. You were a complete innocent."

"An innocent anxious to expand her knowledge," she told him.

He laughed, and kissed her. And the kiss was a new experience. He had never nipped at her mouth before, or used his teeth to tug at her bottom lip.

And, abruptly, he sat up and averted his face.

This time Finch didn't stop herself from reaching for him. She ran her fingers around his arm, rubbed the hair on his chest, brushed her fingertips down his side.

"I should wait," he murmured.

Her breasts flushed, and her thighs. And she grew moist. She caught his hand and took it to her breast. "Can you feel my heart?"

"My God," he said. "I am only a man."

Only a man. She almost chuckled. He was only an incredible man who happened also to be human. She had already seen how he enjoyed looking at her body, feeling her body. And she knew it was the sensation of her breast beneath his hand with nothing but the fine night rail to separate them that made him exclaim.

Men, she had been told, were weak when it came to the female body. Well, she could expand on that now. Women, at least this woman, were weak when it came to the male body—to this man's body.

Wriggling from beneath the sheets, Finch scooted past Ross and got to the floor. There, without ceremony, she pulled the night rail over her head and draped it on a scuffed wooden chest beneath the window. Then she removed what pins remained in her hair, ruffled it loose with her fingers, and let it fall.

She stood where she was, with the high window behind her, and looked Ross full in the eyes.

He looked not at her body, but at her face. His gaze didn't as much as flicker, and he didn't speak. Color gradually rose in his cheeks.

She no longer cared if what she said or did was "appropriate." If this was to be all they had, she wanted to hold every second of it close for as long as she lived. And she didn't want to regret having held any part of herself back.

Ross stood. He undid his breeches and very soon faced her as naked as she was. As naked, but so very different. Without clothes he seemed even larger than when he was dressed.

He beckoned to her, and she hesitated but an instant before she went to him and allowed herself to be tipped against his body. And they stood there, hands at their sides, skin to skin, in a silence broken only by the hiss of fire, the snap of flame. The soft stroke of snow on frosty pane was something felt, not heard.

Ross bent to kiss her shoulder.

Finch kissed his chest.

The hard male part of him rose against her stomach, an insistent pressure that both thrilled and frightened her. But it was a fear she welcomed and marveled at.

His hands cupped her jaw, and he tilted her face up. This time his kiss held a barely contained violence. Between her thighs a pulse began, and the moisture increased, and a deep, insistent ache.

"Finch," he said, holding her away and making circles over her nipples with his palms. "If I do what I want to do, you will never be the same."

She looked into his darkened eyes and could only nod.

"There are many ways I should like to do this with you.

This time what I want most is to feel you welcome me inside you. Do you understand?"

"I . . . no. Tell me."

He smiled. "Yes, miss. First, I should inform you that you are beautiful and to look at you is my delight. To hold you is ecstasy."

Silly tears were in her eyes again. "I am not shapely. I am too thin, I believe, too hard, and too tall."

"Are you? Well, perhaps my eyes and hands cannot be trusted to be truthful. And perhaps what I feel in my body proves it has poor taste. We'll discuss that another time. We have talked enough. If you agree, I should like to make love to you. Completely. That means I should like to put this part of me"—he brought her hand between them until she touched his manhood—"into your body. That is what happens between a man and a woman when they sleep together and are intimate. I put it inside you. Then I stroke it in and out of you and sensation builds until it becomes what you felt on that other occasion—only much more intense. Sometimes you may want to help me move. You may want to touch other parts of me. And I shall want to touch all of you, to kiss every inch of you. If I rub that small part of you—between your legs—while I move inside you, you may find your pleasure is almost too great. But then, we shall both find that worth any price. You want me to continue?"

She took short breaths through her mouth. He hadn't touched "that small part" of her, yet it throbbed. She looked up at him. "I don't want you to say anything else, or I shall become too nervous. So, if you don't mind, I should prefer you to just do it."

Ross whispered, "All right," and took her to the bed.

Lying on his side, Ross watched Finch sleep. Apart from brief snatches of drowsing, he'd been awake for more than twenty-four hours, yet he felt strong and alert. She made him strong. He had tried to explain to her how he felt when they were together, but he'd had too little experience at speaking of love.

Love. Yes, he loved Finch. And today, when she awoke, he would tell her so. Then he would tell her how he needed her to be present with him, how in dark moments of his soul, that presence was a light she must shine on him. He would ask her to be his wife, and he would begin planning for their future.

And this was Ross, Viscount Kilrood, champion of causes shunned by even the most fearless soldiers of fortune? This was the man whose veins ran with melted iron, not blood, so they said? Kilrood who would trifle with women, satisfy his own needs, but who had supposedly taken the only vows of lifelong allegiance he would ever take? Could this possibly be the one of whom it was said that danger was the sole bride he would ever accept?

Snow fell thick and steady and kept the light in the room dim. A pallid, hazy dimness. And against the white bed linens Finch's fair, freckled skin was flushed. Her hair spread in a vivid banner he had to touch again and again.

If he'd never met her, he might have spent the rest of his life chasing the threat of death until it caught him, whether sooner or later. But he had met her, and he didn't want to chase death anymore.

He wanted to take her to Scotland, to Heath's End. She would love it there. And Patrick and Fiona would love her. The house would be filled first with baby sounds, then with the laughter of children. Navigating the path of a husband and father, and overseeing his lands, would be danger enough.

Whatever was to come first—here in London before he could dispatch his responsibilities to Ranthus—he would be ready, and he would win. Drat the bad luck of having the final piece of the box lost in that evil alley in Whitechapel. Chances were that it had fallen into the hands of someone who had no idea what they possessed. That possibility had caused him to take a bold step last night. After he'd searched in vain, he'd gone to the goldsmith he'd retained to join the box again and shown him the sides. He asked the man to fashion a new bottom of heavy gold, and he'd promised to bring the top when it was time to return the treasure to Ranthus. True, the real bottom of the box was also clad in glass but he would try to obtain that final part in time to make the substitution. If he couldn't he'd pray—without great hope—that the difference might not be noted.

"Ross?"

He hadn't noticed when she opened her eyes. "Why are you awake again? You will collapse from exhaustion."

"I'm awake because you're awake," she told him sleepily. "And I shall not collapse. I am very—"

"Strong," he finished for her. "Yes, I know. So you have told me."

Her eyes cleared and opened wide. She stared at him, and he thought her mouth trembled. "What is it, Finch?" Latimer, of course. He wished he could be more confident the other man was safe.

"I am so foolish," she said.

He raised his eyebrows. "What a strange thing to say? You are not foolish at all."

"You say that because you don't know. You don't know what I allowed myself to think when—earlier."

Ross made certain his expression was suitably serious. "Please share this with me."

She looked down, shook her head, and raised her chin as if defiant. "I thought that because we were making love . . . It was wonderful to make love. Wonderful. When you—"

He pressed his fingers to her lips. If she spoke of it aloud, he would not be able to restrain himself from taking her again. "What did you think?" Carefully, he removed his fingers.

Her flush became a brilliant blush. "I tried to convince myself that you were finding it wonderful, too, and that you would want us to . . ."

"To?" He waved a hand.

Working her way deeper into the bed, she drew the covers up to her ears. *"Marry,"* she said on a squeak and covered her head entirely.

His tender feelings for her overwhelmed him. Dragging her near, he caught at the sheet. "Finch, come out at once."

A knock on the door was the most unwelcome sound he ever remembered. "Yes? What is it, Jennings?" Very early that morning his valet, the most discreet and faithful of servants, had taken up his watchful post without a word.

"Something you need to see at once, my lord," Jennings said.

"A moment," Ross said. He leaned over Finch, and whispered, "Stay exactly where you are. We shall continue that last thought."

He climbed from bed, pulled on his breeches, and went to open the door a crack.

"My lord," Jennings said, eyes down and holding out a copy of the *Times* opened to an inside page. "There." He pointed to a headline halfway down the sheet.

Ross read: "Sheik of Ranthus dies. Country in deep mourning."

§ *Chapter* 28 §

Exhausted and panicky, Finch arrived in the foyer of Number 7 to be greeted by Meg and Sibyl Smiles. "What is it?" she asked, panting. "Is it Latimer? Did Latimer come, or send a message?"

The sisters looked at each other. Neither girl was her customary well-groomed self, in fact from the disheveled appearance of their hair, and their wrinkled gowns, they appeared to have slept in their clothes and not to have attended to their *toilettes* since arising.

"Oh, *please*," Finch said. "You sent old Coot out in the snow to get me. You wouldn't do that if it weren't an emergency."

"I told you we should have gone ourselves," Sibyl told Meg.

"If we had we should never have managed—managed it," Meg said.

Coot arrived at the door, having taken considerably longer than Finch to make the return journey from Number

8. Taking off his coat and hat, he sighed heavily. "Is there anything else, please?"

"No, nothing," Sibyl said.

"Nothing," Meg echoed. "Thank you very much, Coot. I'm sure Mrs. Dickens has the kettle on. She always does."

"I can't stand it." Finch heard the wailing tone of her voice but didn't care. "What has happened here?" Light-headedness frightened her. She wanted to lie down. She wanted Ross. Where had he gone in such a hurry and without explanation—and at *such* a moment?

Meg trotted forward and took her by the hands. "It's most mysterious, and we knew you would want to be here to take charge of it."

Not Latimer. Her energy ebbed so rapidly the faintness all but overcame her, and she went to sit on the stairs.

"I told you, Meg," Sibyl said, sounding as if she were about to cry. "I told you we shouldn't have done it this way. Oh, dear. Oh, Finch, you look quite ill. Why are you wearing your hair down? Finch, what has happened to you?" Sibyl's voice sharpened as Finch had never heard it sharpen before.

"Leave her alone," Meg said. "Can't you see she is in some distress? Something has happened to Latimer, hasn't it? Oh, now look what I've done. I am entirely too direct. Forgive me dear Finch. *Has* something happened to Latimer? Oh, I mean—Finch, please tell us what's wrong?"

Ross hadn't been able to take time to explain why he was leaving, but he had told her to wait there for him, and to speak to no one of what she now knew. He warned her that he believed Latimer's safety depended on proceeding with extreme haste. Surely Ross would bring Latimer home. Oh, surely he would.

"This has gone entirely too far." With a resolute air quite unlike her, Sibyl stood before Finch. Such unexpected determination became the more startling in one so slight, and fair, and soft. She tugged a long, escaped curl behind her ear. "Do you hear me, Finch? Entirely too far. You are a gentlewoman alone in London."

"I am not alone," Finch said.

"At present you are most certainly alone. It is clear that something has happened to Latimer. Mr. Chillworth has gone to his commission, and Hunter is in chambers, but we should send for them at once and enlist their help."

"No," Finch said, standing up. "Absolutely not."

"Why?" Meg asked, then pressed her lips together and shook her head slightly.

Finch glanced around to see Barstow proceeding from belowstairs with a vase of white roses in her hands. That lady saw Finch, and an ominous expression made her appear even more gray than usual. Barstow approached the door to 7A and said, "Running errands for the lodgers, now," in aggrieved tones. "Open the door, if you please."

Meg rushed to do so, surprising Finch since the door should have been locked.

"We used our key," Sibyl said, sounding abashed. "Please forgive us, but we were so worried and we wondered if you might have left a note there. All the keys still fit all the doors. There hasn't been time to change them."

"A note?" Finch said. "Why would I leave a note? For whom?"

Sibyl tucked a hand beneath Finch's arm and urged her inside the flat. "Thank you, Barstow," she said, then she stopped and stiffened. "Where did those roses come from? Not *that* man, surely?"

"*That* man?" Finch said. She knew Sibyl referred to Ross. But had he sent them? If so, how had he managed to give instructions when he'd been so preoccupied, and in such a hurry?

"I'm sure I couldn't say," Barstow said, folding her hands over her stomach and drawing her chin back. She'd plunked the roses in the middle of Finch and Latimer's old dining table. "But Her Ladyship may never be the same after all she's been through. Taken to her bed, she has. Shock and

worry. It's all been too much for her. And precious little gratitude does she get for all the love and kindness she wastes
on some people."

"I'm sorry," Finch said, and she was. "I must go and see
her at once."

"She's sleeping," Barstow said. "I'm not one to tell people what I'm thinking. I keep my opinions to myself. Always best. The less said about some things, the better. But
it's a disgrace for a man like that to take advantage of a single woman, even if she should know better."

Finch's cheeks stung. She couldn't think of a response.

"Sinners always know they've sinned," Barstow said, apparently warming to her topic. "There isn't one of us who
hasn't been tempted. The strong turn aside that temptation.
The weak succumb and are lost. Fancy white roses, indeed.
The wages of sin. Roses and silly birds who bite." She
marched away into the foyer and up the stairs.

Sibyl instantly threw her arms around Finch from one
side, while Meg hugged her from the other. "You are not a
sinner," Meg said. "You are good."

She was a sinner. And she wouldn't change a thing.

"An inexperienced girl from the country is no match for a
big, strong, powerful, incredibly handsome, totally scrumptious man who sweeps her off her feet."

Finch made enough room in the group hug to look at
Meg's face. "I take it you rather like Viscount Kilrood."

"No," Meg said, frowning and shaking her head. "Of
course I don't. If Papa were alive, he'd call him an opportunist and a bounder."

"But he's totally scrumptious?" Finch said.

Meg nodded. "Totally."

"Totally," Sibyl agreed.

"Has he—" Meg attempted to straighten Finch's hair. "I
mean, did he . . . Well, you know, whatever it is we aren't
supposed to do, or wouldn't be supposed to if we really
knew what it was? Did he?"

Finch glowed and throbbed in places she'd come to enjoy

glowing and throbbing in, and hoped to do so again—with Ross. What had he been about to say before Jennings had arrived? Oh, what had he intended to say in response to her totally inappropriate comment? She blushed afresh. Really, she had become a slave to her blushes.

"He did," Meg said, indicating Finch's flushed cheeks. "There, Sibyl, I told you he did. Finch, do you suppose you could tell us just a little about it?"

Finch drew back and stared at her. Fractious bird sounds grabbed her attention, and she looked, amazed, at the gilded cage containing Pecker—that unexpected gift with which Ross had presented her. How and when it had been delivered from, she had no idea. In fact she hadn't thought about, or seen the creature since Ross had first given it to her.

Meg flapped a hand before her face. "In the interests of education, of course. After all, we women are all sisters under the skin and have a responsibility to share what information we have on these topics that are forbidden us. I've always thought it unfortunate that we are expected to go into such things in total ignorance."

"Oh, Meg," Sibyl said. "There will be time enough for that. And Finch is obviously deeply upset. Our job is to help her in any way we can. I just know we should get Mr. Chillworth and Hunter to—"

"No," Finch said, desperate to make sure there was no interference in Ross's plans.

"Where is Latimer?" Sibyl asked with another rare show of determination.

"With Ross," Finch told her, suddenly inspired. "They are attending to an important business matter."

The bird squawked again, and Sibyl frowned. "A bird. He wasn't here this morning, was he, Meg?"

"He's mine," Finch said quickly, increasingly puzzled by the arrival of what were evidently Ross's gifts. Even in the midst of extreme trial he had thought of her and of doing things to bring her pleasure, not that she could ever be fond of Pecker, a most unpleasant creature who showed not a shred of charm.

"Sibyl!" Meg leaped away, her eyes huge and troubled. "We have forgotten why we absolutely *had* to make Finch come home."

"Apart from saving her?"

"Oh, indeed," Meg said. Her hands moved restlessly, and she backed up. "The reason we sent that urgent message is because something *appeared*. And we thought it might be something very personal that you would not want to have presented in front of someone else."

"Oh, yes," Sibyl agreed. "Absolutely not in front of someone else. One moment it wasn't here. The next minute it was. And Meg and I are certain we were in this very room, looking through the windows for you at the precise minute when it arrived. It is so mysterious, Finch."

"*So* mysterious," Meg agreed. "Whoever brought it managed to get in and out of this room without our hearing or seeing them."

Sibyl nodded. "Not a sound. So we know it is deeply secret."

"What is it?" Finch asked. She saw nothing unusual, other than the white, hothouse roses, and the gilded cage containing Pecker, who sidled restlessly back and forth on his perch.

"The doorbell didn't ring. Coot didn't come to say it had been delivered. Really, most mysterious." Sibyl swayed from foot to foot. "You should probably change, Finch. You would feel better."

Finch refrained from pointing out that she wasn't the only one whose *toilette* needed attention. "What is this mystery?"

"It arrived for you," Meg said. "Give it to her, Sibyl."

With a self-conscious little smile, Sibyl went to a silver-trimmed biscuit barrel atop the bulbous-fronted sideboard and lifted the lid. She removed several pieces of shortbread Finch did not remember. "We put these on top just in case someone thought to look inside. Here."

Sibyl held out a small package wrapped in oilcloth and wound about with twine.

Knowing what she would find, Finch took it and looked at the label. Then she looked at the two sisters. "You know this is not for me," Finch said. "Why didn't you take it to Viscount Kilrood at once?"

"It's not for you?" Meg said. Then her feigned surprise dissolved. "It's no use. I was never any good at all at deceit. We decided to use the parcel as an excuse to rescue you. After all, it was obviously delivered to the wrong place, so we might as well have made the best of it."

"Why did you feel you had to rescue me?"

"Because we were terrified for your reputation," Sibyl said in a tiny voice. "We were also afraid you had been kidnapped and were being held against your will."

"When you came last night I told you that was not the case."

"He could have some hold over you," Meg said, all defiance again. "That's why we came in here, to see if you'd left a note to say Viscount Kilrood was stealing you away for . . . well, for . . . for *those* purposes."

Those purposes, indeed. He had not stolen her, but she would be perfectly happy if he decided to do so at any time—and for *those purposes.*

"You do see that it was strange for the package to appear here, though, don't you? It was on the floor inside the door. If it had been there when we came in, we couldn't have missed it, could we? And it shouldn't have been here at all, should it? After all, anyone could see it wasn't for you."

Finch gifted Meg with a very direct stare, and said, "Indeed, anyone could."

The bird screamed, literally screamed. Finch snatched up a blanket and draped it around the cage. Muttered angry sounds came from behind the cover.

"We should leave Finch to change, and go and change ourselves," Sibyl said. "Then we'll return and help you decide what to do next. Several heads are always much better than one."

"First, Finch," Meg said, "and I hope you will forgive me for being direct. The boy, the one you introduced to Lady Hester and to Hunter. Who is he?"

She had expected her careless lie to haunt her. "Just someone Viscount Kilrood kindly decided to help."

Meg was not to be so easily diverted. "Lady Hester said there was talk of Viscount Kilrood doing his duty by taking the boy in. The inference was that he is His Lordship's, hmm—relative."

Finch inclined her head. She considered a moment before saying, "Was it now? I shall change my gown and wash. If you'll excuse me?"

She left Sibyl and Meg to gape after her and went into her bedroom. Hurriedly she stripped off the green gown she would rather never wear again. The hem was sodden and dirty. The snow had ruined her slippers.

"Redheads should never wear red." How many times had she been told that by the busybody single ladies of Fowey who fawned upon her father and tried to gain his approval by showing Finch particular attention?

Well, she had a warm dress made of wool the color of oranges and red poppies mixed together. And she loved it. It made her feel warm inside as well as outside, and she had decided it did rather suit her.

Latimer detested it, but in future she would not listen to anyone at all when it came to choosing what she wished to wear.

Washed, dressed in a clean chemise, and with her hair brushed and caught up at her crown, she donned the gown and found her sturdiest pair of boots. There was also a brown-velvet cloak she rarely wore, and a matching bonnet with a golden feather that curled over the brim. She paused to touch a fingertip to the feather. Greville had liked its shade. He said it matched her eyes.

Greville should have lived a long and useful life. She remembered his earnest face, and the old wave of sadness came. He would always have his place in her heart. How simple and complete her existence had seemed when he'd been alive. How comfortable.

Now there was a forceful wind capable of causing turmoil for Finch More, and the name of that wind was Ross.

She carried the cloak and bonnet to the sitting room and set them down, uncertain what she should do next—other than make sure Ross knew another important shipment had arrived. He would expect to find her at Number 8 when he returned. She wanted to be at Number 8 when he returned. But an insistent part of her warned that she should not be predictable, or perhaps not too predictable.

Oh, she was not at all good at games, these games females were supposed to indulge in.

Ross's package must be protected at all costs. This was either the one lost in Whitechapel, or the last piece that he was waiting for. Her reticule was not a safe hiding place. She hurried back into the bedroom and returned with a brown fur muff. Undoing some of the stitching inside was a simple task, and she slid the oilcloth-wrapped treasure into the lining.

The sound of Meg's and Sibyl's voices came from the foyer.

Finch hurried out, anxious to allay the sisters' anxieties and see if she could persuade them to go about their business. What she must do was take Ross's parcel to him. Yes, she must find him and give it to him.

"Oh, Finch, you look wonderful," Meg said. She stood with her arms wrapped around a newel post at the foot of the stairs. "Doesn't she, Sibyl. A picture. A brilliant picture."

"I do not," Finch said, although she rather wished she did. "But thank you. I know I am not supposed to wear red."

"Posh!" Sibyl grinned, a rare sight. "You are a woman intended to set fashion."

Finch waved aside the compliments. "You two are tired. I

feel very guilty about that, and I want you both to promise me you'll go to your beds and rest at once."

"Well"—Sibyl yawned promptly—"no, we can't leave you."

"I shall rest, too," Finch fibbed.

"Look at this." Meg, ever the easily distracted one, pointed at one of the many carvings on the newel post. "Why, I do believe it's Hunter. And there's another face like his."

"Don't be silly," Sibyl told her. "This house is old and everything in it is old—including these nasty carvings."

"They *aren't* nasty. Look at this. It's just like Hunter, I tell you."

Finch closed her tired eyes briefly before going to peer at the face Meg pointed to. Sibyl also looked closely. "Hunter's nose isn't that big," she said. "And he's much more handsome."

"But it does look like him," Meg insisted.

"Sort of," Finch allowed. "But Sibyl's right. Not as handsome and with a bigger nose. Neither is that one."

Meg's grin was impish. "I think Sibyl's rather dazzled by Hunter, don't you, Finch?"

"Meg," Sibyl said, sitting down with a plop on her favorite step.

Finch had no intention of allowing the conversation to stray to matters of love. "I like the baby carvings. And all the girls. It's a lovely staircase. Like a family portrait."

"I wonder who that was supposed to be?" Meg said, pointing at a blank oval almost hidden by a spray of laurel leaves.

Finch all but exploded with frustration, so great was her desire to get away. "I can't imagine."

The doorbell rang, and she had to stop herself from rushing to answer.

After what felt like an exceedingly long time, old Coot made his ponderous way from below stairs. He turned his mournful, bulbous eyes on Finch and the Smiles sisters before carrying on to see who their visitor was.

"I was hoping to speak with Miss Finch More."

She stood utterly still. The voice was faintly familiar but she couldn't identify the speaker.

"Wait here," Coot said, and closed the door again. Carrying a rather tarnished silver tray, he came to Finch and offered her a card with the corner turned down.

As if she didn't already know the visitor was waiting . . . She picked up the card and had to control a gasp.

Whatever happened, she must not show any sign of disquiet—much less of fear. And she must receive her visitor.

"Excuse me, Meg," she said, "Sibyl. I'll come to see you later." Implicit in her politeness was the understanding that they should not remain in the foyer. "Please show in my guest, Coot."

By the time she'd made her rapid retreat into 7A, Finch's heart beat so hard it sickened her. She gulped and took a big breath through her mouth, willing herself to be calm.

"In here, sir," Coot said loudly. "Miss More, Mr. Artemis Gibble."

Finch swallowed again, and said, "Thank you, Coot. Close the door, will you, please?"

The instant the door clicked shut, Finch's visitor said, "I know what you must be thinking."

She was thinking that he sounded almost nothing like the man she had heard speak before.

"I ask you not to be afraid of me. I wish you no harm and will do you no harm. I'm here because I know I've done wrong, and I want to put it right before it's too late."

Only with the greatest difficulty did she turn around and look at the man. Dressed in an expensively cut, dark gray coat and black trousers, his linen was immaculate, his black hair clean and carefully brushed. He held a beaver hat that must have cost a good deal.

"I don't understand," Finch said. What she did and said could determine what happened to Latimer. "Aren't you

Lady Evangeline's coachman?" It would be best if he didn't find out how much she knew about him and his activities.

"I've tricked a lot of people, and I'm sorry."

Her palms were wet. "You don't even sound the same."

"No, well, I'm not a coachman. Not really. I'm just a man who was down on his luck and saw a way to deepen his pockets. But I was wrong. You don't know how wrong I was."

Finch believed she knew a great deal about how wrong he'd been, but the best chance of finding her brother stood before her, and she must be careful not to waste that chance.

"I'm out of my depth, Miss More. I am just a clerk in a solicitor's office. Certain information came into my hands—information relating to Viscount Kilrood—so I got myself in the way of finding a job as coachman to Lady Evangeline so I could have a chance to get close to the viscount. But you're not interested in all that."

He spoke as if she knew nothing of what was afoot. Finch went to the roses and fussed with them, buying time to think. What could he have in mind here?

"But there is something you're interested in, and I must reveal it to you."

Latimer. Something awful had happened to Latimer, that's what this man was about to tell her. She closed her eyes tightly and prayed for the wisdom to do what was best.

"Miss More, I beg your forgiveness."

Latimer must be dead.

"I am sorry for all the trouble I've caused. There won't be any more."

"*Stop* it." She whirled to face him. "Stop talking in circles and say what you came to say. It's my brother, isn't it? It's Latimer."

Artemis crushed the brim of his hat and nodded once. "My fault. All my fault. He's gone inside himself. All he'll say is your name. He hasn't eaten." The man paused and his throat jerked. "He's . . . His mind has snapped."

Finch let out a cry and pressed her hands over her mouth.

"I'm sorry," Artemis said. "I don't think he can go on much longer."

She caught up her cloak, bonnet and muff. "I shall go in search of Viscount Kilrood at once."

"Oh, dear. I went there to find you, first. They said the viscount's left on important business, and they don't know when he'll return."

True enough. She walked in circles.

"I don't blame you for not trusting me," Artemis said. He stood taller, straighter. Rather than dirty, his skin appeared deeply tanned. There was an elegance about him, an almost-foreign elegance. Clean-shaven, his hands scrubbed, nails cut short, and even his teeth miraculously no longer yellow, he was almost an entirely different creature. "I expected you to refuse to accompany me, Miss More. Rest here and try not to worry. I'm just going to have to find a way to force him to come with me. If I have to drag him, or carry him, I'll get that brother of yours into the carriage and bring him here. If I make it, we'll have to get a doctor quickly."

"Oh." Finch's legs trembled. She clutched the back of a chair to steady herself. Then she pulled on her cloak, crammed on the bonnet and tied its ribbons, and pushed the muff onto her left hand. "Take me to him at once. We have already delayed too long."

§ Chapter 29 §

"This is unbelievable. Absolutely, utterly unbelievable. I have placed myself in such terrible jeopardy. Not one of you could possibly imagine my peril. And it has all been in an unselfish effort to help these people—this moon-brained young woman, and this remarkably obtuse man—to find each other.

"Now tell me, can you deny that Viscount Kilrood and Finch More have been placed in the way of having no impediments to their blissful union?

"Oh, an unfortunate comment. Forgive me, I am not myself. I am too old and too much in need of a long rest. These games exhaust me.

"But, speaking of blissful unions—what has happened to the younger generation, may I ask? In my day we knew better than to embark on foolhardy and self-indulgent paths guaranteed—or almost guaranteed—to end badly.

"We will speak no further of that.

"Early this morning they said they intended to "rest to-

gether." Hah! Rest together, indeed. Obviously their interpretation of "resting" and ours are quite different.

"But it is over, and we will definitely put the matter aside.

"I even made certain the package the dratted boy
dropped got where it could serve a useful purpose. It should
have ensured the More girl returned quickly to Viscount Kilrood's home. But what does she do? Well, why should I expect more after seeing how little resolve the foolish snip
has?

"But I shall not give up, not now. I beg you to assist me.
The moment you get the slightest hint of something that will
serve our purpose—that is the purpose of good—shout out
what you know. What good will that do, you say? That is for
me to know, and you to obey."

🙞 Chapter 30 🙜

Ross looked at Jennings and felt complete understanding pass between them. The very worst had occurred. Finch had fallen into the hands of the enemy.

"Finch seemed frightened," the younger Miss Smiles, Meg, said. "Didn't she, Sibyl?"

They had gathered in the shabby sitting room belonging to Latimer and Finch. Just looking at the place and thinking of Finch living there infuriated Ross. "This man you say came for her. You're sure you heard his name as Artemis?"

"Artemis Gibble," Sibyl Smiles, the blond one said. "Old Coot announced him. He came before lunch."

"And you allowed Finch to leave with this disreputable man, this stranger, and did nothing to try to stop her? And she's been gone for hours?" Already the afternoon had grown gloomy, and snow hurtled from a darkening sky.

Meg raised her firm chin and said, "No," while her sister began to cry softly. "How would we interfere?" Meg continued. "Do stop crying, Sibyl, dear. This is no fault of yours. You've done everything possible to help. There seemed absolutely nothing disreputable about the man, my lord. He was well dressed and well-spoken. Not that we heard what was said once he came in here with Finch."

"He came in *here* with Finch? *Alone?*"

Sibyl Smiles cried openly now.

"Och, there's no need for that, lassie," Jennings said. "Sit yoursel' down and we'll get t'the bottom o'this soon enough. His Lordship's a wee bit upset is all."

"Upset?" Ross thundered. By God someone should suffer for this. "My fiancée kidnapped, and I'm only supposed to be a little upset?"

"Fiancée?" Meg said, and her voice cracked. "Finch didn't say."

"She didn't know," Ross said, then recognized how outrageous that sounded.

If Meg noticed, she showed nothing. "My, my, your *fiancée.* I do love a good wedding. That accounts for all the roses again."

Ross frowned at her. "Roses?"

"Roses." She smiled happily toward the dreadful table where a vase of white roses, apparently his own hothouse roses, sat. "The ones you sent this morning."

He stopped himself from asking how the hell they'd got there.

"And the bird. Even though he is rather nasty," Meg said.

Ross looked to the covered cage he still recognized as the one he'd given Finch, but resolved to waste not another second on such things. "Did Finch mention why she returned here when she did?" He would not give Jennings the satisfaction of letting him know he could feel his derision.

"We sent for her," Meg Smiles muttered. "We shouldn't have, but we were worried about her, so we did."

"She shouldn't have come." Ross felt murderous. "I told her to wait for me at Number 8. It's true that I've been gone all day, but I was about very important business—*essential* business—and I expressly told her to wait for me." This was his doing, but given the news from Ranthus, he'd been forced to return to the goldsmith and stay with him until he'd completed as much of his work as he could.

"Finch is very independent," Sibyl Smiles said, surprising Ross. "She is not the type of woman to succumb to boorish male posturing. Where is Latimer? Finch said he was with you."

Jennings cleared his throat, warning Ross to have a care.

"Actually," Meg said. "It was your fault in a way. Finch's going off, I mean. If a delivery meant for you hadn't come here by mistake, we wouldn't have thought of sending for Finch to collect it."

Blood drained from Ross's head. "What delivery?" he asked, very careful to keep his voice low and even.

"Nothing significant I shouldn't think. A rather tatty-looking thing in oilcloth with string around it and a label I could barely read."

"I see." He didn't need to ask whose name had been on the label. "And Finch came for this, er, tatty thing? Do you happen to know what she did with it?"

"Hmm"—Meg confounded him by looking into a biscuit barrel—"well, no, I don't. I rather thought she intended to take it to your house, but then that man came."

"And she left with him."

"We already told you she did."

But he didn't want to believe it. Taking Jennings by the sleeve, he went into the hall. "Thank you both," he said, casting about for some inspiration as to where to go from there. "You have been helpful."

Outside the house he paced the snow-covered flagway while Jennings watched. "Go back to Number 8," he said at last. "Wait for me there. I shall attempt to hold off our thieves. We must hope that telling them we have all parts of the box will whip them to even greater greed. Then they will be more likely to do as I ask and make an exchange for Finch and Latimer. If I send a message telling you to come, and saying that it's time to end it—bring the box."

"Um—including the, er, the piece that remains in the collection, my lord?" The valet's breath turned to clouds of vapor that billowed toward the laden sky.

Ross hesitated, then said, "Yes. I shall then have no choice."

"Very well. May I ask where you're going, my lord?"

Ross glared at him. "You know as well as I do that I haven't the faintest idea where to go. Whitechapel, I suppose, although I don't hold out any hope of finding our pigeons there. You do understand that whatever happens, we must do all in our power to subdue Artemis and Zebediah and retain the box?"

"Och, I think that's become rather clear," Jennings said, his face expressionless.

Despite his frustration, Ross had to smile. "Not one of our usual flawless performances this time, Jennings, hmm? I have committed the ultimate sin in a man such as I, haven't I?"

Jennings's expression was inscrutable. "Ye mean ye've come t'your senses and realized ye *are* only a man, d'ye mean, m'lord? Aye, then, so ye are, and a wise one. Your *fiancée's* a prize."

Such a dour, but sincere declaration from Jennings didn't go amiss with Ross. "You're right," he said. "She's worth more to me than I can explain, but—" He coughed, and resumed his pacing.

"There you are, Viscount Kilrood. Be so good as to stand still, will you?"

Ross flung around in time to see Edwin Oak. He trudged toward them, a muffler wrapped around his head beneath his top hat, and a vast and very long many-caped coat trailing into the snow. The old man's gait was tentative. A step to the side, several forward steps when he raised each gaitered foot high out of the snow, then an occasional backward pace before moving forward again.

"If I didn't know better, I'd say the fellow was in his cups," Ross muttered. "Of all the foul luck. Why does he have to arrive . . . Gad, maybe he knows something. Haven't set eyes on him since the Cock and Jugs. Our friends consider him an ally, don't they?"

"Aye, m'lord, they do at that."

"Afternoon to you, Mr. Oak."

"Hmm. Yes. And a foul afternoon it is. Never could abide snow. Never could understand why some people seemed to consider it *romanic* or some such nonsense." He staggered up to Ross and stood, flapping his wool-clad hands across his chest. "I have done my best to assist Mr. More in every way I could. But after all, I'm a retired museum curator, not a man of action. This position has been far too taxing, but I'm bound to do my duty."

"Yes," Ross said with hope. "We men of honor do insist upon doing our duty."

The old man thrust back his thin shoulders. "I should say so. But really, these past days have been too much even for a most determined spirit. To have those two dreadful . . . You know how those criminals enlisted my help—*my help*—in their nefarious activities. They sought me ought. And I, in an effort to help Mr. More, risked the severe complications death would present. I actually rode through the streets on the back of their carriage to that frightful *place*. You are aware of how I placed myself in grave danger by confronting them there. I can tell you that if I were not devoted to doing what I have undertaken to do, I should have taken myself off by now. As it is, I must be finished with this as quickly as possible. Now, I can tell you where to find them, or not. Depends on you."

Ross stood still and heard the thunder of his heart in his ears. "You can tell me where they are?"

"Oh, I certainly don't have to if it's of no interest to you."

Ross clasped his hands behind his back where he was less likely to be tempted to use them on Oak's neck. "I should be obliged if you would tell me at once. Later I will explain to you exactly how great a service you have done. For Finch, for her brother, for me—and for a certain cause, the importance of which you cannot even begin to imagine."

"If you say so. You'll find them in Piccadilly. If you can get a cab, I'll come part of the way with you and explain exactly what I have discerned."

Leaving Jennings with a reminder that he was to stand by for further instructions, Ross went with Oak, and they picked up a cab at the corner.

By the time they arrived at the Piccadilly address Edwin Oak had given the cab driver, Ross understood exactly what he would confront. His primary anxiety rested on the possibility that the women present would get in his way. And he wished Jennings were with him, but it was important that he be where he could watch over the Sacred Box of Ranthus. Ross carried the key in a hollow bootheel. Once the lid was on and the box shut, it would lock automatically. For the ceremony, the heir to Ranthus must be able to open it. To open it and place the fabulous Ranthus jewel inside. The stone remained there until the birth of the next male heir when, once more, the "old tiger" gave the ruby to the "young tiger." And so the progression had continued for centuries. He hoped the current heir—whom he'd never met—had safeguarded the ruby.

"Well now," Mr. Oak said. "I'd best be off. My relative is expecting me in Hampstead."

Ross had no alternative but to throw himself on the old man's mercy one more time. He asked him to remain outside the house—inside the cab, of course—until Ross could send him a signal to return to Mayfair Square and give Jennings a message.

"I should tell him to come now? That it's time to end it all?" Oak repeated as if the entire idea were humorous. He wrinkled his long nose. "I'm to tell Jennings that? Well, there's no accounting for the fixes some people get themselves into, is there? Least a man can do is end it himself if he doesn't have the courage to carry on. That's what I always say."

Ross hadn't the patience to argue. "Just do that for me, will you?"

With a gusty sigh, Oak said, "Oh, very well. But do make it quick, will you. If I have to exert myself much more, I'm likely to fade away."

§ Chapter 31 §

Ross shielded his eyes against the wind and weather. He blessed the snow that had begun to fall even more heavily, obscuring the view so that anyone coming or going appeared as a wraith materializing from a blanket of white, and quickly disappeared in the same manner. The snow also deadened the creaking of the waiting cab, and horses' blowing.

He now knew the exact house, and who was inside. And he knew that he was one man against two villainous ones, and a hostile woman. Also present were a man who might be too ill to be of any use, and a dear girl who had no place anywhere near such abomination.

Just as Oak had predicted, a gate in a black-iron railing in front of the house was unlocked. A flight of stone steps led down to a small, dark courtyard at the basement level of the house. Ross understood such layouts well and went directly to a door that would open into the kitchens. Not a light showed from within the sash windows. Glancing upward, he noted that the building had about it a cold, empty air. He could not see the street, but had not heard the cab depart as he'd feared it might once he was out of sight.

Oak was a queer one and no mistake. He bore the unmistakable signs of the old bachelor who disliked any change in his habits.

Ross tried the door. Again Mr. Oak was right, for this lock was also open and Ross was able to slip inside the dank, cold corridor. Darkness enfolded him. He groped forward, straining to see, willing his eyes to adjust. A step downward all but upended him. Staggering, he caught himself on the edge of a sink and knew he was in the scullery. Then he moved on with more assurance. Outlines became clearer. The kitchen. A great open fireplace that emitted an acrid scent of old ashes damped and grown hard—and coated with a residue of soot. Pots shone dully on shelves, and he could make out stacks of bowls and platters on tables and counters. Almost as if the staff had left in a hurry.

Windows into the butler's and housekeeper's domains threw back ghostly images of Ross when he passed. "They are evil men," Oak had said. "If you don't deal with them first, they will kill you. I heard them talk about killing you. They also plan to leave no one alive who could identify them."

Very well. He would not feign indifference to such threats, but he did know his own skills. There were too many memories of bitter confrontations for him to want to put faces to his old enemies, but few had risen to a new day after their final "encounters."

The design of passageways and stairs leading to the upper floors didn't disappoint him. Very soon he stood at a door lined with what he knew from feel was baize. This he inched open, but more darkness greeted him.

Ross slipped into a space beneath a staircase and stood perfectly still, listening. He might have closed his eyes to make his hearing more focused but dared not risk reducing his vision for even a second. The faint sounds of the house were all about him. With instincts he'd honed in deserts, bazaars, hill fortifications waiting for attack, and in the so-civilized company of men without scruples, he listened. And he raised his face to feel what the air told him, the subtle shifting of currents—and that certain sense he would never be able to explain to those without similar talents.

Everything about this place was designed to make an intruder think it was empty, or at least that there was no threat here.

Nothing could be further from the truth. Danger soaked his awareness. Not a new sensation—apart from the added, the overwhelming desperation that might have paralyzed a less experienced warrior.

Finch was here. He felt her. And he opened his mouth to breathe, ever so softly. That dear girl was his—he had made her so. And in making her so, in binding her to him so that her pure and loyal heart opened to him, he had thrust her into danger so extreme he ached to race, yelling through this place until he found her.

He did not race, or yell. He did edge forward beside the bottom of the staircase, facing outward but pausing frequently to weigh the atmosphere and to glance upward for any movement.

Then he did hear a sound. A crunching from outside, and he knew what it was. Even the snow didn't mask the grinding sound of grabbing wheels, or the cab driver's yell when he drove away. Damn Edwin Oak's eyes. The selfish old trout had run off to find himself a comfortable bed. Now there would be no hope of Jennings coming with the box if there should prove to be no choice but to give it up—at least until he could get Latimer and Finch to safety. But he would think of some trick. He must.

Doors stood open all around him. A less experienced man might be relieved. Ross recognized the strong possibility that this was deliberate, a means to allow him to eliminate any presence on this floor so that he would move on rapidly.

The rooms were empty. And he did move on. Swiftly, now,

he reached the foot of the stairs and ran lightly upward, certain that other ears listened in the night.

At the top of the first flight of stairs, Ross's training instantly took over, and he looked for other open doors. There was only one. His gut clenched. Every muscle in his body tensed.

Crouching low, keeping beneath the faint but reveling reflection of the snow falling beyond the windows, he reached a wall and remained hunched over. Even the white glimmer from outside would be enough to silhouette a careless man.

Ross couldn't afford to be careless.

He'd already decided that a pistol would be too unpredictable in what could be a very small space. Close combat—with knives—was an old and respected ally. His knife was already in his right hand. A second knife rested in a sheath against his right forearm in case some unforseen development caused him to need it. And if necessary, he would be capable of fighting with both knives at the same time.

His gut unclenched, but he deliberately retained muscular tension. To be as alert as possible required a kind of pain that came from stretching tendon and nerve to breaking point.

Then he heard it, a very faint sob that came on an indrawn breath. He brought his teeth together and drew back his lips. They should suffer for victimizing the weak and innocent.

Until he knew the positions of everyone in that room he could not do other than act with caution. Cautious speed. Only seconds and he reached the wall immediately outside the open door. From his pocket he took a flint device he'd acquired in China. Taking a step inside the room, he ran his thumb over the flint and a spark ignited flame. For several brief moments that flame burned bright and Ross saw all he needed to see. To his left, a pistol in hand, stood the man who must be the newly groomed version of Artemis. He appeared taller, and Ross saw how he'd been duped by the man's former stooped posture.

Ross braced for gunfire but wasn't surprised when it didn't come.

Side by side on the far side of the bed stood Lady Evangeline and Zebediah Swift. Finch huddled on a window seat where her brother, Latimer, also sat.

The flame went out.

"You have been far too much trouble, Kilrood." This was Artemis. Despite a changed accent, the timbre of the voice gave the man away. "All of this drama could have been avoided if you had gone about your business without looking beyond what you'd been told to do."

"Fool," Ross said. "Don't insult my intelligence. You mean all would have been well for you if I had willed myself to be blind to your clumsy efforts, and arranged to present you with what you seek, and without any defense.

"But now to business. This is among the three of us. Swift, yourself, and me. Let the Mores go. And Lady Evangeline. Then we shall work out a compromise."

Artemis laughed. Not a pretty sound but one that echoed from the past for Ross. He had heard that laugh before.

"No compromises," Artemis said. "I shall decide how best to proceed. I believe you have what I require. You will try to fool me into thinking you are still waiting for certain items. Only I won't believe you. We know you already had one early delivery. Then you took possession of four pieces from Whitechapel, from the boy. A fifth was dropped. The dockworker told me before I killed him."

Ross grasped the knife in his right hand so hard the handle dug into his palm. He was careful to keep the blade where it would not catch any light.

"Nothing to say?" Artemis said. "Well, people are no more important to you than they are to me, are they? But there was another piece that was dropped. We searched as soon as we found out. It was gone, but you will know that. Do you have it, too? Of course you do. The boy would have told you."

"Since you know everything," Ross said, "you hardly need to question me."

Artemis made a snarling sound, and Ross felt him coil as if to strike.

"I suggest you control yourself," Ross said. "And do as I ask. Release the Mores. They are no part of this, and if I ask them, they will go home and remain there, without raising any alarm until I get back. You will do that, Finch? Latimer?"

"Yes," Latimer said, his voice stronger than Ross had feared.

"I shall not leave you," Finch said, and Ross closed his eyes. He might have expected her to say something as foolish. "This man is a criminal. He kidnapped Latimer, then tricked me into coming here. Promise him nothing. It's obvious you have things he wants, and he won't get them if he kills you, so he is the one with the biggest problem."

Ah, his courageous Finch. His headstrong, infuriating, lovable, loyal Finch.

"And what of you, Zebediah?" Ross asked. "I thought you were in charge here. Don't you think it would be wiser if we negotiated?"

"I suggest you listen to Artemis," Zebediah said shortly.

The reaction puzzled Ross, but no doubt he would soon be the recipient of whatever the two had planned between them.

"Well, my *lord*," Artemis said, "I do believe it's time for me to discover exactly what you may have on your person that is of interest to me."

Ross saw a movement. "Down on the floor, Finch! You, too, Latimer. Stay there."

"Ross?" Lady Evangeline's voice shook.

"Silence," Artemis thundered. "Don't forget who will decide your future. Do as you are told, and you shall not regret it."

Praying the other man was at least slightly off-balance, Ross launched himself. He shot forward from a crouched position and barreled into Artemis's midsection. He heard a very satisfactory "oomph," and they crashed together to the floor. Killing this creature would be disastrous, at least until his whole story was known.

Any satisfaction was short-lived for Ross. A sickening thud on the base of his skull sent a blade of pain through his brain. Artemis had used the pistol as a club. And he used it that way again and again, raining blows on Ross's head, neck, and shoulders while Ross grappled to gain purchase on the other man. By an evil quirk of fate, his right wrist made contact with a wooden bedpost and the knife flew away.

Artemis laughed aloud, a high, spiraling laugh. "You do not have my skill, Kilrood. So much talk about how practiced you are. How dangerous. What a force to be contended with. But I have worked for this moment, and I must win."

Ross knew then what would be his greatest ally. Artemis loved the sound of his own voice, especially when it proclaimed his own importance.

Artemis rammed the pistol barrel beneath Ross's jaw and threw him to his back on the wooden floor. "Where is it?" he said. "I must have it now."

To Ross's horror, a candle flame spurted to life. Rather than lie on the floor, Finch had found the candle and lit it. She held it aloft and peered at Artemis. "Stop it," she said. "Stop it at once before you do terrible damage."

Ross vowed he would teach this woman to do as she was told, at least in situations of life and death. "Blow the candle out," he said, never taking his eyes off Artemis. Zebediah and Evangeline remained on the other side of the bed but he knew there had to have been an arrangement between Zebediah and Artemis. Zebediah would come in to help finish the job Artemis started.

"Get that beastly weapon away from Ross at once," Finch shouted in a voice that broke. "If you don't, I'll scream."

Ross stopped himself from groaning. This was appalling. The box must go to Ranthus at once. A messenger would arrive in Mayfair Square before morning, and he would expect the shipment to be ready.

"I suggest you make your little ladybird keep her mouth *shut*," Artemis said with a sneer. "I'd have expected you to have better taste. But then, she was convenient."

Oh, he wanted to kill the man. He lay still as if immobilized by the cold pistol barrel against his neck. He lay still enough to wait for Artemis to look around the room, checking on the positions of all players.

And that's when Ross struck. A straight arm chopped upward not only knocked the other's arm away, but it dislodged his grip on the pistol. The latter clattered to the floor and skittered beneath the bed.

Ross closed his hands around Artemis's neck, and received a matching grasp. Ross forced himself to his knees, gasping from the pressure on his neck, but he was the stronger of the two, and the other man's face turned dark.

Surely Zebediah would pile into the fray now.

Ross squeezed Artemis's throat. Artemis squeezed Ross's throat. They fell again, rolled over and slammed into a chair with a table beside it. The table flew to its side, splintering on impact. Glass and porcelain shattered.

Artemis began to scream. With rage, not with pain. And in a language Ross recognized, but did not speak. Artemis poured forth streams of words from the dialect of Ranthus. There was no time to think, but this wasn't the first time Ross had encountered this man.

They scrambled up, landing punches on whatever parts of each other could be reached. Ross saw blood spurt from Artemis's nose, and saw a gash open above his left eye. A blow to his own neck sent him sprawling and panting to the floor at Zebediah's feet.

At once, if coughing, he was on his feet again. He tasted his own blood but didn't know where he was wounded.

He returned Artemis's favor and landed a chop to the windpipe. Gagging, the other dropped back.

"Ross," Finch cried. "Ross, hurt him."

Ross, hurt him? Ah, such viciousness from his lady. "Leave," he ordered. "Latimer, get Finch out of here."

Why hadn't Zebediah come to his partner's aid?

There was no time to consider the mystery further. Artemis came at him, and Ross saw that he had grabbed a leg from the demolished table. He brandished this aloft and landed blows to Ross's shoulders and arms before Ross could cover his head and charge. They locked together and collided with a wall. A painting fell, a corner of the frame gouging Ross's brow. He took a deep breath and bellowed, charging Artemis as he did so. On impact he wrapped his arms around the man's body and crushed him in a death embrace.

Artemis screamed, and kicked. He managed to reach Ross's hair and drag at handfuls.

"That's not fair," Finch yelled, and Ross was dimly aware of a brilliant red, gold gown billowing in the gloom before she leaped upon Artemis's back. "You aren't a good fighter, Mr. Gibble. You cheat." With that she ground her fingertips into the beleaguered fiend's eyes, producing screams that unfortunately stopped when Artemis threw her off. She landed with a thud, and Ross had the impression she didn't move.

If he could be left to deal with this fight, he'd win. Why wasn't Zebediah involved? Breathing heavily, Ross hopped to his feet and spread his arms. He had managed to work his second knife free, and this he used to taunt Artemis into another attack. They circled, and from the corner of his eye Ross finally saw what should have been immediately obvious. Zebediah and Evangeline were tied up, tied to each other, in fact.

"Greedy, aren't we, Artemis? Turning on your own partners. Who are you working for? Won't they have something to say about all this?"

"I worked for Sherwood Trimble," Artemis said, apparently vastly amused at Ross's questions. "Or he thought I did. Actually he worked for me. They all did. And now I don't need them anymore. Give me what I want, or they all die, and then you die."

"You worked for Sherwood?"

"You know what these scientists can be like. Or men like him who are scientists. He always needed money, lots of money for his digs, and he'd spent everything. So when I approached him to discover the details of his agreement with Zebediah, and to enlist his help in getting to you, he was more than happy to oblige. After all, why wouldn't he enjoy being paid twice for his services? He hadn't objected even a little to using his wife to gain entrance to your home. He agreed to pretend Zebediah was her *companion*.

"I managed to take a passage on the same ship as Zebediah. We'd hardly set sail for England when he hired me as a coachman." Artemis chortled. "I made him think we wanted the same things for the same reasons. We cared only for the good of Ranthus." He laughed more wildly. "It was all so perfect. If anything went wrong, everything would be blamed on him. And that's how it will work now. I shall get away with everything, and Zebediah will be found with . . . well, he will be found and there will be no questions asked because it will all be obvious, even to whatever fools come to investigate. He was the one who intended to steal the box for himself. I was merely trying to rescue it for Ranthus, and when I did so I had to race to get back there. When I tell my story in Ranthus, I shall be a hero. We have chatted enough. Give me what I want."

Clattering on the stairs silenced everyone.

The abrupt halt of the footsteps filled the room with utter silence. Then came the sounds of a stealthy advance. The door had all but closed, so whoever was outside could not see what had happened in the room.

The door burst open and Jennings leaped forward. He assessed the situation. Ross knew he must look battered, but even that hadn't prepared him for Jennings's reaction. "I got your message, m'lord. I came as quick as I could. I've the box, just as ye said."

Rather than follow Ross's request that he wait for a sign, Oak must have left for Mayfair Square almost at once. Blessings on the rascal for his impatience.

"How kind of you," Artemis said, holding out a hand. "Give it to me, if you please."

"M'lord?" Jennings said, catching Ross's eye and managing a subtle wink. "Should I give it t'him?"

"Do that," Ross said, praying the valet had devised a ruse.

Jennings tossed a bundle at Artemis.

Artemis quickly pushed the package into a deep pocket inside his coat. "And you, Kilrood? I believe there is one more item I require."

Ross wished the key were not in his possession.

"I said, *yours now,* Kilrood." When Ross made no move to give up the key, Artemis's face contorted. He leveled the pistol not at Ross, but at Finch who continued to lie where she'd fallen.

"Go ahead," Ross said, and the bluff sickened him. "It looks as if she's all but dead already. But I have nothing to give you."

Artemis curled his upper lip and pointed the pistol at Jennings instead. "First your man. Then More, then his sister."

"Aren't you afraid Sherwood will give you away?"

Artemis laughed. He looked at Evangeline, who hadn't uttered another word. "Tell him."

Evangeline, whose pretty face was chalk white, cleared her throat, and said in a small voice, "Sherwood is dead. Murdered by him." She looked at the floor. "Strangled. He's under the bed."

"Here?" Ross said, disoriented.

"Yes," Evangeline told him. "Poor, foolish Sherwood. He could never have succeeded at these games."

Ross felt Artemis snap. "Shut up all of you," he roared. "Shut up and do as I tell you. You. The valet—against the wall. More, you stay on the window seat. Now you"—he backed Ross up—"on your knees."

There was nothing for it but to obey. Slowly Ross dropped to his knees, but remained upright.

"Hands on the floor."

Ross followed orders. Landing strategic kicks to his victim's ribs, Artemis set about searching Ross's pockets. When he could find nothing, he let out a bellow and renewed the kicks to every part of Ross's body. Ross grabbed for an ankle and pushed the leg upward. Artemis overbalanced backward.

He had the man.

Jennings, piling on, threw Ross off-balance. Then Latimer,

moving like a man who had been submerged in water, came into the fray with his fists raised, pugilist fashion, and Ross groaned. He struggled to fasten his hands on Artemis's lapels but was forced away by the combination of Jennings and Latimer. Jennings alone would have helped Ross. Latimer managed the feat of placing himself like a shield before Artemis and giving him an opportunity not only to gather himself, but to come up pointing the pistol at Finch again.

"Stay away all of you," he said, approaching her still form. "I prefer a challenge, but under the circumstances, I have no choice. Put everything on the bed and step away. Or she dies."

This time he wouldn't hesitate to carry out the threat; Ross knew it.

"Who are you?" he asked the man. "Where do I know you from?"

Artemis muttered more words in the tongue of Ranthus.

"Surely you don't mind telling me now."

"You don't know, do you? Take a prince out of his robes and away from his natural surroundings, and you English are too obtuse to recognize him. Especially if he speaks your language as well as you do." He straightened and worked to reveal a heavy chain he wore around his neck and beneath his shirt. Suspended from the chain was a bag fashioned from a mesh of gold. What he produced from inside the bag stunned Ross. A stone, a ruby the size of a quail's egg glinted in the man's palm.

"You see, my lord. All I need is the key to the box, and that I shall soon have. I am Rajab, son of Naren, dead Sheik of Ranthus. I am his heir."

Ross looked blankly at the man. He had seen him in Ranthus, but only at a distance—wearing a turban and flowing robes. Ross would never have known him as this man. But he had heard his laugh . . .

"My father decided I was not good enough to take his place. He would not forgive me for a few youthful mistakes, so he intended to disinherit me by making it impossible for me to take my place at the appropriate time. He had the box dismantled and sent away—by you. So I had to correct that. The box must be where I can find it, and quickly, if I am to claim what is mine."

A shot reverberated in the room, deafening Ross, bringing a scream from Evangeline. And from Zebediah it brought the war cry of a desert tribesman. The huge rock of a man exploded from his place beside Evangeline. He jumped, stretched out in the air, and came down on top of Artemis. The disinherited heir to Ranthus crumpled like a doll made of cloth.

Evangeline rushed forward to hover over Zebediah. "Are you hurt?" she said, and her hand on Zebediah's shoulder left Ross in no doubt as to whose health she was concerned about. "Zebediah, are you hurt?"

"No. Please step back, Evangeline." She did as he instructed and Zebediah got up, pulling Artemis with him. "You did well, my dear Evangeline. I don't believe you even cut my wrists." Artemis hung, unconscious, in Zebediah's arms.

Evangeline let out a small cry and covered her mouth.

Holding Artemis, Zebediah said, "Evangeline saved the day. She freed my bonds."

"You freed mine first," Evangeline said.

"I'm not clear about all this," Ross said. "What exactly—"

"Rajab—Artemis—was banished from Ranthus. That's when he hired an assassin to kill his father, the Sheik. But it was the assassin who died—after he was forced to talk. Then the Sheik hired you, Ross. He had already sent word, asking me to go to him. I was dispatched to Sherwood Trimble because the Sheik knew the man would accept a bribe to help me gain entrance into your house. My job was to make sure you were not followed, and that the box was as safe as was hoped. As long as it wasn't readily to hand, Artemis would be preoccupied. Unfortunately circumstances meant that I did not know Artemis. Our paths had never crossed. It was simple for him to come to me aboard the ship with a so-called message from the Sheik. I was suspicious, but, nevertheless, I told him he should be hired in some capacity once we were in London. And so it was."

"And who are you?" Ross asked.

"I am the Sheik's illegitimate son, Zebediah Swift as you already know me. My father has always been very good to me, as he was to my mother. It is his wish to legitimize me and make me his heir. That is not my desire, but I must help my father."

Evangeline's sigh filled the room.

"I have not made up my mind if I intend to accept what he wants in the end."

"The Sheik is dead," Ross pointed out.

"No. That is not so. I placed the announcement in the *Times*. I merely felt it necessary to draw all this to a conclusion and to deal with Artemis before the issue became too embarrassing to the Sheik. Later a retraction will be printed." He looked at Evangeline and bowed. "Thank you, my lady. My father and I are most grateful for your assistance. You have been very brave when you could not know the outcome of all this."

"I wasn't brave," she said softly. "I followed my heart."

"Trimble came to London to get more money out of Rajab—Artemis as you know him," Zebediah said. Without ceremony, he dropped Artemis to the floor. "It cost Trimble his life."

Ross bent to retrieve Artemis's pistol. "I do believe Zebediah will comfort you, Evangeline," he said.

But with a triumphant cry, Artemis suddenly leaped to his feet and wrenched the gun from Ross's hand. He pointed the weapon at Zebediah. "Never underestimate a man such as me, *fool*. You need not concern yourself with my inheritance. No bastard will ever rule Ranthus."

"Stop him," Latimer cried. He ran toward Artemis, his face contorted.

Ross dashed at him, pushing him aside and bringing up his second knife at the same time.

Latimer fell back. Artemis trained his gun on Ross.

Zebediah made a grab for his half brother and missed.

The only sounds were of scrambling feet and rasping breaths.

Ross managed to twist aside, out of the range of the shot Artemis fired. Instantly the man swung toward him—and stumbled over the broken table.

Ross lunged and sank his knife into the other's breast. Without a sound but for the escape of air, and a clicking in his throat, Artemis crumpled.

On his knees beside Rajab, Zebediah turned the man over. The knife hilt protruded from his chest. "Dead," Zebediah said, and he pulled a cover from the bed to drape over the body.

Ross noted that Finch had sat up, and that she stared, horrified, at the body. He went to bend over her. "Latimer," he said. "We shall have to work hard on teaching your headstrong sister that a woman's place is not in the middle of a fight among men. She might have caused a very different outcome here this evening." But he did love her. He loved her for her fire and even her impetuousness.

"She has always tended to be difficult to control," Latimer said.

"Yes. Well, if she's to make a good wife for a man who has no choice but to follow his star—and that star brings brushes with deadly danger—well, then, she must learn acceptance, and self-control." And while she became accustomed to what his career would mean to them, they would start their life together, and he might decide that his thoughts about farming were worth pursuing. He could still choose to accept particularly intriguing missions.

"Come along, Finch," he said. "We'd better get you home to bed and bring a doctor in."

He gathered her into his arms and smiled at her face. Doubtless she had fainted from excitement earlier. After all, she might be fiery, but she was only a woman.

Her eyes settled on his, not like the eyes of a woman who

had lost consciousness, but like a woman who had decided to keep them closed until opening them suited her.

Ross looked into those eyes. "Why do I believe you were faking, my girl. Well, that's your excitement over. Time for a quiet life for you."

"Kindly release me," she said, and her tone left him in no doubt that he should do as she asked. "I'm glad you've made a success of a very difficult task. I'm sure you will be roundly praised—and compensated. Congratulations."

"Finch, you should get some sleep, then we'll talk."

She wore a heavy cloak over a bright red gown. A bonnet hung down her back from its ribbons. Retrieving the bonnet, she put it on and tied the ribbons beneath her chin. Then she put a hand into her muff. "Oh. This is yours." She removed a packet from the muff and pushed it into his hands. "Good luck, Ross. You are special—in so many ways. Come along, Latimer. Good night, Zebediah. I'm delighted you're a good man. Help Lady Evangeline find some happiness if you can. Thank you for all your kindness, Jennings."

With a sense of amazement, Ross watched Finch leave the room and, shortly, heard the front door open and close.

"Och," Jennings said. "Now look what ye've done wi' your arrogant blather. Will ye never learn how t'treat a woman, especially a woman the likes o' that one? She's a brave, wee thing, and she's no' a woman to be treated like a child after all she's been through. Ye've angered her. If ye can no' get her back, ye'll never be a whole man again."

Shaken, Ross caught sight of a fiery thing on the floor. The ruby. And he still had possession of the Sacred Box of Ranthus, and its key.

Silently, he picked up the ruby and handed it to Zebediah.

§ Chapter 32 §

"Unwell as I am, I have come from my bed before noon to talk sense into you, my girl," Lady Hester said to Finch. "One cannot begin to understand why a man such as Viscount Kilrood would choose you for his wife—even though you are a dear child—but he has chosen you. Such an opportunity should bring you joy and gratitude. Of *course* you will not continue to refuse to receive him."

Summoned to an interview in Lady Hester's boudoir, Finch wished she neither liked, nor felt grateful to Her Ladyship, but she did, and that meant she'd been forced to appear.

"Are you listening to me, gel?"

Seated on the gold-and-black-striped chaise, Finch leaned forward and propped her chin on her cupped hands. Despite her dreams, despite the fact that she had fallen in love with Ross, she had never expected him to propose marriage. Not that he had *proposed* marriage. He *assumed* she would marry him.

"Look at you," Lady Hester said, and to Barstow, "Look at her, Barstow. Hair carelessly pinned, and by the way, that hair is *so* red. I'm not at all certain His Lordship won't prefer you to keep it covered."

"Particularly in bed," Finch muttered, and was instantly ashamed of herself.

"I beg your pardon?"

"I said, it is rather red," Finch said. "And since I'm not the viscount's responsibility, the color of my hair is neither here nor there."

Dressed in unprecedented mauve—be it a dark mauve—and with several short ropes of amethysts set in gold around her neck, Lady Hester looked charming. More amethysts shone at her ears and around her right wrist. She did not appear remotely ill.

At this moment Lady Hester's pretty mouth was set in an uncompromising line. She studied Finch through her lorgnette. "Redheads should not normally wear red. Particularly red with such an orange cast. Oddly enough it suits you. You have such pale, smooth skin. Yes, hmm, quite dramatic in a way, wouldn't you say, Barstow?"

"I would if you would, my lady."

"There, you see, Finch. Barstow agrees with me. You have been compromised. *Compromised.*" Her Ladyship rolled up her eyes as if she might faint away from the horror of allowing such a word to pass her lips. "But you have been smiled upon by the most extraordinary fate. That generous, charming, handsome, powerful, *forgiving* man has consented to overlook your tarnished reputation. Meg Smiles told me so, and Meg does not lie."

Finch stared. Not, *the man compromised you but he wants to do what he should do and marry you.* Not, *that dastardly devil should be whipped for destroying the unsullied nature of a pure woman, but since he wishes to marry you, perhaps you should consider his offer.* Oh, no, she was to positively slobber with gratitude because the man they knew was responsible for whatever offense she had committed, wanted to accept that responsibility. The entire world was gone mad!

He had decided they should marry.

He had decided she would then live without him, waiting for his return after each mission—wondering if he *would* return at all.

She was afraid, afraid to do as he expected, afraid to refuse him.

She loved him too much.

"Are you listening to me, Finch?"

"Yes, my lady."

"So you will agree to receive Viscount Kilrood and entertain his proposal of marriage? And you will accept—with your father's and brother's blessings, of course?"

No doubt Father would be delirious with joy. He would bless Ross for bringing his troublesome daughter to a good end. Not that a woman of nine-and-twenty needed her father's blessings on her decision to marry.

Finch sighed. She had donned the questionable gown once more this morning because she found she hadn't enough interest to decide on another. But even if her hair were haphazardly pinned, she had brushed it well. There was nothing to be done about the dark marks beneath her eyes, or the drawn impression her face gave.

"Finch!" Rising from her brocade-canopied daybed, Lady Hester swished back and forth across the boudoir. "What a very vexing creature you are. Can you tell me you have no interest in Viscount Kilrood?"

"No."

"*No?*" Lady Hester swung to face her, her fine brows rumpled into a frown. "*No?* Yet you have sent him away? Twice in one morning?"

"If he were a sensible man, once would have been sufficient."

"Oh, you are also arrogant, are you? Well, well. Can you tell me you do not find the man attractive?"

"No."

"*No?* Well, so we make some sort of progress." The lady's frown deepened. "At least, I suppose we make progress. Is it possible that you think you ought to *love* him." This last evidently cost her so much energy that she grew still and swayed slightly.

"Absolutely," Finch said.

"You think you ought to love him? Well, I can dispel that nonsense for you. It is of absolutely no importance for you to love him, so put that out of your mind. No, you definitely do not need to love him, to marry him. Not at all."

"I do love him." Oh, exhaustion was taking its toll on her tongue.

Lady Hester positively sputtered. And she tottered to the Chinese daybed and flopped down. She stretched out, cast a forearm over her brow, and allowed Barstow to lift her feet onto the mattress.

"Now look what you've done," Barstow said through her teeth. "You ought to be ashamed of yourself."

"You love him," Lady Hester said faintly. "Has no one explained to you that loving one's husband is a recipe for personal disaster? Didn't your family tell you that men don't love their wives because they don't have to? They accept responsibility for their wives because their wives become the mothers of their children. Love isn't at all the thing in a civilized arrangement such as the one I'm certain the viscount has in mind."

A knock on the door was followed by the appearance of old Coot. His eyes bulging, he advanced with a bouquet of red roses. "They keep me up nights. Order me out in the snow on errands that aren't my duty. And then I'm supposed to run up and down stairs with armloads of flowers."

"Thank you, Coot," Her Ladyship said. "Put them in a vase for me, will you, Barstow? And give me the card. How lovely for someone to think of me in my hour of need."

"For Miss More," Coot said, progressing until he stood before Finch. He dumped the bouquet in her lap. "That man Jennings brought them. He was most insistent that I deliver them now. He told me to say they are a token of deep admiration. Evidently it was felt that a card might not be read."

Finch looked at the exquisite blooms in her lap, and her throat clogged. Tears filled her eyes, and she bowed forward to hide them. He must leave her alone to think. Roses would not be enough to keep her warm when Ross was far away and in danger. And now she knew from experience just how terrible that danger could be.

A sniff made her look up. Tears stood in Lady Hester's clear blue eyes. "Such a display of dedication. Such proof of his honorable intentions. He is a sophisticated man and a catch any girl would swoon over. Love him if you must, but marry him, Finch, before he changes his mind."

Old Coot still hovered. "What is it?" Lady Hester asked.

"Jennings said I was to ask Miss More if she would come to Number 8 with him. Since she won't receive visitors from Number 8 here at Number 7."

Finch shook her head no.

Coot sighed again. "I told him that's what you'd say, you being the kind of difficult young woman you are. But he asked me to plead his case for him. His Lordship may go into a decline without you, so Jennings says. There are already signs of a severe headache and His Lordship hasn't suffered more than two of those in some time."

"Both of them in recent weeks," Finch muttered. "Convenient if you ask me. He uses them to manipulate people."

"I wouldn't know about that, miss."

"You are very unkind and thoughtless, Finch," Lady Hester said. "You have quite exhausted me. I think I must return to my bed."

"Um, there was a message for you, m'lady," Coot said. He went to Lady Hester and bent to whisper in her ear.

She sat up at once. "Hmm. Perhaps so. Yes, yes, we must do everything we can toward that end. Kindly leave me, Finch, I have business of my own to deal with. I will speak with you again later."

Finch didn't wait to be told to leave a second time. She

got to her feet and, holding the roses, made her way down-stairs. When she'd left the flat, Latimer continued to sleep, pale and exhausted from his ordeal. Following the frightful events of the previous evening, they had all spent some hours with constables while explanations for the death of dreadful Artemis were made. Fortunately, Ross's social stature, together with the believable testimony of the rest present, convinced the officials that the villain of the piece was a dead man.

"There you are, Finch," Hunter Lloyd said, altogether too heartily. He ran downstairs behind her. "I've been watching for you. Quite the adventure you've had, hmm?"

"Too much adventure," she told him, smiling. Hunter had the kind of strongly masculine charm that made a woman want to smile. "On your way to chambers?"

"No." he shook his head vaguely. "Actually I was hoping for a chat with you. We don't have nearly enough time to talk."

They reached the foyer, and Finch studied him curiously. Hunter wasn't given to "talks." "As a matter of fact, I'm rather tired. But you're awfully nice to offer to spend your time with me."

"Not a bit of it." He gave her a slap on the back that made her stagger, and promptly tucked a hand beneath her arm and walked with her inside the flat. "Now, let's make our-selves comfortable and catch up on things, shall we?"

Bemused, Finch found herself guided to sit on a couch with Hunter beside her.

"We really should be as quiet as possible," she said. "La-timer's had a dreadful experience. He needs his sleep."

"Oh, Latimer will be fine," Hunter said. "Told me so him-self. Beautiful day, hmm?"

Automatically Finch twisted to look out the window. Snow fell yet again, the flakes huge and soft at the moment. Many inches covered the ground and turned trees and shrubs into white mounds with branches weighted down to the ground. Even the black railings in front of the house had donned high, crystalline coatings that glistened with frosty spicules.

"You ought to go out for a stroll," Hunter said. "Bracing. Very bracing."

Finch transferred her attention from the pristine outdoors to Hunter's slightly reddened face. "I don't think I shall walk outside, but thank you for the thought anyway."

"Yes, well, you might want to reconsider. Good for you, all that fresh, cold air. I say, is that you out there, Chillworth?"

Indeed it was Adam Chillworth. It was also Meg and Sibyl Smiles and they all came into 7A dressed as if planning one of Hunter's "bracing" walks. "Hello there, Finch," Mr. Chillworth said, clapping his hands together as if he'd already been out and was trying to warm himself. "Meg and Sibyl and I are going to . . . er, go out and enjoy the air, aren't we, ladies?"

Meg and Sibyl gave a weak chorus of, "yes." They glanced repeatedly toward the window and the pelting snow outside.

"There, you see," Hunter said with gusto. "Everyone's going to take advantage of an opportunity to take the air. Come along, Finch, you can't let the side down."

She placed the roses on the table, got a pitcher of water from the marble-topped commode in her bedroom, and arranged the flowers.

"It's so romantic," Meg said. "Finch engaged. So romantic."

Finch froze. Her left hand closed on the rose stems and she felt thorns puncture her fingers. The pain scarcely registered. Certainly Ross had sent explicit messages stating his wish to propose to her. His reason for making this public, he said, was that his happiness must be shared with the world. Finch saw through the subterfuge to manipulation—yet again. He knew she was struggling with her feelings. He sought the help of those she trusted in swaying her. But for him to announce that they were engaged?

"You are the secretive one," Sibyl said. "We're very happy for you. Viscount Kilrood is a wonderful man, and he obviously thinks so much of you."

"As long as I don't interfere with his passions."

"Passions?" Meg and Sibyl said in unison. They both turned red. "Well, we wouldn't know about those."

She hadn't the energy to explain how the kind of passions she referred to had nothing to do with a man and a woman together. Finch turned warm at that thought. Only yesterday, early in the morning, she and Ross had entered into the most passionate expression a man and a woman could share. They'd joined their bodies, and she would never be the same. She didn't want to be the same. But how could she, a merchant's daughter, become the wife of a viscount? How would she live that part, especially when he planned to leave her alone most of the time? If she were younger, and more foolish, she would rush to accept what seemed a fairy tale come true. Finch's time for believing in fairy tales had passed.

"A walk—"

"No," she told Mr. Chillworth, much more harshly than she'd intended. "It isn't bracing, it's cold and damp, and the snow will only get inside our boots and bring us chills. You are kind to try to divert me—and I'm certain that is your intention because you think I am unhappy—but I need no diversion. I am perfectly happy."

"Of course you are," Meg said. She cleared her throat and fussed with the ribbons tied beneath her chin. "Well, I suppose we should get along before we become overheated."

"Hmm," Hunter said. He raised his eyebrows and looked from one to the other of the company. "So, then. Shall we?"

"Oh most certainly," Mr. Chillworth said, "we most certainly shall."

"Yes," Sibyl said.

Meg cleared her throat again, more loudly this time.

Hunter stared, and said, "Yes, yes, a pity about the boy."

An instant of concern passed quickly. They were all so

very bad at deceit, yet she did love them for their pure motives. And there was no doubt their motives were the most pure. They wished to see her happy with Ross.

"Do you know about Hayden?" Meg asked, when Finch showed no sign of responding to Hunter's remark. "He's really quite—well, quite."

Poor Meg, lies stuck in her throat. "Quite what?" Finch said. "I expect he has a bad cold."

"Oh, very bad," Adam Chillworth said. "I understand the doctor was called."

"I'm glad to hear that. And what did the doctor have to say? Does he expect Hayden to live?" She was becoming a very cruel person in her hour of extreme disquiet.

"Of course he'll live," Sibyl said, turning pink. "What a dreadful thought that one so young might die from a cold, Finch. How could you?"

"I'm sorry," Finch said, and she was. "I'm not myself." And she wasn't.

"Hayden likes you a great deal," Meg said.

"How do you know?"

Meg showed signs of becoming tearful, and Mr. Chillworth shook his head. He took her hand and tucked it beneath his. "Meg knows because Jennings told her," he said. "Apparently the lad has asked for you. We would be glad to accompany you to Number 8 so that you may visit."

"Do you think I don't know what you're all about?" Finch said, disregarding the need for quiet. "You are determined to see Lord Kilrood have his way. Yet you do not know how I feel—what concerns I may have. And he is exceedingly dangerous and capable of—of—well, he's capable of it, anyway."

"Most men are," Hunter said, and instantly looked horrified. "I mean—"

"I know what you mean," Finch said, and experienced her own stab of discomfort. "You have not seen His Lordship with a knife in his hand, or fighting in the most malevolent fashion. He is a man who knows no fear. There are . . . Well, there are *people* of very questionable character who hire him to do what most men would be afraid to do. This time he survived, but . . . Oh, I cannot speak of this now.

"I do know Hayden is suffering from being wet and cold for too long. And from not having enough to eat. But he is a strong boy and will recover."

"His Lordship wants you," Meg said, her voice rising. "He, he *loves* you. There, I have said it and I am not sorry. I have seen his face when he speaks of you."

"When?"

"Oh, Finch you are unkind and too persistent," Sibyl said. "His Lordship was here before you awoke this morning. He was here before he, himself, had gone to bed. In fact I should not be surprised if he remained up all night. He was distraught. And you know I am not given to exaggeration. His dejection was pitiable."

"No doubt. It certainly achieved what it was supposed to achieve—your pity and support. He has convinced you that I must be made to do as he wishes. And you are all determined to be his little soldiers in bringing Finch, the wicked, ungrateful one, to heel. You do not care that I am also suffering, or that I have concerns of my own in all this. I refuse to be overwhelmed by his declarations, so I am a challenge. He is behaving as he would in the face of any foe to be quelled. Well, I am not ready to be quelled, and I may never be." She considered what she had said. "I mean, I *shall* never be."

§ Chapter 33 ¢

Finch waited until she heard the front door slam and went to the window. She saw Hunter and Mr. Chillworth descend the front steps and face each other in snow that reached their knees. Really, this was ridiculous.

Meg and Sibyl did not appear, but when Finch leaned close to the window she saw them huddled together beneath the overhang above the front door.

They would freeze. Oh, she was beset on all sides. On the one hand there was a powerful man who knew too well that she yearned to be with him. On the other hand there were those who had become her dear friends and who were in league with Ross. And they all intended to convince her that she should have no reservations about doing whatever Ross wanted her to do.

"Finnie?"

She glanced over her shoulder to see Latimer emerging from his bedroom. He was considerably less wan. In fact he appeared quite lively and color had returned to his face. He smiled at her, and the old Latimer glinted in his eyes, her favorite part of him that was really rather mischievous. She'd seen it all too rarely since he'd been preoccupied with the vagaries of business.

"Quite a commotion here today, old thing. Got things sorted out between the two of you, have you? When's the big day?"

"Not you, too." She scowled. "You aren't even supposed to know all this."

He laughed. "Some things are difficult not to know. Should I send for Father?"

"No! Good heavens, no. I'm old enough to make up my own mind about my future."

"I quite agree. A quiet ceremony with your brother to give you away and your dearest friends present is absolutely the thing. Father will be delighted you've made such a fine match."

She gave up. Everyone in her life was determined to conspire against her. "Hunter and Mr. Chillworth are throwing snow at each other," she said. Her breath melted icy etchings on the inside of the window. "As we did as children. Snowballs, no less. I cannot imagine a more unlikely sight."

"Can't you?" He stood beside her. "It's good for people to encourage their more youthful exuberance from time to time."

She looked sideways at him. "You don't tend to encourage yours at all."

"I haven't for some time," he agreed. "But recent events have made me think about what is important in life. I have decided that living is what matters, and I intend to do just that. Within reason, of course."

"You need a wife," Finch said, driven by a wicked desire to delve into her brother's private life as he felt free to delve into hers.

Latimer became so serious that Finch felt remorseful for pressing him.

"First things first," he said. "Your welfare is my responsibility. Oh, good show, Hunter. Look at that. He got Chillworth fair and square. Right in the mouth."

"Men are such violent creatures," Finch said.

"Oh, my," Latimer said, craning his neck and peering outside. "What on earth is Jennings doing?"

Finch looked and saw Jennings scrambling along from the direction of Number 8. Doubled over, he darted this way and that, making grabs into the snow and even falling on one occasion. He disappeared for an instant and came up caked in white. He swept off his hat and brushed it clean, then beat at his coat before setting off once more on some sort of meandering chase.

"What the devil is the chap up to?" Latimer said. "There goes Hunter. And Chillworth."

Frowning, Finch studied the movements of the three men. "They're trying to catch something, but what can it be?"

Hunter collided with Mr. Chillworth, and they both slipped down. Finch watched to see if they would laugh. They didn't.

Mr. Chillworth made a grab at something and yelled loudly enough to be heard through the glass. He leaped up and pulled off a glove to examine a hand. He flapped it and pressed a finger between his teeth.

Suspicion sneaked up on Finch. "No," she murmured. "No, surely not."

"Surely not, what?" Latimer asked. "I can't see what it is they're after."

"No, but I think I know. How could Jennings be so foolish?"

"What?" Latimer asked, sounding impatient. "What are you talking about?"

"Oswin. Hayden's little dog. I do believe Jennings decided to bring her out in front of the house to, well, you know. But the animal is too short. She will be terrified."

"Look at them," Latimer said. "They're hopeless."

"Exactly. They're terrifying the animal." Another figure

arrived, this one painfully familiar. She wished she could make herself leave, but she couldn't.

"His Lordship," Latimer remarked, quite unnecessarily. "I shouldn't have thought he'd enough experience with dogs to be of use."

"Actually he's had a lot of experience with dogs and he's quite good with them." Finch clamped her teeth together. The defense of Ross had come too easily.

She couldn't hear what Ross said, but with his usual "in charge of all he surveyed" manner, he held up a hand and issued some sort of order. The other three men grew still, and the faint sound of Sibyl and Meg squealing from the front steps ceased.

Ross studied the snow where Finch began to see what she hadn't been able to note before with so much dashing about on the part of the men. Repeatedly hopping above the snow, Oswin, her fur soaked and slicked to her scrawny body, dashed in all directions.

"She's terrified," Finch said. "Oh, poor little creature. And she looked so sweet and fluffy when Ross bathed her."

"Ross bathed her?"

She caught her brother's amazed expression. "Yes. And very efficiently, too. I had tried and wasn't doing particularly well, so Ross took over. Oh, dear, she must be taken inside and made warm."

"If she doesn't die of cold before they can lay hands on her," Latimer said. "She's too small to withstand such extreme conditions."

"Hayden will be distraught." Finch gathered up the cloak she'd left in the sitting room when she'd returned home and swung it about her shoulders. She pulled up her hood. "Someone needs to restore calm out there."

She let herself out the front door in time to see Oswin leap into Ross's arms.

"Oh," Meg said, positively cooing. "How sweet. Dogs have a sixth sense about who they should trust, you know.

They only pick the best of people." Hunter and Mr. Chillworth climbed the steps toward them.

"If they don't have particularly poor instincts," Finch remarked. She should return to the house, but she'd like to visit Hayden, and make sure Oswin was all right.

Oh, she was trying to deceive herself. She wanted to get close to Ross.

"Very good, Your Lordship." Ross heard a voice, a dry cracking voice speak, but when he searched around could not match that voice to anyone present. "Just do as I tell you and show how much you dote upon the little mongrel."

Not Hunter Lloyd or Adam Chillworth, that was for sure. They had returned to stand with the Misses Smiles.

Dressed in the brown-velvet cloak that so suited her, and the red gown he'd decided set her wonderful hair afire, Finch also stood there. She stood there looking directly at him but with a speculative light in her eyes.

"Do as I tell you," the damnable voice said.

He looked to Jennings, who was too far distant to be responsible. The valet made subtle motions for Ross to return to Number 8.

"Poor little fellow," Ross said loudly to the ratlike creature Hayden regarded as a queen among dogs. "You are frozen. Inside my coat you go." There was a charm about Oswin's bright, black button eyes. They were moist and sad, and conveyed her serious approval of her rescuer.

Ross tucked her into his coat and fastened the buttons until only the animal's small, scruffy head protruded. Then he nodded to the company on the doorstep outside Number 7, and said, "I'd better get this little soul inside and warm her up before she takes ill. Hayden would be prostrate if anything happened to her."

"That's good," the voice said. "Now mention how you intend to offer Hayden a home—before you ruin your future by taking off on some foolish quest, that is."

"I say"—Ross glanced all about, but saw nothing and no

one—"whoever you are. I don't want any more *foolish quests*."

"Don't tell me. Tell her."

Finch slowly descended the steps and walked toward him, her cloak dragging in the snow. "Is she all right?" she said. "Oswin, I mean."

"She will be," Ross said, and swallowed. "She will be, Finch. I'm sorry."

She drew close enough for him to see how her freckles showed very clearly against her pale skin.

"I know you have been through a great deal. I would never have had such a thing happen, especially to you."

"Thank you." The hood of her cloak covered only part of her extraordinary hair. "These have been emotional times."

"Yes. Zebediah left at first light. There is a ship available, and he will be on his way to Ranthus with the box shortly. Lady Evangeline went with him."

"I'm glad. She has suffered, and I believe he will be kind to her."

"I will be kind to you, Finch," Ross said quietly, conscious of the ears straining to hear every word. "Jennings made a visit for me this morning. To the archbishop. He is an old friend."

"Oh," she said, not understanding his point. Her heart turned. "Are you planning to enter the Church?"

His grin transformed his serious features, his serious, irresistible features. "No, my love. I arranged to obtain a certain document, and I do have it. But it is of no use if we do not share the same wish."

She looked downward. "What is to become of Hayden? They said he is ill."

"He will recover. Then I shall find a place for him. He has a good mind, and he's willing to learn. He shall not be wasted." The dog squirmed, and he scratched her head, earning himself a lick on the nose. "Come, it's too cold. Let me take you home." He must not push her too hard.

"Thank you."

Surely she didn't have to be so amenable to leaving him quickly. "Could I persuade you to return with me to Number 8? You could visit Hayden." When she didn't respond, he added, "And me, Finch. You could visit me. I need you."

Her pale brown eyes met his once more, and he wanted only to take her into his arms. She made no attempt to move.

"At least come closer to the buildings where the wind is less bitter." He held her elbow and walked with her to stand beside the railings. Fortunately her back was to the very quiet assembly on the top step of Number 7, where a stately figure in a swansdown-trimmed gray cloak had now joined the group. Lady Hester stood at the center of her tenants and watched with at least as much interest.

"I got a special license from the archbishop," Ross told Finch. "For us to be married without need to call banns. A word from me, and he will come to marry us himself."

Her eyes didn't leave his face. It was as if she tried to see inside him, to his heart and soul, to discover some truth she must know.

"This very day you could be my wife, and I could be your husband."

Amazingly, Finch did not hear the collective sigh from behind her. "As it is I shall never cease to worry about you," she told him, and she placed the gloved fingers of her right hand on his mouth. "Wherever you are, you will take me with you because I shall never again be free of a part of you within me."

He didn't care what her neighbors made of that, nor that her brother had joined the rest and that he might draw the right conclusions. He caught her hand and held it. "We are a part of each other," he told her. "So why should we deny ourselves the joy of belonging together in the eyes of God as well as of men?"

"I never imagined you would want such a thing."

"I shall find no peace if I cannot have you. Finch, I shall not return to what was my former life. I have decided to do what has called to me for a long time—only I denied it. I wish to go to Scotland, to farm, and to enjoy my wife, and raise our children. We shall keep this house, of course, because we will always love this place."

She swayed toward him, and he almost gave in to the desperate desire to kiss her, but held back.

"Ross, listen to me," she said, "really listen. I beg you to step back. Step back and consider the wisdom of what you suggest. We must both consider."

"For how long?"

She tilted her head and looked up at him. "How can I be certain you will not change your mind when you become bored?"

"Because I am a man of honor who keeps his word."

She leaned against him and placed her cheek on Oswin's head. "You will keep your word even if your spirit longs to be free again?"

He slipped his hand inside her hood and stroked her ear, her thick, soft hair. "I can only ask you to believe that I know what I want. And I want you."

Abruptly she pushed away from him. "I think you believe you do. Please do as I ask and give us a little time. I am too old to be foolish and make rash decisions based only on a woman's fragile heart."

"What then?" he said. "How will you make your decision? And when?"

Her smile bemused him. "Well, I shall make my decision based on my fragile heart of course. What other choice do I have? But I shall be firm with it."

His pulse thundered at his temples. "If you refuse me, I shall lose all will to go on. And I feel a terrible headache sweeping over me. Without you, I shall never recover from the pain."

She wagged a finger at him. "Don't attempt that trickery with me. Jennings already did, and it didn't work, my lord."

He controlled a grin. "But surely you must marry me rather than risk my pining away."

"Marrying out of pity would never work."

"Well"—he narrowed his eyes and contrived to glare at her—"I am a fearsome man, and you'd *better* agree to marry me."

"Marrying out of fear would never work."

He groaned. "I've got to have you, Finch. I've got to have you as my wife."

"And I've got to think. Go away, and let me go away. I will come to you within the hour."

§ Chapter 34 §

Hayden sat before the fire in the red salon with Mrs. Hastings's quilt wrapped around him, and Oswin curled on his lap. The boy's eyes followed every move Ross made.

"What if she don't want to marry you?" Hayden said. "She's gentle, she might not like a hard man like you can be."

"Thank you," Ross said, glancing at his watch. Three-quarters of an hour had already passed. "I can be gentle, too. I'm gentle with Finch. And I'm gentle with dogs. I haven't been particularly rough on you as I remember."

"Nah," Hayden said. "You're a good'un, and no mistake. I was just makin' sure you was ready for the shock if she don't want you."

The front bell rang, and Ross's heart stopped beating.

Please let it be Finch come to her senses.

Jennings looked in on him. "The archbishop," he said. "He says he's here just in case and will be waiting in the library. Mrs. Hastings is seeing to some tea for him. She's also attending to a feast—just in case it's needed." He closed the door before Ross could tell him to close it.

"I'll have t'leave soon, won't I?" Hayden said. "You won't want to 'ave a boy like me around for long."

Ross regarded him. "We shall have to see about that. For now, assume that you will remain here. There are plenty of jobs for a willing boy in a house like this. And if I decide to go to Scotland, I shall have you accompany me there. I think you'd do well with the livestock. But more of that if the time comes."

Hayden's eyes glowed with hope, but he had the sense to be silent.

So tense his head really did ache, Ross clasped his hands behind his back. "I cannot stand this," he said, marching for the door into the courtyard. "If anyone comes for me, I shall be outside. Have me sent for."

The hour Finch had asked for passed while he walked aimlessly about the snow-blanketed courtyard. She was right, of course, he hadn't given her a chance to consider whether she wanted to marry him.

But she did. Of course she did. She would never have given herself to him if she hadn't . . . well, if she hadn't loved him. Finch More was a deal too sensible for her own good, and for his, at least in the matter at hand.

Would she really decide she could not risk committing to him? He shook snow from the naked branches of a slender birch and snapped off several graceful wands. He liked to see their lovely form and often put them in his rooms.

If Finch turned him down, he would still go to Scotland. And he would take Hayden with him. The boy would remind him of Finch, and he wanted to remember her always, not that he was likely to forget.

When the door from the house opened and she walked out with her red gown showing beneath the brown cloak, he held his breath. She carried several of the red roses he'd sent her that morning, and held their blossoms to her face, where she could smell them.

Finch looked at Ross's slender, dramatic face and might have laughed at herself for having thought she could turn from him if he truly wanted her. In one hand, hanging at his side, were long wands from a birch tree. He wore no heavy coat, yet he didn't appear cold. His black hair was rumpled, rumpled in a manner that made her want to rumple it even more, and his blue eyes were turned the intense shade that she never recalled seeing before. The snow gave off its ethereal glitter, and the moment had the quality of a magical, fragile thing.

She went directly to the man. "This is remarkably foolish, you know," she said. "We both know I couldn't deny you even if I wanted to, which I don't."

"I was not the one who suddenly questioned his feelings," said Ross. His stare grew even more intense, then his wonderful smile broke out, sending deep dimples into his cheeks. "You are not practiced in the art of coquetry, miss. No, I don't think you would do at all well if that were a necessary skill for you."

"But it isn't," she said. "Do you love me, Ross?"

"My mouth is dry," he said.

"I didn't ask—"

"I love you, I love you. Yes, I do love you. And I was so afraid you had decided you would not risk agreeing to be with me. You will, won't you? Risk it?"

"Yes, Ross. I'm going to risk it because I'm too weak not to. And I'm glad I'm too weak."

A rustle sounded from behind her but she knew without looking that Latimer and her neighbors from Number 7 had followed her. After all, she'd informed Latimer of her intentions. She heard Lady Hester's voice above the rest. "I knew she would come to her senses. Who wouldn't?"

"Here's his Highness the Archbishop," Jennings announced, coming into view with a jovial-looking man in ecclesiastical garments. "We couldn't find Mr. Oak."

"Such a shame," Meg said. "He's crusty, but that's only to cover a soft heart. I know he'd like to be here."

"No such address as the one he gave in Hampstead," Jennings said. "He's gone. Disappeared."

Finch looked up at Ross, and he took the roses from her. He put them with the birch wands and laid them across her arms before holding her hands. "If you will be my wife, we shall never want for a friend, Finch More. No matter what befalls us, we will always know that the one who matters most, the one we care for most, will be on our side."

She blinked and tried to smile, but her mouth trembled. "We are destined to spend our lives with our best friends."

❧ *Epilogue* ❧

"I suppose I should feel relieved—satisfied, even. Never mind that I am completely exhausted by my efforts.

"Certainly I should be congratulated for persisting under the most outrageously frustrating conditions. Well, I shall take advantage of their silly, emotional little gathering at Number 8 to calm my nerves and gather my strength for the journey I must take. Oh, most would not understand why this journey taxes even one such as me, one whose will has made the impossible, possible. How many can say that they have defied—indeed overcome—even death to complete their life's work?

"Not that I have completed my work.

"This is entirely too much. I shall be forced to rest—possibly for an extended period of time—before resuming the task I must somehow fulfill.

"While they are occupied elsewhere I shall decide how to go about settling in. The trick to these things is to be where you want to be without attracting attention. It's unfortunate *that at least one or two of them are observant. I was horrified when I heard that remark about a likeness to a family portrait. Who could have expected that they would look at a carved staircase and think such a thing?*

"I must be on my way. A likeness to Hunter, indeed. The boy will never gain the distinguished appearance of certain others. And that carving was made well more than a hundred years ago of a man who was—ahem—as handsome as he was noble.

"To think that all I have managed is the removal of one, count that, one intruder into this great house. I cannot even be certain that her brother will follow, in which case . . .

"The work of the dedicated is never done—or rarely done.

"In I go.

"This is a tight fit, and an extremely hard one. Ah, that's better. I must . . . settle down now. One wonders if any of them will pause for long enough to remark on certain changes in a newel post. Probably not. They will merely think they cannot misplace the face that had no form.

"The view from here is certainly excellent. I have always enjoyed being able to see people come and go from the house—and watching them climb the stairs. Keeps one so well informed.

"Good night to you."

A Keepsake Gift
To You
From Stella Cameron

A Private Peek
At Wedding Gowns
From the Early 1800's

Taken From
The Ghostly Writings
of Sir Septimus Spivey

Frog Crossing
Watersville

My dear friends:

Some months ago I wrote to you about an experience I had in Mayfair Square, London. I met an interesting fellow there. Elderly, a bit of a fuddy-duddy, it's true, but intriguing nevertheless and quite charming. Or so I thought.

What mistaken opinions we can form on first acquaintances.

On that occasion I left Number 7 Mayfair Square puzzled, but really revved up to find out more about the place. And find out more, I certainly did. You've just read about some of what I discovered. But now I'm faced with a dilemma. Remember the old man, the one I met and just mentioned again? He wasn't anything like the first impression he gave me. Actually he's an arrogant, selfish, self-opinionated, manipulative . . . Yeah, well, I might as well tell you what I really think about Sir Septimus Spivey. He's a no-good, nasty—sometimes dangerous—pest. And he isn't finished with his shenanigans yet.

Anyway, I got so ticked off with him that I wasn't going to write any of this, at least not the part about the book I found in a trunk in the loft above Adam Chillworth's place.

Then I remembered all those sayings. Ones like, "Why bite your nose to spite your face?" Only I'd be biting your noses to spite your faces if I didn't share some of what was in the book with you.

Okay, because you mean so much to me, here goes. I'll try to keep my opinions to myself, but if I weaken from time to time, please forgive me. You know I'm usually pretty restrained so I guess I should go easy on myself when I slip up.

Enjoy this, if you can.

Stella Cameron

7 Mayfair Square
London

June, 1820

Fellow Sufferers:

I am under absolutely no obligation to chronicle any of this for you, but perhaps I shall gain a certain pleasure from knowing that one day—when I have accomplished all that must be accomplished—whomever of you reads this book will be suitably amazed by my resourcefulness.

A man of my stature should never be reduced to dealing with such feminine foolishness as the details of marriage ceremonies. Or, worse yet, the fripperies that are of such importance to the weak minds of foolish females. However, now that I am set upon my course—to rid Number 7 Mayfair Square of *lodgers*—I must be certain I have allowed for all eventualities. And so I start with that most wasteful of all the clownish trappings of such occasions: The Wedding Dress. Pah!

I foresee five possible weddings. There could be six, but I am determined that with my unequaled brilliance, at least one may be eliminated. Five? Oh, how I shudder.

Could so good a man be expected to tolerate so much inconvenience? It will be perfectly possible to interchange the gowns, depending on the type of ceremony—the circumstances, that is—chosen by the groom. Fortunately I am not bound by some of the restrictions of ordinary men.

For the first gown I have chosen a replica of that worn by Princess Charlotte in 1816. Y'know, considering that mother of hers, she who would love to have become *Queen Caroline*—the hussy—considering all that, the Princess grew to quite a pleasing young woman.

Study my drawing well—I am a man of reputation in the area of drawings, you know, a famous architect.

The dress was of silver lamé over net with a silver tissue slip beneath. The bottom of the slip was embroidered with silver lamé in shells and flowers. The bodice and sleeves were trimmed with point Brussels lace and the Princess wore a manteau of silver tissue lined with white satin and with a border of embroidery to compliment that on the dress. The manteau fastened in front with a splendid diamond ornament (something in paste will be quite good enough for our purpose. All other materials will be of much inferior quality, of course, but good enough to fool the eye at a distance.)

A wreath of brilliant gems that formed rosebuds and leaves adorned the Princess's hair. This will be replaced by a circlet of green leaves interspersed with roses formed from silver tissue rosebuds.

The diamonds appropriate at the ears of a Princess, and the matching armlet, the superb pearls, will be perfectly well symbolized by more paste. I know a fellow who makes a passable job of such things.

7 Mayfair Square
London

February, 1821

And a foul February it is, too. If something could go wrong, it has gone wrong. I have, indeed, accomplished one wedding, but not with the required removal of the bride's brother. And the silly female did not wear a gown at all. She was married in the most shabby of frocks and her mooning groom seemed to consider her appearance beyond fault.

The next nuptial event will be considerably more dignified. I shall make certain of that. And we don't have long to wait.

I have patterned the gown on one that has not yet been worn. So much the better.

Study if you will, the Schaffner Wedding Dress, already planned for 1824. I traveled, at great personal cost to Marietta, Pennsylvania on order to see this.

Note the tasteful use of ivory silk with simple drawstring ties at the neck and around the suitably high waist. No excessively foolish folderolls. The artful tucking of the shoulders into the shapes of blossoms with silk-covered buttons at their centers is charming—if you care about such things. Scalloped cuffs trimmed with inexpensive but striking silver braid will catch every eye.

On the bride's head I visualize a small, crown-like affair, formed of stiffened tulle lined with horsehair to keep it aloft. The whole to be embroidered with seed pearls. I know a dealer in Portobello road who will sell seconds for near nothing. Borrowed pearls at the ears, and the wrist. Stiffening beneath the skirts, and *voila*. Ah, it is both a burden and a pleasure to be brilliant.

7 Mayfair Square
London

July, 1821

Well, Fellow Sufferers:

My troubles persist, but, rest assured, I am not bowed. In fact, I stand straighter and more determined.

I decided to store both the dresses I have to hand, and work on a third. I like challenge and, I assure you, all of these marvelous, yet economically produced masterpieces will be put to good use.

Onward to deal with the next necessary gown. This time I envision nuptials where at least one party will be a person of means—phenomenal means. Not an easy matter when the other party—being one of those I must remove from Number 7—has *no* prospects. *Money, money, lovely money* . . . Ahem, I forget myself. Forgive me for mentioning such an unmentionable topic. But, nevertheless, I am determined to secure someone with deep pockets, who will accomplish the required attachment in an almost indecently short space of time (Why should I care about appearances?), thus lessening the strain on my person.

I have poured myself into this design. In fact, it will not be seen again before 1880 (from which I borrowed the idea) but this will be all the more diversionary in '22, won't it?

The narrow-skirted gown is of the purest white silk. A form-fitting bodice is cut low, and close to the waist. The whole (for modesty of course) is covered with fine rich Belgian lace. This same lace forms long, tight sleeves and forms, in the front, into a single short peplum that opens into triple rows of falling ruffles at the back. These ruffles extend into points over a modest bustle and more lace continues into a graceful train edged with rosettes fashioned from silver faille. At the front of the skirt, when the bride walks an underskirt of white, silk on satin striped material is visible. This is adorned with a ruffled hem.

Finally, a diadem of crystals and pearls, with strands of both draped over the hair, nestles beneath a net veil that completely envelopes the bride and trails even beyond the gown's gorgeous rosette hem.

Ah, a wondrous thing, indeed, but consider the source.

7 Mayfair Square
London

September, 1822

Fellow Sufferers:

I am quite exhausted, but must go on. I must have at least one more gown at my disposal, just in case. Just in case of what? Questions, questions, will they never cease? Don't dare to examine my decisions. What is, is. And what might be, might be. There. More than enough said.

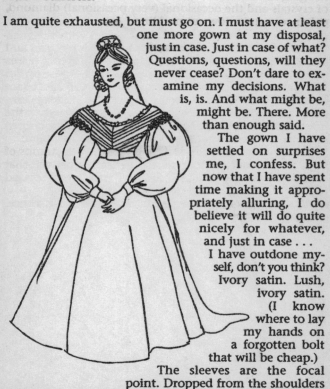

The gown I have settled on surprises me, I confess. But now that I have spent time making it appropriately alluring, I do believe it will do quite nicely for whatever, and just in case . . .

I have outdone myself, don't you think? Ivory satin. Lush, ivory satin. (I know where to lay my hands on a forgotten bolt that will be cheap.)

The sleeves are the focal point. Dropped from the shoulders to bands of lace, then puffed extravagantly, stiffened beneath with net, and clasped into tight satin bands at the

403

wrists. And the bodice. Fine and beautifully draped pleats to the high waist, and a wide belt, also of satin, but with a buckle of mother-of-pearl. In hair pulled to a chignon high at the crown are golden pins shaped like camellias and with crystals at their hearts. More crystals, these hanging like rows of tiny buds, adorn the ears, and a rope of crystals and the occasional (very occasional) diamond, enhances a quite low cut neckline.

7 Mayfair Square
London

February, 1823

Fellow Sufferers:

I had intended to warn you all about a woman who has been a source of extreme irritation to me. Cameron, or some such ordinary name. When I first met her, I thought she might help me. She's a scribbler, you know. A common profession quite unsuitable to anyone who would call herself a lady. But then, well, need I write more on that subject? Anyway, I exhort you, should she find a way to interfere with my plans, let me know immediately and I will deal with her.

Now, I have decided that since I have an obvious flair for this matter of modifying gowns, I shall produce one more—for now. This is for a certain lady whom I consider blameless and far above the station of life that has become hers. I will not say more of her now. Be patient and all will be revealed.

Here is a description of the gown. I'm fading again. Although I'll do my best, I may not be able to sketch the garment now, but my words will paint it for you.

I can only sigh at just the thought of this. Ivory and gold satin damask. Can you imagine a more wondrous medium? The bodice is boned to glorify an already beautiful, ahem, figure. This achieves remarkable, hmm, *roundness* above the very low neckline. The waist dips to a point in front and the bustle employed creates a most beautifully curvaceous shape. Below the dropped waistline in front, and sweeping behind the draperies that reach from the waist, over the bustle, to the hem at the back, the heavy satin drapes most intriguingly. The hem of the gown is edged with lush silk fringe.

Sleeves reach just below the elbow and are ornamented

with tucked bows. Crystal buttons are at the center of each bow, and down the length of the bodice. The entire gown is appliqued with seed pearls.

A pearl tiara, caught at each side of the head by a cluster of pearls, secures an ivory veil. This veil forms a train that spreads into a ruffled edge that brushes the floor.

A gown ahead of its time, but worthy of the efforts I have invested to make it available for your edification, and for, I do so hope, a faultless lady to wear.

I am, your weary servant,
Sir Septimus Spivey

Spivey

Frog Crossing
Watersville

My dears:

Isn't that man something?
I am, your respectful scribbler and fond friend,

Stella Cameron